Judge Suzanne Stafford worked her way through the ballroom of the Percyville Country Club. She glanced at her watch—8:05 p.m. and still no sign of her brother-in-law, Mississippi's governor-elect.

Searching the crowd, she located her sister near the bar. Wearing a polite smile, Taylor sipped vodka and tonic while listening to one of her husband's cronies. With a little help from friends and alcohol, Taylor would manage to play her role to perfection.

Then she spotted Caleb with Annie. As always, the sight of her son gave Suzanne pleasure. She should have guessed that he would find his favorite relative in the crowd.

An eager stir rippled across the assembly. Suzanne stretched to see and through the open doors spotted a black limousine entering the grounds to the club.

"Here he comes!"

"It's Jack!"

"Hey, Governor!"

The limo reached the curb and stopped. Jack himself opened the door and got out. Standing tall, he flashed his famous grin and waved.

For an instant, as Taylor and his two children made their way toward him, Jack stood caught in the light. With this flawless sense of timing, he smiled, opening his arms as if to embrace his fans along with his family.

Mississippi's quintessential golden boy.

The sudden *cra-a-ack* of gunfire stunned the crowd.

Taylor screamed. Jack Sullivan was dead.

KAREN YOUNG

didn't choose writing as a career; it chose her. After
numerous long-distance moves necessitated by her
husband's career, she realized she would never be
in one place long enough to climb the corporate
ladder. So after the tenth move, in sheer desperation,
she decided to try writing a book. When a major
publisher bought it, she knew she'd found a career!
Or, rather, it had found her.

GOOD GIRLS

KAREN YOUNG

MIRA®

For my brother, H.E. Young,
in loving memory.
We miss you, Duck.

Recycling programs
for this product may
not exist in your area.

ISBN-13: 978-0-373-06246-1

GOOD GIRLS

For questions and comments about the quality of this book please contact us at
Customer_eCare@Harlequin.ca.

www.Harlequin.com

Printed in U.S.A.

GOOD GIRLS

ACKNOWLEDGMENTS

To the following people who were helpful and supportive to me, please accept my heartfelt thanks and appreciation. Any mistakes herein are my own.

Robert F. Wood, Attorney-at-Law.
Evan Marshall, The Evan Marshall Agency.
Emilie Richards, Erica Spindler, Metsy Hingle
and Linda West, friends and fellow writers.
Paul Stone, husband and best believer.

PART I

ONE

December 1997

JUDGE SUZANNE STAFFORD's smile had long ago atrophied as she worked her way through the ballroom of the Percyville Country Club, filled to capacity with her brother-in-law's constituents. She glanced at her watch: 8:05 and still no sign of Mississippi's governor-elect. Trust Jack to time it so that when he did arrive, heightened anticipation would have his fans salivating. At a five-hundred-dollars-a-plate fund-raiser, a different kind of man might have thought it only common courtesy to be on time. But then, a different kind of man wouldn't have held a fund-raiser to replenish his campaign chest less than a month after the election.

"Strike while the iron is hot," Jack had said at dinner last Sunday at Riverbend. "The best time to get 'em to ante up is while they're still feeling good about winning."

Suzanne had to admit he was right. There wasn't a sour face in the crowd. The snatches of conversation she'd overheard so far were full of admiration for the evening's guest of honor.

Searching the crowd, she located her sister near the bar. Wearing a polite smile, Taylor sipped vodka and tonic while listening to one of Jack's cronies. With a little help from friends and alcohol, Taylor would manage to play her role to perfection.

Catching her eye, Suzanne lifted her glass imperceptibly. Taylor's face lit up with a real smile. At forty-one, she still retained the looks that had first attracted Jack Sullivan—along with the Stafford name and money, of course. Poised and beautiful in cobalt blue that matched her eyes, she seemed to Suzanne the quintessential First Lady-elect. Perhaps Jack would be pleased, for a change.

Suzanne never ceased to wonder why Taylor put up with him. It wasn't money or fame, and it certainly wasn't the dubious prestige of being a politician's wife. God knows, it wasn't power. Taylor had none. Was it love, however inconceivable that seemed? Was it the kids? Whatever the reason, because Taylor had tolerated Jack, Suzanne had been forced to tolerate him, as well. What would these people think if they suspected that she, Jack Sullivan's only sister-in-law, had voted for his opponent?

She glanced at her watch again. Jack should be here with his family. When he finally did show, the crowd would be literally panting for the sight of him. She surveyed the glittering crowd with a cynic's eye. If they only knew.

Setting her wineglass on a table, she murmured a greeting to a woman she probably should recognize but didn't, then veered toward the doors, checking her watch again. Twelve minutes past eight and still no Jack. She thought of the full briefcase awaiting her at home, but with a sigh she accepted a second drink from a waiter and set out to find Annie Fields. If Suzanne had to suffer through an evening dedicated to praising Jack Sullivan, she wouldn't have to pretend to enjoy it around Annie. On the subject of Jack, she and her cousin were in total agreement.

As soon as she stepped through the doors, she spotted Annie with Caleb. As always, the sight of her son gave Suzanne pleasure. Both were laughing. She should have guessed Caleb would find his favorite relative in the crowd. A political fund-raiser was hardly a fifteen-year-old boy's choice of entertainment.

"What are you two doing out here?" Suzanne asked, greeting Annie with a hug.

"It was too stuffy inside." Annie winked at the boy. "Caleb agreed, so we grabbed a beer and headed for the exit."

"A beer!"

Caleb rolled his eyes. "Mom, she's teasing. Give me some credit."

Suzanne attempted a stern look. "When are you two going to grow up?"

"When you lighten up," Annie said, taking her by the arm. "Come on, let's get out of the traffic." She headed away from the entrance toward a less congested area.

"I'm gonna go check out the security guys," Caleb said, peering over the heads of the crowd.

"Caleb—" Suzanne tried to stop him, but was too late.

"Oh, let him go," Annie said. "He'll be bored enough later sitting through half a dozen speeches from Jack's sycophants."

"*If* the Illustrious One ever shows up."

"We can always hope," Annie said, suppressing a smile.

"Careful," Suzanne said wryly. "We're here to praise the governor-elect, not to trash him." She sobered. "Have you spoken to Taylor yet?"

"Only to say a quick hello." Annie glanced toward the entrance. People were pouring out of the clubhouse. Caught up in the throng were Taylor and the children. "She looks as attractive as ever," Annie said, and shook her head. "Where the hell is Jack? Why can't she share the spotlight? Hasn't she earned the right, for God's sake?"

"When has Jack ever shared anything?"

An eager stir rippled through the crowd. Suzanne stretched to see and spotted a black limousine entering the entrance to the club.

"Here he comes!"

"It's Jack!"

"Hey, Governor!"

"Way to go, Jack!"

"Jack! Jack!"

The crowd picked up the rhythm and began to chant. "Jack. Jack. Jack. Jack…"

The limo reached the curb and stopped. Without waiting for his driver, Jack himself opened the door and got out. Standing tall, he flashed his famous grin and waved. The crowd burst into raucous welcome.

"Can you believe this guy?" Annie muttered.

Suzanne shrugged. "Charisma."

"And bullshit," Annie said.

Plenty of both, Suzanne thought. His dark good looks, rakish confidence and elegant tuxedo were a dynamite combination. She had to admit he was an incredibly handsome man. On top of that, he was a natural politician. During the campaign, and in others before this one, she had often marveled at his style. And guile. Even the media had succumbed. In the final days of the election, he had often been compared with the likes of Huey Long and JFK, to her disgust. When he finally did make it to the podium, within seconds he would have his audience fully engaged. His skill never failed to amaze her.

As she watched, Jack's smile took on an edge. Curious, she followed his gaze and spotted Ben Kincaid. Ah, someone who might know some of Jack's secrets. For the past two months, Ben, now divorced, had been back in Percyville with custody of his twin sons. It seemed odd that a former government agent of Kincaid's rank had settled in a small town in Mississippi. Judging from Jack's reaction, he wasn't pleased to have Ben on his home turf.

The security people seemed intent on urging Jack quickly through the crowd, but he was making it difficult. The consummate politician, he took his time. Over the heads of his eager constituents, he spotted Taylor. He gave her a warm look, letting the voters glimpse the wonderful relationship they believed existed between Jack and his wife. And lest they be forgotten in the crowd, Jack winked affectionately at his children. Gayle, ever the adoring daughter, dashed forward. Less enthusiastically, Trey approached with his mother.

For an instant, as Taylor and his two children made their way toward him, Jack stood caught in the light. With his flawless sense of timing, he smiled, opening his arms as if to embrace his fans along with his family. Mississippi's quintessential golden boy.

The sudden *cra-a-ack!* of gunfire stunned the crowd.

The force slammed Jack back against the limousine. Blood stained the front of his white shirt. For a moment, the crowd simply gaped, paralyzed.

Taylor screamed. The sound seemed to galvanize Jack's handlers. They exploded in a frenzy of activity. Two men went down on their haunches beside Jack. Several others ran toward the darkened line of trees across the drive. A woman tore past Suzanne, shouting that she was a doctor. One man relinquished his place to her.

From the side, Ben Kincaid pushed through the stunned spectators. Flashing his ID, he bent down beside Jack. A moment later, he looked up and saw Suzanne. He said nothing, gave no sign. But she knew.

Jack Sullivan was dead.

TWO

April 1981

SUZANNE WATCHED HER SISTER'S face as she gazed at her bridegroom. Taylor was glowing, her smile adoring. Any woman lucky enough to be marrying Jack Sullivan would be happy, Suzanne decided. Jack was handsome, charming, successful. And *very* sexy, Suzanne thought with just a twinge of envy. To add to that, he was well on his way to the top in his profession. His brilliant defense of the nephew of a U.S. senator indicted for fraud had sealed his reputation in legal circles statewide. The Judge had beamed her approval when she learned that Taylor was engaged to Jack. For Taylor, earning her mother's approval had been almost as important as marrying the man she loved. Suzanne silently congratulated her sister for finally getting it right.

Taylor's behavior for the past few years had garnered so little parental approval. Meaning Judge Lily Stafford's approval, of course. It would have been difficult to gauge approval or disapproval from their father. Although he obviously loved them, Charles Stafford seldom noticed any of his children. He was usually too deeply immersed in the research for his next book to spare anything but the most fleeting thought for his offspring. That left the three of them—Stuart, Taylor and Suzanne—at the sole mercy of the Judge. All three had had to battle her tyranny from birth. There were no exceptions, even in the matter of marriage.

"Get a degree, for God's sake, and find a husband," she'd ordered Taylor after her graduation from Ole Miss. Unlike Suzanne, who knew when she was barely ten that she would be a lawyer, Taylor had flitted from one career idea to another before settling eventually on elementary education. No one believed for a minute that she would ever actually *teach,* but the Judge had laid down the law. "You're twenty-six, Taylor. Another few years and you'll wind up with no man at all, and for you that would be a real disaster."

The Judge was nothing if not a realist. She recognized no burning desire in Taylor for any of the careers she herself would have chosen—the law, naturally, medicine, even politics. From the Judge's point of view, marriage to a man who did have the fire in his belly was an acceptable alternative. Taylor's beauty and sense of style made her an asset to any man, particularly one with his eye on a political career. If it was Taylor's destiny to be the wind beneath the wings of a special man, then it was Jack's destiny to be special. The handwriting was on the wall.

At a signal from the minister, the couple prepared to exchange rings. Jack turned and looked deeply into Taylor's eyes. Suzanne shivered and felt another little pang. Guilt? Jack belonged to Taylor, but Suzanne had been oddly fascinated by him from the moment they were introduced. It was something about the way Jack looked at her, something in the way he smiled at her, as if they shared a secret. She shifted restlessly and fixed her gaze on her bridesmaid's bouquet. Having these feelings about her sister's man shocked and confused her. It was wrong. She had no reason to give Jack a second look. She loved Dennis Scott. She had just accepted his ring. She'd known since high school that she would marry him someday. He was nothing like Jack Sullivan. It bothered her that she had these forbidden thoughts about one man when she was committed to another.

It also bothered her that Jack seemed to be conducting this small, secret flirtation with her. She had given him no encouragement. Could it simply be her imagination?

She had considered talking it over with Annie, who was in Percyville expressly for Taylor's wedding, except that Annie didn't seem to be one of Jack Sullivan's fans. A cousin-by-marriage, Annie had moved to California straight out of high school four years ago. No one was quite sure why. An artist who specialized in greeting cards, Annie was as down-to-earth as she was creative. In spite of being younger than Taylor or Suzanne, she could always be counted on to tell it like it was.

It had unsettled Suzanne to learn that Annie didn't like Jack. She hadn't been shy about stating her opinion to Suzanne at Taylor's shower, but then, Annie wasn't shy. Biting into a thick slice of pizza, Annie had chewed thoughtfully before observing, "He's almost too perfect, don't you think?"

Before replying, Suzanne had glanced toward Taylor, busy advising one of her attendants about hairstyles, to be sure she wasn't listening. "Well, he's handsome and intelligent and successful and…sexy, don't you think?"

"Not really, Suzy. He's too calculating for my money."

"You'd better not let Taylor hear you say that."

"Too late," Annie said, reaching for a beer. "Before they got engaged, I told her what I thought."

Suzanne frowned. "When was that?"

"At the Judge's birthday party last summer. You remember, she brought Jack to Riverbend that weekend for the first time."

"Oh, yeah." The Judge's birthday was the Big Event for the Staffords. Everybody in the family was expected to be there, Annie included.

"Taylor hasn't ever quite forgotten it," Annie said, looking regretful. "I'm surprised she asked me to be in her wedding."

"You're family, Annie," Suzanne said. "Almost a sister. Of course she'd ask you to be in her wedding."

"Maybe, but I wish I'd kept my feelings to myself."

"What do you mean by calculating?"

Annie ran a finger around the top of her beer. "Just a feeling I get. Maybe living in California makes me suspicious, but when I'm around Jack—which isn't often, I admit—he always seems so cool, so self-possessed. He tries to charm everyone. He butters up Uncle Charles and flatters the Judge. I get the feeling he would use them to get what he wants and then just step right over them." She shrugged. "I call that calculating."

"If it's true."

Annie smiled wryly. "I just admitted I'm the suspicious type."

Watching the final moments of Taylor's marriage ceremony, Suzanne tried to forget Annie's cynicism. Jack was marrying Taylor because he loved her, and for no other reason. It might be advantageous for him to have a respected judge from one of Mississippi's most influential families for a mother-in-law, but surely that was just a happy coincidence.

"I now pronounce you husband and wife." The minister smiled benignly on Taylor and Jack. "You may kiss the bride."

As Jack took Taylor in his arms, the sun went briefly behind a cloud, dimming the brilliance of the afternoon. It was barely a heartbeat in time, but Suzanne shivered. Coming so soon after her thoughts, it was too much like an omen. She fought off the silly idea as the piano, moved outside for the occasion, swelled to the strains of *Lohengrin*.

The bride and groom turned, all smiles. Suzanne caught Dennis's eye as everyone stood up, laughing and applauding. She gave him a bright smile. The wedding was over.

Her sister was married to Jack Sullivan.

THE RECEPTION WAS AS LAVISH as any ever seen in Percyville. Anyone of any importance in the state was there, as well as the Judge's friends from New Orleans, Houston and Washington, many of them elected officials. As Suzanne drifted through the crowd, it occurred to her that the occasion was a politician's dream and that Jack seemed more than happy in the spotlight. If she thought once or twice that he almost seemed to forget Taylor and her role in the celebration, she didn't say so aloud.

She knew that from the Judge's point of view, the only drawback to Taylor's choice of bridegroom was Jack's somewhat murky lineage. He had no family, at least none of any consequence. His only living relative, his grandmother, was in a nursing home somewhere on the Gulf Coast. Family was important to Lily Stafford. After thirty-three years of marriage, she knew every twig and leaf on the Stafford family tree. She had little family herself, and they were all dead now, but she'd made it her business to marry a man whose roots went deep into Southern soil and whose blood was decidedly blue. The right connections were important to the Judge. To please her, Stuart had chosen a wife from one of the most powerful families in Jackson, but she was taking a chance with Jack. Perhaps she felt a kinship with him, Suzanne thought, studying the open approval on her mother's face as she beamed at her new son-in-law in the dazzling April sunlight.

Suzanne passed the bar and accepted fresh champagne, then looked around for someplace less noisy. If the bride and groom would leave, she and Dennis could slip away for a few minutes.

She wondered where Dennis was, then spotted him standing with Ben Kincaid and headed toward them. Ben was in law school with her and had been a friend since high school. Catching sight of her, both men grinned and beckoned her over.

"Hey, pretty lady," Dennis said, slipping his arms around her waist. "You're looking too solemn. You need to drink that champagne, not just carry it around."

"I have been drinking it, Dennis," she said dryly, barely managing to keep her glass upright as he parted her tawny blond hair and nuzzled the skin beneath her ear. "And it's obvious you have, too."

"Say, Ben, is my fiancée the most beautiful woman in the state, or what?"

Ben looked directly into her gray eyes. "Yeah," he said quietly, "she is."

"Mrs. Dennis Scott," Dennis said, turning and smiling at her fondly. "Has a nice ring, huh, buddy?"

"Sure does." Ben raised his glass in a toast. "You're a lucky son of a gun."

Chuckling, Dennis gave Suzanne a quick kiss and let her go. "This is some party. The only one that will outshine it will be ours when we get married. Next week okay with you, sugar?"

"Dennis…"

He shrugged, still grinning. "Okay, I'm easy. How about next month?"

"It took months to plan this wedding, Dennis. There's no way we can get married for ages, you know that."

In spite of the champagne, the look he gave her was serious. "So when, Suzy? You name it."

She didn't want to get into this today, of all days. Dennis had surprised her with an engagement ring at Christmas. She had accepted it, but with reservations. She had to finish law school before she could even think about marriage. And Dennis was still working on his architectural degree. Setting the date was out of the question.

She touched her forehead. "Dennis, not now. Please."

Ben cleared his throat. "Okay, you two. No serious talk. This is a party, remember?" He punched Dennis lightly on the arm. "We need a refill, my man. Let your lady circulate. The sister of the bride has duties."

Dennis looked glum, but he drew a deep breath and nodded. He would bring it up again later, Suzanne knew. But for now she was off the hook. She gave Ben a grateful look, then backed away a few steps before turning and hurrying off.

Why did it feel as if she was running away?

SHE SEARCHED THE CROWD for Taylor, finally spotting her with their father, seated on a white wrought-iron bench beneath a cascade of lavender wisteria. With her dark hair and striking blue eyes, Taylor looked as delicate and lovely as Suzanne had ever seen her. If Jack Sullivan hadn't fallen genuinely in love with Taylor, he couldn't love anybody. Just then, Charles rose, leaving Taylor alone.

Holding the hem of her long dress in one hand and her champagne in the other, Suzanne made her way over.

"Oh, give me that," Taylor said, reaching for the glass. "I'm about to dry up from standing in that receiving line and making nice to people I don't even know." She tossed off half the contents in one gulp.

"Looks as if you'll have to get used to that," Suzanne said, her eyes on Jack, who was working the crowd with his new mother-in-law. They watched the two in silence for a moment.

"She looks happy, doesn't she?" Taylor said.

Suzanne glanced at her. "Who, Mother?"

"Uh-huh. She really likes Jack, don't you think?" Her voice held a wistful note.

Suzanne laughed. "I think it's obvious, Tay. From the Judge's point of view, I don't think you could have chosen better. As well as being a lawyer, Jack seems a natural politician. Mother must think she's died and gone to heaven."

"God, I hope not." Taylor finished the champagne and handed the empty glass to Suzanne. "I married a lawyer, not a politician. Today, with Mother to show him around, Jack has a good opportunity to make professional contacts. Some of these people will be future clients."

If Taylor really believed that a career in politics wasn't Jack's ultimate goal, Suzanne wasn't going to disillusion her, not on her wedding day. "You're beginning to sound like a wife already," she said, smiling. "How does it feel?"

"I love it," Taylor said, her gaze now fixed on Jack. "I love *him*."

"I hope so," Suzanne said dryly. "It's a bit late to decide otherwise."

Taylor's eyes were still on Jack, narrowed and intense. "I'm going to be such a good wife, Suzanne. I may have screwed up practically everything I ever tried until now, but this is one thing I'm going to excel at. Just wait and see."

Suzanne stared at her, a little surprised at the depth of Taylor's insecurity. Annie's words came back to her suddenly. What a tragedy if it turned out that Jack wasn't the dream husband Taylor expected him to be.

As if sensing their interest, Jack turned and grinned at them. Saying something to the Judge, he left her with a couple of colleagues and started toward them. In the flattering light of the setting sun, he looked dark and dangerously appealing.

"Hi, darling," Taylor said, her delight obvious.

"Hey, sugar." He kissed his wife lightly on the lips, then smiled directly into Suzanne's eyes. "So, why are the two most beautiful ladies at this party standing here all alone?"

"We're having a champagne break," Taylor said, linking her arm in his.

"Escaping the noise," Suzanne said, touching her forehead again.

"Headache?" Jack asked.

"Probably too much champagne," she said, though she knew she had drunk very little today. "Maybe I'll walk out to the gazebo and grab a few minutes of peace and quiet," she said, giving them a brief smile. "It's the only place at Riverbend that's completely private today." In the split second before she turned away, Jack winked at her as if they shared a secret. She found the small intimacy mildly disconcerting.

SHE MADE HER WAY DOWN the winding path to the fading sounds of the reception. The moment she stepped inside the gazebo, she was glad she'd decided to steal away. She and Taylor and Annie had spent many hours of their adolescence here. It was in the gazebo that Suzanne had first confided her ambition to become a lawyer. Taylor had groaned, vowing she would never consider any career that required so much work. It was Annie's opinion that there were too many lawyers in the world already. Art was her destiny, a fact she never bothered to state. To know Annie was to know that. As for Taylor's plans, they changed from one season to the next. Sometimes from one week to the next.

Suzanne sat down on the ancient lounger, and breathed deeply, trying to relax. For a few moments she did nothing more than stare at patterns of sunshine and shadow. She hadn't really enjoyed this day, and she should have. She mentally ticked off how many things were right in her world. She had fulfilled her wish to get into law school, and she loved it. She had already been tapped for a summer job as a law clerk with a good firm in Jackson. Dennis, the man she was engaged to, was decent, dependable and nice. It dawned on her suddenly that she could be describing her best friend.

Then what wasn't right in her world? It bothered her that she was reluctant to actually name the day she would marry Dennis. Why? She loved him. With a sigh, she closed her eyes and tried to will the headache away. But her thoughts would not be stilled. Maybe Dennis wasn't as exciting as someone like Jack but—

At the sound of footsteps, she opened her eyes.

Jack stood watching her from the entrance of the gazebo. With the jacket of his tuxedo open, his hands shoved in his pockets and a half smile playing on his lips, he was wickedly handsome. "Hi, little sister," he said softly.

Suzanne was startled by his appearance and unsettled by something in the tone of his voice. "Where's Taylor?" she asked bluntly.

"Still circulating, on the instructions of my estimable mother-in-law."

She frowned. Somehow his words were not complimentary to Lily. She watched warily as he pushed away from the entrance and headed for the lounge where she sat. He stopped, still regarding her with that little half smile. "May I?" Without waiting for a reply, he sat. He stretched his arm along the back of the lounge and looked out over the grounds of Riverbend. "I never knew this thing was out here."

"We used to come here when we were kids," Suzanne said. "Taylor, Annie and me." She used his wife's name deliberately.

"Yeah, peace and quiet. It's great."

Unobtrusively, she shifted to the corner of the lounge, putting as much distance between them as possible. "You don't strike me as a person who craves peace and quiet," she said.

He looked at her. "No shit? Then what *do* I look like to you, Suzanne?"

A dangerous man. The last person I should be talking to alone on your wedding day, she thought wildly. Where *was* Taylor? Jack had been married to her less than four hours. No ordinary man would simply walk away, leaving his bride alone with hundreds of guests. But Jack Sullivan was no ordinary man. She knew that without a doubt. She knew also that she didn't want to be here with him. It was inappropriate, but mostly it felt wrong.

"At a loss for words?" he asked in that soft tone. "The promising young law student? You surprise me."

"What's going on, Jack?" she asked suddenly. "What are you doing out here when your wedding reception is still in full swing back at the house?"

He looked playfully astonished. "I craved a moment of peace and quiet, just like you. What do you think?"

"I think it strikes me as odd that you didn't bring Taylor with you."

Ignoring her, he leaned back, stacking his hands behind his head. "I'm one lucky son of a bitch, Suzy. You know that?"

She gave him a wary look.

"You don't follow," he said, glancing at her. "Correct me if I'm wrong, but your mama's family didn't exactly come over on the *Mayflower.* Yet she married Charles Stafford, whose bloodlines are impeccable. Now, God bless her, she's a federal judge."

"I still don't follow you," Suzanne said coldly.

"I've just taken a leaf out of the Judge's book," he explained with exaggerated patience. "I've married *up,* darlin'. Now do you get it?"

Suzanne closed her eyes, sickened that Taylor was married to this man. *Oh, Annie, you were right, and it's too late.*

Jack continued matter-of-factly, "Take Stuart, now, your big brother. Another asset. Here he is, a reporter with the state's top newspaper in Jackson, married to Ellie Baines, a very blue-blooded bitch." His expression was one of pure satisfaction. "Yeah, I'm one helluva lucky man."

Still reclining on the lounge, he turned his head and gave her a lazy smile. It was like watching a snake, Suzanne thought, mesmerized. How had she once considered that smile sexy and seductive? Now it was simply repulsive.

She started up, but Jack's hand shot out and stopped her. For a second she was so startled she didn't think to resist.

"Taylor is pretty," Jack said deliberately, "but you, Suzy, are drop-dead gorgeous."

"Let me go," she said coldly, looking with distaste at his hand on her wrist.

He shifted a little on the lounge, then with a quick jerk he pulled her over, making her gasp. Her face was so close to his that all she could see were his black, black eyes. She still wasn't afraid. She was just sickened at the thought of her sister's lost dreams. Jack could never hide his real nature in the intimacy of marriage. Taylor's joy wouldn't last through the honeymoon. *Oh, Taylor.*

"Beautiful and sexy, too," he said, his eyes running avidly over her face. "I've had the hots for you since the first day I saw you."

"You're talking like an idiot, Jack." She wasn't sure if he expected her to act scared or to struggle, but she refused to give him the satisfaction. "I hope for Taylor's sake that it's the champagne. Now let me up."

"Or what?"

"We're hardly isolated, Jack. One good scream and your public image is ruined."

"And Taylor's girlish dreams, don't forget those."

She studied him, then shook her head. "You really are despicable."

"Cut the crap, Suzanne. You've been coming on to me since the day we met, sashaying around and giving me those big-eyed looks." He grinned. "Well, here's your chance. We can get it on, and I promise you it'll be good. Better than good."

Before she realized his intent, he bent and kissed her. It was a brutal kiss, hard and wet and intrusive. His hand twisted in her hair and brought tears to her eyes. His tongue plunged deep, gagging her. She gasped in shock and revulsion. Dignity forgotten, she began to struggle.

"Cut the act, damn it! You're no goddamn virgin," he snarled. Gripping her shoulders, he shook her hard. "You set this up and I plan to finish it."

Dazed, she shook her head. "I didn't...I don't know what you're talking about."

"You *invited* me, sweetheart. Right in front of my new wife. You know...your big sister. A blind man could have read that look in your eyes."

Still shaking her head, she tried once more to free herself and get to her feet. He shook her again, not as ruthlessly as before, but hard enough to remind her he would get rougher if he had to. She realized with sick dread that he would *enjoy* getting rough. She had to get out of this. But how?

Nothing short of a scream would reach the guests at the house. But she couldn't scream. This was Taylor's wedding. What would people think? Jack was the *groom*. What would happen to Taylor's marriage?

All the while her thoughts raced, Jack was kissing her, pawing at her. He was drunk, that was it. What else could it be? She remembered his wink when she'd mentioned going to the gazebo. How could he have thought she was coming on to him? She was engaged to Dennis.

Oh, Dennis, Dennis, I need you.

"I've been looking forward to this for a long time," Jack said, his voice taut and low, excited. "You're ten times sexier than your sister will ever be." He caught her hair in both hands, heedless of the pain it caused her.

"Jack," she said, trying to keep the panic from her voice. "You don't want to do this."

"I don't want to keep playing games. We both know why we're out here."

"What about Taylor?"

He shrugged. "You don't have to worry about her. I'll do my duty as a bridegroom. She won't have a clue."

She knew then she couldn't reason with him. She began struggling in earnest. "Let me *up!*"

Fumbling inside the bodice of her gown, he found her breast and pinched her nipple. Stinging pain forced a scream, but he stifled it with his mouth on hers.

Only survival mattered now. She pulled back from him, tried to scream again, but he clamped a hand over her mouth. He used his body to trap her hands while fumbling at her skirt to pull it up. "Jesus, look at this! Just these goddamn sexy stockings and a teeny bikini! Shit, baby, you are something else." With a hard wrench, he had the bikinis down.

Again she tried to scream, but his palm stifled her. She finally managed to free one hand and clawed at his wrist, trying to tear his hand away from her mouth, but he was too strong. Nails bared, she went for his face. He cursed and caught her hand, shoving it beneath her, holding it trapped with the other by his body weight. She felt him shift and knew he was unzipping his pants. Her heart thudded in her chest while her mind shrieked denial. With horror, she felt his penis probing.

Then, with one brutal thrust, he was inside her. She felt a searing sting as delicate flesh tore, then agonizing pain as he rammed home. She screamed then, but it was a silent, despairing cry while above her he plunged into her again and again, his breathing labored and hot in her ear, reeking of alcohol. She bucked and fought, mindlessly bent on resisting, distantly aware that he gloried in her defiance.

With each thrust, her neck was banged painfully against the arm of the lounge. Panic assailed her as she sensed his climax. He groaned, arching his back, and ejaculated. The next moment, he had collapsed on her, his weight smothering. She made a sound, and he went still.

"Shit." He withdrew from her without care and pushed himself up. "I guess you'll claim to be pissed now."

She could only stare at him. Without haste, he rose from the lounge and began straightening himself. Briskly he zipped his pants, tucked in his shirttails and smoothed his hair.

"Better get yourself together, babe," he said, finally sparing her a glance. "People wander around at these things."

Suzanne brought a shaking hand to her chest, covering herself. She winced at a slicing pain in her neck. If Jack noticed, he gave no indication. He looked invigorated, a little rakish. He looked ready to resume his duties as a bridegroom. With a quick tug to straighten his jacket, he started toward the entrance.

"Oh, yeah, one thing." He turned on the gazebo steps. The rakishness disappeared. His black eyes were hard. "I know how much you care about your sister, so I think we'd better keep this our little secret, wouldn't you agree?"

Unable to respond, she watched him walk away.

IF SHE COULD HAVE SLIPPED into the woods, curled up in a ball and died, Suzanne would have done so. But that would have meant finding the will to get off the lounge and stand up. That alone seemed an impossible feat. She lay where Jack had left her and stared at nothing.

Her mind refused to function. Somehow, she knew this was a good thing. Necessary. If she moved, if she allowed herself to clear the mist that clouded her brain, she would have to think about it. And to think meant she would start to scream. And if she began to scream, she would never be able to stop.

Vaguely she could hear music and birdcalls, occasional raised voices, loud laughter, car engines.

As she watched a butterfly hover over her, she began to shake. She clamped her teeth together and tasted blood. Her stomach roiled as she thought of his hand clamped on her jaw.

She tried to get up, groping at the arm of the lounge for leverage. She felt battered and beaten. Her shoulder throbbed and her wrist was tender. Her neck ached. The flesh between her legs burned. She managed to turn weakly and slide off the lounge onto her hands and knees. One foot was bare. She stared at it, unable to think of finding her shoe.

After a time, she gazed around the gazebo and suddenly found it horrible. In one moment Jack had stolen the joy of this spot from her forever. She wanted to run a million miles away. But even with panic clawing at her, she knew she could not risk being seen looking like this.

She began feverishly pulling at her gown, straightening the bodice where it had been jerked from her shoulder. She bent, wincing and dizzy, and groped underneath the lounge for her other shoe. She found it and her tattered bikinis as well. Jack's expression as he'd ripped them from her body flashed in her mind. Nausea, quick and sickening, rose in her throat. She wanted to throw them away, burn them, bury them a thousand feet deep.

She could not do any of those things. Shuddering, she picked them up, and with one last look to see that nothing was left behind as testimony to what had just happened, she left the gazebo.

Hesitantly, she surveyed the grounds, then left the path, thankful there was another route to the big house. She wanted nothing more than to get to her own room before someone spotted her. One look at her and the world would know. Miraculously, she met no one.

The back porch, too, was deserted. Closing her eyes in relief, she slipped inside the house and hurried toward the back stairway. Only family and close friends would venture there today. Glancing over her shoulder, she took the first few steps, then turned at the landing.

"Whoa, Suzy!" Ben Kincaid sidestepped just in time to prevent a collision. "They didn't build these backstairs for two-way traffic, huh?"

She froze, thankful that the light on the landing was poor. Ben was sharp and he was never inclined to drink as much as Dennis. She didn't look at him.

"Hey, something wrong?" Angling his head back, he tried to get a better look at her.

She murmured something, shielding herself by reaching up as if to check her hair. As she did so, she saw her bruised wrist and quickly turned it from his gaze. She was thankful it was Ben and not her mother or Taylor—God forbid!—otherwise she'd have had to explain that and her wrecked hairdo.

Her wrecked life.

"Are you sick?" he asked, his tone becoming sharp.

She cleared her voice, trying to get past him. "Just a bit too much champagne."

He reached for her, but she gave a little cry and flinched. In her shattered state, even Ben was to be shunned.

He quickly withdrew his hands. "Should I get Dennis?"

She was already nearing the top of the stairs. "No, I'm okay. Tell him I'll see him in a while."

In her room, she closed the door and locked it. Leaning against it, she wrapped her arms around herself to keep from splintering into a million pieces.

Voices in the hall brought her head up. Hurrying to the bathroom, she fumbled at the buttons and fastenings of her dress. In seconds she was naked. She turned on the shower and stepped beneath the stinging spray. With soap and her bath sponge, she began to scrub herself. The more she worked, the more frantic she became.

A decision had been made. Sneaking away from the gazebo, avoiding people, rejecting a friend like Ben, hiding now in her room—it meant one thing only. She wasn't going to tell. Black despair nearly choked her. It wasn't fair. He would get away with it. Dropping the sponge, she covered her face with her hands.

Oh, Taylor.

Suddenly she was aware of sounds. Then she realized with vague surprise that it was her own voice…mumbling, cursing, wailing. She slid to the floor of the shower and let her emotions take her away. She could scrub and scrub until there was no skin left, but nothing would ever cleanse from her body the smell and taste of Jack Sullivan.

She wept then, long and bitterly, for everything she had lost in those moments in the gazebo.

THREE

SUZANNE BLINKED AND TRIED to bring the phrase she had just written into focus, but the words danced crazily. She closed her eyes, took a deep breath. From the moment she'd arrived for the exam, her stomach had been in a knot. Only a few more minutes remained of the allotted time. In front of her, Ben Kincaid shuffled papers, then resumed writing. They shared several classes. Knowing he was there was reassuring. She waited a few seconds, then read what she'd written. It would have to do.

She collected the exam papers and carefully stood up. When the room stopped spinning, she headed for the front.

A professor's assistant accepted her paper with a smile. He said something, his tone low, but to Suzanne the words seemed as if they were spoken through a tunnel. Turning, she managed to reach the door and escape to the blessedly deserted hall. Somehow she got outside before being overcome by a dizzying wave of nausea.

She leaned weakly against a wall while the world dipped and swayed and stars showered around her. Her notes and purse slipped from her grasp and hit the ground with a muffled thump. She tried to think. Then it ceased to matter. The whole world turned dark and…nothing.

"Suzanne…wake up. Are you okay?"

Her name seemed to come from far away. She floated in a soft darkness. She felt safe, separated from reality. Part of her was tempted to stay there. No thoughts, no problems, no decisions. No nausea.

"Suzy, can you hear me? It's Ben."

Ben. Small things came to her then. A firm shoulder. Hard

warmth. Clean shirt scent. The prickle of grass on her skin. That puzzled her. Why was she lying on the ground?

"Come on, Suzanne, wake up."

She blinked weakly and finally managed to hold her eyes open. Ben was staring at her, his brown gaze dark with concern.

"Ben…"

"Yeah, it's me." He squeezed her hand. "Are you okay, Suzy? You fainted."

"I'm okay," she murmured. Then she glanced past his shoulder. A semicircle of students huddled above them. All were staring at her. She closed her eyes and turned her face into Ben's shirtfront. "Help me away from here, Ben," she whispered. "Please…"

Did she imagine a quick, protective squeeze? He eased her up gently until she was sitting. "Think you can stand up?"

Her throat was thick with bile. She took slow, deep breaths. "Without falling? I think so." She sensed him watching her but refused to meet his eyes. He saw too much. Unlike Dennis, Ben could not be fobbed off with excuses and half truths.

With his help, she got to her feet, leaning gratefully into him as they walked across the grass to his car. It was no more than fifty feet, but to Suzanne, walking on rubbery legs and battling an urge to throw up, it seemed to take forever.

Ben helped her inside and slammed the passenger door. While he came around, she breathed deeply and slowly, praying she could make it home without disgracing herself. He climbed in but didn't start the engine. "You think you'll be okay for a few minutes? If not, we can just sit here until you feel better."

She gave him a weak smile. "Am I looking green?"

"I wouldn't say that." He still looked concerned. "You fainted. I don't expect you to look a hundred percent."

She leaned back against the headrest and closed her eyes. "I may never again be a hundred percent."

He started to reply, then didn't. Instead, he started the car, shifted into gear and pulled away from the curb. Taking it easy, she noted with gratitude, keeping her eyes closed as another wave of nausea rose in her throat.

"Hold on. We'll be at your place in five minutes tops."

She nodded mutely. Ben was a good friend. If she had to faint in front of the whole world, she was glad it was Ben who had arrived to help her. She wondered if he suspected. Incredibly, Dennis didn't. At least, she didn't think he did.

Dennis. She still hadn't decided exactly what to tell him. Not the ugly truth. She would go to her grave with that. She felt her eyes tearing and blinked rapidly. More deep breaths. All she needed was to start blubbering.

"Has this happened before?" Ben asked quietly.

She was so intent on holding herself together that she had to think what he meant. "Have I fainted before?" She moved a hand weakly. "No, this is a first."

A few minutes later, he turned into her street. He stopped in her driveway, climbed out and went around to her side. She was ready to decline his help, but one look at his face and she knew he wouldn't leave until he'd seen her into her apartment and settled to his satisfaction. Ben was the protective type.

Without a word, she handed over her key and stood with her eyes closed while he unlocked the door. He put a hand to her waist, ushering her inside. She heard him clear his throat. "It's probably none of my business, Suzy, but have you seen a doctor?"

She bolted for the bathroom. As she retched into the toilet, she was vaguely aware of Ben in the tiny space with her, rummaging around. He found a washcloth and turned on the water at the sink. By that time, she was collapsed on the floor, too weak to stand. Finally, she leaned against the side of the tub, her eyes closed.

"Here." Down on his haunches in front of her, he put a washcloth in her hand and watched while she used it. She gave it back, murmuring thanks.

He dipped his head to look right into her face. "Okay now?"

She must look like hell. But she nodded and let him help her onto her feet. She went directly to the sink. As she turned on the water, he left her and closed the door quietly behind him.

He was waiting when she came out. "How about some crackers and a cup of tea?"

She gave him a wry look. "How do you know these things, Ben?"

He shrugged. "I read a lot." Then he grinned. "Actually, one of my roommates last year ran into a similar situation with his fiancée." He sobered, looking as if he might have gone too far. "She claimed nothing eased her nausea those first few months like plain crackers and tea."

She sat down, suddenly overwhelmed. "Dennis doesn't know yet," she whispered.

He looked surprised. "You do plan to tell him?"

She studied her hands. His question neatly pinpointed her dilemma. She could have the baby or she could abort it, and when she had first suspected she was pregnant, she had thought of nothing else. But as time passed, the thought of destroying the tiny innocent life within her became repugnant. Such an option was now something she rejected. Besides, even if she chose abortion, she couldn't do it without Dennis's consent and approval. It might be his baby.

Of course, she couldn't tell him that it might not be his baby.

"None of my business, huh?"

She glanced at him, so caught up in her thoughts that she'd almost forgotten he was there. "I'm sorry, Ben." She rubbed her forehead wearily. "These days I hardly know whether I'm coming or going."

"Is there any way I can help? Just say the word, Suzy."

She managed a smile. "Thanks, but I think I'll have to sort this one out on my own."

She felt oddly bereft after he left. For weeks she had kept to herself the knowledge that she was pregnant. She was almost relieved that someone knew. And that it should be Ben Kincaid was somehow reassuring. He had been her friend almost as long as Dennis. Time now to face the next problem.

With a sigh, she got up and made herself a cup of tea, then took it to the sofa, where she curled up under a knitted throw. She could never recall the time immediately after Taylor's wedding with any real clarity. Those days and nights, for the most part, had passed in a dark, tormented blur. One moment she had been livid with rage, trembling with the urge to confront Jack and watch his face when she told him he wasn't getting away with raping her, that she was going to the police. But in the next moment she had acknowledged the futility of that. She had destroyed the evidence vital to prosecuting Jack. In a rape case, if there was any chance of convicting the rapist, physical evidence had to be obtained then and there. Hard on the heels of that, she was swamped with thoughts of Taylor and her parents and the reality of what such a scandal would mean. At those times, her imagination went wild. She felt like a mouse in a maze. She was trapped. Helpless. She was also angry and bitter and frustrated.

One thing had crystallized. Until then, she hadn't actually decided what particular branch of law she was most interested in. Now she knew. She would choose criminal law. And she vowed to be a top-notch prosecutor.

If she ever got over the nausea.

She was in a mindless half-sleep state when she heard Dennis's key in the lock. Her heart began to pound. How could she tell him? She pressed both hands against her abdomen and experienced emotions that were becoming more and more familiar. Protectiveness. Wonder. Love.

How could she love a baby fathered by Jack Sullivan?

She couldn't. It must be Dennis's child. Even though they were careful, a diaphragm wasn't a hundred percent safe. And there were times they did slip up. Actually, not so much since Taylor's wedding. Very rarely since Taylor's wedding. Because she had more or less avoided sex since Taylor's wedding.

"Hey, honey, you got room under that blankie for two?" Grinning, Dennis tossed his notebook aside and sat down on the sofa. He reached for her, but Suzanne stopped him with a hand against his chest.

"Dennis, I have something to tell you."

At the look on her face, his smile faded. He regarded her with concern in his hazel eyes. "What's up, hon?"

"I'm pregnant."

He hesitated for an instant, then gave a startled laugh. "You're kidding, right?"

"I'm not kidding, Dennis."

"This is no joke." His smile was fading fast. "You're serious."

She studied his face carefully but could read nothing except surprise. "Do you wish it were a joke?"

"I know you wouldn't joke about something so serious. Would you?"

"No."

He was shaking his head. "Are you sure? We're pretty careful and we haven't been making love a lot lately."

"This happened eight or ten weeks ago, Dennis. Before the semester ended." She stared at her hands, hating herself.

"Jesus."

"I guess it is a shock."

"Yeah. I mean…well…" He took a deep breath. "Yeah, I won't lie. It's a shock, Suzy. But it's not a disaster, is it? At least, not for me. It's you who'll have to cope with classes and pregnancy. What I mean is, you had concerns about being married while you're in law school. A baby means even more stress."

"Other women survive it."

Something in her tone caused him to look closely at her. "Yeah, and you will, too. *We* will. Hell, you won't just survive it, Suzy, you'll be damn good at it. You'll be a super mom."

"I don't know about that." She spoke the truth. That was one of the things she'd been worrying about. What kind of mother would she be? She'd spent most of her time since adolescence planning her life as a lawyer. Even with Dennis in her life, there had been little room in her plans for marriage. Accepting a ring had nearly spooked her. There had been no plans for a child.

"This explains your moodiness lately," Dennis said as if he'd just figured something out. "I was beginning to wonder—law school, classes back-to-back, exams—it all seemed to be getting to you. You've been so preoccupied that…" His grin was a little crooked. "Hell, I thought we might be giving up sex altogether."

"Pregnancy seems to make me tired and moody." Even as she said it, it sounded like a lame excuse.

He cleared his throat, looking hesitant but needing to know. "About how long does it last?"

She suppressed a smile. "Nine months."

He made a choking sound.

She laughed and punched him lightly on the shoulder. "Relax, Dennis, I'm teasing. The experts say women usually sail through the second trimester."

He looked hopeful. "And that's soon, right?"

"Another month and I'll be my old self." *Please, God.*

A moment passed while they were both quiet, thinking.

"I never thought of myself as a father," Dennis said, a note of wonder in his voice. He studied the pattern on the throw draped across her lap, then reached over and gently rubbed her stomach. "I'll try to be a good one."

Her heart turned over. Dennis was so good, so trusting. Her eyes stung with tears. She owed him more than this. She owed him honesty. But she couldn't tell him. She couldn't tell anybody. "So we'll get married?" she said.

He touched his forehead to hers for an instant, his eyes closed. "Ah…a moment I've sometimes worried would never happen. At last my lady wants to get married." He hauled her into his arms, burying his face in her hair, and held her tight, enveloping her in the familiar scent of his after-shave and his affection.

She swallowed thickly. "You're okay with this?" she whispered.

"Okay? I'm the luckiest man alive! Whether we slipped up

with this pregnancy or not, I don't care. I want to marry you. I love you, Suzanne."

"I love you, too." She lay her head on his chest so that he couldn't see her tears.

THEY WERE MARRIED the next Saturday before a justice of the peace. It was the only weekend Suzanne had free before she was due to begin her summer job. A wedding took time, a commodity neither she nor Dennis had. She had argued that, given a choice, she would have chosen a smaller, more informal ceremony than Taylor's, anyway, but under the circumstances, it was the only way to go.

The worst was still to come. She had to tell her father and the Judge.

Her hands were cold and her stomach in a knot when Dennis finally pulled into the winding lane that led to the big house at Riverbend.

"Nervous?" He reached over and squeezed her hand.

"A little."

"It'll be okay, Suzy. Your folks gave us their blessing when we got engaged. There's no reason why they won't be happy that we got married."

"They didn't expect me to *have* to get married."

"Hell, these things happen, honey. We're not the first. It'll be okay, you'll see."

She closed her eyes and hoped he was right. She wasn't worried about her father, but Lily Stafford wasn't a judge for nothing. She wouldn't be as indulgent as Dennis's mother. She might accept their sudden marriage, yes, but an unplanned pregnancy was another thing altogether. Still, miracles did happen.

Dennis pulled up behind a Cadillac Seville. "Uh-oh, looks like they've got company."

"Oh, my God."

Dennis clearly assumed she didn't recognize the car. "It's okay. It's family. That's Jack's car." He gave her a jaunty smile.

"Courage, wife. The rest of the clan has to know eventually. Now's as good as later."

She moved to stop him, but he was already out of the car. Every nerve in her body was screaming at her to leave. She wanted to lunge for the wheel and drive straight off the face of the earth rather than face Jack Sullivan tonight.

Or ever again.

Cold and trembling, Suzanne found the door handle. Dennis appeared by her side. He was grinning. "Okay, it's show time."

"I'm not telling them about the baby," she said suddenly.

"No?" he said, sounding surprised. They'd talked it over and decided they might as well reveal her pregnancy. It would justify their haste in getting married.

"Later," she said, trying to calm the panic in her chest. Thank God it was dark and Dennis couldn't see her face. "We'll tell them later."

"Hey, your hands are like ice." He caught them in his, rubbed them briskly and brought them to his mouth. His touch was warm and reassuring. He kissed both palms. Then he wrapped an arm around her shoulders and drew her close. "It'll be okay, Suzy. This is your family. They know you. They love you."

Nobody knows me now.

IT WAS EVERY BIT AS BAD as Suzanne had expected. Not looking at anybody except her parents, she told them that she and Dennis were married. Her father had reacted with bewilderment. The Judge had frowned, then gone cold with disapproval. To marry impulsively was unacceptable for a Stafford. There would be more, Suzanne knew, but not before an audience. Her mother's severest criticism would be delivered privately. Taylor had been openly stunned.

But it was Jack whose reaction galled the most.

"Hell, this is a surprise." After a quick look at Suzanne, he pumped Dennis's hand heartily. "To tell the truth, Dennis, I wondered if you'd ever get Suzy to the altar. You must have come up with a powerful argument."

"It took some persuading," Dennis agreed, grinning at the implied compliment to his prowess.

"I'll bet." Jack's gaze swung to Suzanne. She met his black eyes with defiance. "Yeah, she definitely looks like a woman persuaded."

Suzanne fumed silently. Did only she hear the mockery in his voice?

"I think this calls for champagne!" Taylor's breathless voice was a welcome diversion. She turned to Lily. "Mother, don't we have a couple of bottles left over from my reception?"

The Judge was studying Suzanne intently. "I really don't know."

"We do, I'm sure of it."

Jack leaned back on the sofa, his legs crossed at the ankles. "Now, *that* was a party. Didn't you think so, Dennis?"

"Yeah, right. Great band, great food, great time."

"Is that how you recall my wedding reception, Suzanne?" Jack's voice was silky.

"I don't remember much about it. Those things are almost as stressful for the attendants as for the bride. Right, Taylor?"

"I confess the day passed pretty much in a blur."

"Because you had a snootful," Jack said.

Taylor flushed, then got up to get the champagne.

"Still…a moment here and there stands out in my mind," Jack said softly.

"Well, of course," Charles Stafford said in his gentle voice. "That moment when your bride appears. No man forgets that, not even a fellow as forgetful as me." He chuckled, rolling an unlit cigar in his fingers. His wife refused to let him light up anywhere in the house. "And making your vows. Of course, Lily and I didn't write our own like they do these days. We were very traditional."

"Which is the way it ought to be now." Lily's tone was one she'd perfected in the courtroom. "Maybe if we hadn't given people license to monkey around with tradition, they wouldn't ignore their vows at the first hint of trouble."

"You don't have to worry about that with Suzy and me," Dennis said, slipping his arm around Suzanne's waist. "We took those vows to last forever, right, honey?"

"Yes," she agreed, aware of everyone's eyes on her and hoping she sounded more confident than she felt.

"Okay, everyone, here it is!" Taylor appeared, carrying a champagne bottle.

"I'll get the glasses." Suzanne went to the bar. As much as she detested the idea of Jack Sullivan drinking to hers and Dennis's happiness, there was no getting around it. Dennis popped the cork and beamed while he poured the champagne. He took two glasses and handed one to Suzanne. She met his eyes. His look was loving and proud. Unsuspecting. Taylor passed champagne to Lily and her father, and last of all to Jack, still sprawled on the sofa. There were smiles all around. The shock of their announcement seemed to have passed. Suzanne marveled that no one except the bastard on the sofa seemed to sense her misery.

"Here's to your happiness," Taylor said, smiling at Suzanne. "Forever and always, Dennis and Suzanne."

"Yes. Be happy, m'dear," Charles echoed.

Her mother murmured something.

Now Jack was on his feet. His black eyes, holding hers, had a wicked glint. "And may all your troubles be little ones."

Suzanne set down her glass and walked out.

FOUR

TAYLOR WAS STILL TRYING to take it all in as she and Jack drove home that night. Suzanne…married! Her sister was the last person she'd ever expected to elope. For one thing, Suzanne never seemed…well, passionate enough about Dennis to do something like that. Oh, he was a nice guy, but they were more like best friends than lovers. Taylor gazed from the car, not really seeing much. If Suzanne had suddenly moved in with Dennis, that would be one thing. Of course, their mother would have pitched a fit, but Suzanne wasn't nearly as intimidated by the Judge as Taylor was. She sighed. Suzanne's grit was one of many traits Taylor admired about her sister.

She looked at Jack. "You could have knocked me over with a feather when Suzanne made her big announcement tonight, Jack."

Jack didn't answer. He was speaking into his tape recorder as he drove, his eyes on the road. He had a habit of recording everything, and he almost always carried a small battery-powered tape recorder. Jack recorded even the smallest details, junk that Taylor couldn't see there would ever be any need for.

"Jack?"

He punched a button irritably and stopped the tape. "You can see I'm busy here, Taylor. What do you want?"

"Sorry. I just said it surprised me that Suzy eloped. When you think—"

"Later," he snapped, reactivating the recorder.

She sighed and settled back in her seat. There was no point trying to engage Jack in conversation if he had business on his mind. Which was most of the time. She turned her gaze side-

ways and stared into the night. Today was their anniversary—
they'd been married two months exactly. It wasn't very long,
but it was enough for Taylor to know that her husband wouldn't
remember anything like a two-month anniversary. Marriage to
Jack wasn't turning out to be anything like what she'd expected.

But that was too depressing to think about tonight. Ordinarily she'd feel hurt over Jack's neglect, but she'd had enough
champagne to dull her silly insecurities. She would have had
more, but Jack had actually taken her glass away when she had
started to pour that last drink. He had embarrassed her in front
of her parents—especially the Judge—but she knew better than
to defy him. Jack could be pretty harsh when she made him
mad.

She never meant to, but somehow... She blinked slowly, feeling the effect of the alcohol lulling her into sleep. No, marriage
to Jack was nothing like she'd imagined it would be.

Oh, Suzanne, I hope you know what you're getting into.

A few minutes later, the car stopped with a jerk and she woke
up in confusion. It took a second to get her bearings. "Oh, we're
home."

Jack didn't reply. He got out of the car, and she blinked as the
interior light came on. Still a little fuzzy from the champagne,
she picked her way carefully across the lawn. She didn't quite
make it to the front door before Jack had disappeared inside.
She went in after him, her steps lagging. The mellow glow from
the champagne was gone. She shouldn't have fallen asleep, she
told herself. This always happened. She should have turned on
the radio and found something upbeat, kept herself hyped up
with music. But then Jack would have complained about the
noise while he was recording.

She entered the bedroom just as he was coming out of the
bath. Without glancing her way, he began undressing. She
watched the play of muscle on his thighs as he bent over and
felt desire stir within her. Just looking at him turned her on.

"It's really something about Suzanne and Dennis, isn't it?"

she asked while he took off his pants. "Running off like that. It's sort of romantic, huh?"

"It's bullshit." He pulled his shirt over his head and tossed it aside. "Only one thing would send your tight-ass sister to the altar before she finishes law school, and it's not romance. She's knocked up."

Taylor's mouth fell open. "Jack! That's not very nice."

"What? Fucking without a marriage license?" With a hard-edged smile, he sat down on the side of the bed. "What did you think? That she's too pure to do it? Grow up, for God's sake."

She winced, still unaccustomed to the crude manner Jack often assumed when they were alone. It was so unlike the face he presented to the outside world. "You don't know she's pregnant," Taylor chided, feeling honor-bound to defend Suzanne.

"Okay. But…we'll see." He peeled off his socks and tossed them toward the closed hamper. "Time will tell, as they say."

The socks fell short, landing on top of his shirt. Taylor bent and picked up after him. "I wish you'd put your things in the hamper, Jack. How much trouble can it be?"

"That's your job, babe. What else do you have to do with your time?"

She straightened, looking at him. "Why are you acting like this?"

"Like what?"

She hesitated, frowning as several words came to her. Rude, hostile, chauvinistic. But if she answered him honestly, they'd end up in a quarrel, and she could never get the last word in any confrontation with Jack. He was a lawyer. As was Suzanne. She wondered as she removed her blouse if Suzanne would be as skillful in a marital argument with Dennis as Jack was with her.

"Sometimes I don't think you like my sister," she said, stepping out of her skirt.

"What's not to like? She's beautiful, brainy and she's got steel balls."

"You think she's beautiful?"

He gave her a sarcastic look. "Yeah, I think she's beautiful, Taylor."

"More beautiful than me?"

"Different from you."

"Well, she's blond. Is that what you mean?"

"I mean she's different. Don't I always say exactly what I mean?"

"Well…" She heard the uncertainty in her voice and hated it. She'd always been a teeny bit jealous of Suzanne's brains. But she'd never really considered her sister more beautiful. She studied herself in the mirror doors on the closet. She was petite and perfectly proportioned, whereas Suzanne was tall and willowy. In the cream satin teddy that Jack liked and the thigh-high stockings he favored, she looked sexy, didn't she? Or did he wish that she was tall like Suzanne? Or blond? Her own coloring was striking, everyone said so. It was rare to see the combination of truly black hair and crystal blue eyes.

"Come here, dum-dum."

"Don't call me that!" Taylor said sharply, shifting away from him.

"Then don't act stupid." He caught her, anyway, holding her in a hard embrace. "You know why I'm pissed, don't you?"

She shook her head, refusing to look at him.

"Because you got drunk, goddamn it! You knocked back four glasses of champagne in no time flat. I counted. And if I hadn't stopped you, I would have had to pour you into the car. I'm not putting up with it and I'm tired of telling you, Taylor."

"It was a celebration! My sister announced her marriage." She pushed against his chest. He was holding her too tight.

"Next time, two glasses is your limit," he said, ignoring her struggles.

"You can't dictate to me, Jack."

It was the wrong thing to say and she knew it instantly. He caught her chin with his fingers in a bruising grip. "You're my wife. If you get drunk, it's a reflection on me. Don't make me regret that I didn't marry Stafford's other fucking daughter."

She stared at him helplessly, feeling the rush of tears. Why did he talk to her like that? Why did he want to hurt her?

"Now, what's this?" He leaned back a little, glancing at the satin teddy as if he were just noticing it. "Ready for a little action, huh, baby?" The look on his face drew instant response from her. He pushed the tiny straps off her shoulders, baring her breasts, then laughed as her nipples contracted into hard pebbles. She knew it was crazy to feel desire after he'd just bruised her jaw and humiliated her, but her body seemed disconnected from her mind.

"Let's just get rid of this thing and see what happens," Jack said thickly. Before she realized what he intended, he had grabbed a handful of the teddy and ripped it off. She gasped, stunned by the savagery of the act. She was left in nothing except the stockings, but one look at his face, and desire mixed with trepidation. She was suddenly panting.

"Jack—"

"Yeah, baby? You ready for me?" Holding her gaze—smiling—he felt between her legs. "Ahh, sure you are."

He pushed her backward onto the bed and came down on top of her. She tried to slow him down, wincing as he again caught her bruised jaw. With his mouth on hers, he rammed his tongue deep. And then, God help her, there it was—that crazy leap of desire, that heat and hunger smoldering inside her that only Jack seemed to know about.

She wrapped her legs around him, his ferocity feeding something in her that she had never even suspected existed until Jack tapped into it. With a thrill, she felt the onset of her climax. Desperately, she sought it, fearing Jack would come before her and she'd be left wired and wild and unsatisfied. It wouldn't be the first time. Jack didn't always trouble himself to see to her needs, but when it did happen, it was glorious. She wanted that now. Bucking, clawing at his back, she rushed headlong for that goal.

And then suddenly she was there. Tearing her mouth from his, she screamed, coming in an explosion of light and sensation, needing, wanting, craving every last second of it. A heart-beat later, Jack stiffened and threw his head back, thrusting brutally into her one last time as, with a shout, he found his own release. Taylor shuddered, accepting in the depths of her body all that he had to give. When he finally went still, she was smiling.

Suzanne couldn't give him this.

THE LUNCHTIME CROWD FILLED the busy cafeteria. Suzanne stood with her tray looking for a place of relative privacy. Ordinarily she would have delayed lunch until after one o'clock, but she had an appointment with a professor to discuss her class schedule for the next term. Before her pregnancy, she would have skipped lunch altogether, or at least delayed it until midafternoon, but she was afraid to take a chance on going so long without eating. One fainting spell in front of a curious crowd was enough. She spotted a couple vacating a small table in the back of the room and quickly headed for it.

She had taken only a few bites of her club sandwich when she looked up and saw Jack Sullivan making his way toward her. Just the sight of him was enough to turn her stomach. By the time he reached her table, she was rising to leave.

"Hey, hey, hold on, babe." He would have touched her, but she shot him a look of such loathing that he put his hands up in mock retreat.

"What are you doing here, Jack?"

He shrugged, smiling. "I was in the neighborhood and thought I'd offer my personal congratulations to the happy couple."

"Thanks. I'll tell Dennis." She balled up her napkin and began loading her tray.

"Hey, hold on. What's the rush?"

"I have an exam."

He glanced at his watch. "At noon?"

"What do you want, Jack?"

"After last night, it seemed…appropriate for us to talk." He gestured to her chair. "Clear the air, so to speak."

"I don't have anything to say to you."

"Funny, I thought you might, considering all we've meant to each other. But if you want to be that way…"

She sat down. He took the chair opposite her and pulled it around to the side, close enough that she could smell his after-shave, a scent that would forever be repulsive to her.

"Get to the point, Jack."

He folded his arms on the tabletop. "First off, I gotta tell you that you surprised everybody, running off and getting married like that." He shook his head. "What kind of ceremony was that for a Stafford? It was a real disappointment to the Judge, babe. Did you see her face when y'all broke the news?"

"I don't intend to discuss my marriage with you, Jack."

"Then how about the *reason* you got married?"

Her heart was beating fast, but she vowed not to let him see that his words unnerved her. "What's that supposed to mean?"

"Well, hell, a month ago you were telling everybody— including Dennis—you had to finish law school, maybe even work a while before settling down. Now, just like that, you two decide to elope." She watched his bewildered shrug with disgust. "Shit, Suzy, marrying like that causes talk."

"What kind of talk, Jack?"

His glance was sly. "Well, one possibility does come to mind…."

She couldn't believe his gall. "I don't have to sit here and listen to your tasteless insinuations." She bent over to pick up her things from the floor beside her chair.

"Hey, don't kill the messenger, babe. It just looks peculiar, you know what I'm saying?"

"It's no business of yours *how* it looks." She dumped her backpack on the tabletop and began searching for her wallet.

"There wouldn't be more to this marriage than you're telling, would there, Suzy?"

She stopped to look at him. "Okay, Jack. Just spit it out." Her lip curled. "That is, if you can say or do anything straight out."

He ignored her jibe. With a quick look around, he dropped his voice to an intimate level. "I will never forget getting it on with you in the gazebo, babe. That was some welcome into the family."

"You *bastard!*" Although she kept her voice down, all the venom in her heart was in her tone. "How dare you bring that up to me? If Taylor weren't my sister and if there hadn't been three hundred guests at Riverbend that day, you would be arrested and awaiting trial for what you did."

"Aw, shit! Are you still pissed? Come on, we're family, Suzy. It was sex, pure and simple. We did it and we liked it."

"Liked it! You...you..." But words failed her. Nothing was vile enough.

"We need to let bygones be bygones, Suzy. That's what I'm trying to say. There's Taylor to consider and—" he glanced at her waistline "—whatever."

She swept her things up, so incensed that she didn't trust herself to speak. And frightened. Only one thing kept her from panicking; he couldn't know she was pregnant. He was guessing. My God, Taylor was in for a hellish life if she didn't see this man's true colors right away.

"Hit a nerve, did I?"

"Goodbye, Jack."

"Gonna play it cool, huh?" Taking his time, he stood up.

"If playing it cool means I won't discuss my private life with you, then that's the way I'm going to play it." With her free hand, she pushed her hair away from her face, trying to calm herself enough to walk through the crowd of students, some of whom were now looking at them curiously. As she turned to leave, she said, "I mean it, Jack. Stay away from me or I just might decide that there are some things about you that Taylor needs to know."

Jack watched her thread her way through the diners, his expression hard. One screwing hadn't been enough to tame her. Must be the Judge's genes, he thought. As for her marriage to Dennis Scott, he dismissed it with a contemptuous snort. Whether she was pregnant or not, he gave the marriage two, three years, max.

SUZANNE TURNED OFF the shower and slid the glass door open. Before stepping out, she listened for sounds from the bedroom. Dennis wanted to make love tonight, all the signs were there. He'd had dinner ready when she got home. He'd held her chair and nibbled the back of her neck as she sat down. He'd told funny stories while they ate, and teased and promised with his eyes. The whole time she had felt like crying. Or screaming.

Her nerves had been on edge since the scene with Jack at lunch. One minute she was convinced he knew of her pregnancy and, for reasons of his own, was toying with her about it. The next, she knew he couldn't know, not really. But no amount of logic could relieve her anxiety. Now that she knew the kind of bastard Jack Sullivan was, she wondered if she would ever draw an easy breath again.

She dried herself and slipped on an old T-shirt. She never went to bed naked. Not anymore. Turning out the light, she went to join her husband.

"All finished?" Rolling up on one elbow, Dennis lifted the corner of the sheet, inviting her to slip into bed beside him. He was naked. Because he knew she favored making love in the dark, he touched the lamp, extinguishing the light. "I was beginning to think you were going to spend the night in there."

She pulled the covers up. "Sorry, I guess I lost track of time. The shower spray felt good. I was all keyed up."

"Had a hard day, hmm?" When she nodded, he coaxed her onto her side so that they lay facing each other. She was in her eighth week of pregnancy and had actually lost weight. Tense and anxious much of the time over her fears about the baby, she didn't have the voracious appetite that many pregnant women experienced. Dennis began stroking her, gently rubbing her waist and the small of her back.

"Feel good?"

"Uh-huh."

He had edged closer, entwining their legs. His arousal was thick and hard against her belly, and she felt dread building inside her. She closed her eyes, praying that this time it wouldn't happen. That this time maybe she could feel a hint of the warm loving they'd shared in their relationship before Jack.

Dennis pulled her completely into his embrace and kissed her. He tasted familiar. Musky. Male. She fought a wave of panic. It was almost impossible to lie still while his mouth moved over hers. She concentrated on keeping still, on enduring. But terror was creeping in. This was her husband, she told herself. This was Dennis. He was good. Violence was utterly foreign to his nature. They had made love many times before... before...

In desperation, she resorted to a tactic she'd perfected since the rape. She removed herself to a place beyond the bed, the bedroom, beyond her partner. She closed her eyes and saw a spring day, vibrant with blue skies, alive with birdsong. Water from a natural spring made a gentle, soothing sound.

Dennis pushed her T-shirt up, nudged her thighs apart and stationed himself between them. He was at her crotch now, probing. She was dry and unready. Her body's natural ability to lubricate was lost.

Please, please, hurry. Get it over with.

"Suzy...ah, sweetheart...come on, come on, be with me, baby. Just this once."

But she was past hearing. Past responding.

Dennis was a dark shape above her, a crushing, smothering weight. Although her teeth were clamped tight, a cry came from her throat as he forced himself inside her. She moved beneath him, not with desire, but with desperation. His breathing became heavy and labored as his body quickened toward his release. Another deep plunge. And then another. Then one final thrust and a gusting of breath and sound and it was over.

There was silence in the room as she endured the weight of his body. It would be a few moments before she could scramble up and dash for the bathroom to take another shower. There was Dennis to consider. None of this was his fault. And of course there was the charade of their sexual relationship to maintain.

Without a word, he withdrew and rolled away. She turned, curling on her side, praying he wouldn't say anything.

"What's wrong, Suzanne?"

She glanced over at him, but he was just a shape beside her. Thankfully the room was dark. "I'm just tired, Dennis."

"Or you have a headache. Or you're feeling sick because you're pregnant. Or it's Tuesday and you don't do it on Tuesdays. What the hell's the matter, Suzanne?"

"I don't know." She swallowed hard against a tight throat.

He stared at her for another long moment, then pushed himself up until he was leaning against the headboard. "I don't mean to be insensitive, Suzy, but something has to give here. You act like having sex is...is...sick or something."

"No! It's not...I don't..."

"You don't like making love anymore. Don't deny it."

"It's the pregnancy, Dennis. You know hormones are in an uproar during pregnancy, everybody says so. And I'm stressed over exams. Then next week I begin my summer job in Jackson." She rubbed her forehead wearily. "Everything seems to be getting to me. I'm sorry."

With his arms resting on his bent knees, Dennis stared straight ahead. After a minute or two, he wiped a hand over his face. "I don't know how long I can take this, Suzy."

There was no honest way to defend herself, so Suzanne said nothing.

"Are you sorry we got married?"

"No!" She gave him a startled look, but he was staring straight ahead. "No," she added more softly.

"Then what? It used to be good between us."

"I know," she whispered, her tears welling.

He turned to look at her in the dark. "Even with the baby, I shouldn't have pushed you into marriage."

"Oh, Dennis." Her heart ached at the pain in his voice. For a second, she thought of telling him. But buried deep within her was the guilty knowledge that she was not completely without fault. That she had somehow brought this upon herself. She could not put it out of her mind that before she learned his true colors, she had been almost as enthralled with Jack Sullivan as Taylor was. That was what really galled her, that she had been so stupid as to be taken in by the slick, charming facade Jack presented to the rest of the world.

"Suzanne?"

She turned her face, unable to look at him. "I love you, Dennis, and I want to be married to you."

"You don't act like it."

"Maybe after the baby..."

"Yeah." He turned away, then got out of bed and began pulling his jeans on.

"Are you going out?"

"Yeah. I just need some air."

Her throat was almost too tight to speak. "Don't be long, okay?"

He finished dressing silently in the dark, pulling a sweatshirt over his head, ramming his feet into loafers, scooping up his keys and leaving. Still without a word.

She would get past this, she vowed fiercely when he was gone. It wasn't worth ruining her marriage over. It wasn't worth losing Dennis over. No, she would survive it and Jack Sullivan could rot in hell.

FIVE

BEN KINCAID CAME OUT of the admin building scowling as he studied the remarks penned on the margins of his exam paper on constitutional law. At the bottom of the steps, he stuffed the exam into the trash bin. Days like this—*grades* like this— made him want to quit, just forget law school. He had an almost overwhelming desire to get into his car, head out I-55 South and leave Mississippi in his rearview mirror. It hadn't been his choice to study law in the first place, damn it. That was his grandfather's dream.

He had been sixteen when his father, J.T., had died in a fire at an oilfield site in Texas. Lucian Kincaid had insisted that Marilee and Ben come back home to Percyville, thus ending a life-style Lucian had never approved of in the first place. Most of Ben's early childhood had been spent moving from one oil-patch town in Texas to another while J.T. chased impossible dreams, abandoning them like dry gusher holes, only to chase a new one as soon as he put together enough cash.

One of Ben's most painful childhood memories was a confrontation between J.T. and Lucian over a worthless tract of land J.T. had managed to acquire. Located near Woodville, Mississippi, close to the deep, rich petroleum reserve that was discovered in the forties, it was a surefire gusher just waiting to be struck, according to J.T. Somehow, he persuaded Lucian to invest in it—heavily. He'd eagerly drilled, but all the well ever produced was water.

Ben had been about ten at the time. He could still hear the voices of his father and Lucian the day they finally had it out over that sorry piece of land. He could also clearly recall J.T.'s excitement when he was drilling that land. Maybe there was more than a streak of his father in Ben, because he had known from the moment he entered law school that he wasn't burning to be a lawyer. Instead of clerking in a prestigious firm every summer the way Lucian and the Judge insisted he should—the way Suzanne did—he went offshore in Texas as a roustabout. Like J.T., he loved the camaraderie of the men and the excitement of the rigs, the sheer danger of it all. But some of Lucian Kincaid's caution and stern self-discipline lay buried deep inside him, too. It was Lucian's influence that had made him keep his promise to pass the bar before heading out to see the world. It was J.T.'s genes that made him feel restless and impatient to get on with it.

He got into his car, spewing gravel and dust as he gunned out of the parking lot, then headed not for the interstate but for his apartment.

He had his key out to unlock his front door when Suzanne stepped out of her apartment and called his name. Ben waved, pushed his door open and tossed some things inside, then closed up again before jogging the distance between his apartment and hers. She and Dennis lived two doors over. The three of them had been in the same apartment complex for a couple of years. Now that he and Suzanne were both in law school, they saw more of each other than ever.

Suzanne hadn't been herself since that fainting spell when she'd keeled over on the sidewalk. He hoped it was the unplanned pregnancy that was bothering her and not her hasty marriage. He'd felt some concern about that from the start, without knowing why exactly. Suzanne was one of his favorite people—had been from the time he'd first met her when he was sixteen. But she was off limits. She and Dennis were a couple even then.

"Hi, Suzy. What's up?"

"I was afraid I wouldn't catch you," she said, pushing her streaky-blond hair away from her face. "Did you get your grades?"

"Yeah. It's been another red-hot semester for me. How about you?"

She smiled. "Constitutional law was tough, but it's behind us now."

He snorted. "If you're saying nothing could be worse, you obviously haven't studied the new fall schedule."

"Actually, I have." She chuckled. "Tax law, contracts, real estate."

"I don't know about you, but I'm so excited."

Suzanne huffed out an exasperated breath. "I don't know why you're in law school, Ben. I keep telling you, if Lucian knew how bored you are, he wouldn't push you to stay here. Then you could do what you really want and take off for Texas."

He crossed his arms, smiling. "You think my future's in Texas?"

"You've been dying to go back there ever since I've known you, Ben."

He grunted, not bothering to deny it. "You going with Adams and Reeves again this summer?"

"No. I've decided to make some changes."

Surprised, he asked, "Changes? In what way?"

"I'm interested in criminal law, so I got a spot in the D.A.'s office in Jackson."

"The D.A.'s office? Are you kidding me?"

She sighed and fixed her gaze beyond his shoulder. "I know it's different from Adams and Reeves, but if I do well, there might be a permanent job when I get out of law school."

"I don't think there's any question of that. There's always a job in public life for graduates with your credentials."

"I don't have credentials yet."

"You will." He was shaking his head, shifting to get a closer look at her. "I can guess the Judge's reaction when you told her," he said dryly.

"Well, I haven't exactly told her yet," Suzanne admitted.

"Uh-oh." Still shaking his head, he asked, "So will you stay in Jackson?"

"Uh-huh. I've rented a room in a big Victorian house in the Belhaven area, not too far from the D.A.'s office. I'm moving this weekend."

He leaned against the wall, crossing his feet. "How about Dennis?"

"He'll be staying here for the summer session. He needs the extra credits to get his degree at the same time I finish up law school."

"Rough, you two being apart for the summer like that," he said.

"It is. Dennis isn't exactly thrilled about it."

He could believe that. No man married just a few weeks would be happy to see his wife only on weekends, no matter what the long-range plan was. Now, studying Suzanne up close, he saw that there were shadows beneath her eyes. Chances were Dennis was giving her a hard time over it. He'd been moping around a lot lately, hanging out at Freddy's Grille till all hours. Ben hoped he wasn't into something stupid.

"You doing all right, Suzanne?"

"I'm okay." She smiled. "No more fainting spells."

"That's good."

She glanced away as though fixed on some inner thought, then back again. "How about a beer?"

He agreed and followed her into the apartment. It was cool inside. A beer sounded good. He closed the door behind him, struck as always by the difference in their apartments. The only things his grubby digs had in common with this place was the floor plan and the rent. Suzanne had transformed the cramped efficiency into a home for her and Dennis. Must be a woman's touch, he decided.

"You're dry for the duration, aren't you?" he asked, taking his beer from her and popping the top.

"Yes, Daddy, I'm having juice." She twisted the cap off a bottle of tomato juice and wrinkled her nose at him while drinking it.

"Good girl." He raised his beer and toasted her, then savored the first long swallow with pleasure.

She waved a hand toward a striped sofa. "Have a seat."

He did, settling back and crossing an ankle over one knee. "So what's on your mind, Suzanne?"

She laughed softly, staring at her hands. "You mean besides moving, a final research paper for Easton, my summer job, my pregnancy and my mother's disapproving silence on the subject?"

"You told your parents about the baby?"

"Yes, and you wouldn't have wanted to be there."

He wasn't surprised. Her mother wouldn't take kindly to the news that Suzanne's career path had taken a little detour. Not that the Judge didn't approve of Dennis or marriage or a grandchild, but she took a deep personal interest in the lives of her kids, especially Suzanne's. He guessed she would have preferred that Suzanne wait to start a family. Ben had always felt that the Judge identified more keenly with Suzanne than with either Taylor or Stuart.

"She'll come around, Suzy."

"Yes," Suzanne said, examining her hands. "I know that."

"The job, too. She might prefer Adams and Reeves, but hanging out with the elected elite in Jackson isn't exactly a road to nowhere."

"I know that, too."

"So if it's not your mama, what's bothering you?" he asked, balancing his beer on his Nikes.

She looked up into his eyes. "It's Dennis."

Holding her gaze, he drank more beer. "Dennis."

"He hasn't been home before twelve for the past three nights."

"Shit." He crushed the beer can and lobbed it into the trash can at the end of the breakfast bar.

"Have you seen him, Ben? Do you know where he's going?"

"Look, Suzy…" He pulled at one ear, uncomfortable as hell

with this. "It's not me you should be asking these questions, it's Dennis."

"I know, but it's just so difficult."

"Difficult? You can't ask your husband where he's been until midnight for the past three days? Come on, Suzy."

"It's hard to explain, Ben."

"I'm listening and I've got time."

She stood up, walking to the window so that he couldn't see her face. "He's...upset with me. It's personal, but it's hard for us to talk about it."

"That doesn't sound like the two people I know. Your relationship with Dennis began when you were in eighth grade, for Pete's sake. I can't imagine any subject you can't talk about."

She didn't reply, but her expression was so bleak, he thought she was going to burst into tears. He sat there wondering what to say to her. "Did you want me to talk to him?" he asked finally.

"No, that's not why I asked you in." She wrapped her arms around herself. "Actually, I was just wondering if he'd said anything to you. If he'd mentioned that...well, that he's unhappy."

"I saw him a couple of nights ago. At Freddy's. He may have had a few too many beers, but he was alone if that's what you're asking."

She made a small, hurting sound, as though she hadn't thought of that possibility. Then what was she asking?

"Did he talk about me?"

"I think I asked about you, how you were doing. He said that you needed more rest now. He didn't say anything beyond that, nothing I would consider personal—about your relationship, I mean. I don't know what you're getting at, but Dennis loves you too much to talk about that to just anybody."

"You aren't just anybody, Ben." She turned then, and the misery on her face brought him to his feet.

"Jeez, Suzy. What's wrong?"

She shook her head. "I shouldn't have involved you, Ben.

This is something only Dennis and I can work out. I just thought—"

The door opened suddenly and Dennis walked in. For a split second he stared in surprise before crossing the floor to Suzanne. He tossed his car keys on the bar. "Hey, babe. I didn't know we were having company."

"You're not," Ben said, heading directly for the door. "I was on my way out. No matter how hard she tries, Suzy can't convince me I'm cut out to be a lawyer."

Dennis's gaze moved from Ben to Suzanne. "Shop talk, huh?"

"We both got our grades today," Suzanne explained, looking at Ben. "You never said where you're planning to work this summer."

"Offshore—Galveston. I got a call from PetroTex."

"Lucky dog." Dennis went to the refrigerator and took out a beer. "Unlimited fishing in the Gulf, great food, shave only if you feel like it—it's no surprise to me you like that life better than this."

"There are a few drawbacks," Ben said dryly. "Like dislocating a shoulder when a cable snaps."

"And riding out hurricane winds a week before you were supposed to leave last year," Suzanne said.

Ben reached for the doorknob. "Yeah, and how about the occasional world-class bout of seasickness and no hope of going ashore until the next scheduled run of the chopper."

"More than compensated for by indecently high hourly wages," Dennis said.

At the door, Ben spread his hands, grinning. "It's a tough job, but I guess somebody's got to do it."

Dennis glanced at Suzanne, then popped the top on his beer. "Maybe you could put in a good word for me next year."

A short, taut silence fell. Suzanne studied the pattern on the breakfast bar. After a second, Ben rapped sharply on the door with his knuckles. "Okay, you two, I'll see you later. I'm packing tonight, then I'm out of here tomorrow at daybreak."

"Have a safe trip," Suzanne said softly.

"Yeah, take it easy." Dennis said, wiping his mouth with the back of his hand.

When Ben left, Suzanne bent down and pulled a skillet from the lower cabinet. "I thought stir-fry tonight if that's okay," she said, taking vegetables out of a grocery bag. She went to the refrigerator and opened it, but, getting no response from Dennis, she turned to look at him. "Stir-fry okay?"

"I don't really give a shit."

She closed the refrigerator door. "What's that supposed to mean, Dennis?"

"Just what I said. I don't give a shit about discussing the dinner menu. But what I do want to discuss is why the hell I come home and find my wife and her bosom buddy alone together and looking guilty as hell."

"That's ridiculous, Dennis."

"What? That Ben Kincaid is your bosom buddy or that you were looking guilty?"

"Oh, Dennis…" She sighed, unwilling to get dragged into an argument. She just didn't have the energy.

"You can't deny that Ben Kincaid isn't exactly a casual acquaintance, Suzanne. You two have always been close. I'm just now beginning to wonder how close."

Standing at the sink, she stared blindly through the window, unable to deny Dennis's words. It was true. The friendship she shared with Ben Kincaid had begun the first night they'd met. The night Ben's father had died.

Lucian Kincaid was the county sheriff, bluff, straight-talking, a man's man, and Charles Stafford was an introverted, shy writer of nonfiction, but the two men had shared a friendship since boyhood. One Wednesday night in July, Lucian and Charles were playing gin rummy at Riverbend, as usual. Ben, just sixteen at the time, was visiting Percyville for a couple of weeks with his mother. J.T., his father, was in Texas, working.

When someone began pounding on the door near midnight, it had been Suzanne who had answered. Ben, distraught and grief-stricken, was there with his mother to tell Lucian that J.T. had died in a fire on an oil rig. Any distance the two teenagers might have felt at meeting each other for the first time had been bridged by the outpouring of Suzanne's sympathy over Ben's loss.

So, yes, Ben was a special friend.

"What's going on, Suzanne?"

"Nothing's going on, at least nothing like you're suggesting." She turned the water on at the sink and reached for the vegetables. "Since you don't give a shit, I guess the choice is mine. We'll have stir-fry."

"I want to know what Ben was doing here."

She sliced a green pepper in half with one stroke. "We were talking, just as he said."

"About what?"

"Law school. Summer jobs. Life."

"His or yours?"

She paused and stopped to look at him. "Both, Dennis. He doesn't want to be a lawyer and I want to be one above all things. We talked about that."

"Above all things." Dennis nodded slowly at that. "I can vouch for that, babe. You sure want to be a lawyer more than you want to be a wife."

No, never, but being a lawyer was so much easier than being a wife. "I'm sorry you feel that way, Dennis."

"How could I feel any other way?"

She closed her eyes. "I told you, things will be better once the baby is born."

"Sure." He scooped up his car keys. "I'm going out."

SUZANNE BEGAN HER SUMMER JOB as an aide to one of the assistant district attorneys in Jackson two weeks later. Her place in Belhaven was a single room in a rambling old Victorian house owned by an elderly woman and was oddly comforting. Something about it reminded her of Riverbend without the surrounding grounds. Dennis had reluctantly stayed behind after she'd convinced him of the wisdom of her plan. The reality was that she and Dennis would see each other only on weekends. She knew Dennis sensed her relief, which only added to her guilt.

Taylor was thrilled at the thought of Suzanne living nearby for the summer, and when she came to visit she was clearly disappointed when Suzanne refused her offer to live with her and Jack.

"It's only ten weeks, Suzy. We have this big old house—five bedrooms, for heaven's sake! You would be no trouble at all. Won't you reconsider?"

Suzanne's stomach knotted at the thought of living in Jack Sullivan's house. At *seeing* the man every day. "Thanks, but it'll be best if I have my own space, Taylor. I'm close to the job here, and if I have to work late, I can come and go without disturbing anybody."

"Don't be silly! You won't disturb us." Taylor was genuinely distressed.

"Really, Taylor, I appreciate the thought, but…no. You're sweet to offer." She transferred some clothes on hangers from a tapestry garment bag to a beautiful old cherrywood armoire.

"Is it because you think Jack would mind?" Taylor sat on the bed. "If so, forget that, because it was his idea."

With her back to Taylor, Suzanne froze. She turned slowly. "What did he say?"

"You mean his exact words? Just what I said. Tell Suzanne we've got bedrooms going to waste around here. She's welcome to take her pick."

"Well, tell him thanks, but I'm already settled here." Suzanne began tossing shoes into the bottom of the armoire, imagining a few other choice messages she would like to send to Taylor's generous-hearted hubby. She closed the armoire hard, and instantly the room tilted and turned dark as a rushing sound filled her ears. She caught blindly at the armoire, one hand going instinctively to her stomach.

"Suzanne, are you all right?" Taylor jumped up and guided her to the bed. "Sit and put your head down."

"I'm okay," Suzanne said after a few moments. Leaning against the bedpost, she opened her eyes and looked at Taylor. "Just a little dizzy spell. It happens."

"To pregnant women." Wide-eyed, Taylor pressed her fingers to her mouth. "Suz-a-a-anne…"

"What, Taylor?" Suzanne said wearily.

"Jack was right, wasn't he?"

If anything could stiffen her spine, that was it. "About what?"

Taylor's gaze faltered. "I shouldn't have said that."

"What did Jack say, Taylor?"

She shrugged helplessly. "Just that you and Dennis… Well, getting married suddenly like that and not telling anybody…is usually because…um, because…"

"Because I'm pregnant." There was a bottle of orange juice on the bedside table. Twisting the cap off, Suzanne lifted it and drank. Holding it against her forehead, she said, "It's true, Taylor. I am going to have a baby."

"Oh, Suzanne."

Suzanne smiled faintly. "Is that a pleased response or do I detect a note of horror?"

"Well, shoot! I don't know whether to be happy or upset over this." Taylor paused, took a deep breath, then laughed out loud. "Guess what? So am I."

Suzanne looked at her in confusion. "You're what?"

Taylor's blue eyes danced. "I'm pregnant, too. We're going to have babies at the same time!"

"We are?"

"Well, maybe not at the *exact* same time, but pretty close." She sat on the bed beside Suzanne. "When are you due? My doctor's not certain, but I am. I'm positive. I'm three weeks late, but I can tell."

"How?" Suzanne managed to ask. She was dizzy from shock now. Jack was a busy guy. "I never had a clue."

Taylor launched in with symptoms, laughed about losing her lunch in the mall a few days before.

Suzanne nodded numbly. "Does Jack know?"

"Of course. He's thrilled."

"Really."

"Uh-huh. That's one of the reasons he thought you'd like to stay with us. He was just certain you were pregnant, too, and he thought you'd be better off staying with family."

"I'll be fine."

"When did you say your baby's due?"

"Sometime in January."

Taylor paused, counting on her fingers. "It must have happened around the time of my wedding. Isn't that something? I figure March for mine." She gave Suzanne another concerned look. "You're sure you won't change your mind about staying with us, Suzy?"

"Yes."

AFTER TAYLOR LEFT, she was too agitated to sit still. She finished unpacking, then surveyed the room with a critical eye. The place had a decidedly feminine feel. She would have to remember to try to give it a more…married look before Dennis came this weekend.

She would try to act more married when Dennis came this weekend.

With a sigh, she sank down on the side of the bed. It wasn't any concern of hers if Jack and Taylor were expecting a child, she told herself. It didn't affect her in any way. All she had to worry about was her own baby, taking care of herself, keeping fit, eating properly, doing everything she could to bring this tiny life into the world healthy and strong.

Even if it had been conceived in violence.

She rubbed a hand over her abdomen and felt a welling of mother love, undeniable, instinctive and fierce. But the question was always with her. Who was her baby's father?

SIX

August 1981

ANNIE FIELDS BLINKED at the newspaper, gave a little squeak of surprise and set her coffee cup down with a thud. The man sitting opposite her grabbed at the drawings spread over the table before they were soaked.

"Look at this, Spencer." Annie pointed to an article on the society page of the *Percyville Sun*. Not waiting for him, she began reading, "'Among the guests at the Performing Arts Gala Saturday night in Jackson were Jack and Taylor Sullivan. Taylor was radiant in a cobalt linen empire dress with a wide white lace collar. Pregnancy certainly becomes the lovely wife of one of Mississippi's rising political stars.'"

Annie looked at Spencer over the top of the paper. "I bet he did it just to get one up on Stuart."

Spencer frowned. "Did what?"

"Got Taylor pregnant. Stuart is the Judge's firstborn. He and Eleanor have been married for several years now, but no babies. Jack knows that the Judge wants Stuart to produce her first grandchild. It's typical of Jack to want to steal his thunder. Anything to suck up to Aunt Lily."

"Sounds like a real sweetheart," Spencer commented dryly.

"Aunt Lily? Hardly. She's tough as nails and smarter than she's tough."

"I meant Sullivan."

Annie gave a snort. "*Sweetheart* doesn't characterize Jack any more than it does Aunt Lily. The only thing that keeps me from worrying about Jack and what he's capable of is that

Judge Lily Stafford is a match for him. Of course, he doesn't think that, but then Jack is too arrogant to believe anybody's his equal."

"You really detest the guy, don't you?"

Annie picked up her coffee and sipped thoughtfully. "I do, but don't ask me to give you any concrete reasons why. There's just this feeling I have about Jack. And it's wholly negative."

"Then pity his wife."

"Taylor? Yes. But he'll be careful with her, I think. He must realize what an asset she is—she comes from a good family, her mother's an influential judge, she's beautiful, educated and ga-ga over him. As a politician on the way up, she can only help him."

Spencer finished his coffee and set the cup aside. "Which is not the kind of life you would settle for in a million years."

Annie laughed. "Being some man's arm ornament? No."

He frowned, thinking. "I thought you said Suzanne was pregnant. Her baby, not Jack's, will be the Judge's first grandchild, won't it?"

"Yes, and I'll bet Jack's pissed over it. I called Suzanne last week and she told me she'd been at Riverbend the night before to tell her parents. Uncle Charles took the news in his usual way—gently bewildered but pleased for Suzy if having a baby is what she really wants. Aunt Lily was disapproving, of course. She didn't say much then, but Suzy figures she'll find some reason to visit her in Jackson and give her The Lecture."

"The Lecture?"

"Yes. The one about establishing goals—professional and personal—and having the self-discipline, commitment and sheer grit to accomplish both. Marrying in haste is frowned upon. Ditto an unexpected pregnancy, so Jack's still got the edge."

Spencer's mouth moved in a slow smile. "The more I learn about your family, the more I wonder how you managed to fit in. The Judge doesn't sound like a woman to appreciate a free-spirited imp like you."

Spencer seldom smiled, and when he did it was very appealing. Annie chuckled. "She did try her heavy-handed tactics on me a few times, but remember, I already have a mother. If Aunt Lily had been a man, I'd have been in big trouble. Me being fatherless and in need of a father-figure would have been an open invitation for her to meddle in my life."

"You and Eugenia went to live with them...when?"

Annie broke a piece of toast in half and took a bite. "When I was two," she said, brushing crumbs off the glass-topped table. "I was a baby when my mother divorced my father and married Tillman Stafford, Uncle Charles's brother. Unfortunately, Tillman died in a car wreck before I was three. Nobody dares say it, but I think Tillman was sort of a black sheep. He didn't leave any insurance, and my mother was pretty desperate, from what she's told me. That's when the Staffords stepped in. In spite of the fact that we're not related by blood, we've always been treated like family. In the eyes of the Staffords, being married to Tillman made us family."

Annie propped her elbows on the table, cradling her coffee cup in her hands. "Being a true Southern gentleman, Uncle Charles brought us to Mississippi, set us up in a cottage at Riverbend and assured my mother that she would always have a home. That Tillman would expect it."

"From what you've said about Lily, that doesn't sound like something she would do."

"Possibly, but you have to understand her almost fanatical devotion to the Stafford name. She was born dirt poor in rural Arkansas, then used her natural assets—her beauty and her intelligence—to get out as soon as she could. I think she went to some small college in Virginia—on a scholarship, of course. Meeting her and hearing her talk, you'd never suspect her background. She met Uncle Charles when he came to lecture at Emory University when she was in her final year of law school, another scholarship. He was exactly what she wanted— a gentle man—that's two words. He was Southern, from the right family, not too overtly masculine, willing to accept her ambition, even encourage it. She's been a judge for many years. I don't remember exactly when she first sat on the bench."

"Sounds like a cold-blooded bitch."

Annie smiled into her cup. "You'd have to know her."

He gave a noncommittal grunt. "Enough about the first family of Percyville, Mississippi." Shoving plates, uneaten toast, cups and silverware aside, he spread the papers out again. "Let's go over the new production schedule. If we're going to deliver on the date you promised the new clients, we've got to increase production by fifteen percent. Now, here's how I think we can do it."

Spencer pulled the plan and his figures closer and began walking her through the process as he proposed it. Annie heard him out carefully, but as she'd expected, there was little for her to question and nothing to change. Dream Fields, the name she'd coined for her greeting cards, had been a fledgling enterprise when she'd hired Spencer Dutton. During those early days, he'd done practically everything necessary to print her cards. She was well aware of her own creative talent when it came to writing and designing Dream Fields, but Spencer was no less creative in bringing forth the finished product. And in those early years, production had been run on a shoestring. She didn't like to think what she would do if Spencer decided to move on.

He was a loner, she knew that. It wasn't exactly a stretch of the imagination to think of him simply walking away if he should see something more interesting somewhere else. But she didn't think he would do that. They were more than business associates; they were friends now, and he wasn't the kind of man to let a friend down. Actually, Spencer knew more about her life than she did about his, but she trusted him implicitly and she believed her trust was returned.

"So, you want me to go ahead with this?" He looked up at her.

She nodded. "It looks fine. More than fine, Spence."

"Then I'll be on my way." He stood up, collecting papers. "You miss that place, don't you."

She gave him a blank look. "What place? Mississippi?"

"Yeah. And the South. The Staffords."

"Nutty, huh?" She smiled. "Yes, I do. What can I say?"

"Maybe you shouldn't have left."

"Then I wouldn't have Dream Fields."

"Uh-uh. You'd have made it no matter where you were, plus you might have a love life."

"I'm not in the market, Spence."

"You would be if the right guy came along."

They'd been down this road before. "He did, and he chose somebody else."

"Stuart Stafford's the nutty one if he didn't want you, Annie."

She grinned. "*You* don't want me, so are you nuts?"

"I don't want any woman. They're bad luck. Screw up my karma."

"Bullshit. I'm gonna remind you of those words when you finally find the right woman."

His expression revealed what he thought about that. Casually bumping the rolled papers against his thigh, he said, "You could always move your business. Dream Fields greeting cards can be printed anywhere. It doesn't have to be in California."

She laughed out loud. "Oh, sure, I can just see you in a sleepy Southern town."

"You don't need me to produce Dream Fields, Annie."

She leaned back in her chair, cradling her coffee cup in both hands. "Oh, but I do, Spencer. And don't ever doubt it."

After he left, Annie lifted the newspaper again. To keep in touch, she had subscribed to the *Percyville Sun* soon after settling in L.A. Spencer was right—she did miss the South. Her business was in L.A., but home would forever be Mississippi and Riverbend.

She got up and poured herself a fresh cup of coffee and went to stand at her patio doors. Outside was a riot of color—

pink bougainvillea, purple clematis, yellow mums—and yet she wished for wisteria and magnolia and crepe myrtle. She was homesick. As soon as Suzanne's baby was born, she'd go for the christening. She leaned her head against the glass, glad it wasn't Stuart and Eleanor expecting a child. She wasn't sure she could bear that.

SUZANNE'S LABOR BEGAN during the ten o'clock news on New Year's Eve. She had been testy and difficult all day long and had begged off when Dennis tried to persuade her to go to a party. She hadn't admitted it to him, but the last thing in the world she needed was to watch a bunch of people waiting for midnight drinking themselves silly while she sipped ginger ale. After this baby was born, she would never again drink ginger ale.

Besides, she'd had a nagging backache for two days. Smothering a groan, she shifted the pillow at the small of her back and tried to find a comfortable position. She was on a weekly schedule with her doctor now. Tomorrow was a holiday, but the next day she had an appointment. Thank God the baby was due in two weeks. These days she didn't sleep well, she couldn't bend down and pick up anything on the floor, her feet were swollen and she needed help getting out of a chair. She was more than ready to have this baby.

The healthy thump of a tiny foot in her side forced a grunt out of her, and in spite of the discomfort, her face softened. She put both hands on her enormous belly and rubbed. When the baby was restless, gentle stroking sometimes calmed it.

Suddenly she was struck by a sharp, wrenching pain, centered deep and low in her body. Stunned at first, she could do little except ride it out. When it finally eased, she drew several deep, gasping breaths. Was this labor? According to everything she'd been told and almost everything she'd read, the onset of labor in a woman's first pregnancy was supposed to be slow and methodical. Even boring. Pains thirty minutes apart, then twenty, then fifteen and so on. They weren't even supposed to hurt at first.

She gasped again as another fierce contraction racked her lower body. The pain was so intense that she actually saw stars.

Pant. She was supposed to pant. She did, concentrating for several seconds. Four minutes past ten, she saw, glancing at the clock. She'd forgotten to notice when the first one struck, but it hadn't been long ago, she knew that.

First of all, she had to get help. Dennis. She needed to call Dennis to come home. Hauling herself off the sofa, her hands low on her belly, she waddled to the kitchen bar and found the note where Dennis had said he'd be. Hands shaking, she punched out the number. It rang and rang and rang.

"Please, please," she whispered. "Somebody please answer the phone."

"Hello!"

"Hello, this is—"

"Can't hear you, sweet cheeks. There's a party goin' on!"

"Please, I'm trying to—"

"You gotta speak up, baby."

"This is an emergency. Please get Dennis Scott to come to the phone."

"Who?"

"*Dennis Scott!*" She was almost screaming.

There was a rattle as the receiver landed on a hard surface. Suzanne's fingers tightened as she felt the onslaught of another contraction. "No, not yet. Not now," she whispered, bracing herself.

She wasn't supposed to fight it. She dropped the receiver and held on to the edge of the bar while pain bloomed deep inside her, unfurling like a black flower, then bursting through her middle, rising, increasing, peaking in a hellish crescendo.

Helpless and terrified, she sank to her knees, unable to combat the primeval forces invading her body, greedily pushing her beyond the ability to bear them. Whimpering, panting, she waited until the pain passed. Exhausted, she rested her head against the base of the bar and tried to catch her breath. The motion of the receiver dangling over the edge caught her eye. Weakly, she reached for it, praying Dennis would be there. But the line was dead.

Dragging herself upright again, she punched in a familiar number. Tears welled in her eyes as it rang. Hanging on to the receiver, she waited through three rings. Four. Five. He wasn't there. The keening sound was her own anguished cry.

"Yeah, hello?"

"Ben, oh, Ben. Thank God. You've got to help me, Ben."

"Who—Suzanne?"

"It's me. Ben, I need—"

"Suzanne. Jesus, what's wrong? You sound—"

"Ben, please…can you come?"

"You just caught me. I had to come back and get— *Shit!* Never mind why. Are you sick, Suzy?"

"No." She managed a weak laugh. "I mean, I don't think so. I think I'm just having a baby."

HE WAS AT HER DOOR in seconds.

"Suzanne!" Rushing over, he got her on her feet and helped her to the sofa. "What's going on? Did you fall? Where the hell's Dennis?"

"At a party."

"A *party!* That son of a—"

He broke off at her sharp cry. "Another one," she wailed, reaching for his hand. "Help me. Ooooohhh…"

Disregarding her crushing hold on his hand, Ben bent down on one knee. "Suzanne, are you in labor?"

But she was beyond talking. He was astonished at the expression on her face as she took the worst of the pain. He tried to pull away, thinking to call for help, but there was no breaking her grip on his hands. Feeling helpless and useless and scared out of his mind, he waited her out. Endless minutes later, the pain broke and she began drawing deep gulps of fresh oxygen. Her hold on his hands relaxed a little.

"I'm calling an ambulance!" He broke away and lunged for the phone.

"Yes," she whispered, her head falling back against the sofa back. "Tell them to hurry."

"Jesus, where's the number?" Fumbling at the counter for the phone book, he knocked a glass to the floor. "I've gotta find the number."

"On the phone. In red." She hadn't moved. Her eyes were still closed.

With his hands shaking so hard, he misdialed the number, but finally he got through. A bored dispatcher heard him out, then asked for the address. He blanked out momentarily before stumbling through it.

"Hurry, you hear me?" He turned, looking at Suzanne, his eyes wild. "This woman's in labor and I don't know jack about babies, but I can tell you it's an emergency! You got that?"

Suzanne whimpered again and clutched her abdomen. Ben slammed the receiver down and rushed over. She curled into herself as her body was racked with a fresh onslaught of pain.

"I think the baby's coming!" she cried, gasping with the urge to push.

"No!" He bent down and scooped her up.

"Ben…"

"I'm taking you into the bedroom. I'd drive you to the hospital myself, but I think it's better to wait here for the ambulance."

"Don't leave me."

"Never." He reached down and threw the covers back, then placed her on the bed. Before she lay back, he said, "I think you need to get out of those pants."

"Yes." She made no move to obey.

"Suzy…"

"I can't," she whispered, clutching her swollen belly again. "Another one's coming. Ooohhh, Ben, I need to push. I'm not supposed to push…."

"It's okay. If you have to, you have to." Beneath her, he could see a widening pool of bloody water. Shaken, he dashed for the bathroom to find towels, then came back to her.

She looked at him with abject fear in her eyes. "Ben...Ben... God, I'm scared. My baby...I don't want anything to happen to my baby."

Miraculously, his own fear vanished then. "Nothing bad's going to happen," he told her in an unsteady but reasonably calm tone. "Your baby will be fine, I swear it, Suzy." He reached for the top of her maternity pants and began gently tugging them off. Her panties came with them, but he was beyond feeling awkward. "I don't know what those guys do when they find a lady fixing to deliver right in her house, but I know they're gonna have to examine you. Let's get these off, sweetheart. I'm sorry."

"Hurry! I have to push again!"

If the baby didn't wait for the paramedics, he was going to have to help her himself. He'd had some first-aid training in high school. He searched his memory for the basics on childbirth.

Please, God, let those guys get here soon.

Suzanne looked at him. "Is the ambulance on its way?"

"You bet."

"Promise?"

"Swear to God. Now, just lift up a little and we'll slide these towels under you."

She moaned again. "Ben, another one's coming."

He wanted to yell "No!" but he took a deep breath instead. "Okay, we'll ride it out together." He caught her hands, amazed again by the strength still in her. Just in the time he'd been here, she'd gone through enough physical anguish to exhaust a man twice her size.

Where in hell were those paramedics!

"It's coming, Ben! The...baby...is...co-o-o-ming...."

Her legs were bent at the knees. Ben could see movement on her abdomen as the contraction compressed muscles, squeezing the baby through the birth canal. Glancing at her face, Ben saw that she was caught in an ancient, elemental process. She was going on instinct alone. With or without professional help, her baby was coming.

Releasing his hands, she flattened both palms on the bed, then curled her fingers deeply into the bedclothes—seeking traction, he realized. With a deep, guttural sound that seemed to come from the very depths of her body, she gave a mighty push. He felt an answering surge of emotion—fierce and awesome.

Now, he, too, moved on instinct. Urging her knees apart, he helped her brace for the next push. God, the power! How could her body not be torn apart? he wondered. No time to think of that. She was panting heavily and then bracing again for another push.

Limp and exhausted when it was over, she asked breathlessly, "Can you see it?"

Between her legs, he saw the crown of the baby's head—dark, dark hair encrusted with blood and whatever else existed in the womb. His heart stumbled at the sight.

"Ben?"

"Yeah, Suzy. We're almost done."

"I have to push again!"

"Okay, sweetheart, push away." As blood and fluid gushed out, he put his hands in position to receive the baby. He was barely aware of Suzanne's grueling effort as, miraculously, the baby's whole head was pushed out. Ben was still awestruck when, with another gut-deep heave from Suzanne, the baby's small shoulders and upper torso presented.

"Ahhh, come to Daddy," Ben whispered softly, unaware of his words as the baby slithered into his waiting hands. Moving carefully, he lifted the tiny, wriggling newborn. He had an impression of eyes squinched tight, a button nose almost flattened into the round little face. Then the baby made a mewling sound. Somewhere in his inadequate training, he recalled that mucous should be cleared from the baby's breathing passage.

Ben turned him over and frantically curled his finger into the rosebud of a mouth. That done, he gave the baby a gentle shake.

"What's wrong?" Suzanne demanded anxiously.

"We need to make him cry, I think."

"Him? It's a boy?"

Just then, the baby's mouth opened and he let out a short, thin little wail. Then, drawing the first air into his tiny lungs, he began squalling in earnest. With a grin, Ben met Suzanne's eyes. "Yeah, it's a boy." Gently, with the baby still attached to the umbilical cord, he placed Suzanne's son in her waiting arms.

"Way to go, Mama."

FROM THE INSTANT THAT BEN had lifted the baby up and laid him gently over her heart, Suzanne was enchanted with her son. The feeling was startling in its intensity, almost overwhelming in its depth.

"Hello, my precious," she had whispered, caressing his small, unwashed head. He was a squiggly, wailing mass of life and energy and he was hers. *Hers.* She had looked up, meeting Ben's eyes. "Thank you."

Unable to speak, Ben had conveyed a wordless message in his eyes. It was a shared moment neither would ever forget.

Now, in the hospital, at twenty minutes after 2:00 a.m., Suzanne was in a bed, warm and relaxed, her baby safely in the nursery. Fatigue weighed her down, drawing her at last into exhausted sleep.

"Suzy…"

She resisted and moaned, her eyelids too heavy to open.

"Suzy, it's me, honey. I'm sorry. I just got here. I didn't know—"

"Dennis." One hand fluttered.

"God, I'm so sorry, Suzanne. I wanted to be with you. I *should* have been with you." Dennis picked up her hand and squeezed it, then brought it to his mouth. He pressed it hard against his lips.

"It's okay," she said, sighing. He had a boozy smell from the party.

"Are you all right? Did everything—" he shrugged ruefully "—come out okay?"

"Hmm."

He was shaking his head. "I don't know what to say. It wasn't time, Suzy!"

"Surprised everybody, coming so fast," she murmured.

Dennis drew a deep, unsteady breath. "It scares me, just thinking about you being alone and in labor like that. I feel like shit. I mean it, Suzy."

"It's okay," she repeated, too tired to offer comfort. She licked dry lips. "Besides, Ben was there."

"Yeah." He stared at their hands. "Your good buddy comes through again."

"Have you seen the baby?"

"Yeah, he's something else." His tone softened. "Looks like your daddy."

She studied him gravely. "You think so?"

"Yeah. All that black hair. Takes after ol' Charles and Taylor, too, I guess."

She drew a deep, shuddering sigh and felt tears gathering in her eyes.

"What's wrong, hon?" he asked, frowning.

She gave a weak shrug and tried to smile. "Nothing. Hormones again, I guess."

"Let's hope the goddamn things settle down, and soon. They've given you hell for nine months." With his thumb, Dennis wiped away the tear trickling from the corner of her eye. "But it's all over now. Our baby's healthy and handsome to boot. And you're okay. That's all that matters, right?"

She sniffed, forcing a smile. "Right, Dennis."

"How about a name? You got any ideas?"

"Caleb Eli," she said, hoping he would agree.

"Caleb Eli." He wrinkled his face, thinking. "Wasn't that your great-great-granddaddy's name? The one who built Riverbend? Wasn't he the governor or something?"

"A U.S. senator during the Civil War."

"Hey, I'm cool. Caleb it is. Hell, with those genes, he could be president. Caleb. Yeah. Sounds good." He gave her a grin. "Let's do it. And the next one will be named after *my* great-great-grandpa."

She managed a smile. "The one who came to Mississippi from Massachusetts? The Yankee?"

He winked. "The *damn* Yankee."

"Okay." She squeezed his hand. "I love you, Dennis."

"I love you, too, babe."

With a brief knock on the door, a nurse bustled in carrying an electronic thing and medication in a tiny paper cup. Glancing at Dennis, she smiled. "Ah, here's Daddy," she said, setting everything on Suzanne's bedside table. "What do you think about that big, fine boy you've got in the nursery?"

"I like him enough to take him home," Dennis said, smiling back at her.

The aide winked at Suzanne as she popped a thermometer into her mouth. "Hmm, you hear that, Mommy? You did good."

Unable to speak around the thermometer, Suzanne lay quietly while her temperature was taken. She zoned out as Dennis and the aide chatted, her heart heavy. As Dennis said, she should be feeling thankful that the baby was healthy and beautiful. And she was. Oh, she *was*. And that Dennis was so proud and happy.

She submitted to having her blood pressure taken, then accepted the sleeping pill in the paper cup. At the door, the aide clicked the overhead light off and left. Beside the bed, Dennis settled back in the chair to spend the night. In seconds, he was asleep.

The sleep of the innocent. The proud father, unsuspecting.

She watched him, tears slipping from the corners of her eyes. Just as she had never been able to tell him about the rape, she knew now she would never tell him the truth. Maybe he would never guess that Caleb was not his son.

SEVEN

TAYLOR GAZED AT HER REFLECTION in the mirrored doors in her bedroom. Turning slowly, she pressed her hands over the front of her body, outlining her swollen belly. The upper bodice of her maternity dress was layered in ice-pink lace, but nothing could camouflage her grotesque shape.

"Oh, I *hate* this!" Whirling away, she clutched her head in her hands and squeezed her eyes closed. "I look horrible! My body is absolutely hideous. I can't stand to look at myself."

"So don't look." Jack stood at his armoire searching through a velvet-lined tray. "Have you seen my onyx cuff links?"

"No." She flopped down on the bed, propping back on her hands.

Jack made an impatient sound. "I can't find a goddamn thing around here anymore, Taylor. Look at this!" He flung the tray onto the bed, strewing a trail of masculine jewelry everywhere. "Didn't I tell you to have my things laid out when I got out of the shower? We're pushing it to make it on time as it is." Still grumbling, he opened a drawer and crammed a clean handkerchief in his pocket, then turned to look at her.

"However, if you don't think you want to be present at the christening of your own sister's kid, then we'll just kick back and have a late brunch and maybe you can think of something to explain why you couldn't make it."

Taylor got off the bed with a sigh and bent down to pick up the jewelry on the floor. "Of course we have to go, Jack." She handed him the onyx cuff links.

With a deft twist, he slipped the right one in. "Then get your ass in gear."

"I just feel so gross!"

Locking the stud in place, he straightened the sleeve expertly. "Don't start, Taylor."

She spread her hands wide. "Look at me, Jack! Can't you try to understand? I hate people seeing me like this."

He gave her a casual glance before fixing the remaining cuff link in place. "You look like a pregnant woman."

"I feel so self-conscious." She glanced in the mirror. "I'm so...so..." She couldn't find a word. "I'm as big as a cow!"

He sucked in a deep breath. "You're in your ninth month. You're supposed to be as big as a cow."

Taylor winced, wondering if she would ever get used to Jack's casual cruelty. For a man who was careful never to strike a wrong note in public, he could be brutal when they were alone. Because she was his wife, it didn't matter how he treated her.

"I wish we could just stay home," she said wistfully. She rubbed at the small of her back. "I feel terrible. My back hurts. I think I'm having contractions, Jack."

He stood before the mirror knotting his tie. "You've been saying that for two weeks."

"But it's true! I do feel contractions."

"False labor."

"Even if it is false labor, it's still uncomfortable."

"Forget it, Taylor. Grit your teeth and bear it. It's Suzanne's big day. Let her enjoy it while she can. Temporarily."

She frowned. "Why do you say that?"

"Because in a couple of weeks, our son will be born." Staring at himself in the mirror, his tone hardened. "He should have been the first—would have been if she hadn't been stupid enough to screw up."

"I don't see what difference it makes who has the first grandchild, Jack," Taylor said. "And you don't know we're having a boy. What if it's a girl?"

"It won't be."

He turned and faced her, flawlessly outfitted in charcoal

gray, his snowy shirt making his burnished skin seem darker and his smile whiter. "How do I look?"

So gorgeous it almost hurt just looking at him. That was another reason she didn't want to go anywhere lately. Jack looked fabulous, and there were always hordes of women around to let him know just how fabulous. A Stafford family christening was the next thing to a political rally, wall-to-wall people. And here she was looking like a...a...fat, pink cow!

"Well?" he said.

"You look fine."

He laughed and leaned over, pinching her cheek—playfully, yet just hard enough to punish a little. "So come on, Auntie. Let's go gush over your sister's brat. He won't hog the limelight long!"

Taylor moved across the room and opened a dresser drawer to remove a small purse. She had almost given up expecting understanding from Jack. Without looking at him, she walked to the door, stopping when he caught her arm.

"Just a minute." His smile vanished and his dark eyes were as hard as the onyx at his wrists. "Wipe off that sour puss. We're going and you *will* smile and act like I expect my wife to act. I'm sick of hearing you whine about how difficult it is being pregnant. You *are* pregnant. It's what women do. It's easy, a piece of cake. Look at Suzanne. Hell, she had that kid right in her apartment. So shape up." He shook his head. *"Jesus!"*

"Are you finished?" she asked coolly.

He simply looked at her, then swore. "Women!" he said. Turning on his heel, he left the room.

THE JUDGE WAS DELIGHTED with the name Suzanne chose for her first grandchild. "Caleb Stafford was one of Mississippi's most distinguished statesmen," she told a group clustering around her at Riverbend after the christening of the baby. Jiggling Caleb briefly on her shoulder, she was in her element.

It was a gorgeous March day, sunny and mild, the sky an incredible blue. The crowd had naturally spilled out onto the patio and lawn. The affair was catered to the Judge's tastes—drinks, food, chamber music. The baby might have been unexpected, but he was christened as if he were a little prince.

"Caleb Stafford was a voice of reason when the Southern states started talking secession," Lily said, glorying in the colorful past of the baby's namesake. "He'd never owned slaves. Unfortunately, he was outnumbered. Of course, in spite of his radical outlook at the time, he served in the Confederate army," she hastened to add. "He was, after all, Southern born and bred. He knew his duty."

She held the baby away, looking fondly into his tiny face. "This little one will have big shoes to fill, but I have a feeling he'll be special." She gave his small chin a gentle pinch. "We'll show 'em, won't we, darlin'? Just wait and see."

The baby began fussing, prompting the Judge to hand him over to his mother. "He's getting tired," Suzanne said, nuzzling the baby's neck. "And he needs changing. Dennis was supposed to take the diaper bag out of the car, but I'll bet he forgot." She moved away from the group, gently rubbing Caleb's back.

There was no sign of the diaper bag in the car, so she headed back through the crowd, looking for Dennis. It was anybody's guess where he'd put it. He was far more casual about Caleb's needs than she was, she'd discovered. Whether that was unique to Dennis or whether men simply weren't genetically programmed for the intense demands of newborn babies, she didn't know. She didn't want to think her passionate care of Caleb came from anything except the fact that as his mother she felt a compelling and natural need to see to his welfare.

Her head whipped around as Jack Sullivan fell into step beside her. "I never thought I'd see this, Suzy, but with the kid draped on your shoulder like that, you look almost maternal."

Instinctively Suzanne shifted the baby to the opposite shoulder. "You can't know how I treasure your opinion, Jack."

"Sarcasm, Suzy? When I'm trying to be nice?" With a pained look, he clicked his tongue. "Don't you want me to offer congratulations like everyone else?"

"Fine. You've offered. Now, excuse me." She stopped abruptly, looking around. Where *was* Dennis?

"I can't believe you'd want me to ignore an occasion like this—the christening of the first Stafford grandchild."

She gave him a cold look. "Actually, I would."

"Now, that does surprise me, Suzy."

"Why?" she asked in a tone as hard as his black heart.

"Well, hell, hon, I guess I just feel a special…connection to the little rascal." He dipped his head slightly, pretending to study the baby. "I was just saying to your sister that babies all look pretty much alike to me, but I'm damned if I can see much resemblance to your beloved in Caleb."

"Go to hell."

"Yeah, well. Whatever. I guess you're right not to worry. Dennis is hardly the type to think like that, huh? Now, me, I'm not so trusting. My kid better damn sure look like me or it'll be Taylor's sweet ass to pay, I can tell you that."

She turned and looked at him. "You are despicable, Jack."

He grinned. "Yeah, so I've been told."

"Excuse me." Again. "I need to take the baby inside and change him." She started off, but he stopped her with a touch to her arm. "What is it?" she demanded, giving him a cold stare.

"Just thinking…" He tipped his head, indicating the baby. "Since the kid was born, you've given a pretty good imitation of the doting mother. I hope you don't go overboard on this maternal shit, Suze. With your brains and connections… And I'm not talking just the doors that'll open through your mama— I'm making contacts myself that are really going to pay off. Between the two of us, we'd be a dynamite combination."

"Combination? As in working together? You and me?" She stared in amazement. "That's a stretch even for you, Jack. But if you're serious, you're even more deranged than I thought."

Anger flashed fleetingly in his eyes. "I'm going to be in a position to throw you some juicy clients, honeybun. If I were you, I wouldn't be so quick to dismiss a golden opportunity."

"But you aren't me, Jack," she said, lethally quiet. "I'll never need you or your golden opportunities."

"Never say never." He wagged a finger beneath her nose, then glanced at the baby. "So don't get too caught up in the kid. Finish law school, get the bar behind you, then between the Judge and me, we'll see you get a nod from a good firm. As for your little fling this summer with the D.A.'s office, I was against it at first, but now I'm thinking it was probably good exposure. Valuable for the contacts. But we both know public service isn't your destiny, babe. Just ask your mama."

Suzanne breathed in deeply, trying to control her temper. The occasion of her baby's christening was the wrong time to tell Jack how remote the chances were that she would ever speak to him voluntarily except at a family gathering. The man had already turned her life upside down. It was incredible for him to assume he could manipulate her career, as well.

Looking beyond her, he waved at somebody. "Gotta go, sugar. I see a man I've been trying to reach for days." Before she could prevent it, he reached over and chucked Caleb beneath his tiny chin. "Uh-*huh!* That is some fine kid. Must be his superior genes." He winked at Suzanne, but there was no humor in his eyes.

AT RIVERBEND AFTER the christening, Annie Fields strolled through the crowd, savoring the feeling of being home again. As soon as she heard that Caleb was born, she had booked a flight for the baby's christening. When she called Riverbend to announce her impending visit, Suzanne had immediately asked her to be a godparent to Caleb, along with Ben Kincaid.

"What do I have to do?" she had asked, not sure what a godmother's role entailed.

"Nothing. Just send him a special Dream Fields greeting card on his birthday."

"I'll do more than that, but it'll be sad missing out on so many of his growing-up years. California is so far away from Mississippi."

"You can always come back home, Annie," Suzanne had replied. "I really miss you. I've never felt you belonged in California. It doesn't matter where your business is located. What's important is creating Dream Fields, and you can do that right here in Percyville. I wish you would consider it."

It felt good knowing Suzanne sincerely missed her. "You sound like Spencer."

"Your right-hand man?"

"Uh-huh. He's always reminding me that I'll never be a true California person."

"What's he like?" Suzanne had asked after a pause.

"Who, Spencer? Dependable, hardworking, intelligent. A good friend."

"Nothing more?"

"No, Suzy," Annie had said firmly, a mental image of Spencer making her smile. "Honest. He's not my type."

Both knew who was her type. Annie had loved Stuart Stafford since the summer she was fifteen years old. Until then, Annie had thought of Stuart in the same way she thought of Suzanne and Taylor, who, even though there were no blood ties, were like sisters. When she learned of his engagement to Eleanor, she had wanted to die. The only thing Annie could find to be thankful for was that Stuart had remained unaware of her crush.

"You're still getting the newspaper out there, aren't you?"

"Yes, why?"

"Did you see the write-up about Eleanor's trip to Russia?"

"As part of a cultural exchange thing, yes. Ballet, wasn't it?"

"Uh-huh. She managed to get a commitment from the Russians, no less, to perform in Jackson. Jackson, Mississippi, can you imagine?"

Annie had laughed weakly. "Incredible." Thoughts of Stuart and his marriage still hurt. Shifting the receiver, she'd asked casually about him and Eleanor.

"Stuart's doing exactly what he loves—publishing the *Percyville Sun*."

"But is he happy?"

Annie heard the baby murmur as Suzanne moved and guessed that she was nursing Caleb. "Happy? I honestly don't know, Annie. Eleanor had her heart set on a different life-style than the one she's living, you know. She was pretty upset when Stuart resigned his job in Jackson."

"I was astonished when I heard that." It was true. Annie was still trying to figure it out. Journalism was Stuart's life. As a reporter, he was sensitive and incisive but fiercely objective. The job as editorial director for an important newspaper could have been a stepping-stone to bigger things—maybe eventually to New York or L.A. His decision to chuck it all to run the *Percyville Sun* had stunned everyone.

The baby had begun to fuss then and Suzanne had hung up. But the conversation had stayed with Annie, and for the next day or so she had toyed with the idea of moving Dream Fields to Mississippi. Then reality had set in and she dismissed the idea as wishful thinking.

Now, sipping from her wineglass as she crossed the lawn, Annie watched Stuart talking with his father. If his departure from Jackson had been stressful, he hid it well. He looked relaxed and happy. Maybe he had the best of both worlds, she thought. As owner and publisher of the *Sun,* he could please himself. Perhaps he wasn't suited for New York or L.A. Perhaps he was more like Charles Stafford than like Lily. Like Suzanne, maybe his roots were in this small Mississippi town.

He was smiling at something his father said when he paused to sip his drink. As he did so, he caught sight of Annie. With an expression of pleasure, he touched Charles on the shoulder and started toward her. Annie's heart started to beat faster. When did people outgrow these crazy adolescent fixations?

"Hi, Annie-girl." His drawl was irresistible to her California ears. Rich and dark, it was like aged Southern whiskey. His eyes, sky blue, went over her lightning quick. "You're looking good, Annie. California's treating you well."

"Hello, Stuart." He was tall—over six feet—and nearly as lean as he'd been at twenty-one. But there was a solid look to him now. Nearing thirty, he was comfortably settled into adulthood. "You're looking pretty good yourself."

"How's business?"

"I can't complain. How's yours?"

"The *Sun?*" He rattled the ice in his glass as he thought. "Let's see now. Circulation's down fifteen percent from last year, but we haven't had to lay anybody off…at least, so far." He gave a rueful shake of his head. "But it's only mid-March. Ask me again in July."

She was appalled. "Oh, Stuart."

He grinned. "It's not as bad as it sounds. In the year before I took over, circulation was down thirty-five percent from the previous year. We don't call our numbers a success exactly— we call it temporarily slowing the race to the bottom."

Her eyes sparkled over the rim of her wineglass. "And you left the largest paper in the state for this?"

"Call me crazy." For a moment or two, he simply looked at her. "So, how does it feel being back home again, Annie? We still miss you around here, you know."

"It feels good. There's no way I would have missed Caleb's christening."

"Yeah, he's something else, isn't he? Suzy and Dennis couldn't be more proud."

Just then the baby gave a fussy cry, and they both turned to look. With Caleb on her shoulder, Suzanne was talking to Jack Sullivan. Not a friendly conversation, Annie thought, catching the expression on Suzanne's face. What was Jack up to?

"Wonder what that's all about?" she said, speaking her thought out loud.

"I don't know." Stuart frowned, fingering the knot on his tie. Then, after a moment, Suzanne turned away from Jack and went inside the house.

"Jack's a jerk," Annie muttered.

"Uh-huh." A second passed as their eyes met, and then they both laughed.

Annie looked around at the crowd, shaking her head. "We're probably the only two people here whose hearts don't flutter when he speaks, with the exception of Suzanne, of course. Look, even my mother acts silly around him."

Following her gaze, Stuart watched as Jack greeted Eugenia Fields with a kiss on the cheek. Blushing like a teenager, the woman smiled and batted her eyelashes. She began to talk, gesturing with both hands, her face pretty and animated. Beside Stuart, Annie groaned. "Oh, Ma, please!"

Stuart laughed, tugging at one of her wild red curls. "Aw, cut her some slack, Annie."

"She's flirting, for Pete's sake!"

"So?"

Annie sighed. "I guess I'm just not used to seeing my middle-aged mom playing the coquette."

"She's not quite ready for social security, Annie."

"She's forty-three!" Crossing her arms grumpily, Annie shrugged. "I'd rather see her flirt with some of the eligible bachelors your mother is always pushing at her, I guess. Besides, Jack's attention should be on Taylor now. These last weeks are no picnic for a pregnant woman."

"You've experienced pregnancy?" There was something more than surprise in Stuart's expression.

"No, but I'm a woman," she retorted.

"Hmm." Stuart shifted his gaze to his sister. "She does look a little forlorn."

"When we were kids, she'd get that expression on her face when she had a special date and nothing new to wear."

"And I thought we were talking tragedy here."

"Back then, Taylor not having something new to wear for a date *was* a tragedy."

He laughed again and took her empty glass, handing it, with his own, to one of the caterer's staff. "Uh-oh. Speaking of moms, mine is headed this way."

Annie turned, watching Lily Stafford approach. It was no wonder both Taylor and Suzanne were beautiful. With a mother with cheekbones like Lily's, how could they miss? The Judge looked a full fifteen years younger than she was. The ice blue of her suit enhanced her still flawless skin. Her perfectly coiffed hair, tinted a shade of pale champagne, cupped the perfect shape of her jawline. No haircut, however, no matter how skillful, could soften the steely set of her chin. Beside her, Annie resisted an impulse to smooth her own rebellious curls and check that her unstructured blazer hung straight.

"Hello, Aunt Lily." Annie moved to kiss her cheek.

"Ah, Annie. Welcome home, dear." Lily Stafford kissed the air near Annie's ear. "I've been trying to work my way over here for an hour! How was your flight? You're looking flushed. You aren't coming down with something, are you?"

"Not that I can tell. It must be the humidity."

"Yes, well, California's dry as a desert. I always did say that." She turned to Stuart. "Did you know Irving Whitelaw is here, Stuart?"

"No, Mother, I didn't."

"Then you haven't spoken to him?"

Stuart crossed his arms over his chest. "No, Mother, I haven't."

"He's on the subcommittee in Washington that regulates FCC licenses. Surely you know that."

"Yes, but why would it interest me?"

She drew a breath through her nose. "Because you're in the media, Stuart. You're not going to be satisfied running an insignificant newspaper for very long, contrary to what you may think today. As soon as boredom sets in, you'll want to be positioned for something more ambitious. Perhaps you'll want to acquire a radio station or two. In fact, I was talking to Jack about it only a few days ago. Radio is a powerful medium nowadays. Stations strategically located throughout the state could be extremely helpful in a political campaign."

Just then an attendant passed by, and Stuart stopped him.

"Bring me a whiskey over ice, please," he said. The man nodded politely. "I'm not planning to run for political office, Mother."

"I'm aware of that, Stuart. I've given up that dream." The Judge looked across the lawn to where Jack was still chatting with Eugenia. "But Jack definitely will...and soon, too."

"Then *you* buy a radio station, Mother. Or better yet, put a flea in the ear of one of Jack's cronies."

Lily turned to Annie, exasperated. "Maybe you can talk some sense into my stubborn son, Annie. The two of you always seemed to get along well. Here you are barely in your midtwenties running a successful business in the cutthroat environment of Los Angeles, while Stuart is content to sit back in that sleepy little office and grind out the news in a town that never sees anything more exciting than a fire in Will Blalock's chicken coops."

"It was arson, and more than four thousand birds died," Stuart reminded her, "but I guess a good sex scandal would make better reading."

"I don't want the *Sun* sinking to the level of a tabloid, Stuart," the Judge countered, fingering an ivory cameo at the throat of her blouse. "I was simply suggesting that you're never likely to be noticed by any of the big chains, buried here in Percyville."

"Which would suit me fine, as you well know." Stuart accepted the fresh drink from the waiter with a muttered thank you, then tossed half of it down before adding, "You may as well accept it, Mother. I'm not interested in getting noticed by *Time* or the Associated Press. I don't want a huge media group acquiring the *Sun.* And I'm not going to be the voice of Jack Sullivan in his political campaign whenever he decides to run for public office."

Lily smoothed both hands over the short peplum on her jacket and straightened to her full five feet two inches. "Well, I can see nothing will be gained by my saying anything more today." She turned to Annie. "Annie, I still hope you might have some influence on him. Take a walk to the gazebo. You both used to spend hours out there together. See if you can drum some sense into him."

Beyond Annie's shoulder, she caught the eye of a fellow judge and nodded, her smile only slightly strained. "Now, excuse me, if you will. I need to mingle."

As Lily walked away, Stuart met Annie's eyes. With a lift of his eyebrow, he asked, "How about it?"

"The gazebo?" She smiled. "Sure. It sounds good to me."

Feels good to me, she thought, matching her steps to his. But then, it always had felt good being with Stuart. His mother was right. They'd spent a lot of time together—in spite of the six-year difference in their ages—before Stuart went off to Ole Miss. And even afterward—on holidays and special weekends when he was home at Riverbend instead of at some of the fascinating places he'd been lucky enough to visit. How she'd envied that. Skiing in Colorado, trips to Miami, California, Mexico, England and France. In her imagination, she'd been to all those places with him. Still, some of her happiest memories were of time spent with him right here at Riverbend in the gazebo.

"The Judge doesn't seem to have totally accepted your decision to run a small-town newspaper," she said, pushing aside an encroaching blackberry vine from the path.

He glanced at her. "Forget the Judge. What do you think about it?"

"Me?" She touched her chest. "What does it matter what I think?"

He swirled the whiskey in his glass but didn't drink. "I don't know. Everybody seems to think I've lost my mind, but running a newspaper is and always has been an honorable profession. I like it, Annie. I like the feeling that folks open the *Sun* every evening when they get home and find out what's happening in Percyville, beyond their own neighborhood and job and family. I'd rather write about Will Blalock's chickens—and it was a big deal to him because those chickens are his livelihood—than to report on a four-alarm fire in a high-rise in Atlanta. In Atlanta, something like that barely gets noticed."

"Perhaps the Judge remembers how she used to dream of you working for *Time* or *Newsweek*." Annie remembered it and how she used to dream that she'd be by his side, artist and poet and inspiration. Ha.

"That was *her* dream, Annie. *I* used to talk about writing. As an end in itself. The power of ideas."

They'd reached the gazebo. An ancient wisteria enclosed the sides and top, but it was too early in the season for the foliage and lavender flowers. Stuart had to push some of the naked vine aside to climb the steps, then they both sat down on the lounge.

"God, I haven't been out here in years," Stuart said, settling into the corner. "How about you?"

"Not for a long time."

He wore a faint smile. "Why is it that whenever I think of the gazebo, I think of you?"

Because they'd spent a thousand hours together in it. "Speaking of ideas, your editorials always grab me by the throat. That analysis of the controversy over the state's education system was really well done. Very even-handed."

"You get the *Sun* in California?" He looked pleased.

"Of course. How else would I know anything?" Out of habit, she lifted her foot and propped it on the edge of the lounge, draping her long skirt over her knee. "I found out about Taylor's pregnancy when she went to some kind of event in Jackson and it was written up in the Living section."

"No secrets around here."

Annie pushed her unruly hair away from her face to get a clear look at him. "How about you, Stuart? I would have thought you and Eleanor would be parents by now. It's been… what, eight years? Don't you ever intend to be a father?"

He looked away, taking a slow swallow of whiskey. "Once I thought so, but not anymore. Not lately."

"Is that a firm decision?"

"No, Miss Nosy. It's just a wishy-washy 'I'm not sure.'"

"You never used to be wishy-washy," Annie said, studying his firm profile. "You used to know exactly where you were going and how you were planning to get there. And your decision to take over the management of the *Sun* was anything but wishy-washy."

"Yeah, well, I'm wishy-washy about bringing a baby into the world."

She wanted to ask why, but she was no longer thirteen, and personal questions were now off limits. Still, he looked as if the subject was painful. He looked as if he needed a hug, and she had a crazy impulse to lean over and give him one. Definitely off limits. But for a second, as their eyes met, she thought Stuart was thinking the same thing. Or maybe wishing it.

She stood up suddenly. "We'd better get back."

Stuart rose slowly, then reached out and touched the cloud of red curls that reached her shoulder. "I was always fascinated by your hair, did you know that?"

"No."

"It's beautiful, like a fiery summer sunset."

He still used words like an artist used color. "Did you ever finish that novel you used to talk about?"

His hand fell to his side. He shook his head. "Uh-uh."

"Why not, Stuart?"

His mouth moved in a wry smile. "I'm no Willie Morris."

"You used to think you were."

"I used to think a lot of things I'm now embarrassed to remember."

"You should never be embarrassed that you dreamed of writing an important novel."

He studied her intently for a minute. Above them in the trees, a few birds called back and forth. Faintly, in the distance, they could hear the music from the christening. "Why aren't you married, Annie?"

She was surprised she could smile. He hadn't a clue. "That's a loaded question today, Stuart. Would you ask a man the same thing?"

"Probably not."

"Then you won't expect an answer." She turned and took the

two steps down out of the gazebo. Stuart followed her, ducking a little to avoid tangling with the wisteria. They walked in companionable silence, aware of the increasing sounds of the party as they neared the end of the path. Annie shoved at the same blackberry bramble that had tangled in her feet coming out. She straightened up, realizing suddenly that something was wrong.

A group of agitated guests milled around the edge of the patio. As Annie and Stuart hurried toward them, Annie could see Jack and Suzanne crouched beside someone lying on the patio.

"It's Taylor!" Stuart said, hurrying forward. Charles Stafford moved to intercept him, putting a hand on his arm.

"She fainted," Charles said, looking worried. "Jack didn't want an ambulance. He's going to take her to the hospital."

The knot of spectators at the patio parted and Jack straightened up with Taylor in his arms. She was as pale as paper, her dark lashes like black mink against her skin. Jack flashed a brilliant smile. "All this baby-mania is contagious, I guess. Taylor's in labor. We're on our way to the hospital. My son's ready to make his appearance!"

THE BABY WASN'T QUITE as eager to make his appearance as Jack boasted. It was almost noon the next day before Taylor finally gave birth.

"It's a beautiful little girl," her doctor said, beaming at her above his green mask. He placed the baby over her abdomen. "Go ahead," he urged. "You can hold her."

The baby was screaming, her tiny face screwed up so that Taylor couldn't tell anything about her. Because the delivery team seemed to expect it, she touched her. Even with their masks obscuring their faces, Taylor could tell that they were all beaming at her. Expecting something from her that she didn't feel. What she felt was exhausted. It was more than eighteen hours from that first humiliating moment at the party when her water broke. To Taylor, it seemed an endless journey to hell and back. Now with the baby on top of her stomach screaming and kicking and looking nothing like anything human, it was all she could do not to scream herself. She moaned in relief when they took the baby back to cut the cord and clean it up. It definitely needed cleaning up.

Jack came in to see her as soon as she was wheeled into a private room. He had a dozen roses in a green vase. She wished for a moment that they were an expression of his love for her, but she knew better. They were for show—because it was what new fathers did.

He set the roses on the table at the foot of her bed and walked over to her. "See, I told you—a piece of cake."

He didn't kiss her, and the niggling worry that had been with her since the baby was born became full-blown certainty. She had failed. "Have you seen her?"

"Sure. They wheeled her out in an incubator while you were still getting stitched up in the delivery room."

"What do you think?" she asked, searching his face. Hoping against hope.

Jack shrugged. "She's cute. We'll keep her." He laughed.

"I know you wanted a boy." She held her breath, afraid of what he would say. Even if he was really disappointed, he could pretend.

He shrugged again. "Yeah, well…" He went to the window, parting the blinds and looking out. "I was counting on you not to let me down, honeybun. A man needs sons. Maybe you don't understand. It's basic." He turned and looked at her. "Next time, hmm?"

After he was gone, she stared at the roses for a long time.

EIGHT

March 1983

SUZANNE WAS IN THE KITCHEN making spaghetti sauce when she heard that Jack Sullivan was the newly elected president of the state bar association. It was on the six o'clock TV news. She recognized it for what it was—a shrewd move on Jack's part to position himself for attorney general, his next goal before, ultimately, the governorship. From there, it was anybody's guess. She shuddered at the possibilities.

Steam hissed up suddenly as the pasta on the back burner began to boil over. Cursing Jack and his ambition, she grabbed a towel and moved the pot, then turned the heat down. Blowing at a tendril of hair straggling over her eye, she glanced at the clock. Dennis was late again. If he didn't show up within the next thirty minutes, she would have to call a baby-sitter. She had to research defense precedent for a mock trial and had reserved time at the law library at eight tonight.

She rummaged around beneath the counter looking for a colander to drain the pasta, but it wasn't where it was supposed to be. Dennis again. He despised unloading the dishwasher and couldn't seem to remember to put things away in the same place two times in a row. He hated doing any chores around the house. He seemed blind to her schedule—law school, Caleb's care, part-time work for two of her professors. He seldom volunteered to help out. She even managed Caleb's day care most of the time. She honestly didn't think Dennis would do anything other than what was necessary for his personal needs and his own architectural degree if she didn't insist. Even then, when he complied, it was a hassle. Two more months, thank God, and they'd both be finished. Maybe it would be different when they were working.

She had the colander in her hand when she heard a crash from the living room. Caleb's wails sent her dashing to her son.

"Oh, don't move, Caleb!" The baby sat on the floor with the broken remains of glazed pottery strewn around him. He was crying at full volume and looking at her plaintively.

Suzanne bent down and scooped him up, inspecting his face and hands. He wasn't scratched or bleeding, just scared by the crash. "Hush, hush," she crooned, swaying with him snuggled safe in her arms. She pressed a kiss to his glossy black hair. "That old pot made a scary noise when it broke, didn't it, sweetheart? But you're okay. Mommy's gotcha."

"Hey, what's up?" Dennis came in, dumping his golf bag at the door. Clubs clattered and clanked as the bag toppled over with a crash. One look and Suzanne knew he'd had a few beers. "What's the matter with Caleb?" he asked.

"He pulled that pedestal over and the pot broke. He's scared, but I don't think he's hurt."

"Da-da-da-da-da!" Caleb dived into Dennis's outstretched arms. Now, at fourteen months, *daddy* was one of his favorite words.

"Hey, it's okay, guy." Holding him above his head, Dennis jiggled him in the air, then put his face against Caleb's belly and blew. With his cheeks still awash in tears, the baby grabbed a fistful of Dennis's sandy hair and laughed while Dennis yelped in pretended pain. He squealed with delight in the familiar game, his accident forgotten. After a moment, Dennis plunked him on the floor. "Okay, kid, Daddy needs a shower."

"Dennis, you don't have time to take a shower," Suzanne said, exasperated. He'd been on the golf course, not even thinking about his promise to baby-sit. She bent over and picked Caleb up, thrusting him at Dennis. "It's after six!"

With a sigh, he took Caleb and walked to the recliner in front of the television, making a place for Caleb between his legs before settling back. "I'm starved, Suzy. I only had a burger and fries for lunch. Did you get a chance to cook anything?"

"Cook anything?" It was bad enough he strolled in an hour late reeking of beer. Now he expected her to serve up something to eat. "You were supposed to be home by five-thirty, Dennis. I've got to do the research for the mock trial tomorrow. *You* promised to fix dinner and watch Caleb. I can't do everything around here, can I? I've—" She shrieked and dashed for the stove as the smell of burned food emanated from the kitchen. "*Damn!* The spaghetti's burning."

"It's okay. I'll order a pizza," Dennis called, his eyes on the television screen.

"Fine! Just great! But you owe me an extra day!" Dennis could be so maddening. She didn't know what was the matter with him most of the time. Or actually, she did know what was the matter. At least, she had a good idea. He didn't take his responsibilities as a husband seriously because he didn't think *she* was much of a wife.

She folded a towel and grabbed the handle of the saucepan. The pasta was stuck to the bottom, but it was still edible. Barely. She threw the whole mess into the sink with a clatter and stormed out of the kitchen. Dennis hadn't moved.

"There's spaghetti sauce and pasta. Maybe you can salvage some of it," she said, heading for her desk. Her research notes were spread over the top, along with clips, pens and a couple of volumes she'd borrowed from her professor. She collected everything and stuffed it into a worn canvas carry-all.

"Caleb's been fed," she said, slinging the strap onto her shoulder. At the door, she paused. "I probably won't be finished before midnight, Dennis. You don't have to wait up."

"Very considerate," he muttered, dropping his head back in the recliner.

The urge to defend herself was automatic. "I don't think you have much room to talk about consideration."

"And I think that's a matter of opinion."

She turned fully, removing her hand from the doorknob.

"Who does the grunt work around here, Dennis—the shop-ping, the vacuuming, the cooking? There aren't enough hours in the day for the list of chores you manage to avoid."

"You *want* to do all that shit, Suzy."

"You think I *like* working like a slave?"

"No, I think it's something you do out of guilt."

"Guilt?"

"Yes, guilt, my dear wife."

She wasn't sure where he was headed. "How many beers have you had, Dennis?"

"A few, Suzanne, but not nearly enough."

"Because if you're—"

"Don't worry about it, Suze," he said wearily.

"I don't have anything to feel guilty about," she said, driven to have the last word.

"Right."

"I don't!"

"Except for the fact that we never fuck anymore, I guess you could say that."

Suzanne stared at him speechlessly, knowing she'd kept on and on until he obliged her with the accusation. As she watched, he settled Caleb in the curve of his elbow on the arm of the re-cliner. The baby looked up adoringly and tried to reach another fistful of Dennis's hair. He missed, grabbing an ear instead.

"Ouch!" He caught the baby's ears and they rubbed noses. Caleb giggled, in heaven because nobody in his world was as much fun as his daddy.

She reached for the doorknob. "Don't let him stay up too late." There was no reply from Dennis. Sighing, she left, clos-ing the door softly behind her.

AT THE LIBRARY, SUZANNE was soothed by the peaceful familiar-ity of it, the books, the smell, the hushed whispers. She checked in at the desk and then went to the computer station she'd re-served and opened her bag. Her hands shook only slightly as she spread the papers on the surface to try to put them into some kind of order. There was a list of references somewhere. Had she forgotten it? She dug deep into the canvas bag, located a yellow legal pad, flipped the pages and found it. For a few minutes, she simply stared at the jumble of letters and lines and numbers. What she saw instead was Dennis's face as he berated her. Resentful, angry, bitter. So unlike his smile as he rubbed noses with Caleb, making him laugh. Making him happy.

She managed to blunt the misery of her failure as a wife by cramming each day to the limit, by scheduling obligations that could not be escaped in the evenings, then falling into bed exhausted. But when moments like tonight occurred and Dennis's resentment bubbled to the surface, she was forced to face her own guilt.

With a scrape of her chair, she got up to pull one of her references, then went back to her corner and took her seat. Opening the book, she breathed deeply and slowly until she could focus enough to look up the case. For the first few minutes, the words were meaningless, but eventually she conquered the turmoil of her thoughts and began reading.

An hour later, she was ready to write the brief that Professor Rayburn would expect to see in her work tomorrow. After thumbing through her papers, she realized she'd forgotten the outline she'd prepared. It was on the bedside table in the apartment. She stared at her watch. There was still time to write the brief tonight, but she had to have the outline. She rose, walked to the clerk behind the desk, explained that she needed to run a quick errand and got permission to leave her things on the table.

Ten minutes later, she pulled in at the apartment complex but wasn't able to park in her reserved spot because it was occupied. Irritated, she cruised the whole length of her wing without finding an empty space. Some of the residents had complained about visitors parking illegally, and she vowed to add her name to the list. She finally found a spot in the next section of apartments, meaning she'd have a five-minute walk to her door. By the time she reached it, she was out of breath and ready to do battle if Dennis said anything else to provoke her.

The door was unlocked and she pushed it open with fresh irritation. If he was asleep without bothering to secure the apartment, he would hear about it. They'd had it out over this before. Caleb slept in a separate bedroom, and it would be easy for somebody just to walk in. Men never thought of those things. Dennis dismissed the possibility of kidnapping as another example of how overprotective he considered Suzanne to be.

Although the television was going, Dennis wasn't in the recliner. Was he already in bed? Her first thought was for Caleb. She frowned, worried that Dennis might have had more beer after she left. She snapped the TV off, and as she did so, she caught the sound of voices, abruptly silenced. She stood still for a moment or two while a sick dread formed in her stomach. From her bedroom there came soft rustling noises, but her brain rejected them. Wouldn't identify them. She walked down the hall, passing Caleb's room—quiet and gently lit with his Mickey Mouse night-light—and stopped at the master bedroom. Holding her breath, she looked in.

Dennis wasn't alone. Bending over, frantically scrabbling at jumbled clothes on the floor, was a woman. Bare flesh, sleek, long legs, perky breasts. And on the other side of the bed—*their* bed—Dennis stood holding a pillow in front of himself. The bed was a wreck. Suzanne sensed that, rather than actually looking at it. On the floor lay the duvet that had been a wedding present from Stuart and Eleanor. In contrast to the frenzied movements of the woman, Dennis was like a man chiseled in stone. Naked and glistening with sweat, he didn't blink as he met Suzanne's eyes.

"Suzanne. You're early."

"I forgot the outline for my brief."

He plowed a hand through his hair. "Goddamn it, Suzanne."

She stared at him. "What is going on here, Dennis?"

The girl snapped her jeans with a popping sound. "Look, I've gotta run."

Suzanne kept her gaze on Dennis. "This is our home. Our *bed!* Where is your sense of decency?"

"We'll discuss it later, Suzanne."

"Later?"

The girl had wiggled into a tiny T-shirt. With a wary look at Suzanne, she scooped up a denim jacket. To get out she would have to pass her. "Dennis, I've got to go," she repeated.

"Sure, Tiff." Dennis calmly tossed the pillow aside to pick up a towel lying on the bedside table. Suzanne looked at his flaccid penis in disgust as he wrapped the towel around his waist. Ignoring her, he went around the bed to where the girl waited. He took her arm and urged her past Suzanne as if he were helping her through a minefield. They reeked of sex. Suzanne's stomach roiled even as a red haze exploded in her head. With a small sound, she rushed to the window, fumbled at the catch until it gave, then shoved it up as far as it would go so that the sickening scent of Dennis's betrayal was overlaid with chill, clean March air.

She stood at the window with one arm at her waist, her head bent and two fingers from her other hand pressing a spot between her eyes. She could hear their conversation—the girl's tense whisper, Dennis's low, reassuring reply. The door closed and there was silence.

A few seconds ticked by. From the reflection on the windowpane, she watched him walk into the room and toss the towel aside. Silently, he lifted the duvet and replaced it on the bed. His jeans were on the floor beneath it. Without bothering with his underwear, he pulled them on.

"Tiff?" she asked with sarcasm.

"Tiffany."

"Tiffany."

"She's one of the students I've been tutoring."

"And I thought it was something to do with architecture."

"You sound upset," Dennis said calmly.

When she turned to stare at him, she saw that he actually seemed puzzled. "I am upset! What did you think I'd be, coming home and finding my husband having sex with another woman in *our* bed? You're damn right I'm upset."

"Why, Suzanne? Because I'm doing it in our bed or because I was having sex with another woman?"

"What kind of crazy question is that?"

"I thought it was simple enough. If you won't have sex with me, how long did you think it would be before I found somebody who will?"

She turned, slapping her arms against her thighs. "Oh, fine, perfect. Blame it on me." She stopped and whirled back, pointing a finger at him. "We took vows, Dennis. We promised to be faithful. If you were tired of being married to me, then you should have said so. But don't bring some ditzy coed into our home and screw her in our bed!"

"Why not!" Dennis snarled, suddenly angry. "You damn sure don't want to use it for that!" With a savage swipe, he sent a pillow flying across the room. "I'm sick of begging, pleading, trying to figure out ways to entice you into this goddamn bed, so give me one good reason why the hell I shouldn't screw Tiffany in it, or anybody else I get the hots for? In fact, why the fuck shouldn't I screw anybody else anytime I please, *anywhere* I please, because you sure as hell aren't interested!"

She drew in a painful breath. "I'm not going to argue with you, Dennis. You've insulted me and our marriage. I think—"

"Marriage!" He took a step, standing right in her face. "What a goddamn laugh! What a fucking farce!" Waving his hand, he indicated the room and beyond. "You call this charade we've been living a marriage? Well, listen, lady. Marriage to me means something a lot different from what we've got here. It means companionship and sharing and sex and fun. Hell, you never laugh anymore, you don't want to make love anymore. But at least we used to be friends. We talked. We played. We don't even do that anymore. What is the fucking point if that's your idea of marriage?"

"We both have a lot of pressures right now, Dennis."

"Pressures? Yeah, when your wife won't go to bed with you,

that's pressure, all right." He yanked a shirt over his head, then paused. "You know something? I should have cottoned to the truth when you didn't want to change your name. The handwriting was on the wall even then. I'd have seen it if I hadn't been so damn *thick!* So *nutty* about you!"

"That was a professional decision, Dennis."

"Bullshit!" Her eyes fell before his furious look. "The truth is, I don't know why I've stuck around as long as I have."

Suzanne turned aside, walking to the dresser. He was right. About everything. "If you honestly feel that way, Dennis, maybe it's a mistake for us to stay together."

"Say it straight out, Suzanne."

She had known eventually it was bound to come to this, but with her heart beating furiously, with her throat so tight, she just couldn't answer. *Tell him, Suzanne. Tell him why you're not the person he used to know. Why you don't laugh, play, make love. Tell him.* She licked her lips. "I...I..."

"Say it, Suzanne. Say the goddamn word."

"Maybe...maybe we should consider...a d-divorce."

"You want a divorce? You got it!" Dennis stalked to the closet, sliding the door open with a crash. "Hell, I don't know why you haven't brought it up before now. I don't know why *I* haven't." He began pulling hangers out of the closet, tossing clothes on the bed. "Because I'm a goddamn fool, I guess."

"We made a mistake," Suzanne said, forcing the words past the excruciating pain in her throat.

"You were pregnant!" he said savagely. "I did what was right."

"It was a mistake," she repeated.

He turned and looked at her. "Yeah, but whose? If we're doing some straight talking here, Suze, I think we ought to lay all the cards on the table."

She pressed a hand to her stomach. "What are you saying?"

"Only what I've been thinking for a long time. That there's been something funny about this from the start. From the moment I gave you a ring, you refused to marry me or even

set a date. Then suddenly you were pregnant. We've been together since we were both sixteen, so I accepted that the baby
was ours. Mine. Now I'm not so sure."

"I don't think we should discuss this tonight, Dennis. We're
both upset."

"Yeah, that'd be the easy way, wouldn't it? Just sweep it
under the bed, so to speak. You're good at that. Bring up anything that makes you uncomfortable and you start with the
double-talk, using lawyer lingo to baffle me with bullshit." He
slung a drawerful of underwear on the clothes already heaped
on the bed. "Well, just because I haven't pressed you for a
straight answer before doesn't mean that I don't know the truth."

"What truth?"

He made a disgusted sound. "You're good, Suzy, really good.
That's a priceless look on your face. Wounded, shocked. Plumb
pitiful. Only this time, I'm not buying."

"What truth, Dennis?"

"You want me to spell it out? Here it is. I don't think Caleb
is my kid."

She put a hand over her mouth. "You don't mean that."

"He's got black hair. Mine's light and yours is, too. He's got
dark brown eyes—almost black. Mine are hazel, yours are gray.
His skin is dark, we're fair."

"My sister has black hair."

"Yeah, that's right. That's a fact. But she has crystal blue
eyes and pale skin. I read up on recessive genes, Suze. Where'd
Caleb's dark brown eyes and olive skin come from?"

"It can happen," she whispered.

Dennis snorted. "Give me a break. So, tell me, Suzy, is he
my kid or isn't he?"

"Dennis," she implored, "don't do this. Please."

"Is he or isn't he?" He ground out the words.

She stared at him speechlessly.

After a second, he blinked fast a few times, swallowed hard.
"Yeah. Well. I knew it. I just didn't want to admit it." With a
disconsolate shrug, he tossed a bunch of athletic socks onto the

pile of clothes. He stood on one side of the bed, and Suzanne on the other. They looked at each other over the great divide that had been their marriage. Dennis was pale, his freckles standing out starkly on his face. He held his head high, his jaw clamped, but his lips weren't quite steady.

"Who is he, Suzanne?"

"Dennis—"

"It's Ben Kincaid, isn't it?"

"No!" Horrified, she put out a hand. "How can you think that, Dennis? Ben is as much your friend as mine. He's…he…" She shook her head miserably. "Not Ben, you've got to believe that."

"Then who?" With his hands at his side, his legs in a fighting stance, Dennis demanded an honest answer.

"I can't tell you that, Dennis," she said quietly.

"Goddamn it, who is he!"

"You don't know him," she lied.

He stared at her, one quick heartbeat in time, then he groaned, a deep, gut-wrenching sound of denial. He turned away, blindly stumbling to the window. With her heart tearing apart, Suzanne watched him drop his head, shaking it as if to rid it of the hateful truth. He turned then and began pacing the room. Suddenly, with a howl, he struck out, slamming his fist through one of the flimsy sliding doors of the closet. Suzanne cried out, pressing both hands to her mouth as the door crashed to the floor.

"Dennis, please, I'm sorry."

He looked at her from dead eyes. "Get away from me, Suzanne."

"It's not what you think."

"You slept with another man and got pregnant, then you tricked me into marrying you to give your baby—*his* baby!—a name."

"No!"

"I'm wrong? Then explain to me how it was."

Silence again. Stalemate.

"Right." He bent over and yanked at the corners of the duvet, making a huge bundle of his things. "I'll clear out the rest of my stuff this weekend. I don't want to see your face before then because I honestly don't know if I can keep from hurting you, Suzanne."

She reached out to him. "Dennis, please, not like this. Please..."

He gave her a disgusted look. "And you've got the gall to jump me for fooling around. You are some piece of work, lady."

Shaking his head, he lifted the bundle and shouldered past her out of the room. At the front door, he fumbled for the dead bolt, and then, when he had it open, he turned back to look at her. "And you can wait till hell freezes over if you expect me to ante up child support for somebody else's kid!"

Suzanne flinched as the door slammed behind him. But not before she'd seen the tears in his eyes.

NINE

May 1983

ANNIE FIELDS WAS AWAKENED by the ringing of her telephone at one o'clock in the morning. Sleepily she fumbled for the receiver, clearing her throat before managing to croak out a sound.

"Hell, Annie, I forgot the time difference in California."

"Stuart? What…why…"

"I know you get the *Sun* out there, but it takes several days. I thought you'd want to hear the news while it's hot. We have another baby in the family."

"Baby? You and Eleanor…"

"No, not me and Eleanor. It's Taylor. She gave birth to an eight-pound boy this morning."

"Wow, Jack must be over the moon."

"He seemed proud. I'll just leave it at that."

"They didn't waste any time, did they?"

"Uh-uh. It was only about fourteen months ago that little Gayle was born. This one's John Mark Sullivan III."

She chuckled. "And they'll call him Trey, right?"

"How'd you guess?"

"That's for me to know." She was still smiling. "How's Taylor?"

"In good shape. This one came a lot faster and easier than Gayle did."

"Most babies do. That was a difficult birth for Taylor."

"Yeah." He was silent for a few seconds, then said quietly, "There's another bit of family news."

"What is it?"

"Suzanne and Dennis have split, Annie. They're getting a divorce."

"Oh, no." Sitting up against the head of her bed, Annie pulled her pillow close, cushioning her stomach—and her heart—against the news. "When, Stuart? Why?"

"I'm not sure exactly when. You know how self-contained Suzanne can be. She won't say why. Just that it's over. I think it really is, Annie. There's no reconciling them."

"I can't believe this. Suzanne."

"Yeah. I thought you'd want to know."

"Yes. Seems as if it's time for me to come for a visit."

"That's good. Suzanne could probably use a friend right about now, although she'd never ask. When?"

She smiled into the receiver. "When you see me."

"Okay."

"Thanks for calling, Stuart."

There was another stretch of silence. "Bye, now."

Annie sat for a long time thinking. If Suzanne couldn't make marriage work, nobody could. She turned off the light and settled back, only to lie wide awake until dawn.

TEN

June 1983

"SUZANNE STAFFORD?"

Deep in thought about the wording for a motion for dismissal, Suzanne took a second to respond to the low whisper near her shoulder. She glanced up, recognizing the associate professor who was administering the exam for Dr. Rayburn. "Yes?"

"You have a phone call, Ms. Stafford. It's the line in Dr. Rayburn's office."

Suzanne frowned, glancing at the exam papers strewn over her desk. "Phone call? Who is it?" Even as she asked the question, she realized the associate wouldn't know who was calling her. Who *could* be calling her in the middle of a final?

"I don't know who it is, Ms. Stafford," the young associate said, frowning. "I was only told that you have a phone call."

"Thank you." She started to her feet, aware suddenly that the exchange between her and the associate had caught the attention of the other students. Knowing how irritating an interruption could be during an exam, she gave an apologetic shrug meant for the whole group. "Sorry," she whispered.

Leaving her things, she hurried from the room and headed down the hall where the professor's office was located. His secretary gave her a frigid nod and pointed to the telephone. "This is highly irregular, Ms. Stafford."

"Yes, I know. I'm so sorry." With her back to the woman, Suzanne picked up the receiver. "Hello?"

"Suzanne Stafford?"

"Yes, who is this?"

"Caleb Stafford's mother?"

"Yes, what's wrong?" At hearing Caleb's name, her heart began to pound.

"Caleb is running a temperature, Ms. Stafford. You'll have to come and get him. You are aware of the rules of the day care, aren't you?"

"A temperature?" That was all Suzanne heard. "How high is it? What's wrong?"

"Quite high. And we don't know what's wrong. We're not trained for that. As I've just said, you'll have to come and get him. We can't have the other children exposed."

"Exposed to what?"

"Who knows?" She gave an impatient sigh. "We're just not equipped to cope with sick children, Ms. Stafford."

"Of course. I understand. I'll be right over."

She hung up and began scrabbling through her purse looking for her car keys.

"Ms. Stafford, are you all right?" The secretary was watching her.

"What? Oh, yes. I'm sorry." She moved away from the telephone, glancing vaguely in the direction of the classroom. "I've got to go. My little boy is sick. Would you please tell Dr. Rayburn's assistant?" She hurried to the door, slipping the straps of her purse onto one shoulder.

"Wait!" The woman stood up. "You can't just walk out of an exam, Ms. Stafford. You'll have to reschedule—"

"I'm sorry. Please explain to Dr. Rayburn. Thanks." Without waiting to hear any more, Suzanne dashed out into the hall. When she reached the exit, she began to run.

It was the middle of the afternoon before she got back to the apartment. After waiting more than two hours in the doctor's office, Caleb had been examined and diagnosed as having a "virus that was going around." She was told he'd probably be fine by morning, but the ordeal had taken the starch from her backbone. Any threat to Caleb, she realized, was a knife in her heart. With Dennis gone, Caleb was doubly precious. He was, simply, her reason for living.

She was putting him down in his crib when the doorbell rang. Running a palm over his cheek and behind his neck, she could tell that his fever was down. The doorbell pealed again. She left the room, keeping the door ajar. The bell sounded a third time. Whoever her visitor was, he was impatient.

She pulled the door open and almost instinctively moved to close it again.

"Hey, hey, hold it." Jack Sullivan put up both hands, palms out. "This is business."

Still unwilling to let him in, she stood blocking his way inside. "What do you want, Jack?"

He glanced casually at the row of apartment doors to his right and then to his left. "You have no secrets, right?"

Reluctantly, she stepped back to let him in. As he shouldered past her into the apartment, she closed the door but walked directly to the front windows and opened the drapes wide. She was taking no chances being alone with Jack. "Make it quick," she told him.

She watched as he stood in the middle of the living room surveying the apartment and her things and felt vaguely violated. Everything about the man revolted her, but oddly she wasn't afraid of him. Not anymore.

"Nice," he commented, studying an original watercolor given to her by a friend who was an art student.

"Thanks."

His gaze fell on a stack of laundry—personal things—she hadn't gotten around to putting into her dresser drawers. "Not much sign of Dennis left around here, is there?"

"You said this was a business call."

"Hell, it's no great loss, Suzy. I knew it was only a matter of time before you discovered that for yourself. He was never man enough for you, babe. That was obvious from day one."

Suzanne walked to the door and pulled it open. "If this is the 'business' you came to discuss, the discussion is over."

He nodded with approval. "Tough. Very tough. You're gonna make a hell of a lawyer." He rubbed his hands together. "And that's what I'm here to talk about."

"How many times do I have to tell you to butt out of my life, Jack? I don't need your advice or your help. I don't need anything from you."

He was shaking his head. "If you'd come down off that high horse for a minute and just listen, you might change your mind."

"Nothing could make me change my mind if it means dealing with you, Jack."

"Not even to get that job you're interviewing for at Lamar & Wellstone?"

She closed the door with a soft click. "How did you know about that?"

"I told you before, kid, I've got friends. I make it my business to know the movers and shakers in this state. Did you know they had more than sixty applicants for that position? Besides being *the* premier law firm in the state, Lamar & Wellstone employs more than a hundred attorneys. They're in Louisiana, Texas and Arkansas. They're interviewing ten hotshots and you're one of them. How do you think you made the cut?"

Suzanne was trembling all over but determined it wouldn't show. She walked to her desk and picked up the letter that had arrived from the law firm just yesterday. She'd been flattered. Jack was right, the firm was top of the line. Who wouldn't be pleased? Now she wanted to rip the letter to shreds right in front of him, but knowing how much pleasure he'd get seeing her lose control, she managed to lay it down and face him. "You're saying that I wouldn't have made the cut if you hadn't put a word in the right person's ear?"

"Hell, who knows? Maybe you would and maybe you wouldn't. But one thing's certain—you've got the job even before the interview, and you can take that to the bank. I fixed it with the big cheese himself." He gave her a wink. "I'm telling you, stick with me and this is only the beginning, Suzy."

She moved to the window and, with her back to Jack, said, "I suppose you expect me to thank you."

He released a gust of sarcastic laughter. "Hell, no. I know you'll never thank me for anything unless it's for having a fatal heart attack, honeybun. No, I don't expect thanks, but that's okay. I'm a generous guy. You're family, sugar. Haven't I said it before?"

She turned from the window, watching him with narrowed eyes. "So what's the point, Jack?"

"Suzy, Suzy, Suzy…" He moved closer, and before she could evade him, he chucked her beneath her chin. "You'll know it and I'll know it, darlin'. And that'll be all the thanks I need."

Before she could scratch his eyes out, he was gone.

She slammed the door behind him with enough force to rattle the windows, forgetting the noise would probably wake Caleb. She was shaking all over. The nerve! The gall! What would it take to make him stay out of her life? She *hated* Jack Sullivan.

When she'd calmed down and her hands were steady enough to dial, she went to the telephone. With the letter from Lamar & Wellstone in front of her, she punched out the firm's number. A husky-voiced receptionist answered and asked to direct her call. Suzanne requested the name of the person who'd signed the letter. When the woman finally answered, Suzanne canceled her interview. She hung up in the middle of the surprised woman's questions.

Later, she stood over Caleb in his crib and caressed his small, dark head. With his fever reduced and medication to calm his tummy, he was sleeping peacefully. He stirred and turned over, cramming his thumb in his mouth. Suddenly realization of all she'd lost rose up inside her. Her marriage was over, but that wasn't the only price she paid for keeping the secret of Caleb's conception. She'd lost a lifelong friendship and the respect of a man she would always love. She and Dennis had been together since childhood. Now he was gone, and not only was she alone, but Caleb no longer had a father. Somehow in this whole mess, Suzanne hadn't considered the possibility that Dennis would reject Caleb when he walked out on her.

Caleb stirred again, blinked his eyes and saw her. With a smile, he raised his arms for her to pick him up. She did, holding him close, burying her nose in his warm little neck. With her throat tight, Suzanne vowed he'd never, *never* know the name of his biological father.

SOMEHOW SUZANNE GOT THROUGH the next few weeks. Even under ideal circumstances, the last semester of law school would have been stressful, but wading through the ashes of her failed marriage, plus shouldering the full responsibility of Caleb's care made it a time she would gladly forget.

She could barely remember the person she used to be—the confident, eager student, the ambitious career person in the making, the naive innocent believing in the best of people. That Suzanne had been forever altered by Jack Sullivan. Her secret—and her rage—was tucked into a tight, dark box. She told herself she could not waste energy dwelling on it. There were other, more important things to concentrate on now. With Caleb to consider, she had to get on with her life.

He was napping and she was packing boxes getting ready to begin that new life when Ben Kincaid dropped by. Her first thought when she opened the door and saw him was of Dennis's accusation. Her own sins aside, how could Dennis have thought Ben would betray their friendship? No one could mistake Ben's loyalty. He was the straightest of arrows.

And deep in the back of her mind, she acknowledged now that he was also one of the most attractive men she knew. Tall, an inch or two over six feet, he moved with a fluid grace that made feminine libidos quiver. Looking at him now, she realized how dark his hair was, and he did indeed have brown eyes. But where Caleb's were near black, Ben's were a clear, rich whiskey brown.

She let him in and went to the refrigerator to get him a beer.

It was the first time he'd been here since Dennis left. It surprised her just how glad she was to see him.

"What the hell happened, Suzanne?" Ben waved away the proffered beer, watching as she tore open a bag of pretzels. "Law school's finally done, we're all home free, and suddenly you and Dennis are busted up. He's moved in with some airhead and you're looking like Morticia Addams."

"Morticia Addams had black hair."

"I'm serious here, Suzanne. What's going on?"

She laughed, but it sounded hollow to her own ears. "Just your basic death of a marriage."

"But why? You planned to marry Dennis from the time the two of you were in high school."

"Maybe sixteen is too young to decide those things."

"Bullshit. No two people could be more compatible."

Not exactly. But she wouldn't—couldn't—get into that. "We had some problems we just weren't able to resolve, Ben."

"Like what?"

She laughed, more genuinely this time. "I guess I was pretty dumb not to expect a rash of questions, especially from a fellow lawyer."

"Jeez, I'm sorry, Suzy." He settled one hip onto the bar stool. "Maybe I will have that beer." When she handed it over, he popped it open and took a long drink, then stared thoughtfully at the can before lifting his gaze to hers. "It's just that I was sure that if anybody could make marriage work, it'd be you and Dennis. It's painful to see this happen."

"Believe me, it's more painful from where I sit."

He twirled the can, frowning. "Was it really the Tiffany thing? Because I can tell you, she doesn't mean a thing to Dennis. She's just...just a passing fancy. Somebody to—"

"Have sex with?"

He shrugged ruefully. "Yes. If you can accept that."

She dumped the pretzels into a bowl. "Well, I can't."

He took a handful. "No, you wouldn't."

"It isn't just Tiffany, Ben. You knew things weren't exactly going well with Dennis and me."

"What about counseling? Maybe if it was something that could be fixed—"

"It can't be fixed, Ben."

He stared at her long and hard. "You mean that."

"I do."

He nodded after a moment. "Okay." Picking up his beer again, he held her gaze. "Look, if there's anything you need, any way I can help, all you have to do is just call. Will you promise me that?"

"Thanks, Ben." She turned to the refrigerator and removed a pitcher of iced tea. His offer gave her a warm feeling. She was reminded what a good friend he was, and she wasn't taking friendships for granted any longer. Dennis was lost to her forever; she wouldn't let that happen with Ben. "So, how did your interview in Houston go?"

"I got the job. I start July 1."

In the act of pouring tea for herself, she gave him a smile. "Congratulations. I knew you would."

"You knew?"

"Sure." Setting the glass down, she ticked off the reasons on her fingers. "Although you complained a lot, you finished in the top quarter of the class, you passed the bar—"

He raised a hand. "I've only taken the exam, same as you."

"You'll pass," she said confidently. "And you'll walk right into PetroTex's legal department. Every summer since you were seventeen, you've worked for them offshore, you've got a second degree in geology and you wanted to go to Texas with all your heart and soul. That shows. You had it aced, Ben."

"Aced."

"Aced." Smiling, she crunched a pretzel, happy for him. Nobody deserved success more than Ben. He'd longed to get back to Texas for years, so it was no surprise that he was on his way. Still, it left her feeling empty knowing he would no longer be close by, that she wouldn't see him frequently. With

Dennis gone, and now Ben, too, she was really going to be on her own.

"So what's the deal with *your* career?" Ben asked, watching her face as she traced patterns on the bar from the moisture on her glass.

"I'll be working at the D.A.'s office in Jackson again."

With one elbow on the bar, he studied her. "What about Lamar & Wellstone? How'd that interview go?"

"I canceled it."

"You canceled it! Why?"

"I never really wanted to work there, Ben. Dr. Rayburn persuaded me to submit my résumé. For some time now I've been interested in criminal law."

"I know that's what you've said." He fiddled with a small metal car of Caleb's that was lying on the counter. "But I expected the Judge to work on you. Neither she nor your brother-in-law make any bones about wanting you in a big firm."

"Jack has no say in any decision I make," she said stiffly.

His gaze did not waver. "And the Judge?"

She sighed. "It's my life, Ben. Mother made her choices, I have to make mine. You're hauling off to Texas in spite of what Lucian thinks, or your mother. Why can't I do the same?"

"You can. You should. The civil stuff—corporate law, tax, real estate—that was never your cup of tea. Actually, criminal law is a logical choice for you. I guess what really surprises me is that you seem more suited for the defender's role—you know how you used to argue for the rights of the accused?"

She forced a smile. "Can't a woman change her mind?"

"You want to nail those bad guys now, huh?"

"There are a lot of bad guys out there."

He nodded. "That's a fact, and they need lawyers of your caliber in the D.A.'s office, no doubt about that."

"Like you, I'm not a lawyer yet. There's still the bar."

He smiled, shaking his head. "Suzanne, you've been a lawyer since you were fourteen."

"You didn't even meet me until I was fifteen!"

"I heard stories."

"From Taylor. And Annie."

"Uh-huh." Tipping his head, he finished his beer, then crushed the can before looking into her eyes again. "I guess the saddest part is what this will mean to Caleb, huh?"

If he only knew. A week ago, Dennis's lawyer had notified her that under the circumstances there would be no request for any visitation from Dennis. In spite of the "circumstances," she couldn't believe it would end this way. How Dennis could just walk away from their child, she would never understand. Sperm be damned. He was the only father Caleb would ever know.

"Suzy?"

"Hmm? Oh. Yes. Caleb's the innocent one, and yes, he'll pay the highest price."

"Is there a problem with custody?"

She shook her head sadly. "Not really. I'll be getting full custody."

He frowned. "Full custody? What does that mean?"

"Dennis is going with an architectural firm in Dallas. It will be difficult for him to see much of Caleb."

"Tough," he said, studying the mangled beer can in his hand.

She reached for it and put it in the trash. "Enough about my troubles. Tell me more about your job with PetroTex."

"Well, what if I told you I'm not going to work in Houston?"

"No? Why not?"

"I'm going to Abu Dhabi."

"What? Where?"

"You heard me. Abu Dhabi—it's in the Middle East."

"Well, I know that, but—"

"On the Persian Gulf. Part of the United Arab Emirates."

"I know that, too. Sort of." She looked at him with dismay. "Ben, that's so far away."

"Yeah." He grinned.

She shook her head. "I was prepared for Texas, but Asia!"

"I'm not going for the rest of my life, just a couple of years."

"But it's…it's across the globe!"

"And then some. But I'll be home to visit."

With her finger moving slowly around the rim of her glass, she looked at him sadly. "No, that old saying's really true, Ben. You won't ever come home again. Not really."

"My mother's here, Suzanne. And Granddad. I'll be back."

He said that now, but she had a sinking feeling that his visits would be rare. Like his father, Ben was a risk-taker. He couldn't wait to see what was on the other side of the mountain. She envied him, in a way. "Speaking of Lucian," she said, "I'll bet he had a few choice words to say about this."

"He accepts that I have to do what I have to do."

"I suppose so." With a sigh, she went around the bar and took a seat on the stool beside him. "Everything's changing, Ben. We're going out into the real world now. It's scary." Glancing at him, she caught the expression in his eyes. "Not for you, huh? You've been counting the hours."

"I can't deny it. And you wouldn't be having these uncertain pangs if your whole life hadn't just turned upside down." He reached out and touched her hand. "You're feeling low at the moment, Suzy, but it'll pass. You're a lawyer now. It's what you wanted and worked for ever since I've known you. Don't let what's happened to your marriage shake your confidence in that. One has nothing to do with the other. And you're a good mother. You just need to pick up the pieces and don't look back."

She smiled mistily. "Thanks, Ben."

"And remember, even if I'm across the globe, we're still friends and we always will be. If you need anything— *anything*—just pick up that phone."

ELEVEN

July 1983

TAYLOR STOOD BEFORE THE bathroom mirror thinking that she really shouldn't have had that last couple of drinks last night. That was the hell of it; a few drinks made her feel young and smart and pretty, but the reality was that booze actually did the opposite. In the clear light of morning, there it was. Leaning closer, she inspected the corners of her eyes. So far, so good, she thought. Yet she reached automatically for an expensive face cream and smoothed it over her eye areas, her cheeks and around her mouth for good measure.

Coming out of her dressing room a few moments later, she heard the baby's insistent wailing. A boy, thank God. Touching her temples, she waited until the crying ceased. She would never be able to thank Jack enough for allowing her to hire full-time help for the children. Nancy Lovelace was a godsend.

Drawing a deep breath, Taylor slipped into a silk kimono. The baby was quiet now, but she could hear Gayle's chirpy little voice babbling away. Even without a headache it was maddening at this ungodly hour. Were all toddlers such chatterboxes? Her daughter had said her first words before she was a year old. Gayle was definitely Jack's child.

Jack's child she might be, but Jack certainly felt nothing special for the little girl. Gayle lit up like a Christmas tree when he was around, but he never seemed to notice. Or if he did, he didn't seem to care. Taylor wasn't sure which was worse: Jack's unabashed disinterest or her own odd emotional vacuum where her children were concerned.

She was clearly an unnatural mother. Just watching her sister with Caleb proved that. Suzanne thought everything Caleb did was darling. From the moment of his birth, she had been enthralled, enchanted, *enslaved* by her child. None of Caleb's demands was too much. Sometimes Taylor wondered if some vital gene that governed maternal behavior had been bestowed on Suzanne but was missing in her. Oh, she loved her kids— didn't she?—but they took so much time. And energy. God, the energy. She hadn't really bargained for a life like this. One day she was a woman with a very sexy husband and the prospect of lovely, interesting things to come, the next she was having a baby. And before she'd had time to catch her breath, another. Nothing was like she expected. Nothing was like she *wanted.* God, she hadn't had a clue what was in store for her.

Moving away from the dressing area, Taylor checked her appointment book just to make sure there was nothing Jack had scheduled for her today, then she left the bedroom. Jack insisted they have breakfast together, even though he knew she had no stomach for it. Actually, she wasn't sure whether breakfast agreed with her or not. She'd been pregnant for nearly the entire time she'd been married. Before that, she'd skipped it to sleep late. But Jack had this…thing. And there was no reasoning with him.

When she entered the breakfast room, he was sitting at the table, absorbed in the morning paper, as usual. He barely glanced up as she poured herself black coffee, sat down and reached for the sugar bowl.

"Hung over again?" Without looking at her, he turned the newspaper to the op-ed page.

"I'm not hung over, Jack. I only had three drinks last night."

"Five."

She sighed. One thing she'd learned was not to argue with him so early in the morning. "I looked at my calendar and there's nothing there. It's Friday. Why don't you take the day off and we'll drive to New Orleans? The kids'll be okay with Nancy. It'll be fun."

"Sorry, not this weekend. I'm going to Memphis today, did I forget to mention it?"

She put her spoon down with a clink. "Jack, no. Do you have to go? You travel so much. Do you realize I haven't been anywhere that's any fun for ages?"

"You didn't want to go anywhere while you were pregnant."

"But the baby's a month old now. I'm ready to start living again."

"Your life is right here with Trey and Gayle, Taylor, not gallivanting around New Orleans or Dallas. As my wife, you have a public image to maintain right here. In Mississippi. Don't forget, you're a mother now. I expect you to work on that image. I expect you to perfect that image." He folded the paper and reached for his coffee. "God knows, it could use some work."

She felt a quick spurt of fury, but knew better than to argue. If she resisted, he could be vicious. Where she was concerned, Jack was almost a dictator. So instead, she asked quietly, "What time do you think you might be back from Memphis?"

"When I get back." He moved the paper aside to reach for a piece of toast. "How do I know, Taylor? I'll go, I'll do what I have to do and I'll come home."

"Since you don't want to go to New Orleans, I was thinking of inviting a few people over for dinner tomorrow night—mostly family. Annie's coming in from California this weekend. I hardly ever get to see her when she visits anymore. I'd like to invite Suzanne, too. I've hardly seen her since she and Dennis separated. I meant to give a tea in her honor when she finished law school, but the baby came. What do you think?"

"Do it," he said, spreading peach preserves an inch thick on his toast. Jack had a killer sweet tooth. She marveled that he didn't gain weight, while she had to starve herself to stay a size six. Pregnancy wreaked havoc on a woman's figure, which was one more reason she planned never to have another baby. She was going to have one of those tubal ligations, but she knew better than to tell Jack. Next time he went to Washington, or somewhere that kept him away for a whole week, she was having it done.

"I think I'll do a brunch on Sunday instead of dinner Saturday night," she said, tapping her finger thoughtfully against her lips. "That curry chicken salad with grapes is nice. Omelets to order, of course. Croissants. And fruit."

"Do whatever you want."

"We could have champagne mimosas and Bloody Marys."

"By all means get an early start," Jack said dryly.

"Do you think I should invite Grayson Lee?"

He looked up, finally giving her his full attention. "Grayson Lee? Why the hell do you want to invite the D.A.?"

"Well, we've been to his house before. And he *is* going to be Suzanne's boss. I just thought—"

"What the fuck are you talking about? Suzanne's going to work for Randall Lamar."

"I don't think so. I was talking to Mother yesterday on the phone." Reaching for the decanter, Taylor poured herself a fresh cup of coffee. "She's going back to the D.A.'s office. She worked there last summer, remember? She told Mother she withdrew her name at Lamar & Wellstone. She likes prosecuting, she says."

Before she finished, Jack surged to his feet, slamming his chair backward with a crash. "Goddamn her! That stupid, silly *bitch!*" He stormed across the room, hurling the newspaper to the floor. It sailed into an arrangement of fresh flowers, tipping the vase and spilling water onto an antique sideboard.

"Oh, Jack, look what you've done!" Taylor jumped up, grabbing her napkin to mop up the spill.

"She did it just to spite me," he raged, kicking at Gayle's stuffed teddy bear, which was lying in his path.

Now mopping water from the floor, Taylor gave him a puzzled look. "What concern is it of yours what job Suzanne takes?"

"I arranged that job with Lamar & Wellstone," he snarled.

"I went out on a limb for your precious sister. Now what am I going to tell Randall Lamar? That my very civic-minded sister-in-law decided she'd rather spend her days with a bunch of incompetent jerks on the state's payroll than come into his premier law firm? Oh, great. I can just hear it now." With a vicious swipe at the tabletop, he sent his coffee cup flying. "God *damn!* She's going to pay for this, you hear me?"

"Jack! Calm down. For heaven's sake, it's not—"

"Taylor." He silenced her with a slash of his hand through the air. "I'll calm down when I feel like it, and I damn sure don't feel like it now. I'm going to get her for this. Just watch me. You can tell her that for me, too. She thinks she's tweaking my ass thumbing her nose at Randall Lamar. Jesus, he's got so much political pull that half a dozen governors jump when he says 'frog.' She has screwed up royally this time. Nobody embarrasses Jack Sullivan like this. No, sir. She's gonna get hers."

Taylor's eyes followed his movements around the room. "Jack, it's not really as bad as that, is it?"

He turned on her, his eyes hard and black as onyx. "Shut the fuck up, Taylor. You wouldn't understand even if I tried to explain it to you. As for Sunday morning, you go ahead and invite her. Be sure the Judge is here, too."

Taylor knew that look and was suddenly afraid for Suzanne. "What're you going to do?"

Jack grabbed his suit coat and shrugged into it. "Don't worry. She's family, so I can't shoot her." With Taylor anxiously following, he scooped up car keys and briefcase from the hall table and jerked the front door open. "But nothing says I can't stick it to her where it won't show."

She winced as the door slammed.

HOLDING THE RECEIVER to her ear, Annie waited through another couple of rings before finally hanging up. It was unlike Eugenia to forget her. She knew the arrival time of Annie's flight and had promised to meet her at the luggage carousel. With a worried look at her watch, Annie wondered if she'd somehow screwed up the time. At this hour the airport would soon empty and she'd be lucky to find a taxi willing to make the drive all the way to Riverbend.

She walked to the glassed enclosure overlooking the taxi-way. God, it was good to be home. Her irritation was soothed by the sound of soft, Southern drawls around her. When she got outside, she vowed to roll down the car windows and fill her senses with the essence of a Mississippi July, the delicate grape scent of kudzu, the sweet perfume of honeysuckle and fresh-cut grass. Living in California, she sometimes longed for the South with an ache that was almost pain.

"Annie!"

She whirled and gave a glad cry as Suzanne hurried toward her. They met, both grinning, and hugged joyously.

"What are you doing here, Suzy? I'm expecting Mama."

"I'm visiting at Riverbend this weekend. Eugenia called and asked me to pick you up. She's detained in Memphis and—"

"Memphis! She knew I was coming in today. Why on earth is she in Memphis?"

"I have no idea." Suzanne took one of Annie's bags and indicated which exit to take to get to her car. "But I'm sure she'll explain when you get home. Anyway, I was glad to do it. We can talk. Have we got everything?"

Annie slung a garment bag over her shoulder and picked up her overnighter. "This is it. Come on, I'm dying to get out of the airport. It's great to be home!"

Suzanne smiled. "It's great to have you. How long can you stay?"

They paused at the curb to let a van pass. "I'm not sure this time. Spence has everything under control at the plant, so I thought for once I'd take my time."

Talking eagerly, they headed across the tarmac to short-term parking and stopped at Suzanne's aging Toyota. She went to the trunk and opened it. "We'll have to stow your things back here because Caleb's car seat takes up most of the back seat."

"Speaking of Caleb, I'm dying to see him," Annie said when

they were settled in the car. "I wish it weren't so late. He's probably sleeping. Is he as tall as me now?"

Suzanne smiled, glancing in the rearview mirror as she backed out. "Not quite, but he's growing like a bad weed. He's almost eighteen months old, but he's already wearing size two. It's going to be a trick keeping him in clothes that fit."

"Be thankful he's only a baby. Just wait'll he gets old enough to want ninety-dollar Nikes."

Suzanne pulled out onto the highway, merging smoothly with interstate traffic. "You obviously haven't priced children's clothes lately," she said dryly.

"No." From the car window, Annie watched the proliferation of commercial businesses give way to the occasional shop or store and then finally to gently rolling green hills. Most of the trees were pines, with occasional magnolias and a few hardwoods. She faced Suzanne again. "How's it going, Suzy? Are you okay?"

"Yeah, I am. I'm all right. It hasn't been easy, but Caleb and I just take one day at a time. I start at the D.A.'s office next week and I've found a good place for Caleb to stay during the day. It's an older woman who doesn't have any other children to take care of."

"Wow, lucky you. How'd you find her?"

"A friend of a friend. She has a big old house in Belhaven. The best part is that my apartment is only a couple of streets over. I'm also ten minutes from the office."

"Then things are working out," Annie said quietly. "I'm so glad, Suzy."

"Yeah. Me, too." Suzanne slowed for a stretch of highway construction, falling into line behind a dusty pickup. "How about you? Update me."

Annie shrugged. "Dream Fields grew twenty percent this year, so I've had to hire more people."

Suzanne glanced at her in delight. "Congratulations, Annie. That's wonderful!"

"Why wouldn't the business grow? I'm there fourteen hours a day, sometimes seven days a week."

"Having your own business requires more than a hundred percent, or so they say," Suzanne said, accelerating now that she was beyond the construction. "Still, most people would prefer to have that kind of control over their lives."

"Maybe so, but sometimes I wonder where I'll be ten years from now—burned out, or sold out to one of the greeting-card giants, opening a chain of Dream Fields or starting something entirely new and different."

"Knowing you, all of the above is possible," Suzanne said, signaling at the Percyville exit. "In all this soul-searching, have you considered coming home, Annie?"

"You mean relocating the business?" Annie gazed thoughtfully at the familiar piney woods bordering the interstate. "Actually, I have. In fact, I may try to find time to check out some property while I'm here." She glanced over and smiled at the delight on Suzanne's face. "It's just a thought so far, Suzy. Probably a symptom of burnout. I always get a little crazy when I come home."

"Coming home isn't crazy. But whatever happens, I don't think you'll ever be burned out. You're not the type, Annie. Your creativity will see to that. You've always managed to keep things in perspective." She zoomed through an intersection.

"We'll see. I don't—" Annie broke off, whipping around in her seat. "Wasn't that Jack Sullivan?" she asked, craning her neck, trying to get a better look.

"He drives a car like that," Suzanne said, glancing at the rearview mirror. "Who was with him?"

Annie was shaking her head. "I don't know. It was a woman. Not that I'd recognize too many people anymore." She settled back, a faint frown lingering on her face.

"It wasn't Taylor?"

Something in Suzanne's tone drew her attention. "No, it wasn't." She could read the disgust on Suzanne's face as plainly as if she'd spoken. Annie sighed, troubled. If Jack was fooling around with another woman when Taylor had just given birth to their second child, that was a new low, even for Jack.

Taylor, Taylor, you don't deserve this.

"We're invited to brunch at Taylor's house tomorrow," Suzanne said. "She's thrilled to have you back home and wants us to catch up with a good gossip."

"I don't know if that'll work," Annie said with a smile. "The best gossip happens in the gazebo at Riverbend."

"It's been a long time since I was out there," Suzanne said.

"Really?" Annie turned to survey the countryside again. "Lots of memories for me out there." She thought of Stuart and the night he'd told her he was marrying Eleanor. "Good and bad."

"Yeah. Me, too."

"What happened with you and Dennis, Suzy? I thought you'd stay together long enough to celebrate your golden wedding anniversary."

"He brought another woman into our apartment. I caught them in our bed together."

"Oh, no."

Suzanne flicked the signal light and slowed to turn into the lane at Riverbend. "I accept my part in the breakup. Marriage wasn't exactly what I'd anticipated. There was so much stress— law school, part-time work, juggling roles—wife, mother, student, law clerk. Maybe it was a losing proposition to begin with."

"I can't believe that, Suzy."

Suzanne shrugged and pulled to a stop in front of Eugenia's house. "Well, it's a moot point now, as we lawyers say."

Together they unloaded Annie's luggage, then Suzanne backed up to drive back to the big house. Annie didn't turn to go inside right away. Instead, she stood watching the Toyota until the taillights disappeared around a turn in the lane. In spite of the years that had passed as they'd each gone their separate ways, Annie knew Suzanne as she knew no other woman. Suzanne hadn't told her everything about her breakup with

Dennis, but then, Annie didn't expect her to. She turned to climb the front steps. No one knew better than she that some things were never meant to be shared.

The house was dark when she unlocked the front door. Eugenia wasn't home yet. Annie carried a key but it was unlike Eugenia not to be on hand to personally welcome her home. She loved it when Annie came to visit. Almost every time they talked, Eugenia begged her to relocate Dream Fields to Mississippi.

She dropped her bags inside and heard the phone ringing. Hurrying to pick it up, she almost fell over a chair. Balanced on one leg, she rubbed her bruised toe. "Hello?"

"Hi, sugar. I see you made it."

The voice was low and deep, caressing. A lover's voice. Annie gazed at the phone. "Who is this? Who are you calling?"

With a click, the line went dead.

Annie replaced the receiver slowly, frowning. Was it a wrong number or had someone mistaken her voice for her mother's? If so, who was calling her mother "sugar"? My God, did her mother have a lover?

She snapped on a light just as a key turned in the front door. Eugenia pushed the door open and reached automatically for the light switch. Annie took a step forward and her mother screamed.

"It's only me, Mom!"

"My God, Annie…" Eugenia closed her eyes, her hand on her heart. "I didn't know…Lord, you gave me such a fright, honey." She dropped her purse and rushed to hug her. "I'm so sorry I let you down at the airport. Did Suzanne give you a ride home?"

"Yes. It's okay, Mom. Next time I won't schedule such a late flight. Sometimes I forget the time difference."

"It wouldn't have mattered if this trip to Memphis hadn't popped up." Slightly flushed Eugenia slipped her bag from her shoulders and rested it on a table in the foyer.

"Who went with you to Memphis?"

"Oh, no one you know." Eugenia waved airily. "I shouldn't

have agreed to go, I suppose, but sometimes we just can't get out of these things."

"It's not a problem. I got here just the same."

"Any other time I would have just said no, but—"

"It's *okay,* Mom. I understand."

Eugenia chewed anxiously on her lip. "We started home with plenty of time to spare, but he, ah, there was a call, and we had to stop at a...place, and then before we knew it, it was so late..."

"He? You were in Memphis with a man?" Annie smiled. "Mom, are you seeing someone?"

Eugenia touched her cheek nervously. "Oh, no, not really. I just—"

"I think he just called you," Annie said, grinning. "He hung up after mistaking my voice for yours."

Eugenia stared at her in horror. "Called me? What did he say?"

With her finger to her temple, Annie pretended to think. "Hmm, he said something like..." She lowered her voice to a deep, sexy tone. "'Hi, sugar, did you beat your bratty kid home?'"

Eugenia was as pale as death. "Ohmigod."

Annie read the terror on her face. "What's wrong, Mom? I think it's great you're seeing someone. Why are you upset?"

"It's...I... Oh, I'm sorry. I just need—" She rushed past Annie into the small powder room beneath the stairs and closed the door firmly.

Half amused, half concerned, Annie watched the door for a few seconds. She wasn't a prude and couldn't think why her mother would react so oddly to her learning there was a man in her life. She'd often urged Eugenia to get out more. Her mother was very attractive. Annie knew several women the same age, and Eugenia looked ten years younger. It was no surprise that she'd caught the eye of a good man. At least, Annie hoped he was good.

Still smiling faintly, she hoisted her garment bag to her

shoulder and climbed the stairs. The idea that her mother might be involved with someone who wasn't good was absurd.

She stepped into her bedroom, took a deep breath and released it in a pleased sigh. Fresh-cut roses floated in a bowl on an old desk Charles Stafford had given Annie when she was ten years old. She'd discovered it one rainy afternoon while playing in the attic at Riverbend. It had belonged to Stuart's namesake. For that reason alone, Annie treasured it.

The trunk at the foot of her bed Annie had rescued from a load of rubbish the Judge had ordered cleared from the attic a few years later. She didn't know whose it had been, just that its owner was some long-dead Stafford. Many nights she had whiled away the hours making up a history for that trunk.

Most of Annie's childhood had been spent fantasizing about being a true Stafford. It was only after she'd fallen in love with Stuart that she'd realized she didn't want that after all. How could she marry Stuart if she was related to him? She touched one of the roses and watched the red petals fall onto the polished surface. That was how it was when she came home. A part of her rejoiced, but her heart bled for all her lost dreams.

"Annie? May I come in?" Eugenia stood at the door.

"Of course, Mom. Don't be silly."

"No. I've been silly enough for one night." Almost briskly, Eugenia walked to the bed and smoothed the comforter, then plumped both pillows. "If you need anything, sweetheart, just help yourself. You know where everything is."

"Of course, Mom." She watched her mother walk to the desk and scoop the fallen rose petals into her palm. After another look around the room, she went to the door. Was it her imagination, Annie wondered, or was her mother anxious to get away? Some little imp inside her wouldn't let it happen. "Who is he, Mom?"

With Eugenia's back to her, Annie couldn't see her face, but her mother seemed to freeze. "Who, dear?"

"Your man, your boyfriend, your significant other."

"I don't have a man, Annie. I told you that."

"Some stranger is calling you 'sugar'? In a pretty damn sexy voice, too."

Eugenia bent her head and rubbed her temple. Her hand was trembling, Annie realized suddenly. "Mom, what's wrong?"

"Nothing. I—I'm just tired. Memphis is quite a trip."

"If you made the trip there and back in one day, yes, it is. I hope you didn't rush home just because of me." She smiled, trying to understand Eugenia's mood. "I'm used to sleeping in a house by myself."

"Actually, I left yesterday. Didn't Suzanne mention it?"

"No, Mom. So, you went to Memphis with a man who isn't really important to you and you spent the night with him? Am I getting the right picture here?"

"I really don't want to talk about this, Annie!"

Now Annie felt real alarm. Eugenia's reaction was more than just embarrassment at being caught in a compromising position by her daughter. "What is it, Mom? You're seeing somebody and you don't want to tell me about him? Why is that?"

"What I do in my private life is not your concern, Annie."

It was the first time ever that her mother had used such a tone to her. It chilled Annie. "Mom, are you seeing a married man?"

At the look on Eugenia's face, Annie suddenly knew it was true. "I'm right. He *is* married."

"I don't want to talk about this, Annie."

Ignoring that, Annie sank onto the bed. "Does his wife know? Does he have children?"

Covering her face with her hands, Eugenia shook her head wildly. "Can't you leave it alone!"

"And let you break up somebody's home? No, I don't think I can, Mom. Who is he? *Are* there children? Do I know him?"

Her face still in her hands, Eugenia began to sob. "Yes, yes, yes! Yes to everything. *Yes!* Now are you satisfied?"

"Who is it, Mom?"

"I don't have to tell you that. I *won't* tell you that."

"Then I'm not going to stay in this house with you until you do. You said I know him. I've been out of Percyville over six years. I don't know a lot of men, especially anyone you'd be interested in in that way. Who is he?"

"You're going to be so angry with me. You're going to hate me, Annie. I can't believe this has happened." Eugenia walked to the bed and fumbled for tissues on the bedside table.

Annie felt an ominous dread. "You can tell me, Mom. Nothing you can say will make me hate you, don't you know that?"

"Yes, it will," Eugenia said, her voice breaking. Working at the tissues in her hands, she wouldn't look at Annie.

"No, it won't. So tell me."

She buried her face in her hands and whispered, "It's Jack."

"Jack?" Annie lifted her shoulders blankly. "Jack who?"

"Jack, Jack, how many men do you know here with that name!" her mother cried. "Jack Sullivan!"

Annie shook her head, too shocked to believe it. "No."

Eugenia raised her eyes, gazing at her daughter in quiet despair. Tears coursed down her cheeks. "Yes," she said.

"You're having an affair with Taylor's husband, Mom? My cousin? *Your* niece?"

"I didn't plan it. I just—" She shook her head. "It just happened."

"He's younger than you."

Eugenia's laugh was a travesty. "Yes, I know."

"What on God's earth... He has two little children! The baby's just six weeks old. Have you lost your mind?"

"Don't you think I worry about his children?" she asked bitterly. "About Taylor? About the family? About the scandal and the disgrace and the utter shame of it? I've thought about nothing else for six months!"

Annie was aghast. "You've been seeing him for six months?"

"Yes."

"Why? *Why?*"

Eugenia's eyes overflowed with tears again. "I love him," she said brokenly.

"My God. My God." Annie looked around the room, her beloved childhood haven. Her gaze fell on a dozen mementos of time spent with the Staffords—Stuart, Suzanne, Taylor. *Taylor!*

"You have to stop seeing him, Mom."

Eugenia nodded, mopping at her eyes. "I know. I told him that."

"What did he say?"

"He laughed. He refused to believe I was serious."

"He's a bastard, I've always known that."

Eugenia looked at her in dismay. "He's not. Really, he's not, Annie. Oh, I know he seems hard sometimes—"

"Sometimes!"

"Yes, but there were reasons why we—"

"Name one, Mom. Name me one good reason why a man with a small child, a pregnant wife, a man in a political position where such a crazy, nutty thing could jeopardize everything he has or ever has wanted…tell me why such a man would risk it all for…for…"

"For a woman like me?" Eugenia pocketed the shredded tissues and wiped both eyes with her hands. She spoke with a note of bewilderment in her voice. "Don't you think I've asked myself that very question a thousand times?"

"He's scum, Mom. That's the reason. But you don't have to let him drag you down into the garbage with him. You can end it. You have to."

"I know." Eugenia gazed despondently at the crushed rose petals now at her feet. Then she lifted her eyes to Annie's. "But I just don't know if I can."

TWELVE

SUZANNE WAS WAITING when Annie drove Eugenia's car to pick her up Sunday morning. Neither was particularly happy to be going to Taylor's brunch. Suzanne hated being near Jack for any reason, and Annie looked as if she were still operating on West Coast time.

Suzanne snapped her seat belt and settled back. It was a beautiful morning, too beautiful to obsess over Jack Sullivan.

"I've been thinking about Taylor and Jack, Suzy," Annie said after a moment. "Are they doing okay?"

Suzanne turned to look at her. Annie was looking straight ahead, so it was hard to read her expression. "I suppose so, if you can believe the picture they present to the world," she said.

"Last night Jack was with another woman. We both saw him."

"It could have been business," Suzanne said.

"Do you think it was?"

Suzanne leaned an elbow on the window frame and rubbed her forehead. "Probably not."

"Do you know who it is, Suzanne?"

"I haven't the faintest idea, and to tell the truth, I don't want to know. The woman—whoever she is—is probably not important. And even if she were, he's not about to leave Taylor. His public image, you know," she said in disgust.

Annie overtook, then passed a rattletrap pickup. "Do you think Taylor knows?"

It was a question Suzanne had already pondered. "I'm not sure."

"I knew it!" Annie bumped the steering wheel with a flash

of indignation. "I had bad vibes from the day I met him. Didn't I say so at the time?" Pushing one hand through her hair, she ranted on, "How could he, Suzanne? Taylor's just given birth. He has his precious son *and* a daughter. Taylor's life is arranged to his convenience, he's the darling of his party. What the hell's the *matter* with him?"

"When you figure all that out, be sure and tell me." A little pain had started between Suzanne's eyes. She rubbed it gently. "Let's not talk about Jack Sullivan, okay? It's bad enough we have to accept his hospitality this morning. I hate having to watch my sister gobbled up in his ego while almost no one else seems to see anything wrong in him. It's amazing."

"Suits me."

Annie turned into the street where Taylor lived. Suzanne lifted her head and groaned. Cars lined both curbs, everything from upscale imports to flashy Cadillacs and sports cars. "So much for a small family gathering," she said dryly.

While Annie searched for a parking spot, Suzanne watched a tall man with a shock of white hair getting out of a sedate gray Mercedes. "Oh, no! That's Grayson Lee."

Annie zipped in behind a sleek Porsche. "Who's Grayson Lee?"

"My new boss, that's who." Suzanne unsnapped her seat belt, feeling her temper rise. "Taylor's going to hear from me, I swear it! What'll he think, Annie? I don't want to meet him for the first time at a family brunch."

"He's your new boss and you've never met him?"

"No. My job's so low on the totem pole that it wasn't necessary. I was hired by his assistant. Damn it! I've told Taylor—"

"She means well, Suzanne. You said it yourself. She's married to a complete political animal. Watching Jack wheel and deal, she probably thinks she's doing you a favor, that this is the way for you to get ahead."

"I'll get ahead the old-fashioned way, by working my butt off," Suzanne said grimly. "Not Jack Sullivan's way."

Annie shut off the car. "Amen to that."

Suzanne sighed and opened the car door. "Come on, let's get it over with. Hopefully we won't have to stay long."

Annie met her on the sidewalk. "Amen to that, too."

Suzanne gave a short chuckle. "Listen to us. You'd think we were being forced to attend an execution." Their eyes met and they burst into laughter. Suzanne pointed at her. "Shame, shame, I know what you're thinking."

"And it's the same thing you're thinking," Annie said, her eyes still twinkling, and rang the doorbell.

Taylor opened the door, smiling brilliantly when she saw the two women. She was a knockout in flowing white hostess pants and a clinging lace top. In one hand, she held a Bloody Mary; in the other, a cigarette. Smelling of Joy, vodka and smoke, she embraced her sister first and then Annie. "Annie, I love your hair. Is that the newest California look?"

Annie laughed. "Are you kidding?" With one hand, she pushed her wild red curls from her face. "This is not a style, Taylor. As creative as California stylists are, even they can't think of a way to tame this mess."

"Well, I think it suits you."

"Not as well as that outfit suits you." Stepping back, Annie surveyed her. "My God, how can you get into something that tiny after giving birth only a few weeks ago? Do you ever eat?"

Taylor laughed, delighted with the compliment. "Not much, but I think about it a lot." She smoothed her palms over the trim line of her hips. "Do you really like it?"

"It's stunning."

Taylor glanced at Suzanne and winced. Lowering her voice, she gave Suzanne's arm a little shake. "Suzy, damn it, why didn't you wear that yellow silk outfit like I told you yesterday? Do you know who's here? Grayson Lee! I want you to knock his socks off." She twitched at the collar of Suzanne's tailored blouse and made a disparaging sound. "And pants!" She clicked her tongue before sighing with resignation. "Well, at least they're linen."

"My jeans were in the washing machine," Suzanne said impishly.

"Will I do?" Annie asked, holding her long skirt out for inspection.

"Your style is always right," Taylor replied absently, still assessing her sister. She took a swallow of her drink. "It's a good thing your figure is excellent, Suzy. Jack's always saying you've got the best ass in the family. But you're so stubborn! The yellow would have been smashing."

"I think you're the one who's smashed," Suzanne muttered, waving cigarette smoke from her face. She glanced at the drink. "How many of those have you had?"

"Oh, you and Jack are such nags! Only two, swear to God." Before Suzanne could comment, Taylor heaved a sigh. "I'm glad y'all finally made it. These people are *so* boring." She turned back to Annie. "You're staying a few days, aren't you, Annie?"

"I'm not sure. I—"

"You are! You've got to! The three of us haven't talked in *ages.*"

"I do live in California, Taylor," Annie reminded her.

"And my life's a circus right now, Tay," Suzanne said.

Taylor brightened. "I know, I know. But you're here for today, so we need to make a date for the gazebo." She swallowed more of her drink, then pointed at Suzanne with her cigarette. "Someone's baby-sitting Caleb now, right?"

"Yes, but—"

Taylor looked at Annie. "I bet you haven't planned anything, either, have you, Annie?"

"Well…"

"See? There's no reason we can't do it." She frowned at the tiny face of her wristwatch. "This'll be over by two at the latest. I'll have to see that things are tidied up. Jack's a stickler for that. He demands the house look like a magazine in case somebody drops in. Ugh. It's a pain. Even with a maid."

Suzanne and Annie exchanged wry smiles.

"So, is four o'clock good for y'all?" Taylor divided a look between the two. "C'mon, it'll be fun. Just like it used to be. Before we all had such *responsibilities*."

"Well…" Suzanne looked at Annie.

"Fine with me," Annie said with a shrug.

"Great." Taylor glanced at her watch again and grimaced. "However, now we've *got* to circulate. At least, *I* have to. Besides, there are people here I want you both to meet." She turned in a whirl of silk, motioning with her hand for them to follow.

"Wait." Suzanne grabbed at her, stopping her. "Don't drag me over to chat up Grayson Lee, Taylor. I mean it. I don't need my family smoothing the road to success for me."

"I just want him to notice you," Taylor said plaintively.

"The best way for him to notice me is when he sees me hard at work in the office."

"Good girl," Annie said in a low tone.

"I'm sorry, Suzy." With a crestfallen expression, Taylor set her empty glass on a tray. "I'm always doing the wrong thing, aren't I? Jack tells me that all the time."

Suzanne slipped her arm around Taylor's waist and hugged her. "It's okay, Tay. I don't mean to sound ungrateful. You've got good instincts, as Jack damn well knows. And for what it's worth, when he says something stupid like that, I wish you'd knock *his* socks off by telling him where he could kiss."

Taylor blinked, then glanced at Annie, giggling. "Gosh, Suzy, why won't you tell us what you really think?"

"She's right, Tay," Annie said quietly.

For a second, Taylor's smile slipped. Then, eyes bright, she flagged down a maid carrying a tray of yellow mimosas. "You both need a drink, and then I've got to do the hostess thing. See you at four. Don't forget!"

Along with Annie, Suzanne took a mimosa from the maid, murmured her thanks and then watched with troubled eyes as Taylor made her way across the room, smiling and chatting to people she'd just pronounced boring. It was sad how she underestimated herself. Jack couldn't have chosen a woman better suited for the role of his wife than her beautiful sister.

"This is tasty," Annie said, sipping the icy mimosa.

"Umm." Across the room, Suzanne saw Jack in conversation with Grayson Lee and deliberately turned her back.

Over the rim of her glass, Annie casually surveyed the crowd. "I don't suppose we can decently leave for another half hour, huh?"

Suzanne followed Annie's gaze. "There's Stuart. Let's go over and talk to him about finding you a piece of property."

A bit of the mimosa went down the wrong way. Annie coughed, patted her chest, then coughed again before finding her voice. "Oh, I don't know, Suzanne."

"Sure. C'mon. He's the big cheese at the *Sun*—he knows everybody and everything. You can bet he'll know if there's some property suitable for your business anywhere within a fifty-mile radius. And he'll be tickled that you're considering this."

"I'm not sure I'm actually considering it. I—"

"Even so, what harm can come from mentioning it, Annie?"

"It's Sunday. He probably doesn't want to talk business."

Suzanne's eyebrows lifted. "If it means jobs for Percyville? Economic growth for the area? A business that doesn't rely on slaughtering chickens? Give me a break!" She nudged Annie forward. "He'll be delighted."

"Suzanne, just the girl we're looking for."

Suzanne's smile died as she turned to face Jack and Grayson Lee. Jack's smile showed a lot of teeth, but his black eyes were hard. Suzanne knew that he was furious with her for rejecting the job at Lamar & Wellstone. What she didn't know was just how far Jack's fury would drive him. She pushed her misgivings aside and turned her attention to her new boss.

The district attorney's features had just enough cragginess to make his face interesting, if not handsome. In his midfifties, he was tall, lean and impeccably dressed. After twenty-five years in politics, his smile was practiced. He flashed it now at both her and Annie as Jack introduced them.

"Ah, Jack, you've got the devil's own luck with women like this in your family." He held Annie's hand and remarked that he knew Eugenia, who had been a volunteer on his campaign. Annie smiled, said something polite, then murmured an excuse to move away, leaving Suzanne alone with both men. Lee turned to Suzanne, taking her hand in the kind of insipid clasp that men sometimes substitute for a handshake when greeting a woman. "Ah, Ms. Scott—or is it Stafford?"

"Stafford," she said. "I—"

"I can't seem to get in step with this newfangled urge nowadays for women to retain their maiden names," he said, shaking his head, but he spoke without irritation. "Jack tells me you'll be joining my staff Monday morning."

"That's right, sir. Doug Madison called me to confirm the position a few days ago."

He nodded. "Madison, eh? That son of a gun didn't see fit to tell me who you were. Can you beat that? When Jack called, it took a moment before I realized Doug had managed to acquire the daughter of a distinguished judge and the sister-in-law of the state's attorney all in one lovely package."

Suzanne smiled stiffly, not missing the malice in Jack's look.

"I was telling Grayson about your friendship with Madison," he interjected smoothly.

"Actually, I met Doug just two weeks ago," she said, keeping her response as smooth as Jack's. She wasn't going to let him insinuate that she was personally involved with Doug Madison.

"Loyalty," Jack said, winking at Lee. "No trait more valuable in a staffer, right, Grayson?"

"Yes, indeed."

Suzanne watched Jack assume a concerned expression. "Gotta watch these young turks on our team," he said. "One thing I do from time to time to keep a tight rein in my own organization...I shake 'em up. I move 'em around. Doesn't pay to let any one of 'em get a little too big for his britches."

Grayson Lee frowned. "Madison's been a good assistant

D.A. Has a flair for administration. I'd feel it in the organization if I had to replace him."

"Well, it was just a suggestion," Jack said, studying the drink
in his hand.

My God, was Jack going to derail a man's career just because he'd had the bad luck to hire her? Was he that incensed
that she'd rejected Lamar & Wellstone? Appalled, Suzanne said
quickly, "Mr. Lee, I didn't mention my mother or Jack to Mr.
Madison, so he couldn't have known who I was, as Jack seems
to be suggesting."

Grayson Lee reached to pat her on the arm. "Well, no matter
what, my dear, it's nothing you need to be concerned about."

"I'll be very concerned if Doug's job is jeopardized because
he hired me." She refused to look at Jack, but she could feel
him enjoying what he'd stirred up. "In fact, I wouldn't accept
the job under those circumstances."

"Of course you'll accept the job," the D.A. said.

The man was clearly in a bind. Jack was now on the governor's staff with connections that Grayson Lee couldn't afford
to alienate. There would be hell to pay if he didn't act on Jack's
none-too-subtle suggestion that he move one of his best people
to another spot. Or at least demote him. Glancing at Jack, she
longed to rip his throat out. If he managed to do this to Doug
Madison, Suzanne's enthusiasm in working there would take
a dive. She looked up to see her mother heading their way, and
for once, she welcomed the interruption.

"Mercy. None of you look as if you're at a party," Lily Stafford said, shrewdly gauging the dark frown on Suzanne's face.

"Well, you're absolutely wrong about that, Lily," the D.A.
replied, beaming at her. "Actually, I was just remarking on my
good luck in snagging such a talented young attorney as Suzanne."

Not Ms. Stafford or Ms. Scott. Now she was simply Suzanne.

Suzanne looked at her mother. "Mr. Lee wasn't aware until
Jack told him that we were related, Mother."

"That doesn't surprise me," Lily said to the D.A. "Of all my children, Suzanne is the most independent. She'll work hard, you can count on that."

"Then she should make a fine addition to the D.A.'s office," Grayson Lee said expansively. "The backlog of criminal cases is so heavy there's hardly time to break in new junior staff before their case load is overwhelming."

"Nothing much overwhelms our Suzanne," Jack said, enjoying her glare. "As for a backlog of criminal cases, she's eager to get at those nasty criminal types." He appeared to study her thoughtfully. "I'm trying to decide just where she would fit in your organization, Grayson. Do you have any suggestions, Judge?"

"You don't, do you, Mother?" Suzanne stated with a meaningful look at the Judge.

The Judge smiled archly at Grayson Lee. "See what I mean? Independent to a fault."

"And loyal," Jack put in.

Suzanne turned abruptly to Grayson Lee and put out her hand. "It was a pleasure meeting you, Mr. Lee." As he took it, she added, "And please pay no mind to anything you've heard from my relatives. I want to be assigned wherever I can do the best job in your organization."

"Sex crimes," Jack said. "That's getting a lot of press lately. You'll shine there, Suzy."

Ignoring Jack, she pulled her hand free, looking beyond them. "I need to find Annie. I promised her we wouldn't stay too long."

"Who's baby-sitting Caleb?" Jack asked. "Eugenia?"

Lily Stafford glanced around as if just noticing her sister-in-law's absence. "She isn't here, is she?"

"Annie mentioned that she wasn't feeling well," Suzanne said.

"Anything serious?" Jack asked.

"A headache."

"Hmm. Nasty."

With an exasperated look at him, she finally escaped.

ANNIE REFUSED A FRESH MIMOSA from a maid with a loaded tray and headed for the French doors that opened onto the patio. She had almost convinced herself she could be a guest in Taylor's home and not blow her top when she had to look at Jack, but when he'd strolled over wearing that smarmy grin, she had wanted to tell the crowd in no uncertain terms about his despicable seduction of her mother. But, of course, there was Eugenia's position at Riverbend to consider.

Scandal was abhorrent to Lily Stafford. Although Eugenia and Annie had been treated like family for many years, there were no blood ties to ensure it would always be so. Besides, Annie was convinced that in a confrontation Jack Sullivan would always come out on top. It would be Eugenia who paid. And Taylor, of course. With a sigh, she opened the French doors and stepped out onto the patio. It was fun fantasizing about Jack's sins finding him out, but that's all it could ever be: fantasy.

Dazzled by the bright morning sun, Annie didn't realize at first that the patio was already occupied. A bench of cast iron and wood was nestled in a corner shaded by a canopy of artfully pruned English ivy. Stuart occupied it, his long legs stretched out leisurely in front of him, crossed at the ankles.

"Annie-girl. The crowd getting to you?" He patted the space beside him. "Come sit."

She hesitated, but only for a moment. Settling beside him, she stretched her own legs out beside his and sighed. "Hmm. Peace and quiet. Heavenly."

"You were never happy in a crowd."

"I could say the same about you."

He grunted an assent. "You think this is tiresome, you should be at one of Jack's fund-raisers."

"No, thanks."

Stuart studied her profile. "Politics not your game, huh?"

"Absolutely not."

He settled back, squinting up at the limbs of a magnolia tree. "When did you get into town?"

"Yesterday. Suzanne picked me up at the airport."

"Your mama doing okay? I don't see her as much as I used to." He folded his hands over his stomach. His very flat stomach, Annie noticed. He was probably going to be one of those men who looked gorgeous and sexy till the day he died.

"She's fine."

Both looked up as Suzanne came out of the house and headed toward them. "Annie, here you are. Hi, Stuart. Did she tell you what she's thinking about doing?"

"Suzanne—" Annie straightened, aware that Stuart was looking at her.

"What?" Stuart, too, sat up straight on the bench.

"It's nothing," Annie said, giving Suzanne a glare.

"What's nothing?" Stuart demanded, eyeing them both. "I haven't seen that look on your faces since you were both adolescents."

Suzanne spread her hands. "What look?"

"The one you got when Annie would think up something reckless and crazy, then persuade you and Taylor to help her pull it off." Smiling, he crossed his arms over his chest. "I'm curious whether Annie's ideas have toned down some."

Suzanne huffed good-naturedly. "Tell him, Annie."

Annie's heart dipped as his blue eyes met hers. "Yeah, tell me, Annie," he said softly.

"It's hardly a glimmer in my mind, so talking about it *is* reckless and crazy."

Suzanne sat down on the bricks in front of them, crossing her legs beneath her. "It's not reckless and crazy. None of Annie's ideas are or ever were, Stuart. You just persisted in treating us as if we were too immature to communicate as equals back then. But time marches on, as I pointed out to Annie a little while ago." She reached over and gave Annie's dress a tug. "*Tell* him."

Annie pulled an ivy leaf and twirled it in her fingers. "I've been thinking about relocating my business."

The French doors opened again and Stuart's wife looked

out. "I might have known." Eleanor Stafford rolled her eyes eloquently. "Stuart, we need to leave now. I've got a dozen phone calls to make before the committee meeting tomorrow."

For a split second, Annie felt the force of Stuart's reaction to his wife's rudeness. "In a minute, Ellie."

Eleanor's attention moved to Annie. "Oh, hello, Annie. I didn't realize you were in town. It's so incredibly hot here in July. Why in the world would you choose to leave balmy California to swelter in our heat and humidity?"

Annie shrugged. "I was always the odd one in the family."

"Yes, well…" It was clear that Eleanor couldn't disagree with that. Still holding the door ajar, she flashed a smile at Suzanne. "Congratulations on your graduation from law school, Suzanne. I don't think I've had a chance to say that." She looked at Stuart. "I'll make our goodbyes to Jack and Taylor, Stuart. Ten minutes, okay?"

"Yeah."

There was a taut silence when the door closed behind her. Overhead in the magnolia tree, a mockingbird chirped an incredibly complicated melody. The smile that had warmed Stuart's blue eyes was gone when he focused on Annie. "Why would you want to come back to Percyville, Annie?"

"Why not? I've got the kind of business that can be moved almost anywhere. I'm leasing, not buying, space in California. I could purchase land here much cheaper. Or, if I decided to lease, I'm sure I could get something for less than I pay there. The cost of doing business is less here. Taxes are *certainly* cheaper." She raised one shoulder and let it fall. "It makes good business sense. And, of course, my mother is here."

"She needs a good location, Stuart," Suzanne added. "I told her you'd be the best contact for that."

Stuart said nothing for a moment. He was studying Annie's face, his own expression unreadable. "You were barely out of high school when you hightailed it to California. I never could figure out why you wanted to go. Or why Eugenia let you. What makes you think you're going to be satisfied here in Hicksville when you've gotten used to California? Take it from someone who knows, Percyville is nothing like L.A."

"Stuart!" Suzanne was watching him in dismay.

Annie stood up and dusted the back of her skirt. "I shouldn't have mentioned it. The idea was half baked even in my own mind. But thanks for your thoughts, anyway." She flashed a smile at Stuart. "You'd better run. Eleanor's waiting."

THIRTEEN

SUZANNE SLOWLY CLIMBED the steps to the gazebo behind Taylor and Annie. She hung back in the doorway as Taylor headed for the lounge and sat down, bouncing a little on the cushions as if she were still a teenager. Annie, who had changed into jeans, found a comfortable perch on the waist-high railing and leaned back against one of the box columns.

"Come sit here, Suzy." Taylor patted the space beside her.

"I think I'll take a chair. I never felt comfortable on that thing," Suzanne lied, and walked across the floor to one of the wrought-iron chairs. She pulled it away from the tangle of wisteria climbing up the pickets and along the railing.

Taylor shrugged and settled back. "Can you believe this old thing has held up so well? Furniture just isn't built like this anymore, is it? Nowadays, stuff's imported from Mexico or Taiwan. Nothing's American-made, so nothing's as sturdy as it used to be. Especially furniture. Jack says we'd better look out, because with no manufacturing, America will be a Third World nation before long."

Annie studied the worn spot on the knee of her jeans. "Jack's a protectionist now, is he?"

"Huh?" Taylor wrinkled her nose in confusion.

"Forget it, Tay." Closing her eyes, Annie rested her head back against the column.

Taylor smoothed a hand over the fabric of the cushion. "This is a new Laura Ashley floral. Mother must have had it re-covered lately. It's nice."

Nice. Suzanne managed to hide a shudder. It would take more than a designer print for her to admire anything about that lounge. She was already regretting coming here. Her hands were cold, and she was as tense as if Jack himself were here. But—damn it!—it was more than time to face down her fears. Jack would love thinking that he'd destroyed her memories of all the good times spent in this very spot.

Taylor fished out her cigarettes from the pocket of her denim skirt, then lit up. "Now, see…" She lay back, stretching out on the lounge and crossing her ankles. "Wasn't this a good idea?"

Annie's eyes were still closed, savoring the sounds and smells. The call of mourning doves came from a distant pasture, then a cow's quiet lowing. "It is peaceful out here."

Taylor flicked ashes onto the floor. "What'll we talk about first?"

"Annie's decision to move back home," Suzanne said, giving a smiling wince as Taylor squealed.

"Oh, Annie, great decision!" Taylor smiled widely.

"I have made no such decision," Annie said flatly. "And I seriously doubt that I will."

"This is fabulous!" Taylor bounced into a sitting position. "Wait'll I tell Jack!"

"Don't tell Jack!" Annie and Suzanne chorused together.

"But he'll be able to help you, Annie," Taylor said, clearly baffled by their reaction. "He knows *everybody.* If there's property available, he'll put in a word for you to the right people. Why wouldn't you want that kind of help?"

"I'm used to helping myself, Tay," Annie said gently, but with underlying steel in her tone.

"Besides, she's already mentioned it to Stuart," Suzanne said. "You can't deny he knows Percyville and the surrounding area as well as anybody."

"I suppose," Taylor agreed, settling back reluctantly.

Annie was looking at Suzanne with exasperation. "Suzanne, you heard Stuart. He was totally negative about the whole idea."

"He was caught off guard," Suzanne said. "He didn't mean it."

"He meant it." Annie batted impatiently at a mosquito. "And

his reaction was totally appropriate. It was stupid to even mention something as serious as moving my business—no matter what the advantages—without thinking it through. I'm embarrassed that I went off half cocked that way."

Suzanne stared in disbelief. "Embarrassed! Will you listen to yourself. Since when can you be embarrassed by anything Stuart says? I'm telling you, you just hit him cold with this. When he has a chance to think it over, he'll see what a fantastic idea it is."

Taylor nodded. "I like it. We'd all be together again."

"Can anybody hear me?" Annie asked of nobody in particular. "I'm not moving my business to Mississippi. I'm going back to California, and unless I come up with some absolutely wonderful reasons that I haven't thought of so far, I'm going to forget I ever entertained the notion." She slapped viciously at the mosquito as it landed on her arm, then glared at Taylor. "And not one word to Jack, okay?"

"Okay, but—"

Suzanne held up her hand, silencing them. "Wait. Did you hear something?"

"What?" Annie asked, frowning.

"I didn't hear anything," Taylor said, looking around.

"You didn't hear the bell?" Suzanne cocked her head, still listening, but there was only the buzz of insects. The distance from the big house to the gazebo was too great to hear a voice calling. In fact, in exasperation, and to keep from making the long trek, Lily Stafford had finally installed a ship's bell on the back gallery to summon anyone in the gazebo.

"Will you relax," Taylor said, rolling her eyes.

"Are you worried about Caleb?" Annie asked.

"He's with a strange sitter," Suzanne said with an anxious look at her watch. "I couldn't get Mrs. Simpson, so I had to use one of the students at Belhaven. I don't like to shove so many strangers at him. I feel as though I've turned his life upside down as it is."

Taylor blew smoke out impatiently. "Quit worrying about

that kid, Suzanne! He's fine. You are so overprotective, God knows why. Caleb couldn't be more healthy and normal. You need to relax, otherwise you'll make a wimp out of him. Kids pick up on these things."

"Divorce is never normal," Suzanne said. "One day Caleb had a mother and a father, and the next, he had only me."

Annie joined in. "And you're trying to do the job of both mom and dad. Seems to me that's a natural reaction."

"Even so, it's an impossible task." Suzanne broke off a wisteria seedpod. "Caleb misses Dennis so much."

"Speaking of which…" Taylor looked around for something to grind out her cigarette on and finally settled for the wood floor. "I was surprised at the way Dennis just walked away from Caleb. Being divorced from you is one thing, but divorcing your child is another. Jack says in the decree he didn't even demand visitation."

Suzanne stared at Taylor. "Jack looked at my divorce decree?"

Taylor shrugged. "It's public record, Suzy."

"It's no one's business, especially Jack's." She spoke as evenly as she could manage while her heart raced with fury.

"But he's *family,* Suzy." Taylor's face was a study in bewilderment.

"Not my family, he isn't," Suzanne muttered, breaking the seedpod with a snap.

"I'm sorry I mentioned it. Gosh, it's not as though Jack has some kind of ulterior motive or that he's snooping into your life or anything like that. Why would he? He's *concerned,* Suzy. We all are. And it's weird the way Dennis just… disappeared."

"He didn't just disappear," Suzanne said, dying to explain. Dennis's rejection of Caleb still filled her with pain, while behind her back, Jack of all people was snooping into the details of her personal life. Oh, how she'd love to get his meddling rear in trouble, but of course Taylor would be the one to suffer. "He moved to Dallas because he got a fabulous job there."

"And what about legal visitation?" Taylor persisted. "The way it's written, you could keep Caleb from seeing him forever."

"He knows I wouldn't do that. He can see Caleb no matter what is written in the decree," Suzanne said. And she prayed he would want to see him once his anger cooled.

"Okay, if you say so." Unconvinced, Taylor leaned back. "So, did you force him to move there?"

"No!"

"Then give your conscience a break. The man made his choice. There's no reason for you to feel guilty."

Suzanne was shaking her head. "Even if that were true, Taylor, it's Caleb who's shortchanged, not me. And I do feel guilty about that."

Taylor covered her eyes with a bent arm. "Are you listening to this, Annie? Take my advice. Don't get married and don't have kids."

Annie flicked a tiny ant off the railing before it reached her shoe. "As I don't have plans to do either, business will have to fill that void in my life."

Suzanne was still focused on Taylor. "Are you and Jack having trouble, Taylor?"

"Trouble?" Taylor gave a short laugh. "You know Jack. Do you think it's easy living with him?"

"No, but he doesn't abuse you, does he?"

"Of course not. Don't be ridiculous." Taylor sat up, twitching at her blouse to straighten it. "Bruises on the little woman wouldn't look so good."

Annie was now frowning. "There are many ways to abuse a woman besides slapping her around."

"How did we get on this subject, for heaven's sake?" Taylor began patting her pocket for her cigarettes. When she pulled one out and put it to her lips, the cigarette was unsteady. Both women watched her in silence, their eyes following as she got up from the lounge and walked to the railing.

With a quick glance at Annie, Suzanne rose and went to

Taylor. Bending a little to see her face, she touched her on the arm, but Taylor didn't respond. Shiny with tears, her eyes were fixed on a bumblebee busily working the blooms on a thicket of orange lantana. She lifted the cigarette and inhaled jerkily.

"If you want to talk, you know you can call me anytime, Tay," Suzanne said, her voice soft with sympathy.

As if she hadn't spoken, Taylor took another deep drag. Smoke swirled around them, enveloping Suzanne. She waved it away, still watching Taylor with concern. Taylor bent her head and rubbed a spot between her eyes with her middle finger. "It's not the same, is it?"

"What's not the same?" Suzanne asked.

"The gazebo. The three of us here together again. Catching up. Sharing."

Suzanne slowly turned her eyes to the familiar view around them. "I suppose not."

"We're the same people," Taylor said, focused not on the scenic landscape, but on something inside. "But too much has happened for us ever to capture the special feelings we had when we met out here way back then."

"Things change, Tay." Annie linked her fingers around her bent knee. "People change."

"And never how you expect," Taylor murmured. A moment passed and she turned to look at them, leaning against one of the columns. "You know what? Sometimes I like to pretend I'm somebody else. Like an actress. Or a model. Or…get this, Suzy—a lawyer. If I could be any of those, I would only have myself to consider. I wouldn't have to worry about other people, about pleasing other people. I'd get up in the morning, decide how to spend the day and there'd be nobody to tell me different." She gave them a wry smile. "How's that for selfish?"

"At times, all of us fantasize about escape," Suzanne said quietly. "I don't think that's selfish."

"I read something interesting once," Annie said from her perch on the railing. "Sometimes, when a person's unhappy, those fantasies are a sort of preparation for taking action to change things. A dry run, so to speak. Pumping yourself up to take action."

"Well, I'm not going anywhere," Taylor said, dropping her cigarette on the floor and grinding it out.

Suzanne wasn't ready to dismiss Taylor's despondency so fast. "Taylor, the feelings you're describing could be postpartum depression. Have you talked to your doctor?"

"You think I'm mentally unstable?" Taylor asked, her voice rising sharply.

"Of course not. Anyone can suffer from depression sometime in their lives. It's very treatable." Suzanne looked to Annie for help.

"If it is depression," Annie put in quietly, "your doctor will be able to give you something."

"You mean he'll take away something, don't you?" Taylor crossed her arms over herself. "Namely, booze. That's always the first thing anybody says to me." She made a face. "Quit drinking, then quit smoking, don't do this, don't do that. It's pretty frustrating if you want to know the truth."

"Your friends and family care about you, Taylor," Suzanne said as Taylor fumbled for another cigarette.

"Yeah, well, if everyone in my life was so *caring* about me, they'd leave me the hell alone!"

Startled, Suzanne and Annie stared at her. Taylor shrugged with a wry twist of her mouth. "Sorry. It's just that I get so… frustrated sometimes." She managed a smile. "Y'all don't be mad at me, okay?"

"We're not mad at you, Taylor," Suzanne said gently.

"No way." Annie slipped off the railing and dusted the back of her jeans. "If you can't let off steam to your two oldest friends, who else is there?"

"It's so different from the way we thought it would be, isn't it." Taylor drew deeply on the cigarette in her hand, then exhaled, turning her head slightly to avoid the smoke. She fixed her gaze on a small fish pond a few yards from the gazebo. "Odd when you think about it."

"Odd?" Suzanne repeated.

"We spent a lot of time out here planning how our lives would be, remember that? Suzanne wanted to be a lawyer and now she is one. Annie wanted to make it with her art and she's done that. I wanted to marry a sexy guy and live a glamorous life." She turned and gave them a bright smile. "Well, I think we can congratulate ourselves, girls. We made it, we achieved those goals, all of us. But somehow we don't seem so friggin' happy. What went wrong?"

In the silence that settled around them, there was only the hum of summer insects and, in the distance, the soft cooing of mourning doves.

FOURTEEN

ANNIE AWOKE THE NEXT MORNING grumpy and unrested. In spite of the fact that she'd told Suzanne and Taylor there was no chance she'd relocate her business, she still wanted to believe it might happen. There was her mother to consider. If Annie was close, she might be able to keep Eugenia from total self-destruction. In reality, any decision to stop seeing Jack would have to come from Eugenia herself. So, staying for her mother's sake was probably a nonstarter. It was Stuart's reaction that bothered her. There was nothing like the midnight hours to examine a person's motives. If Stuart didn't live in Percyville, would she even think about coming back?

She flung the covers aside and got out of bed. In the bathroom, she stared at herself in a worn T-shirt with her corkscrew curls hopelessly tangled and thought of Stuart's wife as she'd looked yesterday. After six years of marriage, the woman was even more beautiful. She had that special pampered look some Southern women achieved effortlessly—a look Annie could never hope to have. Just thinking about it made Annie feel like leftover meatloaf. She yanked the shower curtain aside and swore. "When are you going to *grow up,* for Pete's sake!"

The stupid part was that Stuart could still influence her, she thought, holding her face under the spray. That was really dumb. The man was a journalist, not a businessman. By damn, this time she wasn't staying a whole week. She was out of here tomorrow if she could get a reservation.

Fifteen minutes later, she was dressed in shorts and a cropped cotton top and ready to kill for a shot of caffeine. Not bothering with shoes, she went downstairs, lured by the scent of coffee. In the kitchen, the pot was on, the coffee brewed, but there was no sign of her mother. She saw the note then, propped against the sugar bowl. With a sigh, she picked it up and read it aloud.

> *"I'm sorry, Annie. I forgot that I'm scheduled to work at the hospital this morning. Too late to get another volunteer. I'll be back for lunch. Make yourself at home.*
> *Love,*
> *Mom."*

She was pouring coffee for herself when the doorbell rang. Taking it with her, she went toward the front of the house, frowning at the outline of a man through the beveled glass. She had her hand out to open it when she realized who it was.

"Stuart." Her heart dipped. She looked at him, then beyond him to see if he was alone. His Mustang was parked at the fence gate, empty.

"Hi, Annie. Can I come in?"

She stared at him, made weak just by the look of him in a white polo and worn jeans. His black hair was a little too long, his eyes too blue, and his arms very tan, with a shadowy sprinkling of dark hair. She became aware of the July heat and moved back hastily. "Sure."

"Thanks." With his eyes holding hers, he stepped inside. "I know it's early, but I was afraid you'd have something planned or that you'd leave before I got out here."

"I don't have anything planned," she said, her mind racing.

"That's good." He looked away finally, his gaze traveling around the foyer, then up the stairs. "Is Eugenia still sleeping?"

"No, she's at the hospital. She couldn't find a replacement."

He glanced at her coffee. "That looks good."

"Oh, sorry." She blinked as if coming out of a trance. "There's some in the kitchen. Follow me."

"Thanks."

No man's voice was like Stuart's. Softly Southern but deeply male. Hearing it gave her the same feeling she got when she heard beautiful music. Or when she finished a sketch that pleased her.

She let him pour his own coffee while she took a seat on a stool at the breakfast bar. With her toes curling over the top rung, she watched him stir sugar into it. Cupping her own between her palms, she asked, "Why are you here, Stuart?" A long moment passed while he stared into the coffee, not tasting it. She wondered suddenly if he knew about Eugenia and Jack.

He looked into her eyes. "Two reasons, but now that I'm here, I guess I'm having second thoughts."

"What reasons?"

"First to apologize for yesterday. I was out of line, Annie. When Suzanne said you were thinking of relocating your business, I was stunned. I didn't expect you to consider living in Percyville again. Ever."

"You were right. It was a crazy notion." Slipping from the stool, she poured her unfinished coffee into the sink and, with her back to him, rinsed out her cup. "Don't worry. I regained my sanity overnight."

"It wasn't a crazy notion. You aren't insane to want to be near your family."

"Well, whatever. I don't want to hex myself. Dream Fields is doing just fine in L.A. I've got a super staff and not a single one has ever even been to Mississippi. They'd probably freak at the notion of moving here. I didn't think it through."

"Are you saying the idea just came to you this weekend? And you thought, 'Oh, wow, good idea. I'll just relocate my business?' I don't think so."

"Why wouldn't you think so? You've always said I was too impulsive." She turned to look at him. Leaning against the sink, she crossed her arms over her breasts.

"I've always said you were impulsive, but not too impulsive. You make it sound like a criticism when it's one of your strengths. It's probably the reason you succeeded as an artist. If you'd sat around and worried about all the things that could go wrong or dwelled on the odds of failure, you never would have left Percyville and your business would never have happened."

"Well, it's all history now. I did go to California and I did manage to start up a business and it's doing well. Why rock the boat by relocating?"

He was shaking his head. "This is my fault. Suzanne said you were serious, that you—"

"You called her? You talked about my plans?"

"Yes, of course."

"What did she tell you?"

"Only that you were thinking about it. That you were interested in finding a good location. That she had mentioned I might know of something."

"I'm going to have to put a gag on her," Annie muttered.

"We're family, Annie, your family. She talked to me about it thinking you planned to ask my opinion."

"It was *her* idea to ask you, not mine."

"You have a problem asking my opinion about something? You certainly never hesitated to give me *your* opinion."

She drew in a sigh, running a hand through her curls. Her fingers caught in the tangles, which reminded her what she had on. And what she didn't. She shifted her feet, rubbed her toes against the back of her bare calf. She'd bet Elegant Eleanor never traipsed around barefoot. "That was when we were kids, Stuart. We're adults now."

"*You* were a kid. I wasn't."

"Males mature later than females."

"I was mature."

His voice was right at her ear. When had he walked over? Feeling edgy, she headed back to the stool at the breakfast bar. With her knees together, bare feet out of sight, she looked at him. "What was the second reason you came by?"

"To show you the sites. Possible locations for your plant. A couple are existing buildings in town, empty dwellings that might work, and the landlords are willing to let them go reasonably cheap. The other is country property with a couple of buildings I haven't looked at lately so I can't vouch for the condition they might be in. We need to take a look."

"Did you hear anything I said?"

"I heard it all, and before you go to the trouble of repeating it, I accept it. But just in case you get back to California and rethink your decision, you'll have some idea of what is available here and how much it'll cost."

She felt a reluctant urge to smile. As if he sensed success, Stuart's eyebrows went up a notch and his blue eyes took on a glint. "So, what d'ya say, Annie-girl?"

She glanced at her bare feet. Looking up at him, her mouth twitched. "Do you think I'll need shoes?"

"Most likely." Chuckling, he caught her hand and pulled her off the stool. "C'mon. We're outta here."

LATER, AS SHE SAT BESIDE Stuart in the Mustang, the wind whipping her hair everywhere, Annie tried to subdue a sense of guilt. It wasn't a feeling she had much experience with. She prided herself on her honesty and forthrightness. She didn't often do things that went against her nature. It was Stuart. He was forbidden fruit, but she was weak where he was concerned.

She had a lined legal pad in her lap. With a sigh, she made a note with a pen, clicked it shut, then turned her gaze out the side window. He was *married*. Maybe there wasn't as much difference between her and her mother as she'd assumed.

"Not impressed, huh?" He wore sunglasses, but he wrinkled his nose, making them drop so that he looked at her over them.

"With the two sites? Actually, the first one wasn't bad. I'd hardly have to do anything to set up a printing operation except to bring in the equipment and start up production."

"That's it?"

Except for convincing Spencer. "More or less."

He drove through the last traffic light in town and accelerated onto open highway. "Okay. One more to go."

They were now out of the town limits. Trees, pine, oak and

sweet gum flourished in the wooded hills bordering the high-way. A few houses surrounded by well-tended acreage were set well back to avoid the sound of traffic.

Stuart slowed down at a small road marked only by a weath-ered mailbox overgrown with morning glory vines. "Notice the rundown condition of the place. The owner died three or four years ago and the heirs are squabbling. They're all out of state, and I think they'd be happy to get a serious bid if you wanted to buy it outright."

He pulled up at an aged cottage. Weathered and badly in need of paint, it had a couple of cracked windows but was other-wise habitable. Behind it stood a long building that once housed some kind of small manufacturing operation. Annie's heart began to thump. Unconsciously, she held the legal pad against her chest.

"You could get it cheap, Annie."

"Hmm."

"No comment?"

"I'm thinking."

They got out and headed straight for the outbuilding. Stuart unlocked the door and pushed it open. It was dirty, but even with a cursory glance, Annie could see that it would be perfect. "I'd need a partition between those two windows to divide the back half into separate areas," she murmured. "One for print-ing and the other for packing and shipping."

"Office space wouldn't take up much of the square foot-age," Stuart said, turning to study the front of the building. "A carpenter could throw up some walls, use Sheetrock to divide the area." He waved a hand at the imaginary wall. "You could put in a wide window to give your manager a view of work in progress."

"Spence."

He looked at her. "Spence?"

"My production manager. I wouldn't consider anything with-out Spence looking it over and blessing it first."

"Sounds like he's an important person in your life." Stuart

turned and followed her out of the building, closing it with a smart bang. "Is he a partner?"

"If you mean does he have a piece of my business, then no. But he's been with me since the beginning, and I wouldn't even want to think of Dream Fields without him."

She headed for the cottage. The door was ajar and she went inside. "Oh, this is just…perfect. Some soap and water, a little elbow grease and paint and Spence could live here. I tease him all the time about being such a loner. He'd love it out here with the possums and quail."

"Is he your lover?"

She whirled, startled. "Lover?"

"I've never heard you carry on like that about any man." He stepped over to a built-in sideboard in the small dining room. One of the doors stood open. He closed it with a firm thump and turned to face her. "So is your relationship strictly professional or is it personal?"

Her arms were straight at her sides, the legal pad in her right hand. "It's a little of both, Stuart. Not that it's any of your business."

"He runs production at Dream Fields and sleeps with you, too?"

"Why does personal have to mean sex?"

"Because it does, nine times out of ten."

"He runs production at Dream Fields and is my oldest friend in California, no sex involved," she said between her teeth.

He clamped a hand to the back of his neck, looking anywhere but into her flashing eyes. Outside, a crop-dusting airplane swooped low, rattling the windows in the cottage.

"Looks like Spence and I are the exception that proves your stupid rule, wouldn't you say?" she said in the silence when the airplane moved on.

Stuart drew a long breath. "I'm sorry, Annie. You're right. This is none of my business."

"Let's go." She turned on her heel and was at the door trying to manage the rusty catch when he caught up.

"I mean it, Annie. I apologize. I was out of line. Your personal life's your own."

With her hand on the catch, she stopped, took in a slow breath and turned around to look at him. "Even so, you don't believe me, do you? You think Spence and I—"

"No, I do believe you. I—"

She searched his face. "Then why did you even suggest such a thing?"

He put out a hand and cradled her cheek in his palm. "We're family, you and I. Can't I be outraged on your behalf?"

"Not really. Even if Spence and I were lovers, it would be okay. I'm old enough to decide these things. I'm all grown up, Stuart. I don't need a cousin-keeper."

His smile was crooked. "I'll try to remember that."

"Good." Closing her eyes, Annie shook her head and, without thinking, moved closer and slipped her arms around his waist, juggling the pad and pen behind him. It felt so right. She sighed with joy. How many years since she'd moved so naturally into Stuart's arms? Not since she had discovered her love for him. Their greetings through the years when she'd been home from California had been stilted and tense. Now, with her head beneath his chin, she murmured, "I suppose I ought to thank you for the thought, but it's so ridiculous when I think of Spence that—"

Stuart's arms, wrapped about her just as securely, tightened. "Shut up about Spence," he muttered.

She rubbed her nose against the clean, starched smell of his shirt. "He's a nice man. Honest. He's really good at—"

He caught her beneath her chin and turned her face up to his. "Shut. Up." And then he kissed her.

Stunned, she didn't move for a second or two. She'd kissed him before, many times. Little hello pecks on the cheek, quick goodbyes with a warm hug, Christmas kisses laughingly stolen under mistletoe, and once in her early teens in the gazebo to make him remember her when he went off to Ole Miss.

But none were like this. Never like this. Nothing about this kiss was cousinly. It was hot and hungry and urgent. *He* was hot and hungry and urgent. Her heart leaped with surprise and shock. And then delight. *This* was what she'd dreamed about for so long. With no other thought than that this was Stuart—*her Stuart!*—she opened to him, allowing the sweep of his tongue, knowing for the first time in her adult life this intimacy, the taste and smell and strength of Stuart. It was heaven. It was better than anything she'd imagined. God, her heart was going to burst with the sheer joy of it.

"Annie, Annie," he breathed, tearing his mouth from hers. "I didn't…I shouldn't…" With a groan, he caught handfuls of her hair, holding her fast until the moment of sanity danced out of his reach. He kissed her again. It was deep and reckless with lust. He ran his lips over her eyes, her cheeks, her ear, then buried his nose in her red curls, inhaling deeply while nearly crushing the breath out of her.

"God, how long I've wanted this," he said hoarsely. "I know it's crazy. And it's wrong, but I don't want to think about any of that right now. Did you know I dream about flying to L.A. and just showing up at your place? I don't think about what you'd do—probably kick me out and tell me to go screw myself—but nothing I imagine seems to help."

Annie closed her eyes, melting with the sweet pleasure of his touch. Finally he was saying the things she'd longed to hear for so many years. She ached to respond but was suddenly frightened. What was she doing? It was *too late!* Bracing her hands on his forearms, she pushed him away. "Stop, Stuart. *Stop!* We can't do this. I don't want this." Her breathing was ragged as she turned away from him, hugging herself, trembling all the way to her toes.

"You feel it, too, Annie. I know you do."

"No, you don't know anything, Stuart. Certainly you don't know me. I have been away from Percyville for years. What we're feeling is leftover childhood stuff. We have no right to do this." She drew in a broken breath, feeling sick that she'd let herself forget the rules for a few mad moments. "We have no right to even think this way."

"Then why does it feel so right?"

"It feels good, Stuart, not right. Sex feels good, but that doesn't make it right between us. Do I have to say it? You're a married man."

He turned away, his mouth grim.

Using both hands, she pushed at her hair to smooth it into some kind of order. Her heart was still slamming in her chest, and the taste of him still lingered. She swallowed against despair and a ridiculous urge to cry.

"I'm sorry, Annie."

"Let's go." She bent and picked up the pad and pen that had fallen to the ground.

He put out a hand. "Annie—"

She closed her eyes, shifting away. "Let's go, Stuart."

He was silent for a moment. "Yeah, okay."

Her vision was blurred as she picked her way through the overgrown grass to the Mustang and, without waiting for him, opened the door. She didn't trust herself to get that close to him again.

"GIVE ME A HUG, sugar-boy." Annie dropped her carry-on to the floor and bent to kiss Caleb. Fluffing his hair, she held him away from her, pretending to study him from head to toe. "Oh, wow. You are *such* a big boy now. I bet the next time I see you, you'll come up to here on me!" She touched her nose as he giggled and turned his face into his mother's thigh.

"I still think it's crazy, you leaving like this," Suzanne said in a tone of dismay. "Please tell me what happened to make you change your mind, Annie."

Annie straightened, slinging her carry-on on her shoulder. "Nothing happened, Suzy. You know I never stay as long as I plan. I get here, I remember the reasons I left in the first place and I hit the road again. I get antsy about Dream Fields. You know how us small-business people are, so obsessed that our little piece of the American dream'll slip away from us."

Suzanne was shaking her head, not believing a word. "Was it Jack? Did he do something? Say something? If he did, I'll—"

"Jack? Puh—leeze. There's nothing that son of a bitch could do to drive me away. I'm telling you, Suzy, I just need to get back."

"But why so soon? You came here with the idea of relocating your business. Now you've suddenly got to get back to California."

"Bye-bye, Annie-Aunt." Caleb waved at her from behind Suzanne's knees.

"Bye-bye, sugar-boy."

"You're running away again," Suzanne said, persisting with a lawyer's tenacity. "I just don't know why yet."

"I'm not running away."

"You are. I recognize the signs. You've done it before, but I understood then. Stuart was—" She stopped, her mouth open. "It's Stuart, isn't it. It's Stuart again. I should have known. He's the only person in the world who can spook you this way."

Annie hitched the carry-on to one side and began rooting in a waist-pack for her ticket. "My plane departs in twenty minutes, Suzy. I've got to go."

"Stuart told me he showed you some good sites yesterday. You liked the Jacobson property, he said. He said you sketched the renovations you'd need right on the spot. He said you thought you could be in production within a few weeks."

"He said, he said, he said." Annie waved a hand. "He talks too much."

"Stuart? Hardly. If anything, he's too closemouthed. Damn it, Annie, what happened?"

Annie looked at her then, her green eyes clouded. "Don't push me on this right now, Suzy. Just believe me, I can't stay here. I can't be anywhere near Stuart. He's...we're..." She shook her head. "I really have to go, Suzy."

"Kiss, kiss," Caleb said at her feet. Overcoming his shyness, he lifted his face and patted his mouth.

"Goodbye, punkin," Annie said, swooping down to kiss him and give him one last squeeze. "Annie-Aunt will send you something good from California, okay?"

"Candy! I like candy!"

Suzanne was shaking her head. "He has such a sweet tooth!"

Annie laughed, blinking back tears. "Okay, candy." She hugged Suzanne, then backed away. "Take care of him, Suzy. He's precious. You're so lucky." She swallowed and managed a bright smile. "And good luck at your new job. Go out and buy a couple of smashing suits. May as well look the part—tough, single-minded woman dedicated to justice and equality under the law."

"Yeah, right."

"I mean it. Give 'em hell." Blowing her a kiss, Annie turned and began to walk rapidly toward the security check.

"Will you come for Thanksgiving?" Suzanne called.

"I'll let you know." Annie dumped her carry-on on the conveyor and slipped through the radar detector. Walking backward, she added, "Oh, one more thing... Will you look in on my mother every now and then, Suzy?"

"Sure."

"Bye now."

"Bye," Suzanne murmured, watching as she retrieved her carry-on and hurried down the concourse to her flight gate, her hair wild and unruly, her legs impossibly long in well-worn jeans. Two businessmen checking in behind her eyed her admiringly. If Stuart had made a move on her, who could blame him? Eleanor was icy-cool, snooty and as loving as a wind-up doll. Beside her, Annie radiated warmth and joie de vivre.

"Annie-Aunt go bye-bye," Caleb said sadly, sensing her mood.

"That's right, sweetheart," she said. She picked him up and buried her nose in his neck, tickling and hugging him at the same time. "But this is home and she'll be back, you'll see."

FIFTEEN

SUZANNE TOOK ANNIE'S ADVICE and went shopping for a couple of power outfits. In the full-length mirror at Maud's, Percyville's best dress shop, she examined herself in charcoal pinstripes. She didn't feel anything like the tough prosecutor Annie envisioned, but in this suit she would definitely look the part, she decided.

Hearing a crash outside the dressing cubicle, she parted the curtain and looked out. Caleb was sitting on the floor, plastic hangers strewn all around him. "Those are not toys, Caleb. Put them back."

"Big, *big* house," Caleb told her.

"You're building a house?"

He nodded rapidly. "Daddy come home."

Staring into his wide, dark eyes, Suzanne felt the familiar stab of guilt. She was almost used to living with the consequences of her choices. At first she'd suffered hours of useless self-recrimination and endless what-ifs. But eventually, even the worst of a person's behavior had to be set aside if life was to go on. But then sometimes—as now—Caleb's need for Dennis was so obvious that she found it almost impossible to justify her decision—*their* decision—to cancel Caleb's right to a home with both a daddy and a mommy. She turned and slipped the jacket off. A horrible emotion, guilt.

She jerked the curtain open. "Pick them up, Caleb. We've got to go."

Caleb ignored her. "Daddy help." He held up his "building," a tangle of hangers strung together.

"We'll go home and build something wonderful with your

Lego," she promised. Laying the suit aside, she began helping him pick up the hangers. She was worried about leaving him in the care of a baby-sitter once she began her new job. It was a given that working in the D.A.'s office, her hours would be long.

"Daddy help?"

She sighed. "You know Daddy's in Texas now, sweetie. He doesn't live here anymore."

He frowned. "No!"

"Yes. Daddy's there and we're here, Caleb." *And we have to make the best of it.* She was instantly ashamed. Caleb didn't understand. How could he? He just felt abandoned by his father, and it was all her fault. How much would Caleb be shortchanged because she was a single mother?

With the suit draped over her arm, she took his hand and led him out of the dressing area. Hoping to distract him, she said, "Want to stop at Riverbend on our way home and you can see Grandpa?" Her father was one of the best people in Caleb's world.

He looked up at her. "Go fishin' Grampa?"

"Not tonight, honey. It's too late for your grandpa to take you fishing, but maybe he'll let you help him tie some flies to put in his new tackle box." *Sorry, Dad.* Little fingers could wreak havoc with delicate fishing lures, but where Caleb was concerned, her father seemed to have no rules.

"Okay." Happy now, his sneakers squeaking on the wood floor, he dashed ahead of her.

And maybe in Charles Stafford's loving company, he wouldn't remember how much he missed Dennis.

At the register, Maud Myrick took the pin-striped suit and slipped it into a plastic sheath while Suzanne wrote out a check. "Suzanne, that teal dress was *so* right for you. Are you sure you don't want to change your mind? It's on sale—thirty percent off—did I mention that?"

"Thanks, Miss Maud, but I'll just take the suit today." She passed the check over. Maud must think her social life was far more exciting than it actually was if she was recommending the slinky cocktail dress.

"You should get out more, Suzanne. I haven't seen you at one of the club functions since I don't know when."

"I'm working in Jackson now, Miss Maud."

"Oh, yes, that's right. Well, that teal dress will look just as fabulous on you in Jackson, dear." The woman played bridge with the Judge every Thursday evening and had known Suzanne from birth. "Lovely as you are, you turn heads no matter where you go."

"Thank you, Miss Maud."

"Now you're divorced, it doesn't mean you have to bury yourself in work and single motherhood," Maud chided gently.

"I'll remember that." She should also remember that if she didn't want a kindly lecture, she shouldn't shop at Maud's.

Maud shut the cash drawer with a snap. "These years go by so fast, darlin'. Take it from me."

"Yes, ma'am." Maud Myrick's divorce had been the talk of the town thirty years ago, according to Lily Stafford. Glancing around, she saw Caleb making a beeline for the door. "Come back, Caleb. Mommy's almost finished."

"He's so cute, Suzanne. Smart, too." Maud took the sheathed suit off the hook and handed it over. "I heard him talking in the dressing room. Really remarkable, and him what? Not even two years old yet, is he? He'll keep you on your toes."

"Yes, he does that, all right." The bell above the old-fashioned door tinkled. "Caleb! Don't open the door. Caleb—" She grabbed the suit and hurried after him. It still amazed her how quickly a small child could cover ground. Before she reached the door, he was out of the shop and across the sidewalk. She sped outside, catching him just before he reached a couple getting out of a car. She scooped him up, trying to avoid his flailing arms and feet as he screamed.

"Caleb, what is wrong with you?" Kicking and squalling, his whole body strained toward the couple.

"Daddy, Daddy!"

Not the couple, but the man. Suzanne's heart caught as if squeezed by a fist. Oh, Lord, it was Dennis. She stood looking into his face for a startled second while Caleb fought against her attempt to restrain him.

"My daddy," Caleb cried. "I want my daddy!"

It had been a month since Caleb had seen Dennis, the day the divorce was declared final. He'd told her then that he'd decided not to be part of Caleb's life. He'd argued that the boy was so young that it would be better to disappear now. In a little while, he wouldn't be able to remember ever having a daddy. She'd been so devastated for Caleb's sake that she still couldn't bear to recall that day. One look at him now and Suzanne knew he hadn't had a change of heart.

"Hello, Dennis."

"Suzanne."

Suzanne glanced at the woman by his side, relieved to see it wasn't Tiffany. She managed a weak greeting while Caleb bucked and screamed in her arms, determined to get to Dennis.

"Looks like you've got your hands full there." He finally looked at Caleb, his features softening. With a rush of relief, Suzanne set the boy down. Caleb instantly ran to Dennis and threw his arms around his legs. Dennis reached down and ruffled his dark hair. "Hey, guy. You and your mama been shopping?"

"Daddy!" Caleb repeated, hanging on. "Go home now."

Suzanne started forward. "No, honey—"

But Dennis stopped her. "It's okay," he said, squatting down at the boy's level. The woman with Dennis glanced about awkwardly, then strolled over to Maud's storefront, pretending to window-shop. Dennis drew Caleb into the curve of his arm. "He's talking pretty good now, isn't he?"

Suzanne nodded. "It happened so fast. One day he was babbling and the next he was saying real words, and a lot of them."

Dennis chuckled, rubbing his nose against the boy's. "Gonna be a lawyer, huh, Caleb?"

Caleb stared at him solemnly, then put his thumb in his

mouth and rested his head on Dennis's chest. Dennis glanced up with chagrin and met Suzanne's eyes. Neither could speak for a moment. He cleared his throat. "How's your new job?"

"It starts Monday." She glanced at Maud's storefront. "I was just—" She shrugged. "How's your new job?" *How's your new life?*

"It's okay." He gently pried the small arm from around his neck and tipped Caleb's chin up so that he looked directly into the child's eyes. "You're a big boy now, aren't you, Caleb?"

Caleb nodded, his dark eyes confused.

"I'm going to be living in a place called Texas." At the dreaded word, Caleb began shaking his head. "Yes, I am, Caleb. And you and your mommy will be here."

Caleb's head still moved back and forth in denial.

"You'll be the man of the house. It'll be your job to take care of your mommy. Okay?"

Caleb stared at him in bewilderment. He teared up.

Still on his haunches before the boy, Dennis glanced at Suzanne. His tone hardened. "This is tough, but it's for the best, Suzanne."

"Daddy—"

Dennis gave the boy a hard, enveloping hug, then stood up and began moving backward, signaling to the woman at the display window. She started toward him. "Get in the car," he told her curtly. With a startled glance at Suzanne and Caleb, she did as he asked. Dennis walked rapidly around the vehicle and opened the door on the driver's side. "Take care of yourself, Suzanne. Caleb—" He managed a smile for the boy. "I'll see you around, sport."

Slamming the door, he started the car and spun out, tires squealing, drowning out Caleb's heartbroken cry.

IT WAS A MIRACLE THAT SHE managed to get Caleb and herself home safely that night. The promised visit to Riverbend was forgotten in Caleb's distress over seeing his daddy and then having him walk out of his life.

Worst of all were Caleb's bewildered questions. She answered him as best she could, putting him off when he wanted to know when they could go see his daddy again. Desperately, she changed the subject, but like a wind-up toy, he was right back to questions about Dennis.

He didn't eat his dinner, even though she fixed his favorite cereal as a special treat. He fussed through his bath and interrupted constantly with more anxious questions while she tried to read *Goodnight Moon*. Finally, when he simply would not settle and go to sleep, she lay down beside him and wrapped her arms around him.

"D-Daddy?" he said, snuffling and burying his face in her breast.

"Oh, Caleb, what can I say?" she whispered in anguish. Drawing in a deep breath, she prayed for the right words. "Your daddy loves you, Caleb. Don't ever forget that. I know you don't understand why you can't see him, why he doesn't live with us anymore, but it's just something that has happened." Maybe the words were as much for her as for Caleb, she thought, rubbing his silky head lovingly. "But you know what, Caleb? We have each other, sweetheart. And we'll be together always, you and me. Someday, when you're all grown up, you can go and visit your daddy and show him what a fine young man you've become."

And it'll be his loss, Caleb. His loss, my darling.

Caleb released a soft, shuddering sigh, and Suzanne realized thankfully that he was asleep.

She cradled his small body and fought against cursing God for hurting Caleb when the sin had been hers. Her earliest memories were of admonishments from her mother that she be a good girl, that she do the chores expected of her, finish her homework every night, display the manners of a lady, send thank-you notes, always be polite to the elderly, dress tastefully and avoid promiscuity. And what had been her reward for obeying all those rules? For trying her best to be good?

Rape and a brokenhearted little boy.

After a while, she got up, moving carefully to keep from waking Caleb, and tiptoed from the room. She had skipped dinner, but it didn't matter. In her room, she sat on the side of her bed and stared around blankly. A woman's room. A single woman's room. A lonely woman's room. When her gaze fell on the telephone, she picked it up impulsively. There was someone, someone who would ask no questions, someone who cared about her. Dear God, she needed Ben Kincaid's undemanding friendship now.

Ben, who shared a special bond with Caleb. He, above all others, would understand. She dialed the number and waited through a couple of rings. Just when she was about to hang up, the phone was answered.

A woman.

She almost cried out, so great was her sense of loss. What had she expected? A man like Ben attracted women almost as easily as Jack Sullivan.

"Hello? Who *is* this?"

She hung up and lay back to wait for the night to end.

HER LIFE AS A JUNIOR prosecutor in the district attorney's office began on Monday morning. She was immediately assigned to assist another woman, Candace Webber, who was reputed to be hard as nails and twice as sharp. Although Candace was more than qualified to be the district attorney herself, after spending only half a day with her, Suzanne realized why she would never be elected. She was too outspoken.

"I understand you have friends in high places," Candace Webber said, shoving a stack of files across her desk toward Suzanne. She was in her late forties, tall and big-boned, with short dark hair cut in a severe wedge. There was no wedding ring on her finger. "And since you do, I can only wonder why you'd ask to work with me."

Suzanne hadn't requested any such thing, hadn't known

enough about any of the D.A.'s assistants to ask to work with anyone. After Jack's attempt to influence Grayson Lee at Taylor's brunch, she had vowed to take any assignment the D.A. suggested and keep her mouth shut and her profile low. At least until she learned her way around.

"It wasn't quite that way, Ms. Webber," she said, sensing the woman would appreciate honesty. "I didn't ask for any special assignment. I don't know enough about the job to even have a preference."

The woman eyed Suzanne from above her narrow reading glasses. "Candace. I'm Ms. Webber to judges in the courtroom and to the media. So you didn't ask to assist me?"

"No, but I'm perfectly satisfied to work with you. In fact, I welcome it."

"*For* me, darlin'. You'll be working *for* me. And you'll be doing more grunt work than you ever knew existed when you were in law school."

"I can handle it."

The older woman's gray eyes were shrewd as she studied Suzanne. "I believe you. So…" She gave a brisk nod to the stack of files. "The top five are urgent. The remainder are only extremely important. We have more cases on the docket than we can ever manage intelligently, so sometimes you'll have to use your best judgment and pray I'd concur. We plea-bargain whenever it's not an absolutely obscene option, but anybody here can tell you that if I go that route, I take a pound of flesh. Now." She pushed her glasses up. "You're on your own as far as work schedule, hours, et cetera. Just don't let me ask for a file and find it incomplete. Do we understand each other?"

"We do."

She nodded again, smiling faintly. "One more thing. I smelled Jack Sullivan's hand in all this when Grayson informed me that I now had a new assistant. You can't be close if he thought you'd have it easy working for me."

"He's married to my sister."

"Yes, I knew that." Candace leaned back, her gaze thoughtful now. "And yet he's gone out of his way to make it tough for you here. Want some advice?"

Suzanne braced for she knew not what.

"Watch out. He's a dangerous man."

Suzanne gazed steadily back. "I'm not afraid of Jack."

After a beat or two, Candace stood up. "Well, then, get to work, girl. Let's see what you're made of."

PART II

SIXTEEN

November 1986

STANDING CURBSIDE SQUINTING in the afternoon sun, Ben Kincaid waited for a chance to cross. The busy street was a maze of taxis, cars and bicycles. Impatiently, he let a gray-bearded cyclist pass, then skirted the rear of a beat-up Mercedes and jogged across, holding his breath to avoid diesel exhaust billowing from a double-decker bus. The address he sought was just around a corner.

He found it a few moments later, an official-looking granite building opening directly onto the street. He pushed through huge carved doors grimy with exhaust soot and went inside, his boots sounding loud on the ancient marble floor. It looked a little better inside than out. The ceilings in the foyer were high. Though now dark with age and neglect, they had once been elaborate and beautiful. Two men in turbans stood talking to a businessman in conventional Western clothing. The conversation was in Arabic. None of the three acknowledged him as he strode to the single elevator and punched the button to go up.

As he waited, his gaze strayed again to the street and the continuous flow of humanity and machines. He was in Istanbul, but he was reminded of Baghdad and Bombay, even Hong Kong, although there was an international flavor to Hong Kong that was missing in other major Eastern cities he'd seen in the past years. He'd wanted to see the world, and he certainly had while working for PetroTex, thanks to the U.S. government.

Suddenly, for some reason, he thought of his grandfather. Lucian Kincaid had wanted him to get his law degree and then work in some area of law enforcement. He almost laughed thinking that he'd certainly fulfilled Lucian's ambitions for him—on a grand scale. Lucian couldn't be surprised that he'd wound up on the payroll of the federal government, but he'd probably expected Ben's assignments to be a little closer to home. Istanbul was a long way from Percyville.

When the elevator groaned to a stop, he waited for a couple of men in military uniform to get out before stepping inside. After punching the button for the sixth floor, he leaned back against the wood-paneled cubicle and felt the heavy fatigue of jet lag settling over him.

He rubbed his face wearily. The flight from London had been long, but what really bugged him was that Sanford Ellis had promised him two weeks' R and R. He'd phoned Jill Pennington, who was assigned to PetroTex London now, and set a date. He'd done that the last time he'd planned a date with Jill, too, and Ellis had screwed it up then by hustling him aboard a jet back to Abu Dhabi.

Refusing Sanford Ellis was not an option. Powerful dignitaries around the world listened when Ellis spoke. Ben himself had been the object of his boss's disapproval only once before. It was not an experience he cared to repeat.

Sanford Ellis had persuaded Ben to join his team a year ago. A career U.S. government operative, Ellis was deep into covert activities in the Mideast. Ben's technical credentials and his willingness to travel made him ideal for Ellis's purposes. His connection to the oil company provided excellent cover.

He spread both feet and braced himself as the cables on the elevator squealed and jerked, but it kept moving. Most of the time, he accepted the unusual demands of his job philosophically. It was still stimulating and the wanderlust in him was still unabated, but it was hard to have much of a private life in his line of work. Fortunately, Jill Pennington was just as career-oriented as he was, so she understood his job much better than most women. However, even Jill had her limits.

He'd met her in Houston. Armed with an MBA she'd earned

at Rice University, she'd landed a job with PetroTex the same time that Ben had been hired. She was an only child of parents in the U.S. diplomatic corps and had been educated in private schools, mostly abroad. Jill herself was determined not to be trapped in the stifling world of political diplomacy.

With both their careers on a fast track, their progress had paralleled for a couple of years. Assignments to Abu Dhabi and Saudi Arabia—her father was presently assistant attaché at the embassy in Saudi—had brought them together in foreign locations fairly often. About the time that Jill was assigned to PetroTex London, Ben had been tapped by the FBI. They weren't together often now. Ben believed their relationship had survived essentially because Jill's commitment to her career was stronger than her need for any man.

Still, she always seemed glad to see him, in spite of the fact that he was away a month or two at a time on assignment. But she never missed him enough for him to feel he had any real claim on her heart. Which suited him fine. Ben was leery of any meaningful emotional commitment. His parents' turbulent relationship had bred extreme caution into him. If that hadn't soured his outlook, he'd then watched Suzanne and Dennis fail at marriage, even though they'd had good, solid reasons to succeed. If love and friendship weren't a fail-safe basis for marriage, he didn't know what would be. He'd decided the smart thing was just to keep relationships casual. Enjoy the friendship, the shared interest in work, play and sex. That's where Jill Pennington differed from most women. They wanted more: marriage, security, a conventional home. He wasn't ready for that. Maybe later.

Jill did, however, expect him to show up when he said he would, especially when she went to the trouble of rearranging her own demanding schedule to be with him. Whatever Sanford Ellis had in mind today had better be good.

He stepped from the elevator into a hallway with half a dozen offices behind closed doors, every one painted a dingy green. He began looking for the number he'd been given before leaving London. He stopped, ran a hand over the left side of his body, comforted by the feel of his weapon beneath his jacket. It never paid to assume the only thing behind a closed door was a friendly face.

Standing motionless, he could hear the muted sound of male voices, then an explosive curse. He laughed silently, recognizing that particular epithet, then turned the knob and went inside.

Sanford Ellis was behind his desk, the collar of his white shirt loosened, the knot of his tie riding at the level of the second button. He was a man of medium height with shrewd eyes the same shade of iron gray as his crewcut and a strong, chunky build that matched an equally strong control of the elite unit of the FBI he managed. He stood now as Ben crossed to the desk and they shook hands.

Slouched deep in a worn leather chair against the near wall was a second man. Owen Jenner's career spanned two decades of covert activities. He was over six two, powerfully built, with a shaved head and a black mustache that might have looked comical until the fierce expression in his blue eyes registered. With his hands cupped to light one of the Turkish cigarettes he favored, he nodded to Ben. Then he shook the match out and grunted a greeting.

Ben hadn't seen Jenner in several months, but they'd worked together before. He admired the man's phenomenal expertise in half a dozen sensitive areas. If Ellis had summoned Jenner, something interesting was up.

"How's it going, Jenner?" he said before turning to his boss. "I got your message, Ellis. Which forced me to forfeit my hotel reservations in London—after bribing an assistant concierge a hundred bucks American to get them in the first place. What happened to the two weeks' R and R you promised me? So far, I've taken—" he glanced at his watch "—thirty-five hours, mostly spent in flight."

"Sit down, Ben. And how is the lovely Ms. Pennington?"

"Maybe if I'd had a couple of hours in London, I could answer that." He went over to a leather couch that matched the chair Jenner occupied and sat down, crossing an ankle over his knee. "Our flights probably crossed over the North Sea."

Ellis donned reading glasses. "Sorry about that, Ben. These things seldom happen at the most convenient times."

Ben glanced at Jenner, who gazed with interest at the smoke curling from the end of his cigarette, then back at Ellis. "What things?"

Ellis straightened, pulled himself forward in his chair and reached for a folder on his desk. It was brown with a cover flap and string. Across the front were the words Restricted—Need to Know. He pulled out a single sheet half filled with text and scanned it before pushing it toward Ben.

"We have a report that Palestinian terrorists are planning an attack on a U.S. oil rig within the next forty-eight hours."

Ben rose and took the paper. "What kind of attack? Missile? Planting a bomb? Mining the surrounding waters?"

Ellis shrugged. "That's just the problem. The possibilities are endless."

He read it swiftly, then gave it back to Ellis. "So what does this have to do with me? Sounds like a job for Navy Seals." He sat back down. "I'm no demolition expert."

"No, but you know the likely places on this rig where explosives might be concealed. PetroTex owns it."

"Shit."

"We'll fly you out to the Gulf and give you as many people as you need to comb the rig. When you locate the stuff, yell. We'll take it from there."

Ben rested his head back against the wall, knowing there was no way he could pass on this one. Most of his assignments weren't as dangerous, but occasionally Ellis came up with a real doozy. He turned to look at Owen Jenner. "What's your role in this one, Jenner?"

Standing, Ellis picked up the folder and tucked the paper back inside. He secured the string, then, walking around his desk, he stopped in front of Ben. "He *is* the demolition expert," he said. "You're partners."

"SIX...FIVE...FOUR...three..." Glancing up from his watch, Ben checked one last time to see that there was nothing occupying the open sea east of the oil rig. At his side, six men waited tensely. He nodded at Owen Jenner, who held an electronic device in his hand. "Two...one. Okay, do it, Jenner."

Boom!

"All—ri-i-ight!"

"Jeez, look at that!"

"Son of a bitch!"

Orange flame billowed thousands of feet upward from the center of the explosion, lighting the nighttime sky as brightly as high noon in Riyadh. The men watched from the deck of the rig. A charge of that magnitude would have decimated the rig, igniting a raging inferno that could conceivably have taken months to smother, plus destroying the lives of every living thing aboard. A terrorist statement to say...what?

Beside him, the men were slapping one another, congratulating themselves for throwing a spoke into some maniac's game plan. At least for now.

He gave them time to settle, then spoke. "We did a good job, men. Everybody on the team. I won't forget it." He gestured with his thumb to the helicopter behind him on the pad. "As soon as we can load up, we're out of here." He turned to Owen Jenner, who was positioned off his right shoulder. "You ready, Jenner?"

"I was born ready." Among Jenner's talents was his ability to fly a helicopter, a skill which he'd honed to perfection in three tours of duty in Vietnam.

Ben grinned. "Then let's haul ass, y'all!"

The men broke ranks, cheering, then headed across the deck to the chopper. With Jenner at the controls, they were airborne in minutes, lifting up from the rig to hover over the now-silent apparatus. As a safety precaution, the rig had been shut down and evacuated when word had gone out that explosives were suspected on board. An expensive proposition, shutting down a producing well, but at least the PetroTex people were safe.

Now, in the distance, the eerie spectacle of fire licking over the surface of the Gulf waters was a grim reminder of disaster averted.

"What a waste," one of the Seals commented quietly.

Ben was shaking his head. "Yeah, thousands of dollars to shut down operations on a rig going up in smoke. Worse yet, startup might not be cost-effective. Depending on the crude left in the well, sometimes a company just writes it off."

One of the men—a PetroTex employee—cursed with disgust. "And we're up shit creek."

"Which is exactly the point these guys are trying to make," another said. He settled back with a grunt, pulling his cap down over his eyes. "I don't know about you guys, but I could use a beer."

"Sounds good." Jenner pushed the stick back and they soared up. In seconds, the strange glow of the fire was behind them. In front of them, clear, bright moonlight showed the way.

AN HOUR LATER, AS BEN climbed out of the helicopter flush with success and the adrenaline high that always followed a dangerous mission, Sanford Ellis was waiting for him. Expecting to be congratulated for the job, he started to grin. Then something about the older man's expression sobered him.

"Ben." Ellis clamped a hand on his shoulder. "A message came for you just about the time you were dismantling the bomb. Blame me for not telling you right away if you want to. It was a judgment call. I thought—"

"What? What's wrong?" He shifted his gear to his shoulder. "Is it Jill?"

"No, no. It's your grandfather. Your mother— Ben, I'm sorry. I don't know how to tell you this." The hand on Ben's shoulder tightened. "There's been an accident, Ben."

"Bad?"

"I'm sorry, Ben. The message came from…ah, a woman. Ms. Stafford?"

Fear bloomed in his chest. "The Judge?"

"No, no, a woman." He glanced at the note in his hand. "Suzanne Stafford."

"Goddamn it, Ellis. Tell me." He reached for the note.

"I'm sorry to be the one—" Sanford Ellis drew a hard breath. "Your grandfather and your mother have been in a car accident. It's bad, Ben. The worst, I'm afraid. They're both gone."

SEVENTEEN

BEN SAT AT THE OLD OAK DESK that had belonged to his grandfather and unlocked the battered strongbox. Blowing away the
dust, he opened it. His chest was seized with crushing pain as
he took out the first item. Not a legal paper or an official document like the stack he'd already sorted out that chronicled
Lucian Kincaid's long life. It was the medal that Ben had been
awarded when he made Eagle Scout. What followed were mementos of *his* life. Guilt assailed him, pushing his grief and pain
to a sharper level. He shoved the strongbox aside, groped for
the mug near his hand and gulped black coffee.

Ah, Granddad...Mama...I can't believe this.

They said it was quick. That there hadn't been time to know
what hit them. That Marilee, who was driving, hadn't a chance
to avoid the pickup passing illegally against the yellow line as
she topped the hill just past Crow's Crossing. The two vehicles
had crashed head-on, the pickup going in excess of eighty. His
mother and Lucian had died instantly. Ben had forced himself to
take a look at the car, a tangle of metal and chrome with twisted
frame and crushed seats. He saw at once that it had indeed been
quick, that they'd died within seconds of the collision. But it
hadn't been instantaneous. He knew they'd had a chance to see
the oncoming vehicle, to feel fear like a fist in their stomachs, to
know they were looking at their own deaths. He hated knowing
that. He hated knowing his mother, as gentle a woman as ever
lived, had been taken that way. That his grandfather, who'd removed hundreds of drunk drivers from the roads while enforc-
ing the law, had been powerless on that day.

At first his pain and grief and rage had centered on the drunk driver, but even that had been denied him when the bastard hadn't survived the night in ICU. Now all he had left was his own lonely grief. And his guilt.

He would have to put it all behind him, pick up and go on. Those words had been offered over and over at the wake and then later, after the funeral service. Sitting now at his grandfather's desk, he pressed thumb and forefinger into his eyes and rested his elbows on the scarred top. He felt empty, devoid of any connection that meant anything. Even halfway across the world, he had felt the affection and approval of his mother and his grandfather, gifts bestowed without obligation. Now he didn't have a single blood relative left in the world.

Jesus. He wiped a hand over his face and blinked rapidly. Reaching for his coffee again, he took a drink and grimaced. Cold. Shoving it aside, he turned back to the task before him. Digging again into his grandfather's strongbox, he pulled out photographs, papers, legal and otherwise, a few stocks and bonds, the deed to the house and other properties, Lucian's will. Ben read it over quickly, finding nothing that surprised him. He read his mother's next. No surprises there, either. He was sole heir to both. Setting the wills aside, he picked up another document, more recently dated, and was reading it when he heard a soft sound at the door.

"Hey, want some company?"

"Suzanne." He pushed his chair back and stood up. Going around the desk, he put his hands out and caught hers. For a second they simply looked at each other, then with a soft sound, she was suddenly holding him close, both arms tight around his waist, her head on his chest.

"I can't believe it, Ben," she said, her words muffled against his shirtfront. "I'm still trying to take it in."

"Yeah." Coming on the heels of his thoughts just now, her sympathy almost did him in. His throat ached and tears stung the back of his eyes. To keep himself from just throwing back his head and howling, he buried his face in her hair and concentrated on how good she smelled, how soft she felt, how damn glad he was that it was Suzanne here with him. He couldn't think of anyone else with whom he'd rather share his loss.

"Your mama…she was the best, Ben."

The sound he made was full of pain.

"And Lucian…I really l-loved that old man."

In spite of his will, a deep, dark wave of grief rose in Ben's chest. His throat closed on emotion so powerful that it hurt. He held his breath, trying to hang on to his composure. But it was too much. Too raw. When he heard her soft sob, his own grief broke in a great, shuddering rush.

Suzanne murmured words of sympathy, patted his back, touched his hair, stroked his neck. God, it felt good to finally give in. Her touch was liberating, like clean water and fresh air. Here was someone who'd loved his family, too.

"I'm sorry," he said hoarsely after a few moments, knowing he was anything but. Turning away, he wiped both eyes with the heels of his hands.

"You're entitled to grieve over your loss, Ben."

The short sound he made was a far cry from a laugh, but it was the best he could do. "Okay, then how about 'Thanks, I needed that.'"

"And I say 'What're friends for?'" She was smiling with him, then sniffing and wiping at her nose with a napkin she found beside his coffee cup.

He dug for his own handkerchief, then blew his nose. "I'm glad to see you, Suzy. I've been sitting here in this big old house trying—"

"You shouldn't be alone right now, Ben. You should stay with my folks. They'd love to have you, you know that."

"Yeah, but…truth is, I don't think I'm fit company for anybody, Suzy. I'm mad as hell."

"Because of how they died?"

"That and because I wasn't ready, damn it!"

"Something like this…no one ever is, Ben."

"If I'd realized, if I hadn't been so wrapped up in my job and my own selfish interests—spending months in places I couldn't even pronounce the names of sometimes…I don't know… I could have come home more often. Seen them on Mother's Day, Father's Day, instead of…" He cleared his throat and looked bleakly outside, where the leaves of a dogwood had turned crimson, almost ready to fall. He'd been six years old when he'd helped Lucian plant that dogwood. "It's too late now."

"Don't torture yourself like this, Ben. Marilee and Lucian would be the first to say that."

He nodded. "Yeah, but I feel it just the same."

After a moment, she waved a hand at the desktop. "You've been busy."

He gazed at the jumble of papers. "It's better to go through everything now. Once I get back to work, who knows when I'll be in Percyville again."

"Don't say that, Ben. This is your home."

"No, I guess that's what I was getting at just now, Suzy. With my folks gone, I don't have a home anymore."

There was sympathy and understanding in her eyes. "Well, is there any way I can help while you're here?"

"Thanks, but it's something I think I should do. A way to sort of—"

"Say goodbye?"

He nodded, giving her a faint smile. "You always know the right words, Suzy." He went back around the desk and sat down. "I remember the first time we ever met. Do you?"

"Uh-huh. At Riverbend. Lucian was in Daddy's study playing gin, which they did every Wednesday night."

"It was June. I was visiting. I was sixteen. Dad was wildcatting in Texas. He'd invested every cent he could beg, borrow or steal in a well near Odessa. A fire broke out and he was killed. Mama didn't want to give Lucian the news on the telephone, so we drove to Riverbend and I waited in the front room while she told him." Ben turned a paperweight round and round, thinking back. "You knew what was going on, so you came into that room and introduced yourself. You were so pretty with that streaky blond hair and those big gray eyes. You took me into the kitchen and made hot chocolate and told me how sorry you were."

"I must have thought how devastated I'd be if something happened to my father," Suzanne said, her eyes on the paperweight, too.

"I knew we'd be staying in Percyville then, and you tried to cheer me up by telling me how neat school would be. You said you'd introduce me to your boyfriend, Dennis." With his hand still on the paperweight, he looked at her. "You did all that and more, Suzy. I never thanked you."

"I never expected thanks. Don't be silly."

A moment passed. "How's it going with Dennis now?"

"I seldom see him. He's married again, you know, and living in Texas."

"Texas. No kidding? Where?"

"Dallas. I saw his wife at his sister's wedding last spring. They seem happy."

"How about Caleb? I never understood Dennis walking away like that."

"Caleb's fine." Her whole face went soft. "He's four now and keeps me on my toes. He caught his first fish a couple of weeks ago and his grandpa hasn't had any peace since. He wants to go fishing every chance he gets. Caleb, I mean, not Daddy."

"I'd like to see him. Before I go back."

"When will you be leaving, Ben?"

"A few days." His gaze went to the window again. "Life goes on, I guess."

On the mantel behind her, the old clock struck three soft chimes. Outside, a mockingbird perched in the dogwood, trilling joyfully. In contrast, Lucian's big black Labrador's bark had a mournful sound.

"I don't know what to do about Buck," Ben said, squinting in the afternoon sun streaming through the window.

"Lucian's Lab?"

"Yeah. He knows something's wrong. Keeps wandering

around the house looking for Granddad. Then he starts to howl." He tried to laugh. "I know the feeling."

"You'll have to find someone to take him, Ben."

"Yeah, I know. The question is, who's going to want an old dog? Buck's at least eleven."

"Have you asked my dad?"

He gave her a hopeful look. "Charles? You think he might?"

"It's worth a try. He and your granddad…" She nodded as the idea took hold. "Yeah, I think he might."

"Buck knows him. That would be ideal…if Charles would consider it."

"Tell you what—let me ask him."

Some of his tension seemed to go. "Thanks, Suzy."

After a second or two, she nodded at the papers strewn across the desk. "Sure you don't need any help with that stuff?"

He went around and sat down again, then picked up the document he'd been reading when she came in. "I don't think so. There's nothing unusual, at least in the stuff I've found so far— just their wills, some stocks and bonds, deeds. I'll take care of probate myself. As for the other stuff, I'll take it back with me and look it over when I'm in better shape for thinking."

As he spoke, he scanned the cover page of the document in his hand. He frowned, reading the names of the principals in the caption. "What the hell is this?" he murmured. Moving his chair closer, he spread the legal-size pages out flat. As he read, his mouth was a tight line. With a quick, furious move, he flipped to the next page. Then the next. Then the next.

"That *bastard!* That *son of a bitch!*"

"What? What is it, Ben?" Suzanne leaned forward, trying to read the caption on the document.

Ben pushed his chair back with a crash and stood up. "Who is it, you mean."

"Who—"

"Jack Sullivan! Your shyster brother-in-law, that's who! That fuckin' asshole. That low-down *cheat!*"

"Ben, what is it? What did he do?"

Ben swept up the document, crumpling pages in his fury. Glaring at her across the desk, he shook the papers in her face. "Do you know what this is, Suzanne? It's the lining for that bastard's coffin, that's what it is. I'll kill him, I swear I will. I always suspected he was a sleaze, but it looks as though I underestimated the depths he's willing to sink to." He stopped then, regarding Suzanne with a sharp eye. "Has my grandfather seemed okay to you lately?"

"What do you mean, okay?"

"Was his age telling on him? Was he getting a little…"

"He was a little forgetful, maybe. He and my dad still played every Wednesday, and I did hear Dad mention that he didn't think Lucian should be driving now. But what does that have to do with Jack?"

Ben was pacing, one hand pressing the back of his neck. "This is crazy. Granddad wouldn't…unless Mama—" He stopped, his gaze going restlessly around the room, to the mallard mounted above the mantel, to the photo of Lucian and the governor in 1975, to his own baby shoes bronzed and dusty on a shelf in the bookcase. "I wonder if Mama knew and just didn't want to worry me with it. Shit. Or has she been giving me hints, Suzanne, and I just didn't listen?"

"That doesn't sound like Marilee, Ben. She was a forthright person. She would have told you if there was something she thought you should know. Or if there was anything you could do."

"I should have been *told!*"

"Ben, what does this have to do with Jack?"

Ben stopped pacing and looked at the mauled papers in his hand. "He swindled my grandfather, Suzanne."

"Are you sure?"

He rattled the papers. "The proof's right here."

She released a deep sigh. "Well, it's not the first time he's done something contemptible or illegal or both, Ben." She glanced at the papers he held. "What is it you think he's done?"

"He's conned us out of the land adjacent to Riverbend."

Suzanne's eyes were wide. "My God. That's hundreds of acres. Lucian would never sell—"

"Forty-five hundred, to be exact. And you're right, my grandfather would never sell it, especially without telling me. It was *my* land, although title was never actually in my name. J.T. bought it years ago with money he borrowed from Grand-dad, so it was in Lucian's name. He was holding it for me." He went back to the papers on the desk, shuffling through until he found what he was looking for. "This is his will. He mentions the acreage as if he still owns it. As if he *thinks* he still owns it."

"He wanted it, he took it. So typical of Jack. But how?"

"Taxes," Ben said bitterly. "The lousy, simplest loophole in the world. How Granddad let it happen is beyond me. He would never—"

Suzanne was thinking. "Jack always has a reason for every-thing he does. I wonder why he wanted that particular piece of property. There's a lot of land in that part of the state, plenty of it for sale if the price was right. He could get mineral rights, too, if he wanted." She chewed on her soft inner lip. "Why this acreage?"

"I don't know the answer to that. Yet." Ben went behind the desk. Gathering the papers up, he stuffed them back in the strongbox, closed the lid with a sharp snap and twisted the key in the lock. "But I'm not leaving Percyville until I do."

BEN WAITED UNTIL THE DAY he was leaving to see Jack Sullivan. It had taken a week after discovering that Jack had swindled his grandfather to sift through the minutiae of Marilee's and Lucian's lives and to clear up all the loose ends. He'd arranged for a real estate agent to lease the house and land. For some reason, he found he didn't want to sell it. He'd stored the best of the furniture and keepsakes belonging to his mother and his grandmother. His flight out of town had a late departure time. At 6:30 a.m., he was waiting in his rental car on the street in front of Jack's house.

His coffee was half finished when schoolchildren began gathering half a block away at the intersection, their laughter and shouts carrying in the crisp autumn morning. More time passed, and then the door to Jack's garage began to rise automatically. Ben heard the Jaguar start up. While Jack was backing out, Ben started his car and pulled forward until the driveway was blocked.

The brake lights on the Jag went on abruptly, and the car stopped with a jerk. The door swung open and Jack got out, frowning thunderously. Ben climbed out of the rental, feeling a high, hot anticipatory rush. Waiting a week had only fed his desire to make Jack pay. He wanted to plant his fist in the bastard's too-handsome face. He wanted to hear him plead when he broke that perfect nose. Loosened a few teeth. Cracked a jaw. His fists flexed involuntarily even as he recognized the sheer lunacy of handling the problem that way.

Jack called something, but it was drowned out in the sound of the school bus trundling past in a cacophony of childish voices, muffled music and noisy diesel engine. Ben made no response. He simply waited, staring.

Ben knew the second Jack recognized him. The pause was infinitesimal, barely a break in his stride. After a quick survey of the street, Jack started forward, his sunglasses glinting in the bright sunshine. He was obviously disgruntled at the prospect of his neighbors getting an earful. Ben felt a small thrill of satisfaction. Any advantage with an adversary like Jack Sullivan was worth grabbing.

Jack *was* a wily one. He cocked his head, while his mouth made a smile that didn't quite reach his eyes. "I didn't realize I had a visitor, Ben. Been waiting long?"

"A few minutes."

"Hell, if you'd come to the door..." He turned, gestured toward the front of the house. "It's not too late to rustle up some coffee. It's been made awhile, and it'll be strong as battery acid, but—"

"This'll only take a minute. I don't want coffee."

Jack paused, as if trying to decipher Ben's state of mind, but his gaze, Ben noted, was guarded. "I thought you were on your way to...where the hell is it you hang out now?"

"The United Arab Emirates. And I'm on my way back in a few hours, but I think you knew I'd be around to see you once I'd had a chance to go through my grandfather's papers, didn't you, Jack?"

"United Arab Emirates. Where the fuck is that?"

"I haven't got time for a geography lesson."

"Okay...no coffee and no geography lesson. Gotta be something in between. That could cover a lot of territory." Jack crossed his arms over his chest with exaggerated patience, still watching Ben intently. "So...what's on your mind?"

"Forty-five hundred acres of land that you swindled from my grandfather, Jack. That's what's on my mind."

Jack was shaking his head before Ben finished speaking. "Now, hey there. Hold on a minute. Where I come from, anybody accusing a man of swindling better be ready to back it up with facts."

"My grandfather is dead, Jack. And the proof died with him. But I know what you did, you son of a bitch, and I know how it was done. Somehow you let him think he was paying his taxes every year, when in reality not a penny was applied to his land. On the other hand, *someone* was paying them—a dummy corporation, I find—and you bought the land from them."

Jack made a dismissive sound. "That's fuckin' nuts! I bought that land fair and square, Kincaid. You're a lawyer. You've examined that deed. It's legal. You might not like it...hell, I can see you're pissed as hell, but what's done is done. Besides, that land's not particularly valuable. I know what J.T. said when he talked Lucian into buying it—Lucian told me all that. Hell, there's no oil and gas underneath. Is that what you're pissed over? The mineral rights?"

"I'm pissed over the whole deal. I'm pissed over you taking advantage of an old man. I'm pissed over your arrogance. Everything about you pisses me off, Jack."

"And here I thought we were friends," Jack said with a mystified look.

"I'm also betting that if I really put my mind to it, I'd find the deal's not legal. I know my grandfather wasn't aware the tax he paid wasn't applied to his land. If he'd had a hint of anything like that, he would have let me know first thing."

"I don't know how you figure that, Ben. The way I see it, since you hightailed it out of Percyville, you haven't had a lot of time for your old granddad. Or your mother." Jack's eyes lit when he saw his shot hit home. "Now, me...I'm a lot more family-oriented than you. That acreage butts up to Riverbend, my wife's homeplace. That alone is enough to make it desirable to me."

Ben made a derisive sound. "You're saying you bought it for sentimental reasons?"

"Among others." Jack shrugged. "Naturally, land's always a good investment."

Ben stared. He had to give him points for gall. "I knew not to expect a straight answer from you, Jack, but that bullshit wouldn't convince a ten-year-old. For reasons I'll dig up—I promise you that—you wanted that land and you set out to get it. Maybe it was as simple as waiting to catch Granddad in a foggy moment, maybe not. Knowing him, I find that hard to believe. But what's done is done. I'm here this morning to tell you this. I know you swindled a man whose whole life was dedicated to public service. He never did you or anybody you care about any harm. I'm going to figure out why you did it. And then I'm going to make you pay."

"Thousands of miles from Mississippi?" Jack chuckled softly. "That'll be a trick, won't it, Kincaid?"

It was a remark calculated to goad him into...what? Actually hitting him? Ben straightened, staring at Jack's smirk. He longed to give him just a taste of the rage churning inside him. His muscles tingled to take action. Blood pounded in his ears, urging him on. With the nerves in his hands quivering, he weighed the pros and cons. God, it would be good. *Feel* good.

But even as his body teemed with wildness, another self—
the trained agent—urged caution. Punching a man like Jack
Sullivan offered only temporary satisfaction. The way to get to
Jack was not open warfare. It would have to be something else.
It would require patience. Time. He had both. Without another
word, he turned and opened the car door.

Jack stepped back, smiling. "Leaving, are you?"

"Yeah, I'm out of here. For now." Ben got in and slammed
the door, then found the switch to open the window and waited
while it lowered smoothly. He touched the bridge of his sunglasses and settled them firmly in place. "It may take me a
while, Jack. Years, even. But you watch your back and cover
your tracks, my man, 'cause I'll be back. You can count on
that."

He looked through the rearview mirror as he pulled away.
Jack hadn't moved. Ben swore softly. The son of a bitch didn't
even look worried.

EIGHTEEN

Suzanne had just put Caleb in the tub when the doorbell rang. She tossed his favorite bath toys in the water and shut off the faucet. "Don't forget to wash, Caleb. Just sitting in the tub isn't going to cut it, kiddo. Okay?"

"Okay." The bell rang again. "Who's at the door, Mommy?"

"I don't know." She gave his nose a friendly tweak. "But there's one way to find out, right?"

"Go and see!"

"You got it." She straightened and headed out. "Remember, wash that neck and those ears and your chest and your face and your—"

"All right, Mommy!" he cried, giggling. "And if that's Grampa, tell him to wait till I get out of here so we can play checkers."

"It's not Grampa. He would have called first."

"Aww." Some of his enthusiasm faded.

She headed for the door. She seldom had visitors at this hour, especially on a weekday. Rising on her toes, she peered through the security hole. "Ben!" she murmured with surprise. She hadn't expected to see him again before he left. Smiling widely, she twisted the lock and opened the door. "Come in… quick," she said, bracing against a gust of icy wind. Catching him by the arm, she pulled him over the threshold. The temperature had dropped midafternoon as rain had ushered in the season's first cold snap. "I thought you'd be on a flight to somewhere."

"Not yet." He smiled, looking beyond her to the interior of the apartment. "It's not too late?"

"Not at all." He was rumpled and a little windblown, and he smelled like crisp autumn air, after-shave and warm male. It was the last thought that sent a little shiver down her spine. She helped him shrug out of his leather jacket. It was the bomber type that pilots wore. She hung it on a coatrack near the door.

"Come into the living room. I've got a fire going. It's the first one this season, so let's hope there's no bird's nest to smoke us out. But it was so chilly, I couldn't resist." She led him to the living room and started to gather up papers spread out on the coffee table and the sofa. "Excuse the mess. I brought some paperwork home on a case." Breathless from…something—she wasn't sure what—she stopped and really looked at him.

He smiled. "Can I get a word in?"

"Right. I'm talking too much." She touched her fingers to her forehead, feeling like an idiot. "How about some coffee? Or wine—I've got that but nothing else, I'm afraid."

"Wine's good."

"White or red?"

"Red."

"Great." She put out a hand as he started forward. "No, I'll be right back."

"Where's Caleb?"

"In the tub. Everything in the bathroom's probably soaked by now except him. I don't know how my son can sit in a tub of water and get the walls, the floor, the towels and anything else within sight wet, but remain virtually dry from the waist up."

"Boys have a natural aversion to real bathing." Ben glanced down the hall. "Is it this way?"

"Second door on the right. He'll love seeing you, Ben. Tell him I want those ears clean and shiny, okay?"

"Yes, ma'am." Chuckling, he headed for the bathroom.

In the kitchen, Suzanne reached for a bottle of cabernet tucked in the back of the pantry. It was only Ben, she told herself, fumbling in the drawer for the corkscrew. She centered the sharp point on the cork and worked at removing it. From

the bathroom she heard sounds of Caleb's laughter, his voice
high with surprised delight, and Ben's deep rumble in reply.
The cork came free with a pop.

"Can I get out now, Mommy?" Caleb yelled.

"Is he clean all over, Ben?" She poured the wine carefully.

"He's wet all over."

Instantly, Caleb began to protest. Suzanne smiled. "Okay,
I'm trusting both of you. Get out and dry off *good.*" Carrying
the wineglasses, she walked down the hall just as Caleb scam-
pered out, the towel dragging on the floor behind him.

"I'm all dried off, Mommy. Ben did it."

She handed the wine to Ben with a smile. "Thank you. Now,
hop into your jammies, Caleb. It's too chilly to dawdle, so make
it snappy. Ben and I are going into the living room. When you're
dressed, you can come in and say good-night."

"Do you like to play checkers, Ben?"

Ben fluffed the boy's hair. "Next time, okay? I've got a plane
to catch and I wanted to talk to your mommy before I left."

Caleb's lower lip poked out. "Nobody ever wants to play
with me."

"Caleb." Suzanne gave him a stern look. "You have tons of
friends who play with you every day. Ben has to fly out of Jackson tonight, so he has to be at the airport on time. Airplanes
don't wait for people who're late."

"Aw…okay." He headed for his room, the towel trailing
behind. At the door he stopped. "But don't leave before I'm
done."

"Right."

Chuckling, Ben followed Suzanne to the living room. She
picked up two cushions from the floor and handed him one.
"You look tired," she said when he'd settled back. "Did you get
everything taken care of?"

"Yeah, as much as possible in the time I had available." He
glanced at his watch. "I've got a couple of hours and I wanted
to see you." He swallowed some of the wine and set the glass
on the coffee table. "I wanted to apologize for losing my cool

when you dropped by the other day. My mother would have washed my mouth out with soap if she'd heard me using that kind of language in front of you, Suzy."

"It's okay. Forget it." She reached out and touched his knee. "You were in shock when you found that paper."

He dropped his head back, pinching his eyes with two fingers. "I saw Jack today."

She set her glass beside his. "What did he say?"

"The condensed version? It's done, like it or lump it."

She nodded. "That's about what I'd expect from Jack." She tucked a leg beneath herself. "Did he explain how he fixed it so the taxes wouldn't be credited to Lucian?"

"No. Just that he now held the property and that the deal was legal. If I didn't like it, tough shit." He made a disgusted sound. "Sorry. Again."

"Stop apologizing, for heaven's sake."

He looked at her, shifting a little. "I wish I didn't have to go back so soon, Suzy. It's been good seeing you again."

She felt a prickle of unease as old fears stirred. *Don't be an idiot. This is Ben, an old and dear friend. You trust him. My God, he helped bring Caleb into the world.* But it wasn't just a matter of trust. It was her inability to get beyond the brick wall of her defense. Five years. When would it end?

"Mommy!" She felt the touch of Caleb's fingers on her face, turning her to look at him. Dressed in pajamas sprinkled with Disney characters, he was smiling at her. "Me and Ben were talking to you, but you were daydreaming, huh, Mommy?"

"I guess so, honeybun. Let me just check you out." She inspected him with unnecessary diligence, avoiding Ben's gaze. "We need to fix this one snap...." She popped it together. "So. Now you're ready for bed. Give me a kiss."

"Aww..."

"Aww, yes!" Laughing, she cupped his face between her hands and kissed him, anyway. "You're never too big for a kiss from your mommy, buddy-boy."

"I'm gonna high-five Ben!" he declared firmly when he'd

managed to dance away from Suzanne. Holding up his palm, he waited for Ben to do likewise. "This is the way men say bye."

Ben laughed as their palms met and smacked smartly. "You're right, pal. No kisses between us real men."

"Straight to bed now, Caleb," Suzanne ordered.

"Okay. G'night, Ben."

"'Night, buddy."

Suzanne watched him dash out of the room, aware that Ben was watching her.

"He's a neat kid, Suzy. You must hear that a lot."

"I do, but we mothers never tire of hearing nice things about our children."

He was hunched forward on the sofa, his elbows resting on his knees. He stared into the wineglass dangling from both hands. "Sometimes I think about that day when he was born. I've never been so scared. Or so awestruck. I never told you this, but I had the strangest feeling when I first saw him. Held him." He glanced up, then back to the wine. "Sometimes I think about it now and wonder if I'll ever know that feeling with my own son."

"It's called bonding."

"Bonding."

"And I hope you won't have to deliver your own," Suzanne said with a smile. "No man should have to do that twice in one lifetime. I know you'll bond with your children. You have too much goodness in you for it to be otherwise, Ben."

"I didn't feel so 'good' when I was threatening Jack Sullivan this morning."

Pleased, she cocked a brow at him. "You threatened him?"

"Yeah, more or less. Of course, it may be years before I can make good on my word."

"Good. Better late than never."

He studied her thoughtfully. "You don't like him, do you?"

"No."

"Mind telling me why?"

She drew in a deep breath. "It's a personal thing, Ben."

"He's family."

"I'm sorry to say."

"Well…" He stood up, placed his wineglass on the coffee table and looked around her apartment one last time. She sensed his reluctance to leave, and the apprehension she'd managed to subdue returned. "Guess it's time for me to go," he said.

With her arms wrapped around herself, she turned and headed for the front door. "I'm glad you came by," she said, reaching for his jacket on the coatrack.

"Me, too." He turned and let her help him get into it, then he faced her again. "Suzanne…" He seemed to lose track of his thoughts. Her heart began beating frantically. Something of her fear must have shown in her face, because he eased back just a fraction, as if he sensed she needed reassurance but didn't understand why.

"Do you see anybody, Suzanne?"

"Men, you mean?" She managed a laugh, knowing what he meant. "I see tons—a daily stream of assailants and rapists and child molesters."

"Jesus."

"No, He's almost never around where I work." She looked beyond him to an arrangement of paper fruit spilling from a cornucopia made by Caleb in day care. "Actually, it's not as bad as it sounds."

"Why?"

"Why isn't it as bad as it sounds? Because my conviction rate is—"

"No, why don't you have a relationship? You're a beautiful woman, I've always thought so. You're smart, successful—"

"Not in that arena, Ben."

"How long are you going to mourn the death of your marriage, Suzanne? Besides, Dennis was the one who cheated. I never—"

"I could ask the same of you, Ben." Her arms were around her midriff again. "Why don't you have a relationship? Why hasn't some intelligent, successful, beautiful woman snapped you up?" She braced for the truth. "Or has she?"

His mouth moved in a half smile. He held up a hand. "Hah! Professor Edwards—The Rhetoric of Debate. Rule number one—turn the opponent's words back on him."

She burst out laughing. "That's the problem when you try to argue with someone who went to law school with you."

"He was dry as dust, but the old geezer knew a thing or two about debate."

They spent a minute in silent reminiscence, but Ben still watched her with an intensity that told her he sensed something wasn't quite right.

Suzanne broke the silence. "I meant it when I offered to help, Ben. If there's anything I can do about your family's things, the probate…anything, just let me know."

"Thanks." He reached for the doorknob, then turned back. "I don't know when I'll be back in Percyville, Suzy. But there's something I've always wanted…"

She frowned. "You always wanted…"

"This." Before the flash of comprehension could reach her brain, Ben moved closer and put his arms around her. In the next split second, he had his mouth on hers. For a moment, there was something so right in a kiss from Ben Kincaid. She was processing fragments of information—his mouth, warm and wine-flavored. Wood smoke. Leather. Spicy after-shave. Arms strong as a vice. Wide, powerful chest. Then shock as his leg sought a place between hers. Fear exploded inside her head.

She pushed with all her might against him, tore her mouth from his. "No! Don't! Stop!" With her hands balled and pressed against her lips, she turned away and felt the hated shudders begin to rack her limbs. She heard the sound of her teeth chattering and hated, *hated* her body for its stupidity.

This was Ben. Not him. *Not an assault.*

"Jesus. Suzy, I'm sorry. I didn't—" Ben put out a hand to touch her, but she spun away, helpless to control the mindless need to protect herself. He made an anguished sound, reaching out to soothe her, but she jerked at his touch.

He backed away then, several steps until he bumped the wall. "It's okay, I'm way over here, Suzy. I'm not going to touch you again."

"I'm sorry, I'm sorry," she whispered, not looking at him. *Unable* to look at him.

"I'm the one who should apologize. Suzy, I didn't mean…I mean, I shouldn't have taken advantage. I didn't know…" He raked a hand over his hair, his gaze on the ceiling.

"It's not you," she managed to say, finally calming a little. She took a few deep breaths as the acid remains of the wine rose in her throat. *Don't let me throw up. Please. Please. This is Ben. This is Ben. A friend, old and dear. I trust him.*

He stayed where he was, watchful. "What can I do, Suzy?"

She closed her eyes, felt the humiliation of it all. "Nothing. I'm okay, really."

"No."

She managed a quick look at his face. "What?"

"You're not okay. That was pure panic just now, irrational, abject panic. What's going on, Suzy?"

She shook her head. "Nothing. Nothing that can be fixed, at any rate. Don't worry, it's nothing to do with you."

The sound he made could hardly be called a laugh. "I think I figured that out. I'm no egomaniac, but I've never had that kind of reaction when I kissed a woman." He edged a little closer, his gaze as sharp as a laser. "You knew I wasn't going to hurt you, Suzy."

"Of course not." Her arms were again wrapped tightly about herself and she wouldn't meet his eyes. "It's just a…a little problem I've developed. I see a lot of violence against women in the cases I prosecute."

"Maybe you should request a transfer. There's an abundance of crime that isn't sexual in nature."

"Maybe I will."

He didn't believe her. It was in the expression on his face, in the compression of his mouth as he looked at her. Inside, she felt the pain of another failure. Ben would never think of her in the same way again.

When she remained silent, he glanced at his watch. "Well, I've still got to catch that plane."

She met his eyes. "It was good seeing you, Ben."

"Yeah, me, too. Give my best to your family, Suzy." At one time he would have touched her, maybe even given her a hug, but not now. He settled for a quiet "Take care."

"You, too."

And then he was gone.

NINETEEN

December 1986

BEN DID NOT RETURN to the Mideast, as planned. Sanford Ellis had paged him at the airport in New York and he'd wound up in Beirut. A few days later, instead of being with Jill in London, he'd spent a week sorting through the rubble of a car bombing on the West Bank in Gaza. When he stood looking at a small, mangled running shoe—the child who'd worn it could not have been older than Caleb—for the first time, he'd questioned what he was doing with his life. What kind of world was it where young children were wiped out in the blink of an eye in the name of religion?

As soon as he could, he'd flown to London. Jill had met him at the airport and they'd gone directly to a hotel, where they'd spent the rest of the afternoon and most of the night in bed. It hadn't taken a professional to analyze what was happening. First, there'd been the death of his family in Percyville, followed by betrayal by a person he'd considered, if not a friend, then certainly not an enemy, then he'd been thrust into senseless violence in Beirut. His need for Jill had been elemental, as though sex would somehow reaffirm his own humanity.

Once or twice that weekend, he thought of Suzanne. He'd finally given up trying to understand her reaction when he'd kissed her and buried it in the same hole in his mind already occupied by guilt and rage from that last visit home. Suzanne was part of the life that had been defined by his mother and grandfather, Percyville, his youth. That part of his life seemed to be a closed chapter.

Then Christmas had come and gone. Sanford Ellis had actually called with an assignment on Christmas Eve. Ben had promised Jill that they'd make up for the aborted London holiday by spending the week between Christmas and New Year's with the Penningtons in their London flat. Ellis had eyed him keenly when he refused the assignment, but in the end he finally accepted that Ben intended to go to the wall on this one.

As it turned out, Jill's parents decided to visit friends in Paris on New Year's Eve, and Jill and Ben had the flat to themselves. Jill loved flashy parties and she had invitations for two that night. Ben was searching for clean socks in his luggage when he heard her throwing up in the bathroom. He had rushed in and found her hanging over the toilet.

"My God! Jill…Jesus, what's wrong?"

She batted at him blindly with one hand. "Leave me alone."

"What's the matter? Here, let me…" He grabbed a hand towel and wet it with cold water. But when he tried to bathe her face, she shoved him away and succumbed to another round of retching.

Ignoring her efforts to banish him from the bathroom, he put an arm around her and supported her until there was nothing left to bring up. Finally, exhausted and spent, she shuddered and would have sunk to the floor if Ben hadn't caught her, flipped down the toilet lid and gently eased her onto it. Ignoring her protests, he wiped her face with the towel, then filled a glass with water and offered it to her. She took it, rinsed her mouth and grimaced with distaste.

"Bed. Have to lie down," she managed to croak. She was so pale Ben couldn't see the outline of her lips.

"Come on, let me help you." He got her on her feet, keeping an eye on her to make sure she didn't pass out.

"Don't look at me!" She turned her face away.

Without a word, he swept her up and carried her to the bed, where she curled instantly into a fetal position, clutching a pillow and facing the wall. Clad only in a gray satin bra and matching bikinis, she looked vulnerable and spent. Ben pulled the comforter over her as his mind reeled back to another time. Another woman. Another bout of violent nausea.

It couldn't be.

"What's going on, Jill?"

She lay in stiff, stony silence.

"Talk to me, Jill. It's only six o'clock. I know you haven't had any alcohol. What'd you have for lunch? A shrimp salad, right?"

She moaned.

"Is that it? Food poisoning?"

"Go 'way." Her words were muffled by the pillow.

"I'm not going anywhere, Jill."

"It's nothing."

"You've just puked your socks up, woman! I want to know what's wrong."

She lay without moving a long moment. Then she mumbled, "I'm pregnant."

"Pregnant."

"Yes. *Yes!*" Shoving the pillow aside, she rolled over and looked at him angrily. "Now you've hounded it out of me, are you satisfied? I'm pregnant, Ben. We screwed ourselves blind when you flew to London six weeks ago and now I'm paying the price."

"Paying the price."

She sat up with a weary sigh, holding the pillow against her stomach. "Stop repeating everything like a robot, for God's sake. I'm pregnant. It happened last month. When I was two weeks late I took a test, but I didn't need to. I knew."

He was trying to take it in. "We've been here together for six days. When were you going to tell me?"

"I wasn't going to tell you at all. I wouldn't be telling you now if I hadn't gagged brushing my teeth a few minutes ago."

"Brushing your teeth."

"You're still doing it, Ben."

"You nearly passed out you were so sick. How could tooth-paste do that?"

Jill sighed with impatience. "I don't know. How does the smell of coffee do it? How does the first movement of my body when I wake up in the morning do it? It just does, that's all." Her blue eyes hardened momentarily. "But not for long."

Ben swung away, rubbing a hand against the back of his neck. "I don't believe this."

"Believe it. It's all too sickeningly true."

He shook his head. "The sickness passes, Jill."

"Oh, yeah? You've had some experience with pregnancy?"

"Not personally, but…well, in a way, yeah, I have. Someone I knew in law school had an unplanned pregnancy."

"Lucky girl."

He thought of Suzanne and Dennis. Of Caleb's abrupt arrival. The turmoil in the marriage afterward. The demise of the marriage. "No, as it turned out, she wasn't lucky."

"Well, I'm not waiting around to see whether or not this disaster is going to turn into something wonderful. I'm taking care of it without delay. I would have done so without you ever knowing anything about it, but I knew it would mess up the holidays and I didn't want to spend a week with you and not be able to have sex." She laughed bitterly. "I didn't know I'd be so damned nauseous that I couldn't have sex, anyway."

"What do you mean you're taking care of it without delay?"

"I'm not having this baby, Ben."

"You're not—" He moved a step closer, frowning ferociously. "Wait. I can't be hearing this right. Are you suggesting what I think? That just because we've been careless and things are suddenly a little complicated, that we schedule an abortion and the problem's solved?"

"A little complicated?" She gave a contemptuous snort. "Babies aren't little complications, Ben, they're major calamities."

"You weren't even going to tell me." He was looking beyond her, to the window where the street lamps were glowing softly. He could hear somebody singing *Auld Lang Syne*. He heard laughter and a shout. The pop of a champagne cork. People getting ready to party. To celebrate the new year. To celebrate life.

He looked at her. "You can't do it, Jill."

She drew a deep breath. "Yes, I can do it. I intend to do it."

"I'm telling you, I won't let you do this, Jill."

She was silent for a moment, studying him intently. Ben thought of her father, Jake Pennington, and his skill as a diplomat. She wasn't her father's daughter for nothing. He could almost hear the wheels in her head turning. But damn it, he wasn't a foreign dignitary and Jill wasn't going to treat their child as a sticky problem. Their situation was a problem, he accepted that. Maybe, to be fair, he might've considered abortion a few months ago, but not now. Although the pregnancy was accidental, it was his son or daughter nestled inside Jill and he couldn't sit by and allow her to destroy it.

"We need to discuss this without getting all emotional, Ben."

"Yeah, well, learning I'm about to become a father is an emotional thing."

"Exactly. This is a child we're talking about. An infant. That means twenty-four-hour care seven days a week for the next eighteen years. *Years,* Ben! Not just for me, but you, too. Are you listening?"

"I'm listening, but don't you realize that—"

"I realize that having a baby isn't something either of us needs right now. I realize that I don't want to be a mother. I don't know anything about being a mother. My career is just starting to take off, Ben. You know how much it means to me. I'm not ready for this. Do you hear what I'm saying? I…don't… want…this…baby!"

He sat down beside her and took her hands. "Jill, listen to me. I've just buried my mother and my grandfather. I don't have another living relative on the face of the earth. If this hadn't happened, I probably wouldn't have kids for years yet, but it has happened. We'll get married. I'll—"

"Married! No, I—"

He squeezed her hands to silence her. "I'll tell Ellis that I want to be based permanently in London."

"What about my job? Having a baby isn't like taking a few days off for a vacation. Kids take a lot of time and energy."

"I won't dump it all on you, Jill, I swear it. I'll be a hands-on dad. I'll get up at night, we'll take turns. I'll change him. I will, honey, I will," he promised. Seeing that she was still unconvinced, he added, "I just can't stand the thought of destroying my baby because he's happening at an inconvenient time!"

Tears sprang into Jill's eyes. Sniffing, she stared down at their locked hands. "Ben, we don't love each other."

He shook his head. "I'm not sure about that. We've had more than two years to get to know each other. We've been together exclusively for half that time. We have similar goals, we're each interested in the other's job. We have great sex—you've gotta admit that. A lot of marriages start off with a lot less."

"Oh, Ben." She closed her eyes and leaned her head against his shoulder. "This is crazy."

"Not crazy, just sudden. Unexpected. Never crazy." He thought of Caleb, saw his bright-eyed smile, heard the little-boy machismo in his voice when they'd high-fived. The child inside Jill might be a boy. His son.

"I'm scared," Jill said. "I can face a roomful of executives and present a cost analysis for a half-million-dollar project, but the thought of a tiny baby terrifies me."

Did she think he wasn't terrified? He kissed the top of her head. "It'll be fine, you'll see."

"Promise?"

He buried his own apprehension and gave her a reassuring hug. "I promise."

TWENTY

November 1987

"WELL, HERE WE ARE—Riverbend." At the outside gates, Annie stopped the car beside an electronic panel, lowered the window and punched in the code. With a creak, the ornate iron gates parted in the center and slid open. She released the brake on her mother's Seville and drove through.

"You didn't exaggerate, Annie." Beside her, Spencer Dutton twisted in his seat, all eyes. "This is something else."

"Wait'll you see the house."

Spencer grunted, taking in the old-growth trees—tall pines, magnolia, river birch, dogwood. The grounds must be spectacular in spring, he thought, spotting camellia bushes and azaleas, their dark foliage set off by the rich rusty carpet of fallen pine needles. Annie slowed for a curve, startling a covey of quail into flight from the underbrush. Just beyond the curve the house itself came into view.

Annie looked at him, smiling. "Well, what do you think?"

He studied the classic antebellum architecture. "Do I get a mint julep with Thanksgiving dinner?"

She laughed out loud at that. "That's such a tired cliché, Spence. Believe me when I say I've never in my life had a mint julep. And no self-respecting Southerner with any taste would ever want one."

"Okay, so long as you don't substitute buttermilk. At least a mint julep has whiskey."

Still chuckling, she shook her head. "You'll get a traditional beverage for Thanksgiving, Spence—iced tea, water or wine,

I promise." Glancing in the rearview mirror, she sought her mother's eyes. "Doing okay back there, Mom?"

"I'm fine, Annie." Except for a slight huskiness in her voice, Eugenia's reply sounded natural. Only Annie knew the toll that these family occasions took on her mother's fragile emotional health.

"How's your headache?"

"I've taken something. It's better."

She watched Eugenia touch a spot above her left eye. At breakfast, she'd refused everything except black coffee, and the smudges beneath her eyes had been camouflaged with makeup. Annie had recognized the symptoms of migraine. How her mother would manage to get through a long, supposedly festive holiday meal remained a mystery to Annie, but failing to attend was not—and never had been—an option. Afterward, of course, Eugenia would be bedridden for three days with a vicious headache. Long ago, she'd given up trying to reason with her mother about her relationship with Jack. She had seen so little of him in the past year that Annie suspected he was tiring of her. Still, Eugenia lived for those increasingly rare moments with Jack.

With a sigh, Annie pulled to a stop at a spot on the side of the big house designated for guest parking. "Okay, everybody out. We're here."

As she closed the car door, she realized someone was on the wide veranda of the house—someone seated in deep shadow. Her breath caught as Stuart rose slowly from a white wicker chair, leaving it in a rocking motion as he gazed steadily into her eyes. Since returning to Percyville, she had avoided Stuart. Four years ago, he'd taken her at her word that she did not welcome an affair. That she intended to put out of her mind the forbidden moments on the grounds of the Jacobson property. She'd been careful since then to give him no reason to think she'd changed her mind. But she was still family and so was Stuart. For today, their differences had to be put aside.

"Do I have time for a smoke?"

"What?" She turned and found Spence looking at her over the roof of the car.

"Oh. Oh, sure, go ahead." As he bent to cup his cigarette and light it, she heard the soft click of the French door closing on the veranda. When she looked back, Stuart was gone.

"Can I carry something, Annie?" Eugenia asked, motioning to the array of things in the back of the car.

"Would you, please? Let me see…" She dived down behind the front seat to sort through the stuff and came up with a basket laden with edibles she'd brought back from California. "This goes to the kitchen, Mom. Suzanne will know what to do. And tell the Judge and Uncle Charles that I'll be in after I see the kids." She reached for a shopping bag she'd stashed behind the driver's seat while Eugenia headed for the front steps carrying the basket. With her hands full, she let Spencer close the door. "I've brought them some stuff. They're playing over there…see, underneath that big tree?"

Spence followed her gaze to a huge live oak where three young children were whooping and hollering and—he looked closer—throwing rocks at each other?

"Acorns," Annie said with a grin. "Those big fat ones that make great ammunition."

"You'd know, of course."

"From painful experience beginning at age four." With a shopping bag anchored on her shoulder, she made for a brick pathway that led off the driveway. "I'll be back in a minute to take you inside and introduce you." She made a face as Spence drew on his cigarette. "Taylor smokes, too. Watch her comings and goings today and the two of you can become fast friends. The Judge banishes her from the house when she gets the urge."

"Nag, nag, nag."

Her grin widened as one of the children—a dark-haired boy—spotted her and gave a shout of delight. The other two—with hair just as dark—went dashing after the older boy, all screeching Annie's name.

"She's not exaggerating."

The voice came from behind Spencer, a husky, feminine voice with an accent similar to Annie's but with a more pronounced drawl. He turned. A beautiful brunette stood watching him.

Cat on a Hot Tin Roof, he thought instantly. With that sultry voice and an incredibly beautiful face, she could have stepped right out of the play. She had a mane of lustrous black hair and startling blue eyes, but it was her mouth that arrested him. It was soft and full, a perfect bow as she smiled and started down the steps.

"You must be Spencer."

"I must be." He took the hand she offered and found it just as soft and vulnerable as her mouth looked.

"I'm Taylor."

"Ah. My smoking partner."

"Annie's a reformed smoker." She smiled slowly but didn't withdraw her hand. "Have you ever noticed that absolutely no one is more intolerant than a reformed smoker?"

His eyebrows went up. "Annie used to smoke?"

"Like a steam engine. She never told you?"

"She never did. When was this?"

"Let me think…" Taylor withdrew her hand and put two fingers against her temple as if deep in thought. "Now I recall. I was about thirteen, so she was ten. There was a thicket of rabbit tobacco along the path to the gazebo, and it kept the three of us supplied with smokes all summer long."

Their eyes met—hers brilliantly blue, his a quiet hazel—and they laughed.

"Gotcha," she said softly.

"Yeah." To tear his gaze from her, Spencer looked over the lawn toward the huge tree where the children were clustered around Annie as she knelt on the ground and divided the contents of the shopping bag. "Two of those are yours, I take it?"

"Gayle, the little girl, and Trey, the youngest." She lit a cigarette and blew the smoke sideways. "They're all nuts about

Annie. She spoils them rotten. She always brings them something from California."

"The feeling's mutual. She talks about them a lot."

They watched the children in silence for a few moments, smoking companionably. "Do you have kids?" Taylor asked.

"No."

"Not married?"

"No."

She nodded. "That explains why you let Annie persuade you to come to Mississippi."

He looked at her. "The fact that I'm not married? How so?"

She wrinkled her nose delicately. "No woman would agree to come to Percyville after living in L.A."

"What's wrong with Percyville?"

"Nothing, if you like being buried alive." She made a little face. "Oops. I shouldn't say that or you might turn around and head back to California."

"Do you feel buried alive?"

She took the final drag from her cigarette, dropped the butt to the brick walkway and ground it beneath the toe of her sandal. The smoke swirled between them, obscuring the expression in her eyes. "I don't live in Percyville."

Her reply didn't answer his question, but Spencer let it go. "Annie has a big family. I'm not sure yet where everyone lives."

"I live in Jackson, thank God."

"But you'd prefer L.A.?"

"God, would I!"

Her passion amused him. "A couple of times trapped on the freeway and you'd soon wish for the green grass of home." His mouth quirked. "Which, I might add, is rare in California, except when we get torrential rains, but that encourages mud slides. Then when there's no rain, we have desert-dry conditions that spawn forest fires. Which are made ten times worse because of perverse winds. Then there're earthquakes, nuts with guns on the freeway, riots, occasional—"

"Okay, okay." Taylor laughed, tossing her dark hair. "I'm ready to move back to Mississippi! You've convinced me."

With his arms crossed, Spencer watched her. "You have a beautiful smile," he said quietly.

The compliment seemed to disconcert her. "Thank you," she said after a moment.

"Have you two introduced yourselves?" Annie asked, approaching from across the driveway. Behind her, the kids still cavorted wildly, but now they were using bright colored paddles, trying to keep a plastic bird aloft.

"We have," Spencer replied, his gaze still on Taylor. He found the soft flush on her cheeks fascinating.

"He talked me out of moving to L.A.," Taylor said, sounding a bit breathless.

Annie, ever sensitive to mood, gave Spencer a thoughtful look before falling into step beside him. "It's a good thing," she said dryly. "Jack would definitely have an opinion about that."

SUZANNE LOVED THE dining room at Riverbend. The cherry-wood table and chairs had been handed down from Charles Stafford's grandparents, who had originally built the house. Over the years, Lily Stafford had added the tea cart, the sideboard and the china cabinet after painstaking searches through antique shops throughout the South. The crystal chandelier suspended from an antebellum medallion had once been gaslit. Today it cast a soft glow on the twelve dinner guests gathered around a table groaning with the weight of roast turkey and all the trimmings. At the head of the table, Charles Stafford spoke a traditional Thanksgiving blessing. With Caleb's small hand in hers, Suzanne thought of the many things she had to be thankful for in her life and breathed her own private prayer. Today she would not dwell on the negatives.

Her father's "Amen" was echoed around the table and conversation erupted in lively Stafford style. On the other side of Caleb, Annie attempted to explain to Spencer Dutton the ingredients of corn bread dressing. No cook herself, she soon gave it up with an airy "Forget the recipe. Try it, Spence. You'll love it."

Suzanne, along with everyone else, had been caught off guard by Annie's decision to move her business to Percyville. Whatever doubts she'd once had were apparently overcome. Two months ago, she'd purchased the old Jacobson property, and in a matter of weeks Dream Fields was in full production. The biggest hurdle, she told Suzanne, had been convincing her production manager to leave California. Once Dutton had agreed, Annie had plunged ahead with characteristic, almost manic energy.

Spencer Dutton seemed nice enough, Suzanne thought, studying him now. He was a quiet, soft-spoken man. Of medium height, he had brown hair and hazel eyes that seemed not to miss a trick. He wasn't handsome, but his face was…interesting. During the hour before the meal, she'd wondered if the Stafford family's conversational free-for-alls might be intimidating to him, but after a while she'd decided he was one of those people who simply preferred watching and listening. For herself, she found something about him just a little unsettling, but Annie obviously thought the world of him, and after observing the two of them together, Suzanne believed they were exactly what Annie claimed—fast friends and business colleagues, period.

As conversation around the table hummed, Suzanne collected the children's plates. On the occasions when Caleb, Gayle and Trey ate with the adults, Suzanne had fallen into the habit of serving them, a task Taylor gladly relinquished. Across from Suzanne, Taylor was ignoring the sliver of turkey and a few salad greens on her plate in favor of a Waterford stemmed glass full of wine. Suzanne frowned, recalling that her sister had consumed a couple of drinks already. Beside Taylor, Jack ate heartily.

He selected a roll from a sterling silver basket passed to him by Spencer Dutton. "Annie, you're a deep one, and that's no lie. I thought I had my finger on the pulse of our little town, so, hell, I was surprised when I read in Stuart's column that you'd bought that rundown Jacobson property right here in God's country and set up production. The presses are already rolling, I heard. So how's business, darlin'?"

Annie sliced an asparagus spear in half. "Unchanged from what it was in California at this point. As to what it'll be when we've filled existing orders, I don't know."

"What kind of deal did you get out of the Jacobson heirs? That place has been on the market for I don't know how long. You should have picked it up for next to nothing."

"I paid a little more than that," Annie said dryly.

Jack looked at Stuart. "Did you do the deal for her?"

"No, I—"

Annie's knife clinked against her plate. "Nobody 'does' my deals for me, Jack," she said. Then she gave Charles Stafford an audacious wink. "Actually, Uncle Charles recommended someone."

All eyes went to Charles Stafford. Inclining his head, he smiled gently. "Not to worry, Jack. I think we managed to negotiate a fair deal. Right, Annie?"

"Hear, hear," Suzanne said. She loved it when somebody outmaneuvered Jack.

Annie helped herself to more asparagus. "I think so, Uncle Charles."

"You should have called me first," Jack said, masking irritation. "Remember that next time. When it's family, I'll see to it personally that you don't get screwed."

"Put a lid on it, Jack," Stuart said bluntly.

Jack's attention shifted. Like Charles Stafford, Stuart was seldom confrontational.

"The kids," Stuart explained abruptly.

"Oh, sorry."

Suzanne picked up her water glass. "I guess your benevolence doesn't extend to close family friends, does it, Jack?"

Jack looked up at her, his knife suspended above his plate. "I don't think I follow you, Suzanne."

"You speak of property deals and family ties. I assume your protective instincts didn't extend to Lucian Kincaid."

Jack resumed cutting the meat on his plate. "Lucian Kincaid's been dead a year," he said curtly. "I don't see your point."

"My point is, Lucian Kincaid was about as close to the Staffords as anybody who's not a blood relative could be. His grandson, Ben, certainly didn't feel the benefit of your concern. Quite the opposite, in fact."

Charles Stafford frowned. "What's this, Suzanne? What about Ben? And Lucian... What property deal? Do you know something?"

Around the table, anxious eyes were on her. The Judge looked disapproving, her father concerned. "Not enough, Dad," Suzanne said, already regretting the impulse to take a potshot at Jack. Thanksgiving was hardly the time to try to discredit him. He was like a snake, anyway. He'd twist and slither and speak out of both sides of his mouth, and it would be Suzanne who'd wind up looking bad. "I shouldn't have brought it up."

"Not at the table," the Judge agreed crisply. "And Jack's right, if you had some concern about Lucian's estate, you should have spoken a year ago. As it is, I'll still be more than happy to look into it, Suzanne. Tomorrow." Her firm tone put an end to the matter.

"That accident was such a tragedy," Eugenia said, her napkin clutched in one hand. "I saw Marilee at the beauty shop the day before it happened. She said she didn't think Ben would be home for Thanksgiving, but she still had hopes he would make it for Christmas."

"Too busy tooling around Turkey to take the time to come home and eat a little of the same with his folks," Jack said, giving his attention to his plate. "No pun intended."

"Jack," Taylor admonished softly.

Jack shrugged. "Well, hell, it took a funeral to bring him back here, didn't it?"

"Annie," Taylor said brightly, fixing her gaze on her cousin, "will you be living permanently at the bungalow with Eugenia?

In your old room? If so, and you feel like redecorating, I know some really nice shops in Jackson."

"I don't see how Annie could need any help redecorating, Taylor," Jack said. "She's an artist, for God's sake."

"Well, sure, but—"

"Thanks, Taylor, I'll remember that." The edge to Annie's smile was lost on Jack. "And yes, I'm staying with Mom. However, as much as I'd like to freshen up my room, I'm afraid I won't have time until I see how my business does."

"Your business will be just as strong here as it was in California," Stuart said quietly. He spooned cranberries onto his plate before passing the dish to Eugenia. To no one in particular, he said, "I've argued all along it doesn't matter where Annie produces Dream Fields so long as she's the creative force behind the business."

"Stuart...nobody's suggesting anything different." All good humor, Jack looked around the table. "Right, y'all?" He tackled a drumstick with gusto. "I'll admit to some curiosity, though. Why now, Annie?" He glanced at Eugenia. "We all know your mama's been begging you to come home for years, isn't that so, Eugenia?"

Eugenia patted her mouth delicately with her napkin. "Yes, and I couldn't be more pleased." She looked at the Judge. "You understand that, don't you, Lily?"

With a discreet tap of her spoon on her water goblet, Lily Stafford signaled the housekeeper to her side. "Refill these if you please, Mattie. All around." That done, she nodded graciously at Eugenia. "I do indeed, Eugenia. It's no secret that I've been trying to persuade Suzanne to go into practice here in Percyville for some time."

Suzanne sighed. "Mother, please."

The Judge refused the gravy boat passed to her. "It would remove you from the risks you face daily, Suzanne. Besides, think how good it would be for Caleb if you were to live here."

"With you and Dad at Riverbend?" she asked dryly.

"Well, of course. The house is certainly big enough. Your

father and I reared three children here with room to spare." She waved her fingers in Eugenia's direction. "Annie chooses to live with Eugenia. I don't know why you can't live with us. One small boy would hardly be noticed."

Caleb looked puzzled. "Where would I stay so you wouldn't notice me? In the attic?"

Everyone laughed. Caleb turned to appeal to his mother. "I don't want to live in the attic, Mommy."

"You won't have to, honeybun." Suzanne patted his hand. "We're not going to move to Riverbend. Granny's just teasing." She looked at her mother. "Aren't you, Granny?"

The Judge clicked her tongue. "If you insist." Then she frowned with genuine perplexity. "I can't understand why Grayson Lee persists in keeping you in that particular section of his organization, Suzanne. The D.A. has cases by the dozen you could work on in other areas. It's a mystery to me why he doesn't give you some variety."

"Mother—"

"It's no mystery at all, Judge." His meal finished, Jack leaned back in his chair and hooked an arm around the top. "Suzanne is far too good just where he's got her for Grayson Lee to even consider reassigning her. Her conviction rate for sex crimes is close to perfect." Although speaking to the table at large, his gaze came to rest on Suzanne. "Right, Suzy?"

"The D.A. demands a high conviction rate. I wouldn't last long otherwise." He was baiting her. She knew what that sly look meant and she wasn't going to oblige him. With her fingers on the stem of her water glass, she added, "Nobody's conviction rate is perfect. I've had my share of disappointments."

"Not lately, you haven't. Take the Mayfield case, for example." He was shaking his head. "I thought for sure your percentages would nose dive on that one."

"The Mayfield case?" Annie said with a puzzled look.

"Diane Mayfield, a female student working at a convenience store, was raped by two fraternity guys," Stuart explained. "She got in the car with them when they offered to drive her back to her dorm on campus. She was found on a remote hiking trail badly hurt the next morning. A fractured skull, wasn't it, Suzy?"

"Among other things."

Jack made a derisive face. "It beats me how you managed to get that airhead to testify."

"Diane Mayfield is not an airhead," Suzanne said, feeling emotion boiling inside her. That he *dared* to even mention this subject to her. "She's at school on an academic scholarship. They don't hand those out to airheads."

"Whatever. She's probably tickled pink over the outcome. I bet she hasn't given a thought to ruining the lives of two promising students."

She stared at him. "No, she probably hasn't spent much time worrying over their ruined lives. For one thing, I imagine a lot of her energy is spent in trying to get through the nights without experiencing the terror of her attack over and over again."

"Hell, I'm not saying they shouldn't have their butts kicked for stupidity or that they should get away scot-free for leaving her in the woods like that." Jack appealed to the others at the table. "That's the trouble with this kind of thing, you know? A woman gets in a car with a couple of guys, what're they supposed to think?"

"That she wants a ride home?" Annie said dryly.

Jack shot her an annoyed look. "I know how you women see these things, but you ask a dozen guys the message a woman is sending when she gets into a car with a couple of randy jocks and ten'll say it's 'Take your best shot.'"

Annie's mouth dropped. "I don't believe I'm hearing this, Jack. Where have you been living?"

"Under a rock," Suzanne muttered, but luckily only Spencer Dutton seemed to hear her.

"Okay, okay." Jack waved both hands in a signal of surrender. "I can see we won't agree on this subject, but we've strayed from the point, anyway. Lily, I don't think you're going to persuade Suzy to walk away from the D.A.'s office as long as she keeps the convictions going—nor is Grayson Lee going to consider reassigning her. Why would he? Actually, you should be proud of her. She's building a reputation as one sharp cookie."

"Oh, please." Suzanne rolled her eyes.

"Hey, I'm just telling it like it is, Suzy. To get anywhere in this business, you've got to draw attention to yourself. Choose your battles, yes, and once you do, go for the whole enchilada."

Suzanne pushed her plate aside. "Is anybody ready for dessert?"

Jack laughed. "Hear that, folks? Sounds a little testy, doesn't she? Well, she's more than testy when she gets in that courtroom. She's a barracuda!"

"Jack!" Taylor protested.

"I kid you not. Suzy goes for these guys like she wants to rid the world of men." He looked directly into her eyes. *Daring* her! "Is that it, Suzy? You have some kind of personal vendetta, and it just happens that as a prosecutor in the D.A.'s office you have the ammunition you need to clean up society?"

"Jack, are you drunk?" Stuart shoved his napkin beneath his plate, his mouth tight. "Suzanne's doing her job. What do you expect her to do? Lose a case now and then and let some lowlife off just to keep up the morale of the criminal element?"

Taylor giggled but quickly smothered it in her wineglass when Jack gave her a glare. Flustered, she hastily set her glass down, wincing when the foot grazed the rim of her plate and some of the wine splashed on the lace cloth.

"Well, shit, Taylor!" Jack said with disgust.

Lily stood abruptly. "Why don't we move on to the living room or the sunroom," she suggested, placing her folded napkin neatly beside her plate. "I think we're finished, and goodness knows we've all had so much to eat that I don't believe anybody will object if we delay dessert and coffee for a while."

TWENTY-ONE

SUZANNE FINALLY ESCAPED to the veranda. Thanksgiving or not, no dessert was tempting enough to keep her in the same room with Jack Sullivan right now. For Suzanne, it never got better. She wondered if she'd ever get beyond those moments in the gazebo. Probably not. Jack was always going to torment her when he had the opportunity. She might scratch back, but she was trapped by her fear that his relationship to Caleb might somehow be revealed.

With her hands on the rail of the veranda, Suzanne felt rage smoldering inside her. She should be used to it, she told herself. His sly references to her successful conviction rate in the sex crimes unit were nothing new. His veiled digs that she had a personal stake in ridding the world of men was an old refrain. Okay, she'd give him that one. She did indeed want to rid the world of men who raped, abused and otherwise victimized women. She rubbed her forehead wearily. And maybe if she was successful enough, there would be some personal consolation, because she couldn't rid the world of Jack himself.

She heard the click of the door behind her. With a dozen people in the house, she'd been lucky to have five minutes to herself. She could have gone to the gazebo, except that nothing short of an impending flood would drive her to the gazebo alone if Jack was anywhere on the premises.

"Looks as if I'm not the only one seeking solitude," Annie said, coming to stand beside her.

Suzanne gave a humorless laugh. "Looks like. Cutting Caleb's day short and heading back to Jackson was not an option, so the veranda seemed the next best thing."

"Is he always so obnoxious?"

"Caleb?" As if she didn't know who Annie meant.

Annie's poke in the side was gentle. "No, not Caleb, you twit. The family's fair-haired boy. Jack."

"The family's dark devil is more like it," Suzanne muttered.

"Your own devil, or at least that's the way it appears. Why's he on your case, Suzy? I know he wanted you to work for that law firm in Jackson, but you've done a fabulous job with the D.A.'s office. Everyone's so proud of you—Uncle Charles, Stuart, Taylor, even the Judge, who by her own admission would love to have you here in Percyville. In spite of the way he talks, Jack must know you're doing a worthwhile job—a necessary job, considering the number of sex-related crimes committed today." She shook her head. "I can't figure Jack on this one, Suzy."

"You don't think I'm too zealous in trying to nail these people, Annie?"

"Is there such a thing as being too zealous in ridding the world of rapists and child molesters? Hardly." She gave a baffled laugh. "This is the first time I've ever heard of a prosecutor being harassed for being too effective. Listen, if these folks don't appreciate you, go to California. The fields are green for harvesting lowlifes there."

Suzanne rubbed a spot on the railing. "I'm not licensed to practice law in California."

"You know I'm only kidding. You belong right where you are, at least for now. Isn't that what we were talking about?"

"In a roundabout way, I suppose so." Suzanne released a sigh. "If my mother is so pleased with my reputation at the D.A.'s office, why does she never miss a chance to try and entice me back to Percyville?"

"The way I see it, one has nothing to do with the other. Naturally, she wants you to come home to practice. If you stayed with the D.A., you'd be well positioned politically, but I don't think the Judge envisions a political career for you. She has Jack for that. He's a political animal to his toenails. You're not." Annie focused her gaze beyond the grounds to the distant line of dark green that marked the Mississippi River. "No, she doesn't want politics for you, at least not yet. In local legal circles, Aunt Lily is a force to be reckoned with. She would no doubt help you get set up very advantageously. That *ain't* to be dismissed lightly, Suzy," she said with a telling look. "Some lawyers would kill for an inside chance like that."

"I know, I know." Suzanne studied her feet morosely.

"And there's Caleb. The Judge and Uncle Charles are good grandparents. They're nuts about him. From their point of view, having him right in the house with them would be just fine." Annie reached over and brushed a fallen leaf from the railing. "Every little kid should be so lucky."

Suzanne sighed. "I'm an ungrateful bitch."

"No, you just want to manage your own career the way you see fit. Nothing's wrong with that."

They stood, side by side, both gazing down at the showy chrysanthemums crowding the beds at the base of the veranda. In September, the Judge planted them in masses. The result was a blaze of autumn-hued flowers visible from all angles of the house until the first hard freeze. Now, in the afternoon sun, their scent—sharp, pungent, spicy—floated up.

"I just can't do it, Annie."

"Then don't. But don't let Jack's ridiculous needling get to you, either."

"Most of the time, I don't. Honestly. I'm used to it. But it would be nice—just once—to have a family get-together without the hassle. Taylor and the kids, of course, sans Jack."

"We could sign him up for a cruise at Christmas," Annie suggested mischievously. "He's so shitty he might get tossed overboard by the other passengers."

"No, he's too wily for that. He can charm the socks off strangers," Suzanne said with exasperation. "Off anybody, actually."

Annie was shaking her head. "Whatever happened to 'You can't fool all of the people all of the time?'"

"Take comfort. There's still you and me without blinders."

"But are we the only two people in the world who can't stand him?"

Suzanne thought of Ben Kincaid. "I'm sure there are others, but he's clever enough to keep his enemies under wraps."

"What about Stuart?"

It was a casual enough question, but Suzanne heard the special tone in Annie's voice that she reserved for Stuart. "Stuart is not fooled by Jack."

Annie was carefully examining a small crack along the top of the railing. "Speaking of Stuart, he's here alone and no one's mentioned Eleanor. What's going on?"

"Nothing like you're suggesting. Eleanor's on a cruise."

"What was I suggesting?"

"Come on, Annie. This is me, the human repository of all your secrets from age four. You're suggesting that because Stuart's marriage isn't exactly a match made in heaven that spending Thanksgiving alone means they're openly admitting it. Wrong. So far, he hasn't thrown in the towel. He keeps hoping a miracle will happen and Eleanor will become warm and loving."

"What do you think?"

"Fat chance."

Annie grunted.

"Stuart knows it's a hopeless cause, but he's as stubborn as Mother, in his way."

"I know."

"It's his problem, Annie." The western sky was turning a brilliant red. The day was almost over. Only a little while longer and she could take Caleb home.

Annie sighed. "What were we talking about?"

"Eleanor taking a cruise."

"Oh, yes." Annie flicked a chip of paint into the mums. "Do fill me in."

"She went with her folks. It's ten days to someplace in the Caribbean and back again."

"Oh, wow."

"Her Aunt Charly—remember her—the artist in Atlanta?"

"I do, actually."

"Well, Aunt Charly came down with a case of shingles and Eleanor's mom and dad offered her the ticket. Pfft! She was gone. Out of here. And Stuart gets to spend Thanksgiving in the bosom of his family."

"He needs children," Annie said, breaking off a fading yellow mum and twirling it round and round.

"If you're suggesting he'd make a super dad, you're right, but not with Eleanor. Please."

"No."

"Don't give up, Annie."

Suzanne stared silently into the perfection of the sunset. *No, don't give up, Annie. At least one of us still has a chance at happiness.*

TAYLOR WAITED ALMOST a whole week before she drove out to Annie's new place of business. It was lunchtime, probably the most convenient moment to catch Annie with a few minutes to spare. Annie was one of the most energetic people Taylor had ever known. Even when they were kids, she was almost never still, always full of ideas. Crazy stuff sometimes, to Taylor's way of thinking.

One time, she had a notion that they could hitch to Memphis and have lunch at the Peabody Hotel. When Suzanne said it was dangerous to hitch, Annie had said she'd carry a small pistol of Eugenia's, one of the few mementos of Annie's dead father she'd considered worth keeping. God knew, there were precious few worldly goods left to Annie and Eugenia when Annie's real daddy died. Too bad Uncle Tillman died only a year after becoming her stepfather. But nothing ever kept Annie down for long. Taylor had always admired that. Annie took the blows and stood right up again.

Sitting behind the wheel of her new Volvo station wagon,

Taylor wondered how some people developed that kind of strength.

She got out, closing the door with a bang. She didn't really like the Volvo. Truth was, she hated it. But Jack had insisted that, as the mother of two, she needed a practical vehicle. Taylor had really wanted a cream Mercedes. It wasn't the money. They could afford it. Didn't Jack drive a Jaguar? But no, the perfect wife, mother and homemaker should drive a station wagon. He never forgot the image they should project to the public. So, nix to the Mercedes.

Bastard. Prick. Son of a bitch.

She winced inwardly when she used language like that, even in her thoughts. She never used to, but being married to Jack, she found she just picked up his bad habits through osmosis or something. He could hardly complete a sentence without using the F-word. Not that he ever said it around anybody who *mattered,* such as her mother. Oh, no. The Judge was never subjected to the worst side of Jack Sullivan. Only his wife.

He treated her like a second-class person. As she strolled up the brick walkway to the door of the cottage, she ticked off a list of grievances: her opinion was worthless, her ideas were dumb, she had no special talent to speak of, she was a lousy mother. Oh, there were a dozen ways a man could make a woman feel like shit, and Jack knew them all.

She hated him sometimes. Really. She had good reason, too. The thing that made her hate him the most was his infidelity. He was having an affair, she knew it, but she didn't know who he was screwing. As she knocked on the freshly painted door, she amended that thought: she didn't know how *many* women he was screwing. It wouldn't surprise her to find out he had half a dozen waiting for him to snap his finger so they could fall into bed with him. After all, didn't she?

The door opened wide and she stared, momentarily startled, into the steady hazel eyes of Spencer Dutton.

"Hello, Taylor." Stepping back, he beckoned her inside.

Hesitant, she peered beyond him, but there didn't seem to be any sign of another person. "Are you alone?"

He smiled. "I live alone."

She frowned. "But I thought Annie—" Still on the outside stoop, she waved at the interior of the cottage. "I thought this was Annie's office. I thought I might catch her at lunch. I was just curious. I wanted to see what she'd done with the place. I don't know a thing about her type of work, printing greeting cards, I mean, and she's been so successful, we're so proud of her, that...well, I had some free time and I just got in my car and decided to see for myself."

He glanced at the Volvo. "Looks like brand-new wheels. Pretty nice. One of the safest vehicles on the road, or so they claim in their advertisements."

"I hate it."

He gave the station wagon another look, then switched his gaze back to her. With his arms crossed over his chest, he shifted so that he was standing with his hips cocked. He looked big, strong, dependable. And kind. To Taylor, there was something about Spencer Dutton when his eyes were on her that was so...good. So right.

So different from Jack.

"Production for Dream Fields is done in the big building behind the cottage," he explained. He had not invited her in. She stood on the stoop and listened. "We did some reconfiguring to lay out space for Annie's office and my own out there. That made the cottage unnecessary from a business standpoint. So Annie suggested I might want to fix it up and live out here myself. I took her up on it."

She nodded. "It's lovely...." She glanced beyond him again. "That is, what I can see is lovely."

"Annie went into town to the post office and to attend to some legal matters."

"Oh."

"Have you had lunch?"

"No."

"I've enough ham to build a couple of sandwiches, I think."

"I love sandwiches."

With a faint half smile, he opened the door fully and stepped back. "Then would you care to join me for lunch, Taylor Sullivan?"

"Yes, thank you." With her heart beating oddly, Taylor went inside. Behind her, Spencer Dutton closed the door softly.

TWENTY-TWO

December 1987

ANNIE SHOVED THE HEAVY carton into the trunk of her car and closed the lid. After checking to see that it was tight, she dusted her hands, glanced quickly at her watch and frowned, trying to decide whether she had time to pick up some wine. The package store closed in less than an hour and there would be no other place to buy it. It was now or never. Some things she missed about California—especially the more relaxed attitudes—but there were compensations.

She decided to get the wine.

She left the car parked where it was and hurried down the street. As she turned the corner, she checked her watch again and didn't see the person coming from the opposite direction until he caught her by the arms to prevent a collision.

"Whoa! Annie."

"Stuart! Sorry, I wasn't watching."

"Where's the fire?" He let her go, keeping his eyes on her face, *memorizing* her face, it seemed.

"Ah, no fire." She pushed stray curls from her cheek. "I was thinking about wine for tonight."

He glanced at his own watch. "Relax. You've got fifteen minutes."

"Well…" She turned and looked at her car as if it was going to start on its own and leave her. "Actually, I've got a few other things to do before I can go partying tonight with a clear conscience."

"Hmm, sounds interesting."

She glanced at the shopping bag he held. "I see you've already made your purchases. Lordy, are you sure you've got enough booze there?"

He laughed. "Only one's for tonight. I was restocking after the Christmas party. Which reminds me, we missed you."

"Didn't you get my RSVP?"

"I got it, but I still missed you."

Annie caught the eye of a friend passing in a car and waved. After a moment, she faced Stuart again. "I've been too busy to do much partying this year." It had been self-preservation, not a crowded schedule that had kept her away from his and Eleanor's home, but she didn't want to tell him that.

"You don't have to avoid me, Annie. I'm not going to step out of line again."

She waved a hand and tried to laugh. "Good heavens, Stuart. That was more than four years ago."

"It seems like yesterday to me."

She lifted her wrist and looked at her watch. "Gosh, I'd better get in there if I want to get that wine." She took a step, but he stopped her with a hand on her arm. Their eyes met and held. A couple came out of the store, giving them a curious look before moving on. Undeterred, Stuart held her fast.

"Are we going to pretend that kiss never happened, Annie?"

"*I* am, Stuart. I don't know about you."

He released a sigh, shaking his head. "I can try, but I think it's going to be like trying to force toothpaste back into a tube, Annie-girl. Once it's done, it's out there."

"Gosh, that's so romantic, Stuart."

His mouth tilted in a half smile. "You always said I have a way with words." While he watched, a small renegade breeze stirred her hair. She caught at it, held it away from her face with one hand. Her bare skin was pale, as befit most redheads, and lightly dusted with freckles.

Stuart's smile disappeared as he cleared his throat. "A part of me wishes I could take it back, Annie, but another part isn't listening. But the worst thing is that I managed to alienate you, and I never anticipated that. I treasure your friendship. I wanted to talk to you at Riverbend on Thanksgiving to tell you that I don't want to lose that with you, but you wouldn't let me get anywhere near you...at least not when you were alone."

"It's not a question of staying friends, Stuart. We crossed a line that day. It was a stupid, foolish thing we did. And it was wrong. We can still be friends, of course, but whether you want to accept it or not, something happened that day that changed the nature of our friendship."

"I really screwed up, didn't I?"

"Oh, cut it out, Stuart! Have you forgotten it takes two? I was as much to blame as you. We need to put it behind us. With my mother in Percyville and now my business here, we won't be able to avoid each other. There's Riverbend, mutual friends, family, there's Kroger's and the Chamber of Commerce, for Pete's sake." She glanced at the storefront just ahead and grimaced. "There's the liquor store." She sighed. "This is a small town. I'm afraid we're stuck with each other, Stuart. But I can be pragmatic about it if you can, okay?"

He didn't answer right away. Instead, his gaze roved over her face and hair, then back to her eyes. "I don't think I can ever be pragmatic about you, Annie."

"Knock it off, Stuart!"

"Sorry."

"You should be." But she was fighting a smile.

He shifted the shopping bag, resting the weight on his hip. "So, are you going to be at the country club tonight or is that wine for another party?"

"Another party."

"Well, hell. I hoped we could have a dance."

"Stuart..." Her tone was a warning.

"At least one dance a year, Annie. In full view of God and everybody. That doesn't seem like too much to ask, does it?"

"Stuart."

"Too much, huh?"

"Yes."

He nodded, looked away. "You'll be celebrating the new year with Spencer?"

"Spencer? No, with Suzanne."

"Suzanne? She's not going to the club this year, either?"

"No, we've both been invited to Candace Webber's house. She's having a dinner party. In Jackson. It's an annual thing for her, I think. Sort of like the Christmas party you and Eleanor have each year. Do you know her?"

"Grayson Lee's first assistant?"

"That's right."

"Yeah, we've met. A lot of people think justice would be better served if she were Jackson's D.A."

"Suzanne thinks very highly of her. I believe the feeling's mutual." She peered beyond his shoulder. "I've really got to run, Stuart. It looks as if they're getting ready to close."

"Sure."

For a heartbeat, she thought he was going to touch her. She clutched her shoulder bag a little tighter, bringing it around toward the front of her as a shield. "Well, Happy New Year."

"To you, too, Annie," he said quietly.

She dashed for the entrance of the package store.

SPENCER WAS IN THE SHOP monkeying around with the computer when Annie finally made it back. "You have a hand-delivered letter, Annie," he said. "Some guy came by while you were out."

"No kidding?" Annie stopped at her drawing board and reached for the envelope propped against the pottery mug that served as a pencil holder. "Looks like Taylor's handwriting."

Spencer's clacketing on the keyboard ceased.

"It's Taylor's, all right."

Spencer pushed a key and the printer began to hum.

"She's at Riverbend to go to the annual shindig at the country club in Percyville. Jack likes to be seen with his in-laws from time to time. Good for his image. The Judge approves, of course." She glanced at Spencer, but he seemed absorbed in the paper spewing from the printer. "Says here they're having a few people at Riverbend before everybody moves on to the club. Last-minute plan. Hopes we'll be able to come." Annie tossed the invitation aside. "I told her last week I had plans to go with Suzanne tonight. The country club hosts a posh affair with a bunch of posh people. Not my thing, and Taylor knows it."

"Who's we?"

She looked at him. "What?"

"You said she hopes we'll be able to come. Who's we?"

"Oh, you and me. She mentions you probably haven't had time to meet anybody, cliquish as Percyville can be. So, if I can't make it, she wants to be sure you know you're welcome."

He grunted and ripped off a portion of continuous feed from the printer.

Annie tossed the invitation aside and looked at him. "What's your pleasure, Mr. Dutton?"

"I'd feel like a jerk without you there."

Annie settled back on her stool, studying him more intently. "But if I went, you'd go?"

He shrugged. "Maybe. Better than spending New Year's with a bunch of rednecks at the Elite." He pronounced it E-lite.

"You're kidding."

"Don't I wish."

The corner of her mouth quirked. "The E-lite?"

Another grunt. "Percyville's answer to the Hardrock Café."

"That is really the bottom of the barrel, Spence."

"Don't I know it."

Annie picked up the invitation and walked to his desk. Tossing it down, she watched his eyes go to it as if pulled by a string. "You mean you'd turn down a chance to spend the evening at the E-lite for a few cocktails at Riverbend?"

"It's tempting."

"Tempting." She still watched him.

"Maybe I'll get to sample one of those mint juleps."

Chuckling, she reached over and tucked the invitation in his shirt pocket. "Then it's yours, my man."

Spencer shut the printer down and stood up. His jacket hung on a rattan coatrack by the door. He took it down and shrugged into it. Annie spoke his name as he reached for the door. He looked back at her from over his shoulder. "Yeah?"

"Be careful, Spence."

He held her gaze for a moment, then with a nod and a ghost of a smile, he opened the door and left.

Annie watched as the headlights of his car swept across the rain-speckled windows. Icy drizzle meant hazardous driving—especially on New Year's Eve, when a few reckless individuals would no doubt get behind the wheel after drinking too much. Tomorrow morning, a few of those would no doubt wish they'd stayed home.

For a few seconds, she toyed with the idea of doing just that. Suzanne's friends were good company, but she didn't know them well. On the other hand, nobody should spend New Year's Eve alone. She moved to the window and rubbed a small spot free of condensation. Outside, there was no sign of movement. A single light had been left on in Spence's cottage. It was on nights like this—times traditionally celebrated with someone special—that loneliness almost overwhelmed her. Maybe it was the curse of living so close to Stuart. The only thing worse had been living two thousand miles from him.

She turned away from the window, unwilling to brood over Stuart tonight. In some ways, she was just as bad as her mother. Even though she wouldn't give in to her feelings as long as Stuart was married to Eleanor, her desire for him was there. Didn't that make her as guilty as if she actually slept with him?

Thinking of Eugenia, she picked up the phone and punched out her home number. Her mother sounded breathless as she answered. Who, Annie wondered, was Eugenia expecting on the other end?

"Mom, it's me."

"Annie." A small pause. "Are you still working? It's New Year's Eve, honey. Can't you get away? It's nearly five. If you don't leave now, you won't have enough time to dress. Didn't you tell Suzanne you'd meet her about seven?"

"Right. And I'm wrapping things up here now. Just a few odds and ends to square away and I'll head on home. I was just checking to see what your plans are."

"I'm going to the club, of course. I go to the club every year on New Year's Eve. Where else would I go?"

Where else? Anyplace where you wouldn't be tortured by the sight of Jack Sullivan with his beautiful young wife on his arm.

Annie dropped into her chair. "Do you have a date, Mom?"

"Actually Tom Perkins is picking me up. We'll stop at Riverbend before going to the club. Lily called and insisted."

Riverbend. Naturally Jack would be there. With Taylor. Rubbing her forehead, Annie forced some enthusiasm into her tone. "Dr. Perkins, huh? This makes the third time you've been out with the good doctor, Mom. You like him, don't you?"

"Of course. He's a very nice man."

"Who is he, Mom? Where did you meet him? He doesn't practice here in Percyville, does he?"

"No, he's from New Orleans. Jack introduced us."

"Jack." So much for thinking the doctor was special.

"Tom has connections to an investors' group or something— I'm not sure about the details. Anyway, Jack is interested in it. He invited Tom to the club tonight to meet a few people who might also be interested."

"And what are you, Mom? An escort service?"

"Please, Annie." Eugenia's tone cooled. "You know we've agreed not to discuss Jack. Or anything that has to do with my... with my friendship with Jack."

"What kind of investors' group? Is this guy really a doctor?" Realizing she was clutching the phone cord in a death grip, she let it go, curling her fingers into a fist instead. "What do you know about him? I mean, other than what Jack has told you?"

She heard her mother sigh. "Annie, it's getting late. I really must hang up now. I know it doesn't bother you to get dressed in a rush, but it does fluster me. And you know how Lily carries on when her guests don't show up on time."

Annie hunched forward, resting her forehead on one hand. "Mom, you don't have to live your life like this—settling for scraps of Jack's attention while your own personal life just withers on the vine. Now he has you entertaining men when he tells you to. There's a word for that, Mom."

"I must go, Annie. I don't want to be late getting to Riverbend."

"Heavens, no. We wouldn't want to keep Jack waiting."

A faint sigh. "Be careful tonight, Annie. It's drizzling rain and the roads will be icy. Happy New Year, honey."

Terrific. Just fucking terrific.

Feeling the urge to throw the receiver across the room, Annie squeezed it instead. "Happy New Year, Mom."

But the line had gone dead.

TWENTY-THREE

JACK STOOD BEFORE THE open doors of his armoire transferring the contents of a small tray to his pants pocket: keys, change, breath spray. Pausing with his money clip, he thumbed through the bills, counting a couple of hundred dollars. Glancing in the mirror, he gave his lapels a last firm tug, twitched at the knot of his tie to center it and cocked his head. Satisfied, he reached for the pocket recorder lying on top of the armoire and pushed the button on the side to activate it.

"December 31. Initial contact for River Run Consortium completed at noon today. Perkins to approach Higgins after January 1." He released the button and stared thoughtfully at the rain-drenched window. He didn't quite trust Tom Perkins. Too cool, cautious to a fault. Son of a bitch wanted iron-clad guarantees to soothe his investors, but damn it, there weren't any guarantees in this business. Especially guarantees in writing. Hell, if the whole thing went down the tubes, there was no recouping the losses. On the other hand, if it went the way Jack knew in his soul it would, the bastards would make a killing. If Perkins wanted security, he should have stayed in the medical profession. Jack squinted through the sleeting rain. Higgins was the key. Shit. Ten to one he'd have to go to New Orleans himself.

With a disgusted grunt, he pushed the record button again. "Reminder—keep flexible calendar first week of January for trip to New Orleans if Perkins doesn't sweeten Higgins." He snapped the button off, paused to think a few moments, then started the recorder again. "Get Eugenia's take on Perkins." He stopped again, paused, then resumed. "Call Franklin Jewelry. Eugenia's earned a bonus."

He snapped the recorder off, slipped it into his pocket. *Never leave home without it,* he thought, patting the small, solid weight with a hard smile, and left his dressing room.

"What'll it be this time, a Rolex?"

Taylor stood by the bed in a short black dress sprinkled with jet beads. His overcoat and her full-length mink were in her hands. She tossed them both on the bed. "She got a piece of Mignon Faget last time. What was it now…?" Taylor squinted at the rain-washed window, her mouth screwed up. "The pendant, wasn't it?" She shrugged, sighed. "I forget."

Jack made an attempt to curb his fury. Goddamn it! She was half lit already. Two hours ago he'd told her to go easy on the booze tonight. If he was going to seek the nomination for attorney general in a couple of years, he needed to solidify his base now. The place to begin was at the grassroots level. For him, that meant Percyville. He'd married into the goddamn family for the connections. Son of a bitch! He wasn't going to stand by and watch it go down the tubes because Taylor was a lush.

"What're you talking about, Taylor?"

"I heard you speaking into that stupid recorder, Jack. I'm talking about Eugenia's bonus. What's it to be, a Rolex?"

"Why? You want one, too?"

"No, but it would be nice if you thought in terms of giving your wife a gift for a change."

He rolled his eyes. "For God's sake, Taylor! It's only a week after Christmas. You got a shitload of gifts then." He went to the bed and picked up his overcoat. "If you wanted a Rolex, you should have put it on your list."

"Why do I have to write a list? Why can't my husband surprise me? Can you understand that, Jack? A surprise from a woman's husband means he thinks of her sometimes. It means she's more than just a…a…a window of opportunity."

He was shaking his head with disgust. "If you could hear yourself, you'd know why I try to keep you away from the booze, Taylor. You sound like one of those idiots on daytime TV." He snatched up a white silk muffler. "I haven't got time for this shit tonight."

"Are you sleeping with her, Jack?"

He turned and looked at her. "What?"

"Eugenia. My aunt." Her lips were unsteady and her eyes glistened with tears. "Just tell me if it's not true, because I know you have some kind of relationship with Eugenia, Jack."

"You don't know any goddamn thing." Wearied beyond belief, he scowled at her. "You must be drunker than I thought. How many drinks have you had, Taylor?"

She turned away. "That's right. Change the subject."

"Did you hear me? How…many…drinks?"

"Two, three. What does it matter?" With jerky movements, she bent to pick up her coat.

He took a breath. "I told you—"

"Jack." She stopped him. "I know something's going on. At least give me credit for having half a brain. I also know that it's important tonight for us to project the right image." She gave him a tight smile. "Us. You and me. So, you see, I do understand my role in the scheme of things, politically speaking. Tonight at the club, I'm the Little Wife. I'm the Cookie-Baking Mother. I'm the Helpmate Extraordinaire." She was suddenly bitter. "And if you just say the word, I can be the Tooth Fairy or Mary Poppins or Mother Teresa. So relax. I won't do anything to jeopardize any long-range plans."

She gasped when he suddenly gripped her arm. He was furious. "You're goddamn right you won't screw up. I'm warning you, Taylor, and this is no empty threat. You keep fucking sober tonight or you'll answer to me tomorrow."

She tried to wrench free, but he held on and gave her a quick, hard shake. "I'm serious, Taylor. Drink some coffee before we leave, you got that? And skip the booze altogether tonight." With a sound of disgust, he let her go.

She stood where he left her, rubbing her arm as he shrugged

into his coat. "Just be sure you have enough leverage, Jack, because two can play this game."

He turned back. She was trembling, but not with fear. Jack realized she wasn't afraid he would hurt her physically and wondered if he'd been too lenient. He could be goaded to violence against a woman. His first victim had been his own mother.

Taylor reached for a black beaded evening bag, then faced him with a smile as artificially bright as the twinkling chain that anchored the bag on her shoulder. "Well. I'm ready if you are."

A FEW HOURS LATER, Taylor was at the bar for a fresh drink. Only her fourth in four hours, she thought, placing her order with the bartender with a rush of confidence. For once she'd been successful in pacing herself. She felt mellow but not too high. It was impossible to party on New Year's Eve cold sober. *Fuck you, Jack.*

As always, when her thoughts about Jack crossed the line, she felt guilty. Maybe there had been a couple of times lately when she'd slightly overdone it. Truly, there was nothing more scary than waking up in the morning without a clue as to what had happened the night before. On those occasions, maybe she did wonder if her drinking was getting out of control. While waiting at the bar, she watched the crowd with slightly blurred vision. People looked happy—talking, dancing, laughing. She wondered if their happiness was genuine, or if, like hers, it was a facade. If only she could reinvent herself into a happy, successful, talented woman. If only she had Jack's ability to manipulate reality. Since none of that was possible, she simply tuned out. After a few drinks, she was blessedly numb to her shortcomings.

She tapped her nails on the bar with impatience and pushed her gloomy thoughts aside. This was a stupid time to be dwelling on her failures. She could safely leave that to her husband.

She took the drink from the bartender and tasted it, savoring the citrusy bite, then flashed him a smile before turning again to survey the crowd, which had been growing more and more rowdy as the clock neared midnight. Good band, she decided. Swaying slightly to an upbeat number, she enjoyed the music until she spotted Jack on the dance floor with Eugenia.

Surely she was wrong about Eugenia. Her own aunt. She watched as Jack said something to make Eugenia glow. How many times had she heard the Judge say Eugenia looked ten years younger than she actually was? And the way she was looking at Jack now... *Fool! Don't look at him that way. I could tell you things....*

"May I have this dance?"

Taylor turned and looked into Spencer Dutton's eyes. Instantly some of the ache in her heart eased. "Yes, thank you, Spencer." She quickly finished her drink, gave the bartender the empty glass and turned into the arms of the older man.

Her first thought was that he smelled good, manly with the added appeal of cold rain and wintry chill. The touch of his hand on her bare back made her shiver. He'd been outdoors, which was why she'd hadn't been able to find him in the crowd. She admitted to herself now that she'd been looking for him.

She shouldn't have added that note inviting Spencer on Annie's invitation. But how else was she going to see him again? Never mind that she shouldn't *want* to see him. At Riverbend tonight, they'd said little. Most of the time he'd spent looking at her in that steady, intent way he had. She told him she would save a dance for him, and now here he was. It was wrong, of course, pursuing him. But wasn't everything she did nowadays wrong?

She followed his lead, not talking but content to enjoy the moment. The music was playing a bluesy rendition of *Poor Butterfly.* He led with just a touch of his body to hers, and she followed easily. If it was wrong, why did it feel so right? Could anything be wrong that helped her forget Jack's cruelty? It was only for the length of a song.

"I didn't know if you were going to be here," she said, careful to keep her eyes on the dancers around them.

Ever so gently, his hand moved over the bare skin on her back. "You asked me, I came," he said simply.

"Why?"

"You know why, Taylor."

Her heart was racing, and it wasn't from alcohol. She was playing with fire, and it was stupid, even dangerous considering Jack's personality, but here was a man who touched the aching, empty corners of her heart as no one had for years. Spencer Dutton actually saw her; he actually looked at the woman she was and did not find her wanting, and she was helpless to resist the seduction in that. She sought in her mind for something safe to say, words that would still keep him interested enough not to walk away, but he spoke before she could.

"What about your husband, Taylor?"

She closed her eyes, unwilling to think about Jack now. "The last time I noticed, he was dancing, so I can, too."

"Yeah, first the blonde with the three-inch heels. Then the mayor's wife. And the Judge. And that woman in the black sequins. And the redhead who's—"

"My aunt."

"What?"

"The redhead's my aunt Eugenia." Her eyes still closed, Taylor inched closer to the broad width of his chest.

"The thing I want to know is, when is it your turn?"

Suddenly Taylor felt dizzy. She opened her eyes wide, focused with difficulty on the cleft in his chin. No more booze, she decided. She'd finished that last vodka too quickly. That would have to be it for tonight.

"Jack has danced with nearly every woman in the room except you," Spence said, almost growling the words.

"He likes to spread himself around." Hardly aware of the words they spoke, Taylor burrowed closer to ward off the dizziness. Sensing her need, Spence brought their clasped hands between them, finding a place between her breasts. It was an intimacy she'd never experienced with Jack. But then, Jack never sought intimacy with her, especially on a dance floor. Taylor wished fervently that she could wrap her arms around Spence, push her body closer still. Hunger and need swirled together inside her. She wished the lights would go out, that everybody would vanish and leave them alone, just Spence and her and the night and the music.

"Don't you mind?" Spence asked.

"What?" Her eyes fluttered open.

"What the hell's the matter with him?" Spence said, impatience tightening the line of his mouth. He had a nice mouth, she thought. She wondered how it would taste.

"You apparently are unfamiliar with politics," she said, speaking distinctly to keep her dizziness under control.

"I vote."

"Yes, well. That's hardly a familiarity with the political scene and the people who live and breathe it."

Spence's reply was merely a grunt. "Can I ask you a question?"

She sighed. "If I wanted to talk politics, I'd be dancing with Jack, Spencer."

"You're here, you're his wife, and yet he's hardly said two words to you all evening. Does he always leave you to fend for yourself? Is it your role just to look beautiful?"

The truth was too ugly to intrude on this moment. Taylor made a move to leave him, but his hold tightened.

"I'm sorry. That was a stupid way to say what I meant." Disoriented by alcohol and hurt, she struggled weakly to get away. "Taylor, Taylor, I'm sorry, sweetheart." The endearment, so softly urgent, stopped her. She held her breath, unused to an open expression of caring from a man.

"I think you're the most beautiful woman I've ever seen," he whispered earnestly in her ear. "You're sensitive and smart, you have two great kids, a nice family, you're educated and polished. But you've told me yourself in so many words that you're unhappy. What keeps you tied to Jack Sullivan?"

Scanning the crowd again, she searched for her husband and found him. Tall, dark, wickedly handsome, he was dancing with Eleanor now, who was gazing with dazed pleasure into his eyes. Taylor wondered if Jack was sleeping with Eleanor. Alcohol must have anesthetized her, she decided, because the thought of Jack's betrayals didn't strike the kind of pain in her heart that it should have. If he was screwing Eleanor and Eugenia, how much longer would it be before he seduced Suzanne?

She moved abruptly, breaking free of Spence's embrace. "I need some air," she gasped. Without waiting to see if he followed, she pushed her way through the crowd.

She was near the wide French doors when she almost collided with Jack. "Hey, what's going on? What's wrong?" he demanded, not realizing that Spencer Dutton was escorting her outside.

"She just needs some air," Spence told him. "I can take—"

Jack shot Spencer a hard look. "No, I'll take care of it." He clamped a hand on Taylor's arm, then turned and gave Eleanor a tight smile. "Catch you later, Ellie."

"Sure, Jack. Happy New Year."

"Yeah. You, too." Jack propelled Taylor through the crowd clustered at the doors. Before stepping outside, he stopped a passing waiter. "Bring us some black coffee and make it strong. We'll be on the patio. And bring my wife's coat."

The man nodded, then disappeared among the gyrating dancers.

Shoving the doors open, Jack forced her outside with a bruising grip on her elbow. Without her fur, Taylor felt the chill instantly. She took a quick, sharp breath of the icy air and felt more dizzy than ever. Her stomach lurched. She pressed her abdomen with her free hand.

"Oh, Jack, I—"

"Shut up." His features grim, he kept walking, giving her an impatient jerk when her foot caught on one of the patio bricks. No one was there to see her stumble or the impatience in Jack as he literally dragged her into deeper shadows.

"Please, Jack, I think I—"

"Sit!" An iron bench was secluded in an alcove beneath rampant overgrowth of English ivy. With a sound of disgust, he pushed her down on the bench and flung her arm away. With her arms wrapped around her for warmth, she leaned her head back against the hard, cold metal and breathed deeply.

Slowly. Take it ever...so...slowly. Don't...get sick. He'll be furious. He'll never forgive that. Punish...he'll punish...he'll...

"If you get sick, you dumb bitch, I swear you'll regret it!"

"I won't." She didn't have strength enough to say it firmly, but she wouldn't. She couldn't. Not here. Besides, he had reason to be disgusted with her. *She* was disgusted with her. *Stupid, stupid, stupid.*

Jack stood in front of her, legs forked in an attack stance. "What the fuck are you trying to do?"

"Jack, I—"

"Didn't I tell you before we left not to drink tonight?"

"Yes, but—"

"But nothing! God *damn* it! You lushes always have an excuse. Just like my stupid-ass mother. Drunk most of the time so you don't have to work, to think, to do anything except plague the hell out of the men in your life. Shit, I oughtta take a leaf from my old man's book and dump your drunken ass, and don't think I won't do it if you don't straighten up, Taylor."

He took a deep breath, raked a hand over the back of his head and held it at his neck. "Listen up, Taylor. The coffee's coming. You drink it and sober up. By God, I want you on your feet at midnight so you can stand beside me in there and smile and at least look good. You got that?"

She nodded, clamping her teeth to try and keep them from chattering. She was freezing, but the nausea had subsided somewhat. She saw movement behind Jack. It was the waiter looking a little wary. Her coat was draped over his arm, and he carried a tray with a polished chrome carafe and two mugs. Jack waited until he'd set the tray on a small table, then took the coat, dismissing the man with a crisp bill and a hard smile. Taylor closed her eyes wearily. Even when his temper was raging, Jack wouldn't let a potential voter see that side of him.

The moment the man was gone, Jack flung the coat at her. Taylor caught it awkwardly, needing no urging to put it on. It was soft and deliciously warm. While Jack poured the coffee, she sat huddled in its furry depths, her thoughts as desolate as the icy night.

"Here. Drink this."

She freed her hands, clasping them around the warm mug. The coffee was strong and bitter, but hot. She sipped it. Waited a moment, then sipped again. She felt nothing, just an abject yearning for the night to end.

With a snap of his lighter, Jack lit a cigarette and inhaled deeply. "What is it with the weirdo from California?"

She warmed her nose in the steam coming from her coffee. "Spencer's not a weirdo." The magic she'd felt in that one brief dance now seemed a thousand years ago.

"Take it from me, he's not your garden-variety production type. He's too quiet. Something peculiar about him."

"He's nice."

"He's nice." Jack mimicked her. "Just don't start thinking he's too nice."

Taylor knew when it was best to say nothing. She put the warm cup to her cheek, but Jack reached out, shoved it aside and, with an ungentle hand beneath her chin, forced her eyes to his. "Answer me when I talk to you, Taylor."

Some tiny remnant of pride stirred. "And say what, Jack? Okay, I won't think he's nice? I will try and think of him as a weirdo?" She sighed. "What difference does it make what I think, anyway? You can't possibly care. We've been here for four hours and not once have you danced with me. Every other woman under the age of sixty, yes. But not me. Your wife."

"Feeling neglected?"

"Shouldn't I, Jack?"

"It beats me how you feel anything. You don't stay sober enough to notice whether I dance with you or not."

"I notice. I see Ellie and Joanna Farnsworth and Christine

Brown and Lila Roberts and Eugenia. Especially Eugenia, Jack. I saw that look on her face while she was dancing with you."

He made a disgusted sound. "Are we back to that again?"

"I saw the two of you disappear into the lounge together."

"Because we had business to discuss."

"Oh, sure."

He reached out and took her cup. "If you're able to nag me about Eugenia, you must be sober enough to go back inside." He glanced at his watch. "It's eleven-thirty-five. Don't piss me off again, Taylor."

She refused to look at him. He swore, then dropped his cigarette and ground it out beneath his foot. "And stay away from the goddamn bar."

Leaving her behind, he turned and stalked back across the deserted patio, kicking at a chair leg that was in his path. Taylor watched him with a sullen expression, feeling angry and abused and humiliated. God, she felt so many awful emotions she longed to lay her head down and sob her heart out. Never mind that she was as much to blame for her misery tonight as Jack; he still had no right to treat her like that. Or to talk to her as if she were nothing more to him than one of his sluts.

Smoothing her hair with one hand, she tried to compose herself. Unfortunately, she couldn't sit here all night. She stood up cautiously. Between the coffee and the cold fresh air, the dizziness had passed. Terrific. Jack, as usual, had prevailed. She was recovered enough to go back inside and play her role at his side when the clock struck the New Year. But she was having another drink. Screw his orders. It was the only way she'd be able to stomach it. Plunging her hands deep into the pockets of her coat, she headed for the French doors.

TWENTY-FOUR

AFTER CHECKING HER COAT, Taylor went straight to the bar and ordered a drink. She lit a cigarette while waiting and surveyed the crowd, desperately hoping for a glimpse of Spencer. But he was gone. She was glad he hadn't witnessed that awful scene with Jack on the patio. If he had, he certainly would wonder what was keeping her tied to Jack. She wondered the same thing herself.

"Here you go, ma'am."

She turned and accepted the drink with a bright smile, then turned just in time to see Eugenia leave through a side exit. There was nothing in that wing except private areas. As she stood puzzling over where Eugenia could be going, Jack ducked through the same exit. More business? She didn't think so. With a defiant gulp of her drink, she left the bar and, bolstered by the kick of the alcohol, decided to follow them.

Once she was through the door, the noise of the party diminished. Strategically placed along the corridor were small conversation areas, each with a couple of chairs, a single table and a low-wattage lamp. Jack was nowhere to be seen, but as she moved silently forward, she heard his voice coming from one of the private dining rooms. The doors were the double swinging type, not designed to block out sound. Ditching her cigarette in a sand-filled container, she edged closer.

She recognized the hard, controlled fury in Jack's voice. He was using some restraint in keeping his voice low, but Taylor knew from experience that his words could be deadly. If he'd stolen a few minutes to have illicit sex, he certainly wasn't bothering with sweet words as foreplay. Sick at heart, Taylor leaned against the wall.

"Don't start with the bullshit, Eugenia. You knew what it meant from the outset."

Eugenia. Oh, God, it *was* Eugenia. Hands pressed to her mouth, Taylor took in a breath that shook her whole body.

"I didn't, Jack." Eugenia's tone was plaintive. "I went out with Tom because you asked me to. You said he was a friend of yours."

"It's business, Eugenia. You knew that."

"Yes, but—"

"No buts, damn it! He wants to hop into the sack with you, what's the problem?"

Eugenia's voice trembled with hurt. "I know you don't mean that, Jack."

"Hell I don't! I need Perkins. The closer you two get, the easier it'll be to keep tabs on the situation with Higgins."

"He's never mentioned anyone named Higgins," Eugenia said, her tone rising desperately. "He never mentions anything about business, Jack."

"He will. And if he needs a little persuasion, it's your job to apply it. Hell, you know some tricks. Use 'em, Genny."

Taylor heard a soft sob. Fool if she thought tears could soften Jack. If anything, weeping made him even more heartless.

"This is not a job, Jack." Eugenia's words were muffled, and Taylor guessed she was mopping at her tears. "You make it sound so...so sordid!"

"Knock it off, Eugenia. I don't have time for this shit from you tonight."

"Please, Jack, I can't do this."

He gave an impatient hiss. "Can't do what, for crissake?"

"You...you know. E-enter...t-tain your friends. It makes me f-feel so ch-*cheap!*"

"God*damn* it! Not you, too." Taylor heard him bump against a chair, then the muted thump as it crashed over. Eugenia would be wise to walk out right now, but Taylor knew she proba-

bly wouldn't. Taylor herself never did. Like a fool, she always
waited until she was slashed and bleeding before she retreated.

"Why is it women pick the dumbest times to get all wounded
and sensitive? You're too good for the likes of Tom Perkins, is
that it, Eugenia? He's a doctor, for God's sake. He's rich. He's
connected to some of the most powerful money in New Orleans.
Jesus, you've been sleeping with me. Why not Perkins?"

Propped against the wall, Taylor felt pain erupt as if her
whole heart were being eviscerated. Here was proof of his infidelity. She pressed her glass against her forehead.

"Because he's not you, Jack." Eugenia was weeping openly.
"Don't you see? He could be the richest man on earth and it
wouldn't matter. It's you I love. I would never have encouraged
Tom Perkins if you hadn't insisted."

"And you didn't have a clue why I'd want you to do that?"
Jack's voice was rich with sarcasm.

"No! You know I didn't."

"Don't give me that shit! You knew!"

"I didn't!" Eugenia wailed. "I didn't…I didn't…"

"I don't believe this," Jack muttered, moving to the door.
"Get hold of yourself, Eugenia. You make me sick. *Women*
make me sick. First Taylor, now you. I'm going back to the
party, and when I do, I want you to find a bathroom and fix
your face. I'll tell Tom you had a personal phone call and that
you'll be out in a few minutes. You got that?"

"It doesn't matter."

"What?"

"Tom's gone."

"Gone? What do you mean, gone?"

"When I told him I wouldn't sleep with him, he left."

For a moment, there was stark silence in the room. Outside
in the corridor, Taylor could actually feel Jack's fury.

"Tell me," Jack said in a dangerously quiet tone, "that you
don't mean what you just said, Eugenia. Tell me you didn't do
something so inconceivably stupid."

Taylor closed her eyes, gathering courage, then pushed the

doors open. "What's the matter, Jack? Things getting a little sticky in here?"

Jack whipped around, only momentarily startled to see her. "Taylor! What the hell are you doing here?"

Taylor waved her drink, indicating the room. "You're not exactly in a restricted area. Granted, it's secluded here, but nothing's secluded enough for the conversation I just overheard."

Eugenia made a pitiful sound. "Taylor, it isn't what—"

Taylor looked at her. "What it seems? Oh, I think it is, Eugenia, but you'll understand if I don't want to hear anything you have to say." She turned again to Jack. "This is a real drag, isn't it, Jack? Both of us giving you a hard time tonight. Me whining over your neglect and now Eugenia refusing to play the whore for you."

"You're both drunk," he said with disgust.

Taylor took a defiant swallow of the drink in her hand. "You're probably right. I'm feeling pretty numb. I must be, or else I'd feel something besides utter disgust now that I know for a fact that you've been sleeping with my aunt."

"It's no big deal."

Eugenia made a small wounded sound.

"I guess the affair's over, Eugenia," Taylor said, her gaze not leaving Jack. "You won't believe this, but you're lucky."

"Oh, Taylor." Eugenia's face crumpled, and she suddenly looked every one of her years.

"Yeah, we're pathetic, aren't we?" Taylor felt like crying, too. Instead, she brought her drink to her lips with a trembling hand. Vodka would have to do instead.

She gave a startled cry when, swearing viciously, Jack drew back and knocked the drink out of her hand. Pain bloomed in her lip as the glass crashed into the wall and shattered. Ice, liquid and shards of crystal flew in all directions. Taylor backed away from him warily, tasting blood. His explosive temper was no surprise. He was mean-spirited and said the first cruel thing that leaped to mind, but until now he'd never struck her.

"I told you to stay away from the booze, didn't I?" he demanded, his face twisted with rage. Catching her by the wrist, he pulled her from the doors and kicked them shut. Pain shot up her arm as he twisted her around and shoved her into a seat, cracking her elbow sharply on the corner of the table.

"Did you think I didn't mean it? Are you really as stupid as you've been acting lately?"

Eugenia took a step and touched his arm. "Jack—"

"Shut up, Eugenia! You've done enough tonight."

In the chair, Taylor cradled her throbbing arm. "Why Eugenia, Jack? Did you get some kind of bizarre satisfaction from seducing my aunt? Did it amuse you to see your wife and your mistress together at Riverbend?" Her voice quivered with pain. "Do you realize how sick that is, Jack?"

"God, you *are* drunk." He rammed a cigarette in his mouth and lit it. "Spare me the whining."

"I'm not going out there, Jack."

Inhaling once more, he studied her through a haze of smoke. Taylor could almost read his mind. Gauging her anger. Wondering how far she would go. Assessing the potential for scandal.

Still silent, he handed his cigarette to Taylor, and she took it and drew the smoke deep into her lungs. The nicotine steadied her instantly. She'd needed it and he knew it, damn him. She didn't thank him. She owed him nothing. Nothing.

"Did you hear me, Jack? I'm not—"

"Shut up." His eyes flicked from her to Eugenia, who was weeping silently. If he forced them to play out the evening, there was the possibility one or the other would embarrass him.

Suddenly Taylor was desperately tired. "I want to go home," she said. She couldn't speak for Eugenia, but a public appearance was truly beyond her. Jack apparently agreed. With another muttered curse, he walked to the doors and pushed one of them open far enough to check the corridor.

"Stay here, both of you," he said in disgust. "I'll get my car and pull it around to the service entrance. Wait a few minutes, then take the exit through the locker rooms near the pro shop." He paused, giving them time to digest his instructions, then added, "I'm not playing games here. I don't want either of you to say or do anything else stupid tonight. *Anything.* You got that?"

He stalked out without waiting for a reply.

IN THE SUDDEN SILENCE after he left, Eugenia moved to a chair and sat down heavily. She looked into Taylor's eyes and knew the full extent of her folly. She had always known that her obsession with Jack could destroy her, but somehow she'd managed to push from her mind what it would do to Taylor—and others—once her secret was out. Well, now she knew. The price was going to be paid in broken hearts—Taylor's, the children's. And Annie's. For Eugenia could not imagine that Taylor would close her eyes to what she'd learned tonight.

Oh, Annie, you were right. What happened to me? To my pride? Where was the shame that should have forced me to end it?

Sounds from the ballroom suddenly crescendoed. Eugenia looked dully at her watch.

"Ten! Nine! Eight!"

The countdown started. "We should go now, Taylor."

"Seven! Six! Five! Four!"

Without a word, Taylor stood up. She appeared to sway momentarily. Closing her eyes, she groped for the back of a chair until she steadied herself.

"Three! Two! One!"

"Are you all right?" Eugenia put her hand out, but stopped when Taylor shifted to avoid her touch.

"I'm okay."

"Happy New Year!"

All hell broke loose in the ballroom, but neither woman noticed. Before Eugenia could do it for her, Taylor pushed blindly through the swinging doors, beyond caring whether anyone saw them or not. And no one did. The corridor was empty. Eugenia glanced at her with concern. Taylor was deathly pale, her face dewy with a fine sheen of sweat, but her expression warned Eugenia to keep her concern unspoken. Another thirty feet and there was the exit. Jack was waiting.

He flipped his cigarette away. "Where the hell were you?"

"Happy New Year to you, too," Taylor said, but with no more defiance. She looked empty of any emotion.

He shoved her full-length mink at her, then tossed Eugenia's lined cape over. Eugenia slipped into it gratefully, while Taylor fumbled with her coat in a search to find the sleeves before finally getting it on.

"I want you to drive," he said to Taylor, then jerked the door of the car open at the driver's side. "Get in."

Eugenia felt alarmed. "Oh, Jack, I don't think Taylor—" But one look at his face and Eugenia's protest died.

"I want Taylor to drive because I've got some things to say to both of you. Now, into the back like a good girl." He waited with impatience while Eugenia climbed in meekly, then closed the door. Before he made it into the passenger's seat, Taylor had started up with a roar.

"Goddamn it! Go easy on the gas pedal. The engine's been sitting. It's cold. Hell, it's twenty-five degrees." Slamming his door, he yanked at his tie, pulling it loose and undoing the collar button, all in a few practiced moves. Then with a quick look through the rear window, he told Taylor to go.

He swore again when she peeled out too fast. "Slow down! Son of a bitch, we're trying to get out of here without attracting attention, Taylor. Can you, just once, do as you're told?"

"You said go, we're going." She braked abruptly at the end of the drive, sending Jack forward toward the dash. Before he recovered, she pulled out into traffic and accelerated in a screech of tires.

He cursed viciously and fumbled to fasten his seat belt. He looked up as she wrenched at the wheel to avoid sideswiping a line of parked cars. "Are you gonna slow down or do I climb over this console and give you a driving lesson, Taylor!" he yelled.

Eugenia scooted forward in the back seat. "She wasn't feeling very well as we were leaving the club, Jack."

"I'm fine now." Taylor squinted hard at the headlights approaching in the opposite lane. She swerved at a blast from another driver's horn, missing him by a hair. Cursing, Jack ordered her to stop. "Are you trying to get us killed?"

"What does it matter?" She took the next corner on squealing wheels, and Eugenia realized Taylor was weeping silently. Tears glistened on her cheeks.

"Pull over, goddamn it! I mean it, Taylor. Pull over!"

She didn't respond. They were now on a residential street, but the speedometer was climbing fast. Ahead was a four-way stop, but Taylor ignored it, zipping through and narrowly missing a car halfway across the intersection. The driver stood on his brakes while blasting his horn angrily. Accelerating again, Taylor drove another half mile at a fast clip before rounding a curve. Water lying in the street shone in the headlights. She hit her brakes and the car began to fishtail. Jack lunged for the wheel but was hampered by his seat belt. He ripped it off as the car jumped the curb onto a grassy median and plowed down a row of small trees. He had his hands on the wheel now, cursing viciously, but the console was in the way when he tried to get his foot on the brake. When he finally managed it, he brought the car to an abrupt stop. Taylor cried out as her head banged the side window. Eugenia flew forward, landing in a tangle of arms and legs against the back of Jack's seat. Only Jack managed to come through the ordeal unscathed.

For a few seconds, there was silence in the car. Jack, enraged rather than scared, breathed like an angry bull. Taylor whimpered in pain. Eugenia was dazed, barely able to comprehend their narrow escape. She struggled weakly to get back into her seat, then leaned back, utterly spent.

"I can't believe this *shit!*" Jack wrenched open his door and climbed out. "Be out by the time I get around there, Taylor!" he ordered, rocking the car with the force of his temper as he slammed his door.

Taylor was dazed, but not enough to ignore Jack. She fumbled at the handle, trying to get the door open, but her fingers seemed unable to obey her brain. Giving up finally, she rested her head on the steering wheel in abject misery.

"Just hold on a few minutes longer, Taylor," Eugenia managed to say. Shaken and aching from her tumble, she felt near collapse herself. Closing her eyes, she prayed the night would soon end. Beyond that, she would not think.

Jack yanked the door open. "Did you hear me, Taylor? I said get out."

"I can't," she whispered.

"Knock if off, damn it! I'm not in any mood to coddle you after that stunt. Why didn't you tell me you were drunk?" He grabbed her arm and dragged her out of the car.

Still fuming, he spotted a twig stuck in the side mirror and yanked it off. "Fuckin' women drivers. When I dump you two, I'm going back to the club, where I'll be with people who aren't fuckin' drunk or whining and I'll try to patch up the damage with the folks I invited tonight. I've still got to do business with them Monday morning." His lips curled with contempt. "If that's all right with you ladies, of course."

He expected no reply and there was none. Then he noticed that Taylor hadn't moved. "What are you, deaf or something? I said get in the other side."

Taylor's hand went out to steady herself against the car. She rested her forehead against the cold metal and closed her eyes. Her face was as pale as milk. "I can't, Jack. I think I'm going to be sick."

"Don't...even...*think* it, Taylor," he ordered, "or I swear I'll get in this car and drive off. I'll leave you here for the buzzards if you get sick now."

She clamped both hands over her mouth and gagged.

"Shit." Quickly sidestepping, Jack moved a safe distance away as Taylor bent forward and vomited. While she retched, Jack radiated disgust and exasperation and seething rage. In the car, Eugenia could do nothing except wait in misery. Never had she felt such despair.

Taylor, too weak to stand, had sunk to her knees. Jack eyed her coldly. "Can we go now?"

Trembling, her teeth chattering, Taylor nodded, then waited wretchedly for him to help her. Muttering curses, he grabbed her by the arm and pulled her roughly to her feet. Grudgingly, he thrust his handkerchief at her, then opened the back door, where Eugenia sat huddled in the seat. "You two can keep each other company. I must have been out of my mind to ever get mixed up with either one of you!" He shoved Taylor onto the seat beside Eugenia, then slammed the door and threw himself into the driver's seat. He started the car with a roar, rammed it into gear and pulled out into the street.

Taylor moaned with the rapid acceleration, and Eugenia tried to help her get more comfortably situated. She was deathly pale. And so still. Eugenia imagined the scene tomorrow morning between Taylor and Jack and sighed at her own ugly part in it.

In the driver's seat, Jack glared straight ahead, obviously intending to ignore them. Eugenia guessed he'd drop her at her cottage and then Taylor at the big house. She wondered if he would leave Taylor to manage on her own. She wondered if Jack had any feelings left for Taylor. Eugenia knew he had no feelings left for her.

"Taylor might need a doctor, Jack," Eugenia said. There was a trickle of blood on her temple where she had bumped the window when the car went out of control.

"She doesn't need a doctor," he growled. "She needs to sober up."

"But there's some blood on—"

"Good. Maybe next time she'll listen when I tell her to lay off the booze."

"Alcoholism is a disease, Jack," Eugenia said wearily. "Taylor needs help."

He swore viciously. "Do you fuckin' hear yourself, Eugenia? What are you now, a marriage counselor?" He rolled his eyes, thumping the wheel with the heel of his hand. "I can't believe what I'm hearing. Do me a favor, will you? Leave me the pleasure of dealing with my lush of a wife."

Closing her eyes against the cruelty of his words, Eugenia turned her gaze to the side. The last thing she wanted was to talk about Jack's relationship with Taylor. She was dazed and sickened by what she'd glimpsed tonight and bitterly disillusioned by the things Jack had wanted her to do for him so he would profit on a business deal. Eugenia touched her forehead. How could she have been so blind? So gullible?

Opening her eyes, she stared at an oncoming car. It zipped past and she realized that Jack was driving very fast. And although there wasn't much traffic on this road, there were icy patches, and they'd already barely escaped tragedy once tonight. They shouldn't count on unlimited good luck. She thought about cautioning him but feared another scathing attack.

She saw the clock on the dash. Not yet thirty minutes into the New Year and her whole life had unraveled. The way she felt right now, she simply didn't care. With her gaze fixed on a single red light ahead, she thought of the shameful, selfish lie she'd been living and knew the time had come to pay the piper.

The red light was drawing closer. It was a biker, she thought, only now catching the muted rumble of his machine. She gasped, realizing that Jack was gaining on it too fast. The roar of the engine was loud now. She could see clearly the biker's black-and-yellow helmet. Long blond hair straggled out, blowing in the wind. He wore a leather jacket. A huge eagle was formed in a pattern of silver studs on his back.

"Goddamn bikers," Jack muttered. "Freaks and druggies."

Eugenia braced one hand against the armrest, suddenly frozen in horror. If Jack didn't slow down, he was going to plow right into the boy.

"Jack! Watch out!"

At the last second, Jack swerved, but still grazed the biker's rear tire. Motorcycle and rider were catapulted in a high arc. To Eugenia's horrified gaze, bike and rider seemed to separate in midair. The biker was hurled head over heels down the steep gulley and disappeared abruptly, while the motorcycle bumped and bounced, tumbling end-over-end before slamming into a stand of small trees.

"Omigod, omigod…oh…oh…oh…" Eugenia realized she was close to hysteria and clamped both hands to her face. Jack was not stopping. *He wasn't even slowing down!* With a squeal of tires, Jack accelerated and the car shot ahead. Eugenia turned frantically in her seat and looked behind, but there was no sign of the biker. Of anything. It was too dark. There was nothing. No winking red taillight. No biker with an eagle on his back.

She leaned forward and shook Jack's shoulder urgently. "We have to stop, Jack!" she cried, looking back again. "That biker took a horrible tumble. He could be—"

"Shut up, Eugenia!"

"But Jack—"

"Shut…up." If she'd learned anything tonight, it was to heed that tone. *But the biker could be dying!*

She gathered courage. "Jack, we have to go back."

"We're not going back, Eugenia." He captured her gaze in the rearview mirror. "At least not now. Do you realize what would happen? As soon as it came out that I was involved, there'd be a shitload of publicity. Bad publicity."

She stared as if she'd never seen him before. In fact, she never had seen the Jack Sullivan she was seeing tonight.

He made a disgusted sound. "Oh, for God's sake, stop looking at me like that. I'm not going to abandon the kid. I'll drop you off at Riverbend—it's only a couple of miles from here— then I'll go back. Whole trip won't take more than ten minutes."

"He could die in ten minutes, Jack."

"Yeah, well, he was hogging the road. He should have moved over when I honked."

"I didn't hear your horn, Jack."

The look he gave her was deadly. "I honked."

Eugenia settled back, shaken. She felt trapped in a nightmare. She looked down at Taylor's white face and almost envied her being unconscious. The sad part was that Taylor would wake up tomorrow morning still married to Jack Sullivan.

It was only a few more minutes until they reached the gates at Riverbend. Jack slowed, pointing his remote at the ornate iron, drumming the fingers of his left hand impatiently while the gates swung slowly open. Tossing the remote on the dash, he gunned his car and they sped through, then up the winding lane to the turn just past the big house that led to Eugenia's cottage.

Jack stopped the car at her front steps, but she didn't wait for him to open the door. Whether he would extend that small courtesy now, she seriously doubted. Once, that thought would have hurt cruelly. Tonight she was too disillusioned to feel much of anything. Only emptiness. And a bleak acceptance of the inevitable. Pulling her cape closely around her, she hurried to her front steps.

"Hold up, Eugenia." Jack stopped her before she made it to her door.

"It's late, Jack," she said, not looking at him. "I'm cold." She didn't think she could ever be warm again.

"Hey, now…" He chucked her beneath her chin suddenly, all easy charm. "I know you're upset. That was a bad scene back there. Hell, these things happen. And on New Year's night yet." He grinned wryly. "Sometimes you can't buy a break."

"It was certainly a bad break for that biker."

"Can you believe how he was weaving on the road? And talk about bad timing. Just four more miles and it would have been somebody else who clipped him."

His callousness was appalling. Not meeting his eyes, she rubbed her forehead. "I need to go inside, Jack."

"Not before we talk." The charm vanished.

She clutched the cape at her throat and raised her eyes to his. "All right. Say what you have to say, Jack."

"I don't have to explain the facts of political life to you, Eugenia. You've been in this family long enough to know." He shifted suddenly, putting his weight on one leg, and looked away from her to the quiet, beautiful grounds of Riverbend. "This is a gorgeous place, isn't it?"

"I've always loved Riverbend."

"And you'll always have a home here. Many times I've heard Charles and the Judge reassure you about that, Eugenia."

"They've been very generous," she said stiffly.

"You wouldn't want to do anything to screw that up, babe."

"No." Her hold on the cape was tighter than ever. He was so calm. Whatever devil that had possessed him for the past hour was now safely under control. It would have been amazing had it not been so sinister.

"I'm going to turn around now and dump Taylor's ass at her mama's house." A nod of his head indicated the big house. "And then I'm going back to see what I can do about that kid. He's probably okay. Maybe knocked out from the fall, but I just barely scraped the back wheel. Hell, it's not as if I hit him broadside or anything like that."

Eugenia felt a despair so dark that it was true pain.

"And you're going to let me take care of it, right, Eugenia?" He waited, but she was incapable of giving him the answer he demanded. "You're not going to do anything, are you, Eugenia?" he repeated.

"No," she whispered, feeling tears fill her eyes.

"Because you surely wouldn't want to jeopardize your sweet little setup here at Riverbend, would you?"

"No." She barely moved her lips.

"But in case you were thinking you should say something, it makes me wonder how the family would take it—an outsider trying to stir up scandal or bring shame on the Staffords. No, I know you wouldn't want to be responsible for that, would you, sugar?"

She shook her head.

"Oka-a-ay." Before she realized his intention, he took her face in his hands and kissed her on her lips. Once. Just a brief touch. "You've always been such a good girl," he whispered in a low tone that had always thrilled her. She was chilled now, and she shivered.

"Cold, babe?" He kissed her again, ever so softly. "Then you'd better hurry inside. It's cold as a witch's tit out here."

She stepped away from him and reached blindly for her key. Thankfully, she found it quickly and slipped inside. Before she closed the door, he spoke again in a tone as sweet as a lover's.

"'Night, sweetheart."

TWENTY-FIVE

LEANING BACK AGAINST the door, Eugenia waited until the sound of Jack's car faded into the night. She put her fingers to her lips and imagined she could still taste him there. Musky, erotic, irresistible. Her throat tightened and her eyes filled. Shame and despair welled up with her tears. How could she still feel anything—*anything!*—except disgust for Jack? Tonight proved how cruel he was, how heartless and completely without honor, so why was the thought of cutting him out of her life so devastating? How could she still long to feel the dark power of his passion? Savage sometimes, even frightening, but compelling, enslaving. How would she live and never again run her fingers through his black hair, never again know the taste of his mouth, never feel the hard, flat plane of his stomach, never trace beyond the silky arrow of black to that curling nest and the promise of ecstasy? How could she still yearn for just one more night with him?

It was sick. It was deranged. It was evil.

She was all those things.

Covering her face with her hands, she sank in agony to the floor. Her cape billowed around her like a dark blot. There was something evil in Jack, and her obsessive need to have him in her life made her evil, too. After tonight, after he'd expected her to whore for him, why didn't she hate him? She had to find the strength to cut him out of her life or she would truly lose her soul.

She had already lost her daughter. Sometimes the look on Annie's face was a knife in Eugenia's heart. How it hurt to sit across the breakfast table on a morning when Annie knew she'd been with Jack and see the look in her eyes—sadness, bewilderment, pity, loss. And anger. Annie was so angry with her. Her obsession with Jack had blighted the beautiful relationship they'd once shared. A torrent of grief overwhelmed her and she wept brokenly.

And the boy. The biker on the motorcycle. He could be dead. If he was, his death was on her hands as much as if she'd driven the car herself. She should have forced Jack to stop. And if he wouldn't stop, she should have opened the door and jumped out. She should have screamed at him, demanded, begged, grabbed the wheel. Oh, God, she should have done *something*.

She looked dully toward the telephone. She could call the police department and find out if they had discovered the accident yet. If not, she could report it. But Jack would be furious. And if she didn't call and Jack didn't go back to check on that boy...

Rising shakily, she went to the phone and dialed the police department. On the mantel, the clock struck two. More than an hour since it happened. Maybe there was still time....

"Percyville Police."

Eugenia opened her mouth, but no words came.

"Percyville Police. Hello? Hello!" the dispatcher prodded with irritation.

The phone cord was knotted in her hand. "I— Is— I wanted to know if—I mean..."

"Who is this?"

"Just a—I'd rather not say. What I wanted was—"

"Yes? You wanted..."

"Has there been an accident on Lincoln Road?"

"What kind of accident?"

"A motorcycle?"

She heard the dispatcher say something to someone nearby, but the words were muffled. She caught "witness...kid on the bike..." but nothing more.

"Did you see it, ma'am?"

"Uh, not really." Eugenia closed her eyes. Another lie.

"If you'll give me your name..."

"Just tell me, is he okay?"

"You tell me, ma'am. Were you a witness?"

"Is he okay!" she demanded frantically.

"I'm afraid not. He's dead. So, if you—"

Dead. Oh, God. Eugenia replaced the receiver. A boy was dead, and his death was on her hands as well as Jack's. She stared at her shaking palms, imagining them red with the blood of an innocent. Shuddering, she buried her face in her hands. She had never meant to hurt anyone. Anyone. She'd just been so lonely when Jack noticed her. Annie gone to California. No career of her own. No identity, really. Jack made her feel alive. Desirable. Utterly female. Now all of it wiped out in one black night.

She flung her cape aside and rushed into the bathroom. Fumbling in the cabinet, she found her prescription of Valium. Hands shaking, she shook two tablets out and put them in her mouth. Then she took another and swallowed. Still trembling uncontrollably, she filled a glass with water and drank.

She stood at the sink for a few moments, then lifted her eyes to look in the mirror. She was a repulsive person. Weak. Annie was right. Jack was like a drug and she was addicted to him. He was a liar, a cheat, an adulterer...a murderer. As was she. It was hit and run, pure and simple.

She stood with tears streaming down her face. The sequins on her dress were a thousand eyes winking slyly. Suddenly she fumbled to find the zipper. Out of the dress, she threw it at the open door of her closet. Her bra and shoes and panty hose followed. She fumbled at the diamond earrings—gifts from Jack—and hurled them across her bedroom. They fell on her carpet and lay like ice chips on sand.

Stripped now, she wouldn't—couldn't—look at herself. Uncaring of her nakedness, she walked to the living room and found a bottle of whiskey. Unlike Taylor, she had no particular love for alcohol, but for what she had in mind, it was necessary. With a glance at the label, she emitted a short, bitter laugh.

Southern Comfort. She chose a beautiful Waterford tumbler, one of six that Lily Stafford had given her, and filled it. As she walked back to her bedroom, she forced down a big swallow. The Valium was kicking in. She was more calm now, almost numb. Black despair was giving way to a resigned melancholy.

When she reached her closet, she rifled through her clothes until she found a soft, rose-colored robe, a gift from Annie for Christmas the first year she'd been in California. She put it on and tied the sash belt. Then, stroking the satin lapels of the robe with sadness, she walked over and sank down on the bed.

She was deeply, mortally ashamed of her obsession with Jack. She did not believe there was a way to make amends to Taylor for what she'd done. There was no act of contrition great enough to absolve her. And all for a man who had never really cared. Who didn't seem capable of love.

She opened the top drawer of her bedside table, where she kept a box of stationery. She found a pen, and using the box as a hard surface, she wrote on the cream-colored vellum, "My darling Annie." But the words blurred and she had to find a tissue to dry her eyes before she could continue.

She wrote steadily for a few minutes. The words came without difficulty, as if she'd been thinking them for a long time. She didn't have to pretend with Annie. Annie knew everything. She would understand. She might not forgive such an act of cowardice right away, but she would after a while. She had a big heart, Annie.

When the note was done, she signed it and sealed it in an envelope and wrote her daughter's name on it. She didn't want anybody else reading it first.

Then she picked up the bottle of Valium and poured all the pills into her palm. It was a new prescription, so it should be enough. She swallowed them, four at a time, taking a small gulp of Southern Comfort with each dose. She didn't want to take a chance that she would gag and they'd come up, half dissolved, before they'd had time to work.

When she lay back, the whiskey sloshed alarmingly in her

stomach, but she kept very still. She was truly numb now. In every way. That was good. She had been in pain for so long.

I am not a whore.

Don't hate me, Annie.

Jack...Jack...I love...you...so....

ANNIE INSISTED ON STAYING with her mother in spite of the paramedics' insistence that she leave. They'd pushed. She'd refused again. One of them had even taken her arm, thinking in her shocked state that she would go along with whatever was suggested to her, but she'd flared up, her red curls fairly crackling. She would not leave her mother.

Eugenia was dead, of course. All the procedures and the gadgets in those little black bags and the electronic gizmos and the medical wizardry couldn't change that. She was dead and she had been for hours.

There had been an accident on the interstate. Suzanne had been anxious because she'd been forced to use a new baby-sitter. Her regular one, a student from Millsaps, was home for the holidays, and if Caleb woke up and heard the inevitable noise—firecrackers and rockets, car horns—she didn't want him to find himself with a stranger.

In the end, it was Annie who had cause to regret the delay. If only they'd left fifteen minutes earlier. If only the accident had affected eastbound travelers instead of westbound traffic. If only she'd gone with her mother to the club as Eugenia had asked.

"We're going to have to take her now, ma'am."

Annie blinked, then nodded dully. "Yes. Where?"

The paramedic shifted, moved his gaze to the stretcher where her mother lay covered in something white. Not a sheet. Surely not plastic. Not yet. Please. The black belt fastened across the white drape seemed too harsh for Eugenia. She never wore black and white. Too stark. Too strong. Eugenia liked pastels. Her dress tonight had been pale pink, the sequins iridescent. Never black and white for her mother.

"The hospital."

"Oh. Okay." Hospital. Morgue. Autopsy.

Oh, Mama. Why?

"Is there someone you'd like to call?"

Suzanne, but later. Not yet. She shook her head. "No."

"Are you sure?"

"Yes." She looked at the envelope in her hand. "I'm fine."

"Well, we'll be off, then."

"Yes. Thank you."

She watched dully as the gurney was rolled out of the bedroom. There were a couple of turns to be made as they headed for the front door. She saw their faces as they wheeled her mother out of the cottage for the last time. Blank. How did they do that? Annie wondered. How did they mask all feeling in these moments? Did they see suicide so often that they felt nothing?

"You take care, now, ma'am," the paramedic said, then nodded respectfully. Solemnly. As befitted the occasion.

She watched them slide the gurney into the ambulance, then flinched when the doors were closed with a final, solid thud. Beside the ambulance, the blue lights of the accompanying police car pulsed obscenely. There was no one home at Riverbend, she guessed, otherwise someone would have seen the commotion. Someone would have come. If it had been Jack, she honestly believed she would have pulled out the old shotgun that had belonged to her stepfather and shot him dead.

But no one came.

She waited until they'd pulled out, then closed the door and took the single piece of folded stationery out of the envelope. She'd read it only once, but she could almost recite the last few lines.

You will be disappointed in me, Annie, for taking this way out. You were right all along about Jack. He doesn't love me. He's like a drug and I'm addicted, but there's no clinic that can teach a person how to stop loving, is there?

I don't think Taylor can forgive what I've done, and so I don't think I can bear to face the consequences. I've disgraced myself, you, and the Staffords.

One final thing, my darling Annie. You will be so angry, you will want to confront Jack. Don't do that and don't blame him, I beg you. I take full responsibility for everything I've done.

I do love you, Annie, and I'm so proud of you. I pray that you will find happiness someday and that it will be as bright and shining and as free as your spirit. Don't make the same mistakes I did.

She had signed it simply "Mama."
Annie crumpled the paper in her hand and wept bitterly.

TWENTY-SIX

IT WAS ALMOST NOON when Taylor finally woke up on New Year's Day. From experience, she knew to lie perfectly still. The smallest movement sent painful shock waves through her head, followed by sickening nausea. Whether or not she made it to the bathroom was a toss-up. So to speak, she thought with black humor, and breathed slowly, slowly.

After a few minutes, she stirred ever so slightly and pain burst in her head like fireworks at a carnival. God, she was going to have to get a handle on this. What had made her sneak that first drink so early in the day when she knew—she *knew!*—that she'd need to be in control for the party at the club.

The club.

Something flashed in her memory, then vanished. Just a slip of a thought, a tiny peek behind a dark curtain. Not enough to pin down anything concrete. Just enough to bring her heart to her throat. Something bad, she felt it. She hated when that happened. A glimpse of a picture was worse than no picture at all. It was so frustrating.

She lay still for a few moments and tried not to think. About anything. But of course that never worked. With her body immobilized, her mind moved in frantic circles. She remembered how nasty Jack had been before they left for the club. She remembered leaving for the club. She remembered dancing with Spencer. She remembered what he'd said and how nice it had been until Jack had dragged her out to the patio and she'd felt so sick. And cold. And miserable.

She remembered going back in. She'd needed another drink to fortify herself for the moment when she would have to stand beside Jack in front of all those people and pretend everything was all right. Pretend that Jack was as nice as he looked. Pretend that she was as nice a wife as she looked. Pretend that she hadn't made a mistake in marrying him. Pretend to be the good girl her parents had reared.

She moaned, bringing her hand to her splitting head, gathering the strength to open her eyes. Holding her breath, she took a first fleeting glimpse of the day and realized that she was in her old bedroom at Riverbend. Why Riverbend? Oh, God, this was what she hated about the blackouts. They'd been supposed to drive home to Jackson after the party. But no. Again, she had a quick flash of memory. *She* was driving, not Jack. Leaving the club with Jack beside her. And in the back seat...Eugenia. Oh, God, Eugenia.

She flung the covers aside and stumbled toward the bathroom, beginning to retch before she reached the door.

A few minutes later, Jack found her standing at the dresser, pulling her hair away from her face with a comb. No makeup had been invented yet for masking a hangover. Their eyes met in the mirror.

"Jesus, you look like hell, Taylor."

She reached for a T-shirt and pulled it on over jeans she'd found in a chest of drawers. Thank God he hadn't come in ten minutes earlier. At least she'd had time to brush her teeth and swallow three aspirin.

"I'd like to go home now, Jack," she said quietly. What she had to say to him could wait until they were back in Jackson.

"Worried about the kids?"

She felt a sharp pang. She'd barely thought about Trey and Gayle since she woke up. They were safe, of course, with their nanny, but what did it say about her that she hadn't even checked? Worse yet, it had been her responsibility to call Nancy last night to tell her of their change of plans. Had she? God, she didn't even remember last night. She was going to give up drinking. This time she really meant it.

"I thought so." Jack wandered to the small television set

recessed in a bookcase and turned it on. He adjusted the volume and appeared to be watching it. "Don't fret, babe. I took care of it for you."

"Have you checked on them this morning?"

"I have."

"They're okay?"

"We'd be on our way to Jackson if they weren't."

They would. Of course. She was a nitwit. She stood twisting her hands, then remembered Eugenia. Anger rekindled inside her. "I still want to go home. We need to talk."

"About what?"

"You know, Jack. I didn't drink too much to wipe out *that* memory."

"You admit you don't remember everything that happened last night?"

"I remember Eugenia."

"Yes, a real tragedy there."

"The tragedy is that you even started it in the first place."

He gave her a look of polite puzzlement. "I don't think I follow you, Taylor."

"You follow, all right, Jack. Don't try that bogus innocence with me this morning. You want it in plain English? I'm talking about your affair with my aunt Eugenia."

"Oh, that. Hey, people do strange things sometimes. I guess she was lonely. With Annie in California, she had no one. I was sympathetic." He shrugged.

She stared, amazed at his insouciance. "You played the Good Samaritan, is that it, Jack?"

He appeared to give that some thought. "Well, considering what's happened, I guess you could call it God's will and all that."

Fury made her tongue-tied for a moment. He was so damned arrogant. And glib. He'd never admit to being in the wrong. But if he thought she was going to overlook an affair with her own aunt, he was crazy. "We shouldn't discuss this now, Jack. We should wait until we're back in Jackson."

"Discuss what, the affair or the tragedy?"

"Tragedy?" She shook her head irritably. "Why do you keep using that ridiculous word?"

"I don't know what you'd call suicide if not a tragedy. I'm sure that's the way Annie would look at it."

"Suicide?" Taylor covered her forehead with her fingers, as if to cushion the throbbing pain behind her eyes. "What are you talking about, Jack?"

"You mean you don't remember?" He turned to the TV set and found a station in the middle of a news broadcast. With a glance at his watch, he faced her again. "I thought they might have something on the noon news, but we must have missed it."

Taylor was shaking her head, recognizing a ploy Jack used when he wanted to torment her. A hint here, a suggestive remark there, then the thrust straight to her heart. "For once, Jack, would you please dispense with the games? You're dying to tell me something. What is it?"

He shrugged. "I guess there's no tactful way to say this, but...Eugenia's dead."

"What?" She stared at him with disbelief.

"You heard me, babe. She's dead. Killed herself."

"No."

"Yes. It happened last night after we left her at the cottage."

"No. She wouldn't. I don't believe it."

"Hell of a shock, huh?" He lifted the curtain at the window and gazed out.

Taylor slowly sank down on the side of the bed. "But... she didn't...I mean, she seemed...upset, but not..." Frowning, she tried to picture Eugenia's face when the two of them talked while waiting for Jack. "She really was upset, but not... suicidal. She tried to apologize, but I wouldn't let her. I didn't want to hear anything she had to say just then, but she still didn't seem...I mean, you'd have to be *devastated* to take your own life, wouldn't you?"

She glanced up and found Jack watching her with an unreadable expression on his face. "Are you sure about this, Jack?"

"Annie called early this morning."

"Why didn't you wake me?" she cried.

"She had Suzanne with her. I guess she called her sometime in the night and she drove down from Jackson. Your folks are over there now."

Taylor got to her feet, moving slowly. Not from the hangover, but from shock. She began pacing the room. Snippets of memory were zipping through her brain like tiny bright arrows, too fast to catch. She simply couldn't remember.

"We were in the car," she began, her gaze fixed in front of her as she paced. "Eugenia was in the back seat. Oh, it's so hard...I just don't...." She stopped and looked at Jack. "Did you suspect she was that upset?"

"Who can tell with women?"

For once Taylor ignored his sarcasm. She put two shaky fingers to her head, thinking hard. "She was talking about somebody while I was outside that room. A man. Somebody who wanted to—" She looked up at Jack. "No, *you* wanted her to sleep with one of your business cronies. It hurt her, what you wanted her to do."

Jack dismissed her words with disgust. "She knew the way the game was played. She has a few drinks, then when it comes to putting up or shutting up, she suddenly regains her integrity. She picked the wrong time to play coy."

"Eugenia doesn't drink much. I don't think she was drunk."

"How would you know? *You* damn sure were."

"I've just told you, Jack. I remember more than you think about last night."

"Oh, yeah? Well, how about weaving all over the road, do you remember that? You were an accident waiting to happen."

"Then why did you make me drive?"

"Yeah, that's the question I was asking myself last night."

She stopped suddenly, searching the room as if some answer lay in its corners. "This is getting us nowhere. I need to go to Annie. I can't begin to imagine what she's thinking...feeling.

Her mother—" She looked at Jack, chilled at her thought. "You don't think she knows about your affair with Eugenia, do you?"

He was reaching for his jacket, draped over the back of a chair. "Nah. Eugenia was paranoid about keeping it from Annie." He shrugged into the jacket, then gave it a couple of tugs before checking his reflection in the mirror. "Uh-uh, no way."

"I'm going over there right now."

"Suit yourself."

With her own jacket in her hand, she stared at him. "I don't understand you, Jack. Don't you feel anything?"

"Yeah. I'm just about fed up with the screwups women can cause in a man's life." He pocketed his keys and stalked irritably to the door. Pausing, he looked back at her. "Oh, one more thing. Last night will be the last time you're gonna embarrass me by drinking yourself shit-faced. I've made an appointment for you to check in at Greenbriar in Atlanta."

She stared at him, stunned.

"Six weeks and they guarantee you'll come out clean and sober, a reformed alcoholic."

"A hospital?" A jail. Oh, God.

"No, not a hospital, a rehabilitation center. What's wrong? You think you don't need it? After last night, you think you can still handle it? You think it's normal to lose twelve out of twenty-four hours once or twice a week? Well, it's not. So I've decided to take care of the problem, and you will cooperate like a good girl."

"Oh, but, Jack—"

"No buts. It's a done deal, Taylor." He reached for the door-knob. "No sense in both of us hanging around here today, so I'm heading back to Jackson. I'll send Nancy back with the kids in the Volvo. Hang around as long as you feel you need to."

She flinched as the door closed with a bang.

After he was gone, she stood clutching the denim jacket, feeling as if she were falling into an empty black well. Shipped off to be dried out like the troublesome lush he believed her to be. She crushed the jacket to her chest to keep her heart from falling right out.

What would everyone think?

The truth, of course. That she was too weak to handle the job of being Mrs. Jack Sullivan. She had no formal career, and the only responsibilities she had were to be a good wife and mother, and she was a failure at both. God, what would the Judge say when she learned that her oldest daughter was going to be shipped off to sober up? Taylor closed her eyes in despair. At least it was out of the state.

She moved across the room to the television set. Before she reached it, she heard the newscaster's wrapup of local news.

"Death on Lincoln Road…Percyville youth…motorcycle… apparent hit-and-run…"

She realized she was standing with her hand suspended in midair. The words had produced a quick flash of memory, something dark and sinister. She struggled to bring it into focus, but the pain in her head was suddenly too much. She groaned, barely hearing the announcer reporting the dramatic reduction in accidents from the night before. Credit went to the designated-driver program and joint efforts of law enforcement and civic groups.

And no thanks to idiots like me.

She snapped the television off and shoved her arms into the denim jacket. Annie. She must get to Annie.

SUZANNE HELPED ANNIE sort through the cards and letters and expressions of sympathy after the funeral. There were many. Eugenia had been a loving and caring person with dozens of friends. Why someone with so much to live for had chosen suicide was a mystery to Suzanne. There was nothing to be learned from Annie. She was bitterly silent.

Suzanne checked off a name from the list in front of her and pulled another card from the stack. Without reading the return address, she slipped the folded note from the envelope. For a moment, she simply gazed at the gray embossed letters that danced on the white paper. *Mr. and Mrs. Ben Kincaid.*

She lay the note down and rubbed a finger gently over the embossed words. Who was she, Ben's wife? Was she beautiful? Was she smart? Was she good enough for Ben?

With an ache in her heart, she opened the note with hands that weren't quite steady. Her face softened at the sight of his handwriting. Bold and slashing, yet gentle in his expression of sympathy to Annie.

Suzanne's gaze stayed on his name a little longer than it should, then moved to the postscript.

My wife, Jill, and I are now the parents of twin boys. They're four months old.

Suzanne set that note aside for Annie to answer.

PART III

TWENTY-SEVEN

October 1997

"MOM, CAN I DRIVE this morning?"

"Hmm?" Suzanne sorted through the files stacked on her bedside table until she found the two she needed. Reaching for the briefcase on the bed, she popped it open and tucked the files inside, then straightened up, gazing around her with a vague frown. "Caleb, have you seen my desktop calendar?"

Caleb walked straight to her dressing table, picked up the small electronic notebook and took it to her. "You always look at it when you're putting on your makeup, Mom."

"Oh. Yes, thanks. 'Preciate it." She opened the calendar, checked to see when she and Taylor were on for lunch, re-checked the time court convened this morning, snapped it closed and tossed it into her briefcase. Only when she was satisfied that she had everything she needed for the day did she straighten and really look at Caleb.

"Now, what was it you asked, honey?"

He was shaking his head, smiling. He moved his hands on an imaginary steering wheel. "Car. Me drive. You passenger."

Suzanne drew up her shoulders with real regret. "Oh, Caleb, don't do this to me again. You know you have to wait until you're sixteen."

"Aw, Mom, everybody drives now."

"Except you. And that's the way it is, at least until you get that learner's permit, which you will have in a couple of months."

"Nobody'll know, Mom."

"But what if we have an accident?"

"We're not going to have an accident."

"But what if we did, Caleb? How would it look, me running for district judge and my fifteen-year-old son driving illegally?"

"You're unopposed, Mom. You *can't* lose the election."

"Oh, yeah? Shows what you know. If I'm caught acting as if I think the law doesn't apply to me, I would definitely be in for some rough publicity."

"Who're they going to vote for, 'None of the above'?"

She chuckled, hefted her briefcase from the bed and tossed it to him. "Here. Make yourself useful."

He caught it deftly, then waited for her to collect two more files before following her down the hall. "I feel like a wuss sitting there while you chauffeur me around."

Suzanne smiled. "I sort of like it. Reminds me of when you were little. You were so cute, buckled up in your car seat, pretending to drive with your little yellow plastic steering wheel."

He groaned. "Mom, please…"

She shrugged. "I can't help it. You *were* cute."

"I can't wait to get that permit," he grumbled, snagging his jacket from a coat tree beside the front door.

"And then you'll be agitating for a car." Suzanne stopped at a cherrywood table. "Where are the keys, Caleb?"

He dangled them in front of her. She made a grab for them, then punched him playfully on the arm. "Let me guess. You've already backed the car out of the garage."

He grinned. "You don't have to thank me. It was nothing."

"Truly." Closing the door behind them, she gave him a gentle shove, and together they went down the steps. As usual, he forgot her legs were shorter than his and took off across the lawn, forcing Suzanne to try to keep up. He'd just finished a growth spurt and was now almost six feet tall. And still he hadn't completely grown into his big feet and hands. She was continually amazed when she looked at him. It really did seem only a few short years since he'd been content to ride in the back seat in his car seat.

Caleb waited until she unlocked the car, then climbed into the passenger side. "Actually, Mom, I've been meaning to have a talk with you about a car."

She backed out and pulled away from the house. "Sure, son. What'll it be—a Jag, a Porsche or a garden-variety BMW? The sports model, naturally."

He crossed his arms and gazed straight ahead. "That's okay, be funny. I know you're thinking about it, too."

She slowed at the intersection and gave him an amused look. "You're reading my mind nowadays?"

"Jason Briggs is getting a motorcycle."

"In your dreams, kiddo."

"See, it could be worse. I'm only asking you to consider a safe, conventional mode of travel for me. Say, a…well, a '94 Mustang.' Previously owned, naturally, but hey, I'm easy."

"Then how about a '96 Toyota Camry?"

"We've already got one," he retorted.

"We can share."

They turned and looked at each other, then both burst out laughing. "Good try, buddy-boy," Suzanne said, feeling a rush of love, "but I think we'll leave such decisions on the back burner for a while."

Caleb slouched back in the seat, making himself comfortable. "Okay. I'm a patient man. Besides, that was a trial run for the real argument when I'm ready to present my case."

He'd been talking about becoming a lawyer ever since he was old enough to understand his mother's job. And his grandmother's. And his uncle's.

Dear God, maybe it was in the genes.

She zipped through the traffic signal at the intersection where the school was located and turned into a curved drive leading to the entrance. Caleb had the door open on his side before she was completely stopped. "Have you got lunch money?"

"I'm not the one who misplaces my notebook, loses my keys and forgets to eat, Mom."

"That reminds me, did you eat breakfast?"

"Cereal, toast and juice, a banana, a cinnamon roll and a piece of that pound cake. Did you?"

"Caleb, you know better than to eat cake for breakfast!"

"Just kidding. I had a couple of those ice cream sandwiches instead."

"*Now,* you're kidding."

"You claimed they were low-fat when you were eating one last night."

She rolled her eyes. Lately, she never seemed to get the last word. "Be careful at football practice, okay?"

He climbed out, then glanced back at her with a grin. "Yes, ma'am. And I'll try not to get my clothes dirty, Mommy."

"Watch your mouth, you hear me?"

"Uh-huh." He got ready to close the door, then leaned in to look at her. "Don't you hear the Kent Group case today, Mom?"

She sighed. No matter how she played it, he always seemed to know her judicial calendar. It came with the territory, she supposed, but she hated the idea of Caleb feeling any concern about her cases.

The whole scene was still new to her. It was hard to believe that she was a chancery judge. She'd been appointed by the governor when her mother had suffered a stroke eight months ago. After more than fourteen years in the district attorney's office she had been ready for a change, but filling her mother's shoes hadn't been the change she'd expected. Still, she was flattered and pleased and fiercely determined to show the governor that he hadn't made a mistake.

"I know it's today, Mom, and that citizens' group that brought the suit is gonna be all over you like white on rice. If your decision goes against them, they could get mean."

"The courtroom is a very safe place, Caleb. There are armed guards everywhere, you know that."

"Yeah, well, there's no armed guard watching your back in the parking lot, Mom. Just be careful, you know what I'm saying?"

"I will, honey." Behind him, Suzanne could see his friend Jason approaching. She blew Caleb a kiss. "Love you."

"Yeah, Mom, me, too."

She stayed where she was, watching as he and Jason loped off across the lawn. They were soon joined by several of their buddies. In the way of teenage males, they met with a lot of high-fives, backslapping and general horseplay. Suzanne smiled with amusement. There was enough testosterone flowing in that group to conduct a small war.

She put the car into gear, warmed with the conviction that Caleb stood out even in a group of kids generously blessed with good health and driving energy. Beyond his dark good looks and intelligence, there was something about him that drew people. Suzanne knew she was hardly an unbiased observer, but any mother would be proud of a son like Caleb. He seemed to have it all.

Except a father.

With a sigh, Suzanne checked the rearview mirror and pulled away from the curb. She made it a point never to dwell on Caleb's fatherless state, and she definitely couldn't afford any distractions this morning.

SUZANNE HEARD THE amplified voices of the protesters before they came into view. Although she had expected something, the size of the crowd was a jolt. Protesters lined the sidewalk, their hand-lettered signs moving up and down in rhythm with their chants for justice. Police units were parked at equal distance from each other, their pulsing blue lights adding to the general chaos. Uniformed cops with their billy clubs at the ready kept the demonstrators confined to the sidewalk.

Suzanne sped past the courthouse, relieved to see that the entrance was relatively free of traffic. If the crowd surged into the courthouse itself, there really would be chaos. Caleb must have second sight, she thought, turning at the corner. The best she could hope for would be to avoid recognition until she could park and get into the building from the rear entrance.

Two uniformed policemen guarded the gate shed at the parking lot behind the courthouse where she had a designated slot. She nodded to the cop on her left who waved her through, then drove the Camry into the space marked Judge Suzanne Stafford. She took a moment to collect her briefcase, her shoulder bag and a couple of loose folders that were too bulky to fit into the briefcase, then opened the car door.

People seemed to erupt out of nowhere, including the press and their terrifying paraphernalia. Microphones were shoved at her. The black eye of a camera materialized in front of her. The *zsit-zsit* of rewinding film hissed from all directions. A protester jiggled his sign so close it brushed her shoulder. Someone yelled, "The Kent Group wants to poison our kids! You got an obligation to this town, Judge Stafford!"

The rear entrance to the courthouse was about forty feet away, but the distance yawned as wide as the Sahara Desert. Clutching her briefcase and the files close to her body, she ducked her head and made straight for the door.

"Judge Stafford, will you rule in favor of the citizens' of Caldwell County or will you cave in to big business?"

Suzanne recognized Amanda Mason, a journalist whose write-ups about her were consistently critical.

"Do you know the identity of the Kent Group as individuals, Judge?"

Another hostile reporter. What *was* this?

"Is the rezoning legal, Your Honor?"

A protester this time, a farmer in a plaid shirt wearing a baseball cap with John Deere over the bill, said, "That land butts up to mine, Your Honor. I ain't gonna stand for it."

Suddenly her bag was jerked from her shoulder, snagged by the pole of the protester's sign. Suzanne made a grab for it, lost her grip on the bulky files and felt them slipping from her grasp. A hand shot out and caught them as a masculine arm went around her waist. There was no time to think. She was lucky just to stay on her feet as her rescuer propelled her through the crowd, up the back steps and into the courthouse.

The door banged shut behind them, and she sighed with relief at the sudden hush inside.

"Are you okay?"

It was the chief of police. She closed her eyes, holding a hand against her chest. "Wow. I think so, Jim. Thanks."

He watched her with concern. "You're sure? You're pale as a ghost."

She reached for the files he held and managed a shaky laugh. "I'm fine, just a little shaken up. How on earth did they get beyond the police barrier?"

"Who knows? Here, take your bag, but let me carry these files and make sure you get into your chambers without another incident." Jim Rankin's military background showed in the hard glint in his eyes and his rigid jaw, not to mention the crack efficiency of the department since he'd taken over a year ago. Suzanne suspected that somebody would answer for the breach in security. Rankin was reputed to have zero tolerance for screwups. That aspect of his character made her feel a bit wary sometimes, but right now it wasn't unwelcome.

They crossed the wide marble foyer quickly, then took the stairs to the second floor, where her chambers and the courtroom were located. She went inside, calming her law clerk's anxiety with a few words before entering her own private domain. She went directly to the credenza behind her desk, put her briefcase down and dropped her bag into the top drawer. Then with a sigh she slipped out of her coat. Jim took it out of her hands.

"Sit down and collect yourself." He hung the coat neatly on a hanger. "That was a sorry stunt out there. You need to put it out of your mind before court convenes."

She hid a smile. "You mean I'll need all my wits about me on this one?"

"It's a nasty case, Suzanne."

She sat down abruptly, her smile gone. "Don't I know it."

"A bunch of ill-informed citizens have no business trying to tell you how to do your job."

"It's still a free country, Jim. And they may not be ill-informed. That man's life will be directly affected if Kent is allowed to develop the land the way it's rumored they intend to. I can't help but sympathize with him."

"It's zoned for a landfill, for God's sake. Kent can put anything they want on it."

"And that farmer's within his rights to object."

Rankin gave her a sharp look. "Have you decided against the Kent Group? Is that what you're telling me?"

"I wasn't *telling* you anything. We were discussing the rights of individuals under the constitution." Her expression turned cool. "Thanks for your help getting through that crowd. Next time I'll keep a sharper lookout and hopefully avoid another ambush."

Rankin rubbed his neck, looking chagrined. "I'm sorry, Suzanne. That was out of line, wasn't it? You can't discuss a case. I, of all people, ought to know better."

"Actually, you should." She smiled to take the sting out of her words.

"You'll do the right thing."

"The *legal* thing."

"Well, sure. Goes without saying."

"Thanks again, Jim," she said, wanting to be alone now. "If you'll excuse me..."

At the door, he stopped and looked back at her. "We're still on for the dinner theater tonight, right?"

"If there's anything left of me after court recesses," she said. Apparently taking that for assent, he nodded and left, closing the door quietly behind him.

Suzanne had held Jim Rankin off firmly at first, as she did all men, but he was so persistent that she'd finally gone to dinner with him. To her surprise, she had enjoyed it. An attractive man in his early forties, Jim kept much of himself private, and she sensed that in a romantic relationship he would be complicated and moody. Like herself, he was long divorced, although he never mentioned his ex-wife. But, then, she never mentioned Dennis Scott.

It would be the fourth time she and Jim had been out together, and she wished she'd remembered which case she had scheduled today when she had agreed to the date. Dating anytime was stressful to her. Today she was sure to be spent by the time court recessed.

She pushed her worry over the upcoming date aside. A lot could happen between then and now. With a glance at her watch, she opened a brief filed by the Kent Group. Forty minutes to show time.

"ALL RISE!"

With the bailiff's call, the courtroom quieted abruptly. Suzanne followed him out of her chambers, her black robe flowing around her ankles. In spite of the quiet, tension hummed in the packed courtroom. She allowed the faces of the spectators to blur in her mind but felt the force of their attention just the same, in spite of the peculiar tricks she had devised to distance herself. As she quickly climbed the steps to the bench, she prayed for wisdom to deal with the sticky case today with half the skill of Lily Stafford.

"Chancery Court of the State of Mississippi," the bailiff was intoning. "The Honorable Suzanne Stafford presiding." With a nod, Suzanne indicated that all present be seated.

Her gaze went directly to the plaintiff's table, where Candace Webber was to present the case for the citizens' group. "Is the plaintiff ready?"

Candace rose, unsmiling, no hint of their prior history in her expression. "We are, Your Honor."

Your Honor. Suzanne wondered if she'd ever get used to hearing that form of address, especially from Candace, who'd mentored her for five years in the district attorney's office. But that had been a long time ago. While Suzanne had stayed on for another nine years before leaving Grayson Lee's little empire,

Candace had opted for private practice. Now she specialized in cases such as the one before the court today.

"Proceed, Ms. Webber."

"Thank you, Your Honor. We request an injunction from the court against the Kent Group, Your Honor," Candace began without benefit of notes. "On the fifth of September, the Friday before Labor Day this year, the County of Caldwell called a special meeting to hear a request for a variance in the zoning of a ten-acre tract of land. That variance was granted. But it was an illegal procedure, Your Honor, in that the citizens of the County of Caldwell were not given sufficient time to consider the matter and to exercise their rights, whether for or against the request for variance."

Suzanne had read the briefs outlining the case for the citizens' group. It was a sleazy act by the county commissioners. The meeting had been held late at night just before a major holiday weekend and had escaped the attention of many residents who might have complained had they been aware of it. The intent, but not the letter of the law, had been violated. Candace knew that, of course, but was arguing persuasively, in spite of the fact that the citizens' cause was all but lost.

Suzanne settled back as the attorneys wrangled back and forth, but unless Candace came up with a miracle, the citizens were doomed. Suzanne was going to be forced to dismiss the injunction, and the investors comprising the Kent Group would capitalize once again on a project that smelled to high heaven of political patronage.

"This is reprehensible, Your Honor. It's another example of corporate greed, a bunch of fat cats taking advantage of the good people of Caldwell County."

Vincent Terry, Kent's attorney, was shaking his head. "Candace, Candace, we all know the way your heart bleeds, and your argument tugs at my heartstrings. But you're on very shaky ground here. I think you should go back and have a look at the facts in this case. My clients—"

Suzanne banged her gavel and motioned with both hands to the attorneys. "Approach, please."

With a bewildered look, Terry dropped his notebook on the table and walked to the bench. Slick and polished, he wore his six-hundred-dollar suit as if he'd been born in it. He was confident and arrogant and almost too handsome. His law firm was based in Dallas, Texas, with offices in Jackson, Little Rock and New Orleans. He was the best money could buy. Candace, smiling faintly, rose from the plaintiff's table and approached with him.

"What's the problem, Your Honor?" Terry still wore a perplexed frown.

Suzanne signaled a pause to the court stenographer, then leaned forward, covering the microphone with one hand. "In my courtroom, Mr. Terry, you will address Ms. Webber properly and with respect, is that clear?"

Still feigning confusion, Terry shrugged. "Why, sure, Your Honor. Of course. Haven't I been doing that?"

"Do not use Ms. Webber's given name again, Mr. Terry."

He rolled his eyes.

Suzanne's eyes flashed. "And other such wordless expressions of disdain will not be tolerated, either, Mr. Terry."

He cleared his throat. "Sorry, Your Honor."

Suzanne nodded. "Now, if you think you understand the etiquette of my courtroom, we can proceed."

"Understood," Terry said, his mouth a tight line.

"Thank you, Your Honor," Candace said without expression. Suzanne dismissed them both with a nod and signaled the court reporter to begin again.

TWENTY-EIGHT

SUZANNE WAS BREWING tea when Candace stuck her head in the door a few hours later.

"Got a minute, Your Honor?"

Suzanne smiled and waved her inside. "Tea?"

"If you'll lace it with something stronger than lemon."

"How about Southern Comfort?"

"Perfect." Slinging her briefcase onto the leather couch, Candace flopped down, pushed her shoes off and leaned back with her eyes closed. "What is it they say in Texas? I feel like I've been rode hard and put up wet."

Suzanne set a steaming mug on the coffee table in front of the couch and finished filling it to the brim with whiskey. "It was a heartbreaker, all right."

"Is that a note of sympathy I hear?"

"You know as well as I do that I would have loved ruling against the Kent Group. I had no choice. The variance was legal." She sat down and cradled her tea in both hands. "Sneaky, sleazy, underhanded and, to use your word, reprehensible, but legal."

Candace opened one eye. "Wait. Next you're going to say lifting the injunction hurts you more than it hurts me."

Suzanne grinned and sipped her tea. "Consider it said."

With a disgusted snort, Candace straightened up and reached for the mug. "This is why you're going to make such a fabulous judge, my friend. You did the right thing up there today with such style. Lily would be proud."

"You think so?" Even if Candace was teasing, the words felt wonderful. But deep down Suzanne was worried that her mother would have found a way to let the injunction stand, at least until there was less public furor. She said as much to Candace.

"Your mother wasn't a miracle worker, Suzy. She couldn't conjure up law that wasn't written, even if the defendants are sneaky, sleazy and all those other things you said."

"I suppose." Suzanne stared into the bottom of her mug. "But this makes three times the Kent Group has been represented in my court, and all three times I've been forced to rule in their favor. I just hate it, Candace."

"They're good, Suzy. They have the best money can buy."

Suzanne wrinkled her nose. "If you're referring to Vincent Terry, then all I have to say is yuck."

"Me, too, even if he is pretty as a pup." Candace took a healthy swallow of her drink. "You know who he reminded me of?"

"Jack Sullivan," Suzanne said promptly.

"You, too?"

"Maybe Jack coached him."

Candace was instantly alert. "You think Jack is part of the Kent Group?"

Suzanne sighed. "You know I can't say that, Candy."

But how she'd love to give Candace ammunition to link Jack with this sleazy deal and hopefully blow his chances at the governorship. Who else but Jack knew the inside workings of this county's government so well? Who else knew out-of-state firms were searching for a hazardous-waste landfill site? Who had the connections in Jackson to smooth the way so the fat cats who own it could cut a deal? Moreover, Jack's fingerprints were all over the land in question. But only she and Ben Kincaid knew he had swindled Lucian to get it. And Ben was on the other side of the earth.

"Anyway—" Candace frowned, tugging at her ear "—since the Kent Group is rumored to have ties with gambling interests in Las Vegas, it wouldn't be a good thing for Jack's name to be linked to them right now."

"Not with his campaign in full swing, no."

"You know something, Suzanne?" Candace sipped from her mug. "Jack Sullivan is such a charmer that I don't think people would shy away from voting for him even if he was linked to shady interests."

Suzanne gazed through the window, where sounds of angry protesters mixed with the noise of rush-hour traffic. "You're right, of course. No matter what comes up, he stays fifteen points ahead of Jude Blanchard in the polls. He's going to be the next governor of the state, like it or not."

Candace got up and poured more Southern Comfort into her mug. Turning to Suzanne, she chuckled. "Maybe it's Jude's name."

Suzanne shrugged. "He's a nice guy, but he's a loser. I can't think of a candidate who stands a chance against Jack. He's handsome, he's glib, he's uncannily adept at tapping into things that interest ordinary people."

"Worse than that," Candace said, tossing off the rest of her drink, "he's smart."

Suzanne was at her window, peeping through the blinds. "Right. The election's his to lose."

Candace moved to the window. "What's going on down there?"

"I think I've pissed off my constituency from the looks of those placards," Suzanne replied.

"Forget the placards. Look at their faces," Candace said, grimacing. "You're going to need a police escort to get away from here, honeybun."

A sharp knock at her door startled them. "It's open," Suzanne said, moving to her desk.

Jim Rankin opened the door. He gave Candace a brief nod, then said to Suzanne, "If you're ready to leave, I've got a team waiting at both exits to get you out of here. One of my men will drive your car and I'll take you home personally."

"Do you think that's necessary, Jim?" Suzanne couldn't remember Lily Stafford resorting to such dramatic measures after a controversial decision.

"That crowd's pretty hostile. I can keep them away from you until you get into your car, but you shouldn't be on the road alone. Whether you let me drive you or not, I'm going to see that you get home safely."

"My subdivision has security gates," she reminded him.

"Yeah, but there are several miles between the courthouse and that neighborhood, Suzanne. No use asking for trouble."

"He's right, Suzy." Candace walked to the couch and slipped her shoes on. "I can go out there and try to reason with my clients, but I can't guarantee they will listen. You have Caleb to think about. Let the chief take you home."

The decision was made easier when glass crashed into the wall just below her window and a roar went up from the crowd. "I'm ready if you are," she said, taking only her shoulder bag and holding it against her midriff.

"Come on," Rankin said, catching her beneath her elbow. "They've got both exits covered, and most of the television cameras are at the front. I think there's less chance of a serious effort to harm you if half a dozen Minicams are on hand to record it."

They rode downstairs in the elevator, accompanied by two of Rankin's men. But the moment Suzanne stepped into the lobby, she felt the full force of the crowd's anger. No amount of armed policemen could make her feel safe plowing her way through the sea of protesters lining the steps and walkway to the police cruiser twenty yards away.

Again, she tucked her head and prepared to be hustled through the crowd. The protesters who'd accosted her earlier were like Sunday school students compared to this crowd. The bright lights of a Minicam blinded her momentarily and she stumbled, clutching at Rankin to stay on her feet. Somebody yelled an obscenity and she cringed, understanding why famous people sometimes cursed their celebrity.

"Give us a statement, Judge Stafford," Amanda Mason demanded, thrusting her microphone in Suzanne's face. "Why did you rule against the citizens of this county?"

"No comment!" Jim Rankin growled, shoving the microphone aside.

"Hey! Let's hear what she has to say," the man in the John Deere cap yelled.

"You're unopposed this term, Your Honor, but just wait until next election day!" This from a woman carrying a baby.

"Poisonous waste kills!" a bearded youth screamed, waving a crudely lettered sign.

"Hold on," Rankin said in her ear. "Just a few more steps to the car."

Suzanne nodded, looking around apprehensively until she met the gaze of the youth carrying the sign. He seemed no older than Caleb, but there was a look in his eyes she prayed never to see in her son's. In the next moment, he had shoved the sign at an older man and something changed hands between them.

It happened so fast. One second she was looking at the boy, and the next, he was ripping the top from a plastic cup, leaning back and winding up to throw. Suzanne saw it all as if in slow motion. The liquid was a dingy yellow color. That's all she saw as it flew at her in a long, suspended splash. She screamed, dived sideways and came up hard against the deputy on her left. The mess splashed on her sleeve and skirt, drenched her legs through her panty hose. It was so quick that she didn't smell the stench until the boy darted past the startled deputies and disappeared into the crowd.

"Son of a bitch!" Rankin literally swept her off her feet and carried her to his cruiser. Suzanne felt the odd pressure of a hand on her head to protect her as she was thrust inside, then she was on the seat, the breath whooshed from her when she failed to catch herself with her hands. Blocking the door with his body, the chief fanned his men out with a few succinct orders, then climbed in beside her. His pale eyes were furious. "Are you okay?"

"Y-yes." She made a face and brushed gingerly at her soaked sleeve. "Wh-what do you think this is?"

"I don't know," he snapped. "But it had better not be anything worse than stinking water."

She laughed nervously. "I think it's rotten eggs."

He shifted and pulled his handkerchief from his pocket. "Here, you can try and mop some of it off with this. Murphy! You got a roll of towels up there, or some tissues?"

The driver groped on the floor beneath his seat and came up with a roll of kitchen towels. The chief took them, ripped off a long strip and wiped some of the mess from Suzanne's foot. "Take off your shoes," he ordered. "They're ruined."

"And my skirt," Suzanne said. Her hands were shaking so badly it was all she could do to tear off more towels. After a moment, she leaned back against the seat and closed her eyes. "I can't remember my mother ever coming home smelling like a waste-treatment plant," she said, feeling as though her bones would never be solid enough to hold her again.

"There's nothing worse than a bunch of environmentalist wackos," Rankin said with disgust.

"People are frightened," Suzanne said, taking a deep breath. "I wish I'd had any other option today."

"Well, you didn't. The law's the law. This is a black-and-white issue, and the law's on the side of the Kent Group. These idiots will just have to accept it." He settled back, jamming his hat more firmly on his head. "I'll tell you one thing, that punk kid is going to wish he'd stayed home where he belongs. If I can find a way, I'll nail his ass. Teach him and anybody else who gets another cockamamy idea like that a lesson they won't soon forget."

"He's too young to prosecute, Jim."

"I'll find a way."

"Just see me before you do anything," she said, too exhausted to argue with him. Caleb was uppermost in her mind now. She needed to get home before the evening news. It would be less shocking if she was with him when he saw the attack.

When they finally turned into the main street in her quiet neighborhood, it had never looked so good. But instead of soothing her, everywhere she looked were Sullivan for Governor campaign signs.

Beside her, Jim Rankin whistled softly. "Your brother-in-law doesn't have to worry about the politics of your neighbors, does he? Judging by the number of signs, he's got these folks in his pocket."

"Hmm."

He shifted to get a better look at her. "You don't show much interest in Jack's campaign, Suzanne. Why is that?"

The cruiser turned onto her street. Two blocks to go. "The last thing Jack needs is my input on his campaign."

"Maybe not directly, but you want to let the voters know you're on his team. Hell, the sky's the limit for Jack Sullivan. He's the most charismatic politician to come down the pike in a long time. Anybody in his inner circle is going to be set for life."

And you'd like to be one of them.

Suzanne rubbed her forehead, ashamed of the nasty little thought. It was probably unfair of her to lump Jim Rankin with all the others hoping to ride on Jack's coattails. Besides, her own mother had often made the same observation. Suzanne almost shuddered at the thought of Jack Sullivan as the wind beneath her wings. She'd rather walk on hot coals.

Thankfully, they were pulling into her driveway. Her hand was on the door to get out before the car stopped. "I guess I'm old-fashioned, Jim, but I'd rather make it to the Supreme Court on merit, not because Jack Sullivan is married to my sister."

"Damn," he said softly, his look almost comical. "Seems like I put my foot in it on that one."

She pushed the door open, scooping up her soggy shoes in one hand. "Seems like."

"Mom! *Mom!* Are you okay?" Caleb was charging across the lawn toward her.

"I'm okay, son. Oh, watch it. Stay back." She held him off with her free hand. "I smell to high heaven."

Caleb grabbed her shoes. "What was it that guy threw on you, Mom? I couldn't tell on TV. It looked nasty. Really gross. It wasn't acid or anything like that, was it?"

"No, nothing like that." So much for shielding him from reality. "It wasn't toxic, unless a person can be poisoned by stink alone."

"Go get your mother a pair of slippers, Caleb," Rankin ordered while handing her purse to the boy so that he was free to assist Suzanne.

One look at Caleb's face and Suzanne said hastily, "That's okay, honey. I don't need shoes. I'll just—"

Rankin frowned. "Your sidewalk is rough, Suzanne. Tell him to—"

"She can walk on the grass," Caleb said, his dark eyes stormy. "She does it all the time."

"She's had a shock, for God's sake!" Rankin snapped. "Can't you see that?"

Caleb's eyes flew to Suzanne, all guilty concern. His quarrel was with the police chief, not his mother.

"I'm fine, Caleb." Suzanne took her soiled shoes from him and dropped them onto the ground. Her son wasn't one of Jim's rookies, she thought irritably, working her feet back into the wet pumps while holding Caleb's arm. For some reason, Caleb had rejected all Jim's efforts to be friendly. Couldn't Jim see that barking out orders to Caleb like a marine drill instructor was guaranteed to alienate him further? With a tight smile at both of them, she started across the lawn, squishing with each step.

"Mom, wait up! That's gross."

"It certainly is!" she rejoined, aware that both males were trailing after her. The moment she reached the front door, she kicked the shoes off. "Thanks for the ride home, Jim. I would invite you in, but I'm heading straight for the shower."

"Yeah, Mom, you need to wash that stuff off. Right now."

Rankin managed a smile for Suzanne. "He's right about that, Suzanne. But don't forget our plans for tonight. I'll be by to pick you up around seven-thirty."

"You're going out? After what happened?" Caleb looked at Suzanne with disbelief.

Rankin glanced at his watch. "That'll give you a little more than two hours, okay?"

No, she wanted to scream. She wasn't used to having garbage hurled at her or to being verbally abused by the citizens of Percyville or having to endure harassment by the press. She needed a bath and, above all, solitude. The last thing she needed was to mediate a turf dispute between Caleb and Jim. "I don't know, Jim. I—"

"Tell you what. I'll come by and we'll play it by ear. You don't want to go out, we won't. We'll order something in."

"Well…"

He touched her cheek. "Trust me." With a sharp little salute and a quick look at Caleb, he turned on his heel and walked back to the cruiser.

"Come on inside, Mom." Looking concerned, Caleb held the door open. Both her shoes were in his hands and her purse was tucked beneath his arm. "Are you sure you're okay?"

With a grimace, she held her skirt away from herself. "I'm fine, honestly. Just wet and sticky. Ugh! I'm going straight up to shower. Let the answering machine pick up any calls. I don't want to talk to anybody." She started up the stairs.

"What'll I do with your shoes, Mom?"

She glanced back at him and couldn't help smiling at the expression on his face. "Trash 'em. The quicker the better."

"Boy, they really stink."

"And so do I."

"What do you think it is?" He held them out gingerly.

"Who knows? Probably rotten eggs. Nothing else smells quite like that. Don't worry. It washes right off and it's harmless."

Caleb glanced toward the television screen in the living

room. "I think I recognized that guy who threw the stuff on you, Mom. He's a year older than me and a little bit weird. He lives out in the county. Near where they want to dump all that stuff."

"I bet you're right, honey."

Caleb's gaze returned to her. "I guess he must have felt pretty strong about the situation to do something that drastic."

"No doubt."

"What'll happen to him, Mom?"

Standing at the foot of the stairs, Caleb looked up at her anxiously. Now that he saw she wasn't harmed, there was no question where her son's sympathies lay. He recognized the dilemma of the beleaguered landowners, something that hadn't given Jim Rankin a moment's concern.

"Mom?"

"He's a juvenile, Caleb. He'll get a stern lecture from a judge and have to do some community service."

He nodded. "That's cool."

"Glad you approve." She turned to climb the rest of the stairs, smiling. At the top, he called her name again.

"Are you going to let that guy pressure you into going out when you don't want to?"

"I made the date several weeks ago, Caleb. This case was on my calendar and I knew I'd be stressed out. I should have taken that into consideration. It would be rude to cancel at the last minute."

Caleb gave the bottom step an irate kick. "Yeah, well, the chief's an asshole."

"Caleb..."

He put up his hands, backing away. "I'm going, I'm going."

SHE GOT OUT OF THE SHOWER considerably refreshed, but no more enthusiastic about going out with Jim. Was Caleb right? Was she being pressured? Probably. She tossed her towel aside and reached for sheer black panty hose. Jim was no different from the other men she'd dated over the years. After a reasonable number of dates, they all expected the relationship to progress to having sex. She opened her lingerie drawer and chose a gray satin teddy. So far, Jim had been more subtle than the others, but his impatience was there. She felt it simmering just below the surface and knew he was waiting for the right moment. Unfortunately for him, she didn't think the right moment was even close. And why?

With a sigh, she took a short black dress from a hanger and slipped it over her head. She was a normal woman with all the usual needs of a woman. She wanted—longed for—a man with whom she could enjoy sex. Damn it! Why couldn't Jim Rankin be the one?

She came downstairs at seven-thirty, and right on time the doorbell rang. She went to answer it, smiling faintly. Caleb had ducked out well in advance of Jim's arrival. He was the quarterback for the junior varsity football team, and the coach had asked for his help in tutoring a couple of his teammates who were struggling with various subjects. One encounter per day with her suitor was the most her son could tolerate.

To her surprise, Jim was dressed casually. For him. He wore a starched blue oxford shirt but no tie. He came inside in a cloud of cologne, a musky scent she disliked, but he couldn't be expected to know that if she'd never shared her feelings with him. In one hand, he held up a large carry-out bag bearing the logo of the local Mexican restaurant. "It's chicken fajitas," he told her. "I know you like them."

"What about the tickets to the play?"

"I guessed you'd rather stay in tonight." Closing the door behind him, he handed her the bag. "We can still go if you want to. I can stop by my place and get into the right clothes. Won't take ten minutes."

She headed for the kitchen. "No, no, it's fine. But I hate for you to waste the tickets."

"No problem. They were freebies, anyway."

"Oh. Well, then…" She turned, smiled brightly and took a

deep breath. "How about some wine? I've got a merlot that'll be good with Mexican."

"Sounds great." He touched her arm and guided her gently but firmly to the door of the kitchen. "I'll open it while you go upstairs and change into something more comfortable. Not that you aren't beautiful, but you said you were tired, and I'll bet you'd rather spend the evening in something else."

She would. With another bright smile, she left him and headed quickly for the stairs. If he would just balance such moments of thoughtfulness with some tact in dealing with Caleb, she might feel a bit more optimistic about their chances at something lasting.

Once inside her bedroom, she slipped out of her high heels, considering his actions. Maybe she found it a little irritating that he'd canceled their evening without consulting her. Suppose she wasn't in the mood for chicken fajitas? And she'd really rather decide on her own if and when she wanted to change clothes. She rolled her eyes. God, she was so contrary these days.

The telephone rang as she was removing the black dress and trying to avoid catching the delicate fabric on her earrings. She started toward it, then stopped when it failed to ring a second time. With a shrug, she walked to her closet to find a hanger for the dress, then quickly perused her casual outfits, looking for something comfortable but nice. It was a date, after all, and she didn't want to look too informal.

"That was Caleb," Jim said, appearing suddenly at the door of her bedroom.

She turned, startled. For a split second, she did nothing as he stared at her in the brief teddy and panty hose. Recovering, she snatched a shirt to hide herself. "Jim, I'm not dressed!"

He nodded, smiling, and walked toward her. "I can see that."

"What are you doing?" She held the garment against her chest.

"Relaying a message from Caleb." At her confused look, he added, "He called to say he'd be late. Asked to extend his curfew. I told him to take his time, midnight was okay." His eyes were devouring her. "Jesus, I was just about to run out of patience, but this is definitely worth waiting for."

Suzanne's heart raced. Forget that he had no right to answer her phone or grant permission to Caleb for anything, or even that he'd entered her bedroom without invitation. The man was close enough to touch her now, and that was all that mattered. With the shirt clutched to her body, she drew in a breath and told herself there was no reason to panic. This was the chief of police. She said quietly, "Jim, please leave my bedroom until I get dressed."

"Leave? Suzanne, baby, this is me, Jim. It's taken me months to get into your bedroom. I know you have a reputation as an ice queen, but I never believed it." He touched her cheek, making her earrings sway. "You're too beautiful to be frigid. Too much a woman to deny what's natural."

"It's not natural for you to be in my bedroom uninvited," she said, striving to keep her voice steady. She sensed he wasn't used to rejection and prayed that she would handle this right. "Wait for me downstairs. Please."

"Hey, you don't really mean that." Before she realized his intention, he gave her a lingering kiss on the mouth. "God, I've been dying for this."

"Jim, for the last time—"

"Damn, Suzanne. How long are you going to hold out?" There was exasperation and something else showing in his pale eyes.

"I'm not holding out, Jim. I don't play sexual games."

"Fine. I'm glad to hear it." He reached for her again, but she put out a hand to hold him off.

"Don't do this, Jim."

"C'mon, what's a kiss?" He took her wrist and pulled her closer. "You're so damn beautiful," he muttered hoarsely, trying to kiss her. "I don't think you know how crazy I am about you."

She strained her face away. She shouldn't panic, she told herself, but her heart leaped wildly. He was the chief of police. He wouldn't resort to violence. Would he? But his mouth was

on her throat, and even though she pushed at him, resisting, he
was bent on getting past the teddy. He shoved a strap aside and
bared both breasts. Suzanne gave a frightened cry, fighting him
in earnest now.

"Oh, shit. Oh, baby. God*damn,* you're perfect! C'mon, sweetheart, don't fight me now. Ahhh..."

Oh, God, he was *licking* her! Licking and panting and
making awful noises. She shoved at him while flashes of another time, another man forcing her, added to her panic. *Please,
please,* she prayed silently, *let me get away.* She twisted and
tried to lift her knee to deter him, but her panic only served to
excite him. "I'm not trying to hurt you, baby, I'm gonna love
you."

He curled a hand around her breast and immobilized her
with a hand in her hair while he sought her mouth. His tongue
was thrust all the way to the back of her throat and she gagged
with disgust. Then she felt the strength of his penis pushing past
the satin teddy, seeking the softness between her legs, and she
gave an anguished cry, fighting with the strength of a crazed
animal.

Not again! No, please, not again.

"Baby, baby, just let me feel—"

"No! Let me *go!*" she screamed, and shoved mightily
against him, causing him to stumble backward. Even in her
panic, she saw how stunned he looked. Suzanne seized her
chance. Snatching the fallen shirt, she bolted from the room and
made for the stairs. At the top landing, she cast a frantic glance
behind her and screamed again when she saw him framed in her
bedroom door. Fully panicked now, she raced down the stairs
in a desperate sprint for the front door.

It was only then that she realized someone was banging on
it. Through the oval glass, she could make out a shape. A man's
shape. Caleb? Oh, God, let it be Caleb.

She fumbled at the lock, sobbing. Her fingers were shaking so violently that throwing the dead bolt was almost beyond
her. She turned for another look at the stairs, and sure enough,

Rankin was coming down fast. He was saying something, but
between the banging and the peal of the doorbell, she couldn't
hear him. She didn't *want* to hear him. She only wanted to get
away from him. To be safe again.

She wrenched the door open, and the person on the other
side wasn't Caleb. It was Ben Kincaid.

TWENTY-NINE

FOR A CONFUSED MOMENT, Suzanne stared in disbelief. "Ben? Oh, Lord, Ben, is that you?"

He was frowning thunderously, looking beyond her to the stairs. "Yeah, it's me. What's wrong, Suzy?"

"Oh, Ben…Ben…" Drooping suddenly in vast relief, she closed her eyes. "I can't believe…"

He reached for the shirt in her hands. By the time Rankin got to the bottom of the stairs, Ben had helped her put it on. He wrapped her in an embrace, but over the top of her head his gaze was leveled at Rankin. "What's going on here?"

"Who the hell are you?" Rankin straightened his shirt and smoothed his hair.

"I asked you a question, mister," Ben said.

"This is a private matter," Rankin said. "Tell him, Suzanne."

Suzanne turned, still safe in the haven of Ben's arms. "I want you to go, Jim. Now. Please."

Rankin's nose flared as he took in a quick breath. "You're upset, Suzanne. I realize that I came on too strong upstairs, but this guy can't just walk in here and—"

"Oh, yeah?" Ben said softly. "I can and I did. And from what I heard, it's a good thing."

Rankin's gaze narrowed. Watching him, Suzanne thought that she'd never noticed his eyes were too close together. Wasn't that a sign of something in the animal kingdom? A predator? He shifted his weight from one foot to the other as if preparing for an attack. "I don't think you know who you're talking to, buddy."

"Okay, then you tell me."

Rankin looked at Suzanne again. "Who is this guy, Suzanne?"

But Ben had had enough. "I'm your ticket to hell if you don't get out of Suzy's house in about ten seconds, you bastard. When she came down those stairs a minute ago she was in full panic. No woman looks like that because she's just had a happy experience. Now, do we do this nicely or do you want to take me on? Because I'm just pissed enough to beat the shit out of you."

Conscious of the vast amount of leg revealed in the shirt, Suzanne nevertheless stepped away from Ben and made an effort to pull herself together. "Leave now, Jim. I mean it. Don't force me to call one of your deputies."

The force of Rankin's fury throbbed in the air. It was a humiliating moment for a man in his position, but she couldn't care less about his ego. He hadn't been thinking about *her* ego when he barged into her bedroom and tried his heavy-handed seduction. With a short puff of disgust, he shouldered past them and stalked out.

"To you, too, buddy," Ben muttered, closing the door with a firm slam. Outside, they heard Rankin's car start with a roar and then the scream of his tires as he accelerated. Still looking grim, Ben squeezed Suzanne's shoulder. "Are you all right?"

Suddenly she put her face in her hands. It had been a near-miss. If it had happened again, it would have destroyed her. She'd come so far, now this! *Goddamn you, Jack Sullivan. And Jim Rankin. And all the other insensitive, selfish males in the world.*

She felt Ben move close and gently pull her back into his arms. Struggling to hold herself together, she released an unsteady breath. "I was so scared, Ben."

"Yeah, I noticed." She was still shaking, so he simply stood there rubbing her shoulders. He stopped only when she tried to laugh. Stepping back, she kept her arms wrapped around herself, holding back hysteria. She tried for a light note. "That was the chief of police of Percyville," she said, and wondered if he could hear her teeth chattering.

"You want to tell me what was going on here?" Ben asked,

studying her from whiskey-brown eyes that were still familiar and warm, even though more than ten years had passed.

She glanced down at herself and tried another shaky laugh. "Only after I get some jeans on to complete this ensemble."

He rubbed the back of his neck. "You won't get any complaints from me if you stay just like that."

She smiled then. A real smile, and she felt no threat. "Thanks, Ben, but I've had enough sex for one night if you don't mind." When his eyebrows shot up, she gave a little yelp. "I didn't mean that like it sounded. Honest. I didn't have sex with that jerk."

He waved her off. "Go. Change. I'll wait."

"There's a very nice merlot in the kitchen," she said as she reached the top of the stairs. "I'd much rather share it with you than a dumb ex-marine."

SHE WAS BACK DOWNSTAIRS in five minutes, reaching for the wine that Ben held out for her. "Thanks. Come into the living room and let's talk. I can't believe you're here." She went, knowing he was following, and took a seat on the sofa. Patting the cushion next to her, she asked, "Why *are* you here, Ben?"

"Early retirement. Sort of," he said, settling beside her. He took a sip of his wine. "Hmm, this is good."

"You're too young to retire. Try again."

He stared into the wine. "Jill and I got a divorce six months ago, Suzy." He managed a smile when she made a sympathetic sound. "Thanks, but the truth is, my marriage lasted about five years longer than it should have. We married for the wrong reasons, but because we had a lot in common careerwise, and frankly because we traveled so often we avoided seeing much of each other, we managed to hold it together until it was way past time to call it quits. She stayed in London. The good thing is, I got the twins."

"Twins," she murmured, trying not to appear shocked that a mother would accept such a long-distance relationship with her sons. "I knew you had them—boys, right?"

"Uh-huh. They're ten now." He leaned back, cocking an ankle over one knee. "We've moved into the Kincaid farmhouse along with a buddy of mine—Owen Jenner—who's retired, too. He's the boys' nanny. Sort of."

Suzanne laughed. "A sort-of nanny? A former soldier of fortune?"

"He's a pussycat at heart. But how'd you know he was a soldier of fortune?"

"Oh, I manage to hear things now and then." At his frown, she patted his hand. "Don't worry. My source is Stuart, naturally. He's a great admirer of yours."

"I get an annual subscription to the *Sun*. It's tops, as small-town papers go. But I guess you know that."

"Uh-huh."

He lifted his wineglass and drank, then twirled it between his palms while looking at her. "So, what was that all about just now, Suzy?"

"I'm not sure. I've had a few dates with Jim, but I've never given him the idea that I'd welcome him into my bedroom. At least, not intentionally. He seemed to think otherwise."

"When he came on to you, did you tell him to stop?"

"Of course. I pushed him away. I struggled. Hard. He was just so excited." Frowning at the memory, she shook her head. "It shouldn't have happened. I don't know how it happened."

"You've never married."

She gave him a look. "I was married to Dennis, remember?"

"Not much of a marriage, as I recall."

"Well, it's the closest I ever came."

"Many must have tried."

She ran a finger around the rim of her wineglass, smiling faintly. "Actually, I'm pretty good at heading them off before they get the kind of ideas Jim had tonight."

"God, there must be a lot of frustrated men around here."

Startled, she looked at him. He stood up quickly. "Forget I said that. Hell, I've always had a crush on you, Suzy, you know that, but you made it clear it was hands off that time I tried—"

She bent her head, touching the bridge of her nose. "Please, I still squirm when I remember that."

"Was it that bad?"

"No!" She looked at him in surprise. "I mean, I overreacted. I was stupid. I wish—"

He inclined his head. "Yeah, you wish—"

She stood up then and laughed. "I wish a lot of things. I wish I knew why you were back in town, for starters."

"I've given a dozen years to Uncle Sam. You might say I'm on sabbatical. Anyway, now that I've got sole custody of the boys, I thought I might try a nice, safe place, somewhere we don't have to lock the doors and bar the windows. A place where folks respect one another, where everyone knows his neighbor."

He bent and placed his empty wineglass on the coffee table. "So I'm sitting in my house watching the six o'clock news and there you are riling up the citizens and getting a good dose of their appreciation splashed all over you." He chuckled as she groaned. "Then I charge over here to find out what the hell is going on and I find you being victimized by the town's top cop." He shook his head wryly. "A man could wonder just how nice and safe Percyville is, after all."

"I was forced to make a very difficult decision, one that was unpopular."

"Then I know it was the right one."

"Thanks for the vote of confidence, but being right doesn't make me popular, as I learned this afternoon."

"But it'll make you one hell of a judge."

She smiled at that, then sipped her wine. "So you're staying in Percyville for a while?"

"Yeah, I am."

"What are the twins' names?"

"Luke and Jakey. Short for Lucian, of course, and Jacob, which was my dad's name."

"Jacob was J.T.'s name? I didn't know that. It's nice."

"Yeah."

"Won't your sons miss seeing their mother? They're a long way from London."

"She wasn't much of a hands-on mom, to tell the truth. Now she's married again, but this time to someone who won't nag her for her maternal failings." She waited, sensing past pain by the expression on his face. "He's had a vasectomy."

"Oh."

He shifted his weight from one long leg to the other. "So how's the campaign going?"

"I'm unopposed." She made a face. "Luckily, I suppose, after the fiasco today."

"Don't sweat it. Congratulations, by the way. The present governor showed great wisdom in appointing you to replace Lily."

"Thanks, Ben."

"It was Jack's campaign I was referring to. How's it going?"

"He's going to win unless something utterly vile happens."

"In the immortal words of the governor of Louisiana a few years back, Jack would have to be caught in bed with a dead girl or a live boy to lose this one."

She laughed. "All too true, I'm afraid."

He shook his head.

"Me, too," she said dryly.

"Still don't cotton to your brother-in-law, huh?"

"Still don't."

They were smiling at each other when the sound of a key unlocking the front door made them turn. Caleb came inside, slinging his backpack to the floor with a plop and dropping his headphones on top of it. He stopped short when he saw them.

"Hi, honey. I didn't expect you for another hour."

"Hi, Mom." But his eyes were on the tall stranger. "Mr. Kincaid, right? Ben Kincaid?" He walked right up to Ben and held out his hand. "I'm Caleb, sir. How are you?"

"Fine, Caleb." Ben shook hands, smiling. "Nice to see you again."

"Yes, sir. It's been a long time."

Suzanne looked with confusion from one to the other. "A long time? Do you remember Ben, Caleb?"

"Nah, not really. But I know he was the guy who delivered me when you couldn't get to the hospital in time, right?"

"Don't remind me," Ben said, still smiling.

Suzanne was staring. "I never told you that, Caleb."

"These things get around in families, Mom."

"Is that right?"

"Actually, it was Uncle Jack."

"Jack told you." Her tone cooled.

"Uh-huh." He watched her face. "Are you mad?"

"No, no, of course not." She put a hand to her throat, cleared it, then looked at Ben and managed a smile. "Just wait. When the twins get a little older, you can experience these lovely moments, too."

Enjoying himself, Ben crossed his arms and studied Caleb. "I don't know. My boys didn't experience such an exciting birth. They came the old-fashioned way."

"Lucky for Jill," Suzanne muttered.

Caleb crossed his arms across his chest, too, and chewed the inside of his lip to keep from grinning. "C'mon, Mom, haven't I been worth it?"

Her face went soft, and, getting her own back, she ruffled his hair just as she'd done when he was five. "Ask me again when you graduate from college."

He ducked with a yelp and headed for the stairs laughing. "See y'all. Don't stay up too late."

Suzanne's mouth was still gaping when he disappeared. Her son granting approval for her to entertain a man? She turned and found Ben watching her. It had been a long time since she'd let herself think about Ben, how much she'd always liked him. And just now, something in his eyes made her own gaze falter.

She would have to give this some thought.

THIRTY

TAYLOR STEPPED INTO THE whirlpool bath and sank slowly up to her neck in frothing warm water. Another day in the campaign over, thank God. How many more to go, she wasn't sure. She'd lost count. Reaching for a clip, she fashioned her long dark hair into a knot and anchored it on top of her head. What difference did it make, anyway? Jack would win, and she would be under the media's microscope even more intensely than now.

God, how she hated politics. Even after so many years and never an unsuccessful campaign, she still hated the charade of endless smiles, meaningless chitchat, repetitive speeches, everlasting fund-raising and eternal pandering to people whether she despised them or not. And mostly she did despise them.

No, mostly she despised Jack.

She leaned wearily against a pink bath cushion. How long now had she fantasized about divorcing him? For about half of the sixteen years they'd been married, more or less. The thought had been a vague one for the first few years, but it had crystallized on the night Eugenia Fields had killed herself. The night she, Taylor, had killed that boy on the motorcycle.

She pushed that thought hastily from her mind; otherwise she would need a drink to drive the demons away, and she couldn't have a drink until the campaign was over. Jack would go ballistic if she did. Then he'd start threatening to send her back to Betty Ford; she'd done that twice already and she didn't care how nice everybody said it was. You had to be the *patient* before you understood the reality of having your life taken over by other people.

No, she didn't want to do Betty Ford again.

"Taylor! Are you gonna spend all night in there?"

"I'm finished." Not really, but she stood up, anyway, dripping, and wrapped herself in a bath sheet, not wanting to irritate him if she could avoid it. Always, in the madness of the final days of a campaign, Jack's temper was notoriously uncertain. She never knew how far he would go. One thing she did know—*she,* not Jack, was the one who invariably ended up crushed and humiliated.

He pushed the bathroom door open before she finished drying herself. "You didn't forget we have that rally on the coast tomorrow, did you?"

"No, Jack." She dropped the bath sheet to reach for a teal silk kimono hanging behind the door and slipped it on. She might have been a mannikin for all the notice he took.

"The goddamn flight leaves at seven in the morning," Jack said, studying some handwritten notes. He flung them onto her dressing table and raked a hand over his face. "Jesus, I'm bushed."

"You're burning the candle at both ends, Jack. You should slow down a little. Everyone knows you've got the election in the bag. I'm wondering if we can keep up this pace two more weeks."

"Ten days," he snapped. "And what the hell difference does it make to you? All you have to do is stand there and look good. I'm the one making the decisions, memorizing speeches, eating mushy broccoli and kissing babies."

"You don't memorize speeches, Jack. That stuff rolls off your tongue like…like…" Snake oil, she wanted to say, but if she told the truth, she'd be subjected to one of Jack's raging fits. Testy and irritable as he was now, she dared not pull his tail.

"Like what?" he demanded, his jacket half off.

"Like honey," she said, tying the sash on her kimono.

"Be ready at six in the morning," he ordered, pulling the belt from his pants. "Since you're sober lately, maybe you can move before lunchtime."

Giving her a mocking look, he reached for a decanter of

Scotch and poured himself a generous drink. "Sorry we can't share, darlin', but one of us has a lit-tle bit-ty problem with this stuff." He tossed half of it back.

She looked away. "I don't think you've had any cause for complaint in this campaign, Jack."

"Only because I've been on your case constantly." He finished the Scotch and set the glass down before yanking his tie loose. "You start on the booze now and screw everything up and I'll have your ass, just remember that."

"I'm clean. I'm sober." *I'm miserable.*

He stopped in the act of unbuttoning his shirt. "I don't like that tone, Taylor."

"Sorry." Taylor moved warily to the other side of the bed. She didn't know what got into her to tweak him like that. She knew it made him furious. She knew what happened then.

"You know, it beats me what would make you happy, Taylor." Jack shrugged out of the shirt and threw it in a corner of the room. "You live like a queen. You're married to the next governor of the state, barring some disaster. You don't have to work, yet you're bitchy as hell. You complain about having to campaign when all that's required of you takes no effort. No talent. You dress up, you shake a few hands, you smile, you look pretty. I don't know what more a woman would want."

"Maybe the chance to use my brain," Taylor said. She knew he was giving her one of his incredulous looks, but she refused to turn around.

"What brain? Hillary Clinton you're not, little darlin'."

She pulled the duvet back and climbed into bed naked, as Jack liked. Demanded, actually. "I'm tired, Jack. The alarm is already set, the coffee's timed for five-thirty and your suit and shirt for tomorrow are hanging on the caddy."

He replied with a grudging grunt.

See, damn you, I am good for something. After a couple of hard thumps to her pillow, she lay back and turned on her side away from him, but inwardly she raged bitterly.

I know your schedule and I'm prepared. The outfit I'm to

wear at the rally tomorrow is already chosen, I've alerted Nancy that we'll be away, so that she can pick up the children at school. In the unlikely event that I'm asked to say a few words, I've memorized a two-minute speech. I know the names of the people who are hosting the event and I can recognize their faces. Take a look at me, Jack. I'm not just a pretty face. I'm an asset to you, damn it! Furthermore, I can do this whole routine with my eyes closed. It doesn't take a rocket scientist to master the art of politics.

"C'mere."

She closed her eyes as he reached for her, wishing she had the nerve to tell him to go to hell. And then he was turning her, his palm moving over her still-flat belly down to her curly nest. She made a small sound as his fingers dipped between the soft folds. His touch was not tender, but she felt instant arousal, anyway. At the same time, he plunged his tongue into her ear and sent both warmth and chills through her.

She wanted to resist. She tried. She hated him. Hated this. But already she was wet and panting as if her body were possessed. She felt herself flushing, and, God help her, she loved the feeling. His hard penis probed her from behind and she knew how he'd decided to do it this time. He knew it would hurt her. She was to be punished.

"Feel that, baby?"

"Don't, Jack." She whimpered, resisting. "Let's do it some other way."

"Missionary style? Oral stuff?" He laughed softly, finding her with his fingers, tweaking the sensitive nub. He bit her earlobe. "I don't think so."

She whimpered again with pain and—oh, God—pleasure.

"You like it, you know you do." He shifted, and then his body covered hers, his weight and strength pinning her down. She fought, but her struggles simply spurred him on. It was a familiar game. Then he was straddling her, both hands lifting her up so that her buttocks were in the right position. With a satisfied grunt, he plunged brutally into her.

First there was pain, but he quickly found the kernel of her passion again and worked it. Desire mixed with pain, bringing perverse pleasure. Above her, Jack growled animal sounds of lust and domination, and something dark inside her leaped in wild harmony. Both were now building to mutual climax. It was coming, it was coming, she thought, greedily seeking. When Jack finally shouted out his release, Taylor screamed her own pleasure.

He collapsed on her, panting. Half a minute passed, no more. Then his chest rumbled as he started to laugh. He pulled his penis from her body abruptly and gave her a solid slap on her butt. Groping on the bedside table, he found his handheld recorder and clicked the record button on. "Reminder to check connection to Pink Paradise Casino in Biloxi. They're still short five thousand bucks." He flicked it off, tossed it on the table and turned out the lamp.

"*Now* you can go to sleep, darlin'."

HE WAS SLEEPING WHEN she came out of the bathroom after another hot, steamy bath, but no flushing and scrubbing could erase the self-loathing she felt. She'd learned long ago that sex with her fulfilled a need in Jack at the end of his day, but it was no more important than the nightcap he allowed himself. The mystery was: why did she still respond to Jack sexually? His motives were all too clear—to humiliate, to dominate, to reduce her to a level so low that she would make no more demands than a puppet. God, it was sick. *They* were sick.

Moving silently across the carpet, she slipped into the walk-in closet and found her jeans. With only a few rustling sounds, she soon had them on. Next, she slipped a black cotton sweater over her head, not bothering with a bra, and picked up her Nikes. Finally, a glance at the bed to be sure Jack was snoring, then she was slipping out the door, tiptoeing down the hall. At the bottom of the stairs, she paused to put her shoes on, then made for the back of the house to the breakfast room, where she slipped out through French doors that she'd had the foresight to leave ajar to keep from triggering the security alarm.

Outside, she paused, feeling the keen, heady anticipation that came with these nighttime trysts—and not a flicker of guilt. A quick look around assured her that no one was lingering on the grounds, and she took off at an eager jog.

Her life was a mess, she supposed, although she'd given up trying to figure out how it had all happened. Divorcing Jack was simply her favorite fantasy, and he knew it. The first time she'd mentioned it, he'd been waiting for it. He'd delighted in telling her that she was the hit-and-run driver who'd killed the biker on New Year's Eve. According to Jack, they'd arrived at Eugenia's cottage and he'd left Taylor in the car while he walked the other woman to the door. Then Taylor had driven off in a jealous fury, leaving him to go to Riverbend himself. It had been devastating not to be able to dredge up any memory of that moment, or of anything else that night. She remembered only driving away from the club with Jack and Eugenia in the back.

Two deaths on her hands, she thought now, looking up into the starry sky as she skirted the open grounds, heading for the rear of the property. Eugenia and that poor young man. It was a secret shared by her and Jack, a chain that bound her to him. If he told it now, Jack would probably gain a few points for sticking by a wife who was guilty of vehicular homicide, while what was left of her life would be utterly destroyed. Just the thought of the Judge's reaction was enough to make her stomach hurt. And what about Gayle and Trey? Her children would be branded as having a drunken murderer for a mother. And how about her father? And Suzanne. And Annie. She shuddered at the prospect of incurring the wrath of everyone who loved her, and hurried toward the shadowy figure leaning against the railing inside the gazebo. Solace and sympathy and tenderness just seconds away.

When Jack had hired a contractor to build a replica of Riverbend's gazebo at their Jackson estate, Taylor had been amused.

But now she thanked her lucky stars. Were it not for the gazebo, there would be too much risk involved and she would not have been able to have this man in her life. The thought was unbearable.

He saw her, and his lighted cigarette made an arc as he cast it away. With a soft cry, she flew up the steps and threw herself into Spencer Dutton's waiting arms.

He rained kisses over her face as he murmured loving words and wiped at her tears with his thumbs, tangled his hands in her hair and breathed deeply, as if he could live on her scent alone. Taylor, safe in the haven of his embrace, felt loved and protected. He rocked her as gently as if she were a baby. She kissed his throat. He was so strong, so good, so understanding. She would die without him. Her soul would literally perish.

"Are you okay?" he asked, leaning back to search her face.

"Now I am."

His mouth was a grim line. "Did he hurt you tonight?"

"No."

His arms tightened. He always asked and she always lied.

"Make love to me, Spencer, please."

He cupped her face in his hands. "It's too chilly tonight, love. We can't."

"Oh, please, please…I need you." She pushed at the sides of his denim jacket and fumbled at the buttons of his flannel shirt. He sucked in a sharp breath as her hands found bare skin and she ran her mouth over his chest. She urged him toward the settee, and he went down with a groan. Taylor got on top of him, moaning as he shoved her sweater up and kissed her breasts.

"Open your pants," she demanded, breathing hard and wriggling to work her jeans down over her hips.

"God, you're naked down here," he muttered, squeezing her buttocks.

"For you, for you," she chanted, and closed her fingers around his penis just as he found her—soft, wet, throbbing. He shuddered and she smiled with the sheer joy of knowing she pleased him. This—*this*—was the way making love should be. Sexual but fulfilling, pleasurable and warm, a sharing. No pain.

With a strong grunt, he held her in the right place to take his first thrust. He was big, bigger than Jack. He filled her and it was heaven. On top of him, frenzied and gasping, she threw her head back. Her black hair flew around wildly and she was keening in rhythm with each thrust. Then, just before she climaxed, he reached for her, meeting her mouth with his, driving his tongue deep in a kiss that was carnal and possessive, so that when she screamed in pleasure, the sound was taken into him. To keep her safe.

God, how she loved him.

"Mom, is Ben Kincaid the one?"

Suzanne paused at the toaster, glad that Caleb couldn't see her face. "What one?" But she knew.

"Is he my biological father?"

She breathed in silently, slowly, then reached for the popped-up toast and slid it across the table to him. "No, he isn't your biological father."

"Promise?"

She sat down and cupped her hands around a coffee mug. "You know I've always tried to be honest about this, Caleb."

"I guess, but you might hide certain facts to keep me in the dark, Mom."

"What facts, Caleb?" She watched him pick up a piece of toast, smear it with a sickening amount of grape jelly and bite into it. He munched a minute, then drank some milk.

"Like who you were dating around the time you got pregnant."

"You know the answer to that—it was Dennis Scott."

"Yeah, I know. You were engaged, but he wasn't the one."

She sighed. "Do we have to discuss this right now, Caleb? I've told you everything that is important about that time. I was in law school, engaged to Dennis. I was foolish enough to get into a situation where things got too…got out of control."

Caleb started on another piece of toast. "You were seduced."

"Uh-huh." She took a bite of grapefruit and forced herself to swallow it. She'd been through this many times with Caleb, but it never failed to rattle her when he brought it up. Her story was that she'd been seduced, since she'd never been able to say the word *rape* when telling him about his conception. She didn't look very virtuous with her version of the truth, but she'd never figured out any other way to explain it. She couldn't say the man who impregnated her was dead. Caleb would want to know his name, his family, his…everything. Above all, she couldn't tell him it was Jack, that he'd grown up seeing his father at every family gathering.

She sighed and tossed her uneaten breakfast in the sink, then poured herself fresh coffee. Sometimes it seemed as if she'd spent her whole adult life guarding this secret….

"It happens, Mom." Caleb dipped into the jelly jar again. "I just wish you'd tell me his name."

She set her coffee down. "What do you mean, it happens? You haven't…you aren't experimenting with…" She cleared her throat. "Caleb, you're fifteen. I know what boys are thinking about at that age. I just want you to be careful. Think carefully before asking a girl—"

"Mom, Mom, Mom…" He was shaking his head. "We're not talking about sexual responsibility on my part. I've had the course. I've been there, done that. We're talking about you. And 1981. If I was born in January 1982, then it must have happened in April 1981."

"What do you mean, you've been there, done that?"

"It was a figure of speech, Mom. What I want to know is this—when are you gonna tell me the name of the man who got you pregnant?"

Never. *Never!* She put her hand to her head, prayed for wisdom and got up to make more toast. She didn't know if she'd ever get used to these sessions with Caleb. It used to rip her heart out when he'd come home from school saying everybody had a daddy but him. Even the divorced kids had a daddy, whether he was a regular presence in their lives or not. He'd beg her then for a name. Someone he could weave into the fantasies a little boy needed to scare away the ghosts and goblins of childhood.

But she just couldn't give him a name.

Now, at fifteen, he was even more determined to drag it out of her. It had been a few months since they'd had one of their "talks." She yanked open the dishwasher. She had Ben Kincaid to thank for letting this horse out of the barn again.

With her back to him, Caleb picked up the orange juice carton and drank from it. "You know, I'm sorta disappointed it isn't Ben Kincaid. He's okay."

"How many times do I have to tell you to use a glass?"

"Man, I bet he could tell some war stories, being in the Middle East with some kind of government agency and all. And did you notice that bulge under his jacket last night? He was packin' heat, Mom." He tossed the empty OJ carton and helped himself to the last piece of toast, cramming it into his mouth. "I just wonder what he's doing in Percyville."

Suzanne frowned. "Ben was wearing a gun?"

"You mean you didn't notice?"

"No…" She stared thoughtfully through the breakfast-room window. No, she hadn't noticed, but it was something she would definitely ask about the next time she saw him.

"You're sure he's not the one?"

"What?" She swung her gaze back to her son and caught the mischief in his eyes. Shaking her head, she stood up and began gathering the plates. Caleb didn't have an inkling that Jack was his father, but as much as she hated to admit it, he had inherited a lot of Jack's characteristics—sharp wit, tenacity, stubbornness and intellect. Good stuff, fortunately.

Thank God.

THIRTY-ONE

CALEB TRAINED THE LENS of the camcorder on the family clan as they milled about the patio. It was *the* Stafford occasion of the year—Grandma Lily's birthday. He'd already filmed everybody singing happy birthday, which came right after Jack delivered a champagne toast. Next was the cutting of the cake, *very* awkward because Grandma Lily hated not being able to do everything the way she used to when she was healthy, and sure enough she flubbed it. First, she couldn't blow out the candles. Then she dropped the knife and a big section of the cake toppled over. When the maid tried to patch it up, Grandma Lily lost her temper and was now parked under the big vine-thing apart from everybody. It hurt to see a lady like his grandmother brought down. Having a stroke was a real bummer.

He brought her into focus, using the anonymity of the camera to observe her. He thought he understood why she'd chosen that spot. She was out of the limelight but still in a position to watch everything. Just because she couldn't manage her motor skills anymore didn't mean she didn't like to know everything that was going on. Grandma Lily was disabled, not dead.

Braced on a tree shading the patio, Caleb panned away from his grandmother to focus on Jack. Even at a good fifty feet away and talking on his cell phone, Jack sensed the camera's eye and turned, flashed his thousand-watt politician's smile and gave a thumbs-up signal. Keeping his voice down, Caleb muttered, "There he is, folks, the next governor of the state, our very own uncle and favorite son, *Ja-a-ck Su-u-ll-i-van!*" Glancing around to see that no one was listening, he added, "And God help us if he's as shitty a governor as he is a husband and father."

Right now, as Jack spoke into his cell phone, Gayle stood by his side. A couple of times today she'd shyly tried to talk to her dad about something in the campaign, but he'd brushed her off, as usual. Caleb felt like belting Jack sometimes because he was so neglectful of Gayle. Couldn't he see how she worshipped him? She never got tired of listening to him talk about his friggin' campaign; she loved running and fetching for him; she constantly nagged Trey to be more supportive and take an active part in Jack's rise to the political mountaintop.

But Gayle was no miracle worker, and any meeting of the minds between Jack and Trey would be a miracle. Those two hadn't got along since Trey was old enough to think. Caleb panned the area looking for his cousin, but Trey was nowhere to be found. Which meant he was probably in the house nerding on Grandma Lily's computer. There was nothing Trey couldn't produce on a computer if he had enough hard drive. Besides, it was an excellent way to zone out of family stuff.

Speaking of which, where was Aunt Taylor? Oh, there she was, bright and brittle, playing Candidate's Wife to the hilt. Yuck. She was having to schmooze that sleazy guy from the coast—somebody connected to the Pink Paradise Casino. On orders from Jack, no doubt. Damn it, Jack knew the rules. Grandma Lily's birthday was closed to everybody except family and close friends, but with the campaign closing in, he probably had some vested interest in sucking up to Mr. Pink. Caleb panned the area again. Mr. Pink wasn't the only stranger. There were a couple of other VIPs who'd arrived with Jack. So much for sticking to the rules. From Jack's point of view, rules were made to be broken. Caleb lowered the camcorder. And Jack wondered why Trey grabbed every chance to stick it in the Great One's ear.

Being older than Trey, Caleb sometimes felt he should try to persuade Trey to dwell on his dad's good points rather than

everything that was wrong with him. The trouble was, Jack…
well, there was a *lot* wrong with him. Although Caleb had been
around him all his life, there was still something about his uncle
that put him off. He'd done a lot of thinking about it and finally
decided that it was because of his mother. If Jack was around,
Suzanne was different…uptight. She just didn't like him and
she'd never been able to explain why—at least, to Caleb's satisfaction. Lucky for Jack, the voters had no inkling of his dark
side.

Moving around the perimeter of the crowd, Caleb hefted the
camcorder again. This time, he panned around until he found
Annie, his favorite relative, chatting with his grandfather and
her manager, Spencer Dutton. Some of Caleb's best memories
were times spent with his Annie-Aunt. When he was a little
kid, she'd had a way of making him feel special, as if what he
had to say was important. It'd made him feel good about himself. He filmed her a little longer talking with Spence. Nice guy,
Caleb thought. A little different, maybe, but…okay. While he
had them centered in the lens, Spence walked away and Caleb
used his zoom to enlarge Annie's face. She wasn't beautiful the
way his mother and Taylor were, but he liked her face. Maybe
because she smiled a lot.

She was smiling now. He panned back and realized her smile
was for his Uncle Stuart. Aunt Eleanor wasn't here because of
some business in Washington. Her job had something to do
with economic aid in the state. Jack had gotten her the job—
naturally. But he'd heard his mom say more than once that
Ellie could have succeeded without anybody's help, she was
that smart. Possibly his mother and Uncle Stuart were the only
two people Caleb knew who refused to let Jack muck around in
their lives. Oh, and Annie, of course. Her greeting-card business was one of the few things in the state Jack didn't have his
hand in.

With Annie and Stuart centered in his lens, Caleb zoomed in
real close. When he did, he went very still. Seeing people like
this was almost like an invasion of privacy, he thought, watch-

ing the look on his uncle's face. Stuart's soft spot for Annie sure showed today. Caleb couldn't say how he knew that Stuart liked Annie. It was just something he'd always known. At least, he'd always *sensed* it.

He panned away and again caught Spence Dutton in his lens. Just for the heck of it, he followed Spence as he moved through the group. He seemed to have some destination in mind. Odd. The guy hardly ever did anything to make you notice him. With a little huff of surprise, Caleb realized Spence had sought out Taylor. "Geez, Aunt Taylor's lit up like a Christmas tree," he murmured, zooming in for a clearer shot. For the second time in two minutes, he felt he was intruding where he didn't belong.

"Getting in some candid moments, hmm?"

"Hi, Mom." Without lowering the camcorder, he turned and trained it on her face. "Smile, pretty lady. Ok-a-a-ay, ladies and gentlemen, the *real* statesperson in the family, Judge Suzanne Stafford!" He groaned when she mimed a goofy smile and stuck both forefingers in her cheeks. "Gimme a break," he begged. "You politicians all wanna hog the camera."

She rapped him on his arm, bumping the camcorder into his nose.

"Ouch!"

"Serves you right," she said, then her smile faded when she looked beyond him. Caleb followed her eyes.

"Uh-oh, here he comes," he muttered. Swinging the camera back into position, he focused on Jack heading their way. He had his professional smile in place, but at least he'd put the cell phone away and no bootlickers trailed in his wake.

"Hey, hey, Uncle Jack."

"Keep it up, Caleb, and I'll get you a job at Channel 16 this summer."

Jack was always saying stupid stuff like that. Caleb kept the camera in position. "Heck-fire, I wanted to start at CNN in Atlanta," he said.

"No problem-o. Atlanta it is." Jack pinched him on the cheek. Hard. "Now, disappear while I talk to your mama."

Caleb moved the camera just enough to catch his mother's eye. She nodded, and after a brief hesitation, Caleb moved away.

"You look like a million bucks today, Suzy." Jack cocked his head to get a better look at her. She was wearing a hunter green skirt that swirled to midcalf and a matching long, slim sweater that ended at her fingertips.

"Thanks," she said shortly, sipping her wine. "What was it you wanted to talk about?"

"Telling a beautiful woman she's looking her best is talking, isn't it?"

She gave him a hard stare. "I'm not in the mood, Jack."

He chuckled. "I'm here to proposition you, but it's not that kind of proposition, honey."

"I'm not interested in any proposition from you."

"Still hard as nails." He shook his head, his smile broadening. "Some things never change, do they?"

"No."

After a quick look about, he dropped his tone. "I know what you need, sugar, but I guess you'd scream and carry on if I were to try and demonstrate. By the way…where's Jim Rankin? I heard you two were seeing a lot of each other."

"This is a family gathering."

"Plus close friends. And you two are close, aren't you?"

"Not in the way you seem to think."

He studied her for a moment. "You know, one of these days—and it has to be pretty soon because you're not getting any younger, darlin'—you're gonna have to thaw out a little. I know you and that lezbo Candy Webber have been thick as thieves for years, but I for one never believed you were…you know, like that."

"I think the Judge needs me right now, Jack." She made a move to walk off, but he stopped her with his hand on her arm.

"Or, on second thought, maybe something else is going on." She shook off his hand. "Nothing's 'going on,' Jack."

"Maybe I should say, some*one* else."

"Such as?"

"Ben Kincaid."

"Ben— What about Ben Kincaid?"

"You tell me, sugar. That bastard's been on the feds' payroll for a dozen years. Now he shows up in Percyville and first thing he does is look you up. I want to know why he's here and what he's up to. And don't give me that bullshit about him being retired. If he's retired, I'm taking up chicken plucking. No, he's nosing around here trying to sniff something out."

She would wonder later how Jack knew Ben had been to her house, but right now she was more interested in finding out why it mattered to Jack one way or the other if Ben was back in town. "Why can't he be here for the reason he's stated? He's at a point in his life when many men reassess where they want to go. He's divorced. He has his boys to think about. He even has an old friend with him—also retired—to help him with his sons. After junketing around the globe, why wouldn't he want to settle in Percyville? It's a nice place."

"I repeat, bullshit."

She shrugged. "Whatever you say. But don't look to me for answers. I don't know any more than you do."

"Oh, yeah? You knew about his kids, his old army buddy, his divorce and his plans to settle down. Hell, you're a goddamn gold mine of information. Just keep it coming and I'll see you get rewarded…generously."

"Oh, puh-leeze." She rolled her eyes.

He grinned. "Just so we understand each other, babe. Now, about that little matter of business I mentioned."

She could walk away now, but he'd just show up later, and the time and place might not suit her as well. "Make it fast, Jack."

"I've been trying to catch you on the phone for days," he said, patting his jacket pockets in search of something. "To give you this." He had a business card in his hand, and when he turned it over, she saw a name and phone number scrawled by hand.

"What is it, Jack?"

He indicated with a nod of his head the three businessmen he'd brought with him. "A couple of my friends are very interested in meeting you. I told them you'd be here today. The guy in the gray-and-red tie is Fred Grimaldi. He, along with the other two, have some interest in that land that you ruled on last week." At her puzzled look, he explained, "The landfill deal that riled up the citizens. These guys are shareholders. They were very pleased when you refused to grant Webber's injunction."

"I had no choice but to rule the way the law dictated, and you know it, Jack," Suzanne said coldly. "If you're suggesting anything different to those men, then I'm warning you that not even the fact that you're probably going to be the next governor will keep me from causing you extreme embarrassment. I don't think you'd like that right here in the closing days of your campaign."

Jack stood watching her for a moment in silence. He smiled. "I can see I picked a bad time. In spite of the fact that you look gorgeous, you're grumpy. No problem. I'll drop by your office tomorrow. We'll thrash this out, just the two of us."

"Sorry, but I have a full calendar tomorrow, Jack."

Beyond her shoulder, he caught the eye of one of his casino pals and gave him a thumbs-up. "Don't I know it, baby-cheeks. Time's a commodity none of us has enough of. But I'm gonna try and swing by your place tomorrow, anyway, okay?" Before she realized his intention, he bent and kissed her on the cheek. To the family, it must have looked benign enough, but instant fury spiked in Suzanne. He turned and lifted his hand to everybody as she fumed. Caleb, still filming, zoomed in on his face until it filled the whole frame. Jack gave him his best grin. "Hey, I've gotta get a move on, guys. Miles to go before I rest." He caught Taylor's eye. "Honeybun, I'm leaving the limo here so you and the kids can ride back to Jackson. I'll see you tonight, but it'll be late."

Taylor, talking to Spencer, nodded. When she realized Caleb was filming her, she produced a bright smile. Jack was nearly across the lawn, his arm draped across Mr. Pink's shoulder, while the other two guys drew up the rear. As much as Caleb hated to admit it, once Jack was gone, the party went kind of flat.

THAT NIGHT CALEB LAY in his bed mulling over the events of the day. He'd picked up on several interesting points during the party, and the most interesting was that conversation with his mom and Uncle Jack. With his head resting on his palms, he stared at the play of moonlight and shadow on the ceiling. Although he'd moved away when Jack took his mother aside, he'd heard some of their conversation. At one point, he'd been tempted to move to his mother's defense. Jack had a habit of bugging her about business stuff, and as a judge, she had to remain totally distanced from anything that cast a shadow on her integrity. Making deals with Jack's casino cronies was a definitely questionable move. But his mom had held her own, making Caleb fiercely proud.

Of course, Jack would show up at her office in spite of the fact that she'd told him flat out not to. Jack was so friggin' arrogant that he did most anything he pleased. Caleb wished there was a way he could make Jack back off from his mom, but he was realistic enough to know that the time wasn't right. Someday he would be in a position to challenge his uncle, but not yet.

Yeah, all that was interesting and frustrating, but the *most* interesting thing was Jack's paranoia about Ben Kincaid. Caleb felt a little tingle in his belly. He'd been right, after all. Ben Kincaid wasn't just some hometown guy seeking to settle down in peaceful retirement. Like Caleb, Jack thought that Ben had another mission in Percyville. What the heck could it be?

Caleb squinched up his face, thinking. Also very intriguing was his hunch that his mother wasn't being exactly honest about Ben and their history. He'd never thought his mother would actually lie to him, but a lot of coincidences sort of came together here, enough to make him wonder. Kincaid was in law school with his mom. He was a good friend of hers and Dennis

Scott's. He was at the big family wedding in April when Taylor married Jack, which was about the time Caleb figured Suzanne got pregnant. Ben, not Dennis, was in the apartment when she suddenly went into labor, and Ben, not Dennis, had actually assisted in his birth.

Jeez, could Ben be the one after all?

THIRTY-TWO

JACK WAITED A COUPLE OF DAYS before showing up at Suzanne's office. She knew he hadn't said all he wanted to at her mother's party, and from long experience dealing with Jack's compulsive need to control everything, this visit had to be.

She glanced at the small Victorian clock on the bookcase wall. "I have less than thirty minutes to be in court, Jack. You already know that because I'm sure you charmed it out of my secretary. So let's dispense with our usual sparring and get right to the point."

He put a briefcase on her desk and took a seat in the deep leather chair directly across from her. "You know, Suzy, you puzzle me sometimes. Don't you understand what most Southern women are born knowing? You can catch a lot more flies with honey than vinegar."

"We're going to spar, anyway?"

"I'm telling you this for your own good—as you set out on your new career. Be a little less rigid, darlin'. Softer, you know what I mean? Here I am in your office—on official business, whether you know it or not—and right away your back's up. I've gotta tell you, Suzy, if this is the way you act with everybody, you might find you've sabotaged your career as a judge before it gets off the ground."

She leaned forward in her chair, lacing her fingers in front of her. "Be a good girl, play it the way you good old boys like and who knows how high I'll rise, is that it, Jack?"

He shrugged elaborately. "In a manner of speaking."

"Well, how about speaking in a manner that explains why

you're here." She glanced again at the clock. "Now I've got twenty-five minutes."

He hitched forward, pulled his tape recorder out of his pocket and pushed a button. She lifted her eyebrows as the docket number and legal caption of a case on her calendar three weeks from now was recited in Jack's voice. He tucked the recorder back into the inside pocket of his jacket with a chuckle. "Stupid to take chances on not getting it right when talking to a judge."

"And stupid of me to let this conversation go any further if you plan to discuss a matter pending before the court. Be very careful, Jack. As you well know, I'm severely limited in what I can say about any active case."

"You met Fred Grimaldi at your mama's party Sunday. I believe I mentioned then he had some interest in that landfill property out in the county."

"So?"

"You ruled right on that one, Suzy. The next one up is this case I just mentioned, and this time it's vital that you rule right again, because this one deals with something far more important than the use of a few acres for dumping waste."

"Toxic waste." She was sitting straight in her chair now.

"Whatever." He reached for his briefcase, popped it open and pulled out a document. "This is land that borders on the river. Grimaldi and others want to build a floating casino. To get the project off the ground, they've drawn up this petition." He shoved it across to her. "Take a look."

She didn't glance at the document. "I can't believe you, Jack. Even if I wanted to, I couldn't look at that document. I'll read everything pertinent to the case when it's filed, and not a second before."

"This is no time to mount a moral high horse, Suzy. We're talking the real world here, not some Utopia the way you liberals want it to be. If this decision goes the wrong way, my friends stand to lose millions. On the other hand, if it's right, we make millions."

"We?" she asked dryly.

"We. And that includes you, sugar. You don't think you'll go unrewarded for playing ball, do you?"

She stared at him. "Don't bother saying another word, Jack. I know what's going on here. You need to go back to your Las Vegas pals and tell them you've fixed it with the judge to ram something down the throats of the people of Mississippi before they've had a chance to decide it for themselves. Putting aside the fact that what you're asking is illegal, do you think I'd be stupid enough to risk everything I've worked for to do that?"

"Everything you've worked for?" he repeated. "You think you got this appointment because you worked hard? Or because of the sheer brilliance of your legal mind?" He was shaking his head. "Give me a break. Look, here's the way it is, Suzy. *I* was the one who fixed it with the governor to name you to replace your mama after she had that stroke. Hell, you weren't even on the short list for that appointment, whether you want to believe it or not." He leaned back. "You're going to have to get real here, for a change. Dump these starry-eyed notions about equal justice for all. Save it for the bleeding hearts of the world, who I might add, don't wind up on the Supreme Court, either in this state or in D.C. You need to keep that in mind, Suzy-baby."

Suzanne didn't give him the satisfaction of showing her dismay. He could very well be telling the truth. Deep down she'd wondered the same thing when she learned she had been named by the governor. But she'd put it out of her mind, vowing that even if she'd gotten the job through her mother—*her mother, damn it!*—she'd be the best judge she knew how to be. She'd be fair and impartial, thoughtful, just, honest. Above all, honest.

"My answer is still the same, Jack," she said quietly. Let him do his damnedest. She could always get work as a lawyer.

He studied her in silence for a long moment. "I'd hoped I wouldn't have to go any further than reminding you that you owe me, Suzy."

"I don't owe you," she said fiercely. "I didn't even know you were pulling strings behind the scenes."

"I guess you leave me no choice, then. Either you cooperate with us or I'm having a talk with Taylor."

"Taylor? What does she have to do with this?"

"Nothing, but I think she'll be interested in what happened at our reception."

Suzanne went cold inside. For years Jack had danced around the suggestion of revealing the secret of Caleb's birth. But in all his manipulations, he'd never actually come right out with it. He'd always backed off just short of blackmail, leaving her shaken and full of rage, but with her secret intact. Could he be serious now?

"What's the matter, darlin'? Trying to figure out if I mean it?" He still wore a smile, but it was far from the one he showed voters.

She glanced at the clock, her shaking hands pressed hard on her desktop. Anything she said now was a bluff and they both knew it. "Fifteen minutes, Jack."

"Okay, if that's the way you want to play it." He put the document back in the briefcase and snapped it shut. "Here it is straight out. I'm Caleb's father and you know it. It suited me to go along with the fantasy you fed everyone all these years, but as of this moment, it doesn't suit me anymore."

"It was *rape!*" she cried, leaping to her feet.

"Your word against mine."

"You *bastard!*"

"And who do you think Taylor will believe?"

She thumped her chest. "Me! She'll believe me because you've been such a lousy husband all these years."

"And I'll say you and I have been lovers all these years."

"That is too ludicrous for words," she said, her voice trembling with rage.

"No, this argument is ludicrous. One look at Caleb is all it takes to see he's mine, and I think that's what you've worried about ever since he was born." He stood up, straightened his tie and gave the edges of his jacket a tug. "Caleb's your prime concern, Suzy. You've been like a mama bear protecting that kid from me, the big bad biological papa. Just think. All that mollycoddling down the tubes if you don't play ball."

His arrogance was almost more than she could stomach. She curled her fingers into fists to keep from lunging at him and scratching his eyes out. "The election's only a few days away," she said in a voice quiet with loathing. "I don't believe you'll want to take a chance on something like this getting out."

"And I don't believe you've got guts enough to call my bluff. You're too hung up on protecting Caleb and Taylor and your folks and your fuckin' family name." He chuckled. "Hey, it could be ironic if it weren't so pathetic. The thing that keeps you from playing ball with my friends is what keeps you from blowing the whistle on me. But it ain't integrity, sugar, it's pride. Pure and simple. Mustn't let the world know how nasty we are, right?"

"Get out, Jack. Now."

He picked up his briefcase, looking at her with hard black eyes. "I'm giving you a week to think it over. The election'll be behind us then, and as my sister-in-law, you'll be even better positioned for a seat on a higher court, whether you admit it or not." He walked to the door and put his hand on the doorknob. "If I were you, I'd think about that before doing something that could prove very stupid."

She dashed across her office to slam the door but stopped short when she saw Ben Kincaid standing at her secretary's desk. Jack, too, seemed startled, but he quickly recovered.

"Ben Kincaid. How the hell are you?" He stuck out his hand and flashed his practiced smile. "I heard you were back in town."

"Hello, Jack."

Jack made some hearty remark as they shook hands briefly, then Ben's clear, calm gaze went to Suzanne. Knowing she looked rattled, she managed a smile, but she knew she didn't fool him. He knew her too well. "Got a minute, Suzy?"

"Bad timing, Ben." Jack made a production of looking at his watch. "She's in court in exactly six minutes. Right, Suzy?"

"Come in, Ben." Ignoring Jack, she beckoned Ben over, but before she took him inside, a woman entered and walked over to her secretary.

"Amanda Mason," she said, flashing a press card. Then, spotting the three people at Suzanne's door, she quickly left the secretary to approach Suzanne. "Judge Stafford. Jack." She nodded at him before glancing at Ben. It was clear she was curious. "I wonder if I could have a couple of minutes of your time, Judge Stafford?"

"I'm sorry. I'm due in court momentarily." Suzanne motioned Ben inside her chambers, leaving Jack to deal with Amanda Mason.

"A reporter, huh?" Ben said, studying Suzanne's face.

"Yes, and one who's on a fast track to the big time." She moved to the front of her desk and rested against it, crossing her ankles in front of her. "The woman is always on a hunt for scandal. It makes the frenzy of the campaign even more frenzied, if there is such a thing." She touched her forehead, smiling wryly. "I've learned to dread the six o'clock news. Her sound bites capture me speaking words I could swear I never said."

"She can forget sullying your name," Ben said, his eyes still on her face. "She might try putting the wrong spin on your words, but she can't find scandal where there isn't any."

Lord, if he only knew. Rape, her son branded a love child, her family's name dragged through the mud, her sister's marriage destroyed, her career in ashes. It was scandal on a grand scale, more than enough to propel Amanda Mason's career into the big time if Jack decided to make good on his threats. To her dismay, Suzanne suddenly felt close to tears.

"Suzanne..." Ben's voice was rich with concern. "What's the matter? What's wrong?"

She laughed shakily. "Oh, it's nothing. Really. I've just had a very trying morning."

"Jack? I thought he looked pretty cocky when he came out of your chambers. You looked as if you'd like to choke him... or worse."

For a mad second or two, she felt like telling him everything. He had been such a good friend when her marriage to Dennis was going sour. But she wasn't that young and fragile rape victim anymore. She'd managed to handle all the curves Jack had thrown her so far, and she could handle this one, too. She looked up to find Ben watching her intently.

"I was right, it's Jack," he said. "Is he threatening you in some way?"

"It's nothing I can't handle, Ben. Truly." She glanced at the clock and pushed away from the desk. "Jack was telling the truth just now. I've got about five minutes until court convenes. Was there a special reason you dropped by?"

"I can't just show up because I want to see you?"

She gave him a startled look. Was he flirting with her?

"Anyway, you didn't answer my question about Jack. Is it something more personal? Is he coming on to you?"

She felt herself flush. "Why would you ask that?"

"Because you're beautiful and smart and he can't stand rejection."

"You think I've rejected Jack?"

"Let's just say that his attitude struck me as frustrated and testy."

"Then he can be frustrated and testy until hell freezes over," she said bitterly. Then, realizing Ben was still watching her with that same shrewd intensity, she managed a laugh. "You're something else, do you know that?"

"If you mean I'm stubborn when I sense a woman is being harassed by a man I know to be a snake and a bully, then I guess you're right."

"I absolutely have to get to court, Ben."

He touched her arm as she started out. "Okay, but just promise me one thing, Suzy. If he tries anything that makes you feel threatened or pressured, or if he tries to use the power of his office to intimidate you in any way, will you tell me?"

"No."

He looked startled. "No? Why the hell not? I want to help

you. I can't just stand by and watch that bastard hurt someone else I care about."

She squeezed his hand. "And I can't be calling on a friend to help me in a situation I should be able to handle myself. I'm not a twenty-one-year-old student anymore, Ben. I'm a Chancery Court judge. If I'm not tough enough to handle the job, then I shouldn't have the job."

With a brief knock at the door, Suzanne's secretary stuck her head in. "You're going to be late in about a minute and a half, Judge Stafford."

"Thanks, Betsy. I'm on my way."

Suzanne walked to a closet, opened it and took out her robe. As she put it on, she gave Ben a smile. "Don't be upset. I know where you're coming from and I appreciate it. Truly."

"Uh-huh." He stepped back so that she could leave her chambers ahead of him. As he closed the door behind them, he said in a tone low enough that no one else could hear it, "I'll see you in court on this one, lady."

The thrill of his words stayed with her all the way to the courtroom, and when she took her seat on the bench a few seconds later, she was smiling.

TAYLOR RUSHED UPSTAIRS knowing Jack would be furious because she was late. She'd called on her car phone to tell him she'd been caught in a traffic jam on the interstate, but at this stage in the campaign, he wouldn't accept anything short of her death as an excuse.

Three more days, thank God.

She heard his voice before she reached the bedroom. He was talking into that silly tape recorder. He must have miles of tape, she thought, peeling off her jacket. In these last frantic days, it seemed his every thought was recorded. Uh-oh, he sounded furious. Then she heard Suzanne's name.

She listened a moment. Apparently he'd seen her today to talk about a case and Suzanne had not cooperated. Taylor wasn't surprised. Suzanne was one of the few people who defied Jack even though it was like waving a red flag at a bull. No effort on her part to smooth things between them ever worked.

Jack punched the button with savage force and tossed the recorder on the top of the armoire, where it landed with a clatter. He shrugged out of his trendy suspenders and flung them against the wall. "Stupid bitch!"

Taylor crossed the room and bent to pick up some papers scattered on the floor. "Jack, I don't like you talking about Suzanne that way."

As usual, he ignored her. "She's on her high horse again." He balled up the shirt in his hand and threw it on the bed. "She'd better come around or I'll see that judgeship snatched away from her as easy as she got it."

"Come around about what?"

"The Grimaldi thing. If she doesn't rule on that case the right way, it means millions down the drain. And this time I've got a personal stake in it. Dumb broad."

"Is this about casino stuff?"

"First off, *I* don't want to be on their shit list. Those guys in Vegas play hardball. I'm telling you, Taylor, it'll be her ass if she keeps on like this."

"Whatever you want from Suzanne, is it illegal, Jack?"

He kicked off his shoes. "A judge rules in a case like an accountant crunches numbers. There are ways to cook the books and there are ways a judge can circumvent the statutes."

"But is it illegal?"

"What the fuck difference does it make?" he snarled, hurling his socks against the wall.

"Suzanne won't do anything illegal, Jack. Of all the people I know, with the possible exception of my parents, Suzanne has the most integrity. She'd sacrifice everything before compromising her principles."

"And 'everything' is exactly the price she'll pay if she doesn't come around." He jerked open a drawer in the armoire and yanked out a fresh shirt. "I'll have her job, and then see how much her precious principles matter." He ripped off the paper strip on the shirt. "See how she feels when she's got nothing left but that kid she's so goofy over."

Caleb? Taylor frowned. What did Caleb have to do with anything? "What are you talking about, Jack?"

He threw the shirt at her and she automatically began unbuttoning it for him. "They're so tight, let them figure out how to handle the fallout together," he muttered.

She stood unmoving in the middle of the room, his shirt in her hands, and watched him pace and rant and rave until everything whirled dizzily in her head. With a sigh, she sat down on a love seat. "You're not making any sense, Jack."

He stopped suddenly. He was looking at her, but she had the feeling he wasn't seeing her, that, as usual, his thoughts were elsewhere. He turned on his heel and headed back to the armoire, where he grabbed the recorder again. Ignoring her, he began outlining in clipped and vicious terms a scheme so diabolical that even for Jack it was pushing the envelope. Taylor was dumbstruck. If he did what he said, Suzanne would be ruined. He snapped the recorder off and stood thinking.

"Jack, what—"

He quieted her with a snarl and snapped the thing on again, adding a couple of new thoughts, then he punched the Off button and took his shirt from her hands. "That'll take care of Miss High and Mighty, I think."

"Jack, you can't be serious. I heard that. It's all lies. Suzanne's whole career—"

"Will go up in smoke," he said, shoving an arm into his shirtsleeve. "Forget your candy-assed principles, Taylor. This is not a game. Think of what you just heard as an insurance policy."

"Insurance! For whom, Jack? Grimaldi and his sleazy friends? This is Suzanne. My sister. I've known you to destroy the lives of other people, Jack, but you can't do something like this to Suzy."

"I won't have to if she comes around." He stood in front of the mirrored closet doors tucking his shirttails into his pants. "Come on, get dressed. We've got a long drive ahead of us."

"She won't come around, Jack." Taylor went to her closet for a dress. "And what about Caleb? He'll be hurt, too."

Jack fixed the knot of his tie, then stood in front of the huge mirrors. "Don't worry about Caleb. He's tough." He smiled at himself. "He's from good stock."

SUZANNE HAD A LUNCH DATE with Taylor the day before the election. Her sister was tense, her gaze darting here and there, almost never meeting Suzanne's eyes. She fiddled with the silver, folded and unfolded her napkin, crumbled crackers, sipped water. Suzanne realized exactly how rattled Taylor was when she opened her purse and took out a cigarette.

"I thought Jack's handlers advised against smoking during the campaign," Suzanne said.

"After they've walked a mile in my shoes, then they can advise me on that." Turning her head, she blew the smoke away from Suzanne.

"Is that why you asked me to meet you at this restaurant? Because you knew there wouldn't be any reporters and you wanted to sneak a cigarette?"

"I just wanted a moment of blessed privacy," Taylor said, touching her forehead with unsteady fingers.

Suzanne reached over and covered her hand with sympathy. "Taylor. Forget privacy for the next four years. It's not going to happen. You'll be living in a goldfish bowl. You've got to prepare yourself."

"I know. Don't remind me."

"Then why did you go along when Jack told you he intended to run? This is your life, too."

Taylor gave her a bland look. "You've got some experience telling Jack something he doesn't want to hear?"

Nothing she could admit. "Well, I just—"

"Forget it, Suzy." Taylor withdrew her hand and began toying with the silver again. "Like everyone else in the campaign, I'm just feeling last-minute jitters. It'll be better tomorrow when it's all over. At least Jack will calm down."

He would win, there was no doubt about that. He was so high in the polls that editorial cartoons had featured his opponent conceding before election day. Suzanne leaned back, wishing she could believe things would be better when Taylor was Mississippi's First Lady. But she would be even more in the public eye.

"This has been so hard on you, Taylor."

"Nothing like what it's done to Trey." She stubbed the cigarette out, only half smoked. "I guess that's one thing I can be grateful for—at least one of my kids is never going to be a politician. He despises this stuff almost as much as I do."

"Yes, I know."

"And it makes Jack hate him." She paused while the waiter placed their salads in front of them. "He came home Friday night with alcohol on his breath."

"Who, Jack?"

"No. Trey."

Suzanne closed her eyes. "Oh, no."

"Like mother, like son, right?"

"Taylor, you have to get some professional help."

"I've done Betty Ford twice, Suzy. Besides, I can't disappear for another rehab just as Jack is inaugurated as governor." She made a face. "Imagine the scandal."

"I meant counseling. And not just for you," Suzanne said. "I meant the family—yourself and the children."

"Oh, for a second, I thought you were including Jack in that cozy picture." Taylor gave her a bitter smile. "I can just see it now, one big happy first family, all of us pouring out our miseries to some shrink. Get a grip, Suzy."

Alarmed by her sister's morose mood, Suzanne watched her lean forward suddenly to get her purse. She rummaged through it and came up with a bottle of pills, which she finally managed to open. She shook three of the pills into her palm before closing the cap.

"What's that, Taylor?" Suzanne asked sharply.

"Something for my nerves. Don't you think they need calming?" But ever mindful that someone might see, she placed the pills on a piece of boiled egg in her salad, then swallowed them along with the egg.

"Clever," Suzanne said dryly.

"You get to know a few tricks."

"How's Gayle doing?"

"As possessed as Jack, at the moment. She eats, breathes and lives the campaign. It'll be a good thing when it's over and she can return to the life of an ordinary fifteen-year-old girl."

"In the governor's mansion?"

"Let me have my little fantasies, will you, Suzy?"

It took only a few minutes for the pills to work. As they talked, Suzanne noted that the edge was off Taylor's words. She was more mellow, her sarcasm blunted. At least the pills brought her some peace, even if it was only temporary. Suzanne's heart ached, watching her. How had it all turned out so tragically? Mixed with her concern was Suzanne's own guilt. Was she responsible in any way for Taylor's unhappiness? The marriage would have ended before it began if she'd reported the rape. In keeping her secret all these years, had she done her sister a grave injustice?

With a sigh, she gave her attention to her salad once more. She was pushing grilled chicken around her plate when she looked up and saw Ben Kincaid making his way toward their booth.

"Look who it is," Taylor said, smiling brightly. "Ben, hi. Come join us."

"Hi, Taylor. Suzy. I thought that was your car I spotted outside." In jeans and a sweater, he looked as if he didn't have any particular destination in mind. But Suzy knew better. Had he followed them? She watched him take off his baseball cap and rub a careless hand over his hair. It was a boyish gesture, even though in those jeans he didn't look like a boy.

Taylor started to rise, dropping her napkin on the table. "Here, you can have my place. I was just heading for the ladies'

GOOD GIRLS

room." She slipped out of the booth, still smiling, and said in a singsong voice, "Back in a sec, ya'll."

Ben sat down and smiled at Suzanne. For some reason, she felt flustered. What was it about Ben Kincaid that got to her this way? "Surprise," he said.

"Is this a coincidence or what?" she asked, giving up altogether on the idea of eating.

"Or what," he replied, glancing in the direction of the ladies' room. "What's she taking?"

"Excuse me?"

"Taylor. She's glassy-eyed and her pupils are as big as saucers. What's she taking?"

Suzanne drew in a breath. "Ben, she's under a lot of stress right now."

"Tell me about it. But handling it with drugs is a dumb idea."

Suzanne nodded. "I know. She knows it, too. Her life is… difficult." When he only grunted, she took half a roll and began pulling it to pieces. "Does your relocation to Percyville have anything to do with Jack?"

"Why do you think it might?"

"Hey, you two aren't talking business, are you?" Taylor, back from the ladies' room, slid into the booth beside Suzanne and reached across the table for her salad. She picked up her fork, wagging it in front of Ben like a schoolmarm. "I leave you two alone hoping you'll use the time to say something interesting and I come back and find you both looking serious as a heart attack. My sister is a gorgeous woman, Ben, single and smart. What's the matter with you?"

Suzanne made a dismayed sound. "Taylor!"

Taylor shrugged. "Well, I happen to think you've gone long enough without romance in your life."

"Taylor, are you drunk?"

Taylor's vivid blue eyes went wide. "You know I'm not allowed, Suzy."

Suzanne began folding her napkin, but she couldn't leave the booth unless Taylor let her out. "I've got work—"

Taylor sighed dramatically. "Oh, chill out, as Trey would say." She gave Ben a cheery smile. "Gosh, I've hardly seen you since you got back to Percyville, Ben. How are you? How are those twins? Somebody told me they were the cutest things."

"They keep me on my toes." Smiling, he leaned back. "How about yourself, Taylor? How does it feel knowing that when the polls close tomorrow you'll be the First Lady of Mississippi?"

"Numbing."

"Numbing? Is that good or bad?"

"Neither. You don't feel anything if you're numb." She sprinkled a few grains of salt on her salad. "You don't have to tell Jack I said that."

"No problem."

Suzanne touched Taylor's hand. "Taylor, I think we should go now."

Taylor looked at her, blinking. "But Ben just got here."

"So Jack's pretty confident, hmm?" Ben asked after sending Suzanne an enigmatic look.

"The polls don't lie," Taylor said, popping a small cherry tomato into her mouth.

Ben watched her carefully push sliced onion to the side of her plate. "He's full of plans for the state, I bet."

"Big time." Taylor speared a pink shrimp. "Nothing's too insignificant. He's got voters' groups positioned strategically all over the state—agriculture in Greenville, economic development in Tupelo, telecommunications and the arts in Jackson, shipbuilding in Pascagoula, gambling in Biloxi—it boggles the mind."

"I thought the state was pretty much saturated with gambling," Ben stated, tapping a thumb on the table.

"That's not the way Jack's Vegas connections see it."

"Would that be Fred Grimaldi and his pals?" Suzanne asked. "Those guys Jack brought to Mother's party at Riverbend?"

Taylor paused, holding her water glass. Dividing a look between Ben and Suzanne, she said, "I'm talking too much."

"Don't sweat it, Taylor." With a rap of his knuckles on the

tabletop, Ben slid out of the booth. "I've got to get back to the house. The twins have a soccer game at three."

Both women watched him thread his way through the tables. He said something to the woman at the register, who perked up and smiled in response. "Notice his ass, Suzy," Taylor said. "Cute."

"Yes," Suzanne said dryly.

"He's dangerous, though," Taylor said with a thoughtful look on her face. Suzanne gazed at him through the restaurant window as he threaded his way through the parking lot. She agreed with her sister, but not in the way Taylor meant.

"You like him, don't you?" Taylor asked.

"We're old friends."

"Yes, but he's got a different look in his eye these days, Suzy. I just had the oddest thought when I came back from the rest room and saw the two of you talking." Knowing how her sister's imagination could run amok, Suzanne slid out of the booth and dug in her purse for her wallet. Taylor stood up, too. "What if you'd married him instead of Dennis?"

The thought was not new to Suzanne.

THIRTY-THREE

SUZANNE'S CELEBRATION ON election day was quiet, as suited her taste and the fact that she had run unopposed. Caleb said that took some of the fun out of it, but she was touched by the look of pride in his eyes as one by one members of the judicial community came by to congratulate her. He videotaped her receiving warm wishes and hugs from family and friends—Candace Webber, Ben Kincaid and his twin boys, her law clerk and Betsy, her secretary. Actually, she was surprised there were so many others. She had assumed her own accomplishment would be totally eclipsed by Jack's monumental victory.

Charles and Lily Stafford had been forced to leave for Jack's campaign headquarters in downtown Jackson, where the size of the celebration was comparable to the size of Jack's margin of victory over his opponent. There, hundreds of constituents were delirious with success. Food and beer were everywhere and, after the official announcement, champagne. A live band blasted rock and roll, with a country song thrown in every now and then. The cheers were deafening when Jack stepped up to the podium to thank everyone with rakish charm and apparent modesty. A cloud of balloons was released into the sky amid cheers and whistles.

Suzanne and Caleb watched it all on television with Annie and Spencer Dutton at her cottage at Riverbend. By that time exhaustion had set in and they were glad to spend the rest of the night relaxing and pigging out on junk food.

"He's going to be even more obnoxious than ever, take my word for it," Annie said, sipping beer from a frosty can.

"And nobody'll ever know it but the family," Caleb said, stuffing a handful of popcorn into his mouth.

"Maybe he'll be so busy carving out his place in history he'll spend most of his time in the governor's mansion." Suzanne crunched a chip. "Which will make it hard on Taylor."

"There's Uncle Stuart," Caleb said suddenly. "Boy, look at his face. I bet he'd rather be here with us. Whoa, Aunt Ellie's getting her picture taken beside the Great One. Now, *she* looks like a happy camper."

"Ellie's right where she wants to be." Suzanne slipped off her shoes and sighed with relief. "Believe it, she's going to get a plum of a job when Jack takes office. Which is only what she deserves. She worked her tail off during this campaign."

Annie studied the label on her beer. "What do you think it'll be? The job, I mean."

"I don't know, but she'd jump at a lobbying job in Washington. She tells me Jack's working on that. Or he might get her in at the commerce department."

Annie set the beer down carefully. "But what about Stuart? I can't see him leaving the *Sun* to become a pundit in D.C."

"Maybe Stuart won't mind her getting an apartment there." Suzanne took another chip. "It'll mean they're apart a lot, but they don't have a traditional marriage, anyway. We all know that."

Suzanne frowned suddenly, watching the antics of Jack's inner circle on the podium. Champagne was flowing freely and now Taylor was holding a glass. "I hope Taylor isn't drinking that champagne."

Annie groaned. "Damn. She's been so good this time."

Spencer spoke quietly. "She can't hold out when she's surrounded by other people who're drinking. AA preaches not to get into those situations unless you're with your AA buddy. That's why she should join and attend regularly."

Suzanne gazed at him in surprise. Was he speaking from experience or from a personal concern for Taylor? "Have you mentioned that to her?"

"A hundred times." Spencer poured soda into his glass. "She thinks she can handle this by herself."

A hundred times. Suzanne met Annie's eyes. Did that mean Spencer had had a hundred conversations with Taylor?

Spencer set his glass down with a thump. "The problem is, Sullivan doesn't do a damn thing to support her. He's so wrapped up in his own ambition—wheeling and dealing with anybody he thinks can make it worth his while—that he doesn't even *see* Taylor. She could be a shadow on the wall for all the attention she gets as his wife." He seemed to realize they were all staring and his expression was suddenly embarrassed. "But I guess all of you know that."

"Right," Annie murmured, shooting another look at Suzanne.

"We'll have to try to pick up the slack," Suzanne said. "Being in the limelight will be hard for her."

Everyone turned to look at the party on the television screen. Jack was beaming, shaking hands, hugging folks, backslapping. At his side, Taylor was beautiful in a red dress with a dramatic design of black sequins on one shoulder. Unlike Jack's, her smile seemed fixed. Someone came through with fresh glasses of champagne and she took one. Suzanne winced, watching her drink it quickly. It might be too late to pick up the slack.

"Mom, you're drunk."

Taylor gave Gayle an admonishing look and put her finger to her lips. The limousine driver might look like a robot, but Taylor knew he heard everything. Jack warned her constantly that anything she said or did in the limousine was likely to come back to haunt *him* on the six o'clock news.

"Put a lid on it, Gayle," Trey said, slumping back on the seat, his hands resting on his bony knees. Jack had insisted he wear "something decent" tonight. In khaki Dockers, a blue oxford shirt and navy jacket, he looked as if he were ready to enroll in an Ivy League university. It couldn't have been more unlike Trey's preferred grungy look.

Taylor drew in a deep breath and was instantly so dizzy that she was glad they weren't home yet and that she didn't have to prove to Gayle that she wasn't drunk. Just a little buzzed, maybe, because she'd finally succumbed to the temptation of a sip or two of champagne when the evening had stretched out so endlessly. Glad, too, that Jack had sent them home when he realized she was drinking. It would delay her chastisement.

"Why do you do it, Mom?" Gayle demanded, her tone high with distress. "This was supposed to be a special night. You've ruined it."

"Shut up, Gayle!" Trey hissed, jabbing a thumb at the driver. "Leave her alone. Save your shit for when we get home."

"Be quiet, both of you," Taylor said tiredly, her eyes still closed. "We've all been through an ordeal, but it's over now. We can relax. Your father's the governor of the state. We're the first family." She giggled then and popped her fingers over her mouth before darting a playful look at the driver. "We have to remember that at all times."

Trey, sitting across from her, met her eyes and laughed. "She's right, Mom. You're bombed."

She opened her eyes wide and whispered, "Don't tell your father."

"This is *disgusting!*" Gayle said, turning her face to the window.

"*You're* disgusting," Trey said, enjoying the poisonous look she shot him. "But except for that, you're perfect." He patted his mother's hand. "Me and Mom, now, we have lower standards. So there's still room for some fun in our lives."

Gayle rolled her eyes and didn't give him the satisfaction of a comeback.

"Fuck you," Trey said mildly.

Oh, God, she was in hell. Taylor began to weep silently.

THE COTTAGE SEEMED TOO EMPTY and too still after everyone left. Annie walked around picking up glasses and napkins and left-over food. She brushed crumbs off the coffee table and wiped up the ring left by her own beer can. Ordinarily she wasn't much of a housekeeper. A lady came in twice a week—the same one who'd cleaned for her mother—but she wasn't due until Friday. She finished finally, then turned the lights off and went into the kitchen, where she dumped everything in the trash and stowed the dirty things in the dishwasher.

She looked at the clock. One-thirty in the morning, past bedtime even on a special night, but she was wide awake. She could have another beer, but she had a rule about drinking alone. She could go to the drafting table she'd set up on the sunporch and try to do some work, but the way she was feeling she probably couldn't produce anything worth keeping.

Shit.

She knew what her problem was, but she hated admitting it. That picture of Stuart at Jack's celebration party was stuck in her mind. Stuart and Ellie. Goddamn it, why didn't she just divorce him? How could she waltz off to Washington trusting him to wait like a good boy as if he didn't have the normal needs of a man? Did she just take it for granted he'd bury himself in his editorials and not even notice his wife was gone?

Annie snapped the light off in the kitchen and stalked down the hall. The devil that had been riding her lately was alive and well. A little tormentor inside her head wanted to know why Stuart put up with Ellie? Why didn't *he* divorce *her?*

She pulled her sweatshirt over her head viciously and was on her way down the hall in a camisole and her jeans when she heard a soft tapping. Holding her sweatshirt in a wad against her chest, she went back to the front of the house. Someone was on the other side of the glass door.

Stuart.

Her heart began to pound, and when she got to the door, she didn't open it. She just stood there. It was not a good night to see Stuart. She hadn't been with a man since—God, she didn't know how long it had been. There had been that halfhearted affair with one of the attorneys who worked with Suzanne at the D.A.'s office, but it hadn't come to anything. He was just too...

He wasn't Stuart.

And there was the marketing guy in New Orleans who wanted to do her while he was doing her ad account for Dream Fields. He was wrong, too.

"Let me in, Annie." His tone was low and subtly compelling.

Let me in, Annie.

She threw the dead bolt and opened the door slightly—but not enough that he could come inside. She didn't turn on a light. From what she could see of his face, he was troubled. He hadn't easily made the choice to come here in the middle of the night.

She rested her forehead on the edge of the door, still making no move to let him in. "It's late for a visit, Stuart."

He nodded. "I know. I sat in your driveway a long time before I got up the nerve to knock."

"What do you want?"

"Ellie and I had a terrible fight."

And you thought I'd kiss it better. She gave a strangled laugh. He was like so many men in unhappy relationships—ripe for an affair. But it could never be that casual for her. She was her mother's daughter, and she'd watched Eugenia succumb to her passion for Jack Sullivan and then end her own life because of it. Once she slept with Stuart, all her principles would be shattered. She wasn't sure who she would be anymore.

"Don't tell me," Annie said, still barricaded behind the door and the bulk of her sweatshirt. "She's going to take a job in Washington and you'll see her two weekends out of the month."

He didn't answer for a minute. "Am I the only one who didn't see this coming?"

"Probably."

He was shaking his head. "Anyway, that wasn't what we argued about. She was so fired up—" he frowned in bafflement "—so enthralled with Jack and the victory and what it meant to her that she never even thought to talk about what it would mean to me. To us. Our marriage. Without a word to me, she's already told Jack she's thrilled and asked when he wanted her to leave."

"I'm sorry."

"No." He pressed a hand to his nape, then dropped it. "Don't be. I'm not here for sympathy or anything like that. I just seem to see things better when we talk." He glanced around the dark porch then back to her. "Look, could I come in?"

"It's not a good time, Stuart."

For several moments he simply stood there. "What do you have on behind that balled-up sweatshirt?"

She blinked as her heart thudded. She glanced down at herself. "Ah, a camisole."

He nodded, considering that. "You should probably put the sweatshirt back on. It's hard for me to think while my imagination's galloping off into forbidden territory. Unless you're ready to put an end to about fourteen years of torture."

Annie turned and managed to shake out the sweatshirt and pull it over her head. She stood for a minute wondering why she didn't feel any safer. Impulsively, she opened the door wide. "Come inside, Stuart. I want to tell you something."

His look narrowed, but he did as she said. Not bothering to turn on the lights, she headed back down the hall, past the dining room and kitchen to the den. She'd enclosed the porch with glass years ago so that she could work at home, but it was drafty when the temperature was chilly. She closed the French doors that separated the two areas and sat down on a big, soft sofa that was piled with cushions. Tucking her legs beneath her, she waited until Stuart was seated. Then, knowing this was going to be an ordeal, she wrapped her arms around a cushion.

She met his eyes and saw the puzzlement on his face. Along with dread and hope and desire. The same feelings teemed inside her. They had so much history, yet their feelings for each other—whatever they were—had survived in spite of their efforts to resist the irresistible. She couldn't stop to wonder now about his reaction when he heard what she had to say.

"My mother and Jack Sullivan were lovers, Stuart."

He didn't move. Didn't blink. For a second, she was thrown off, wondering if he already knew. "Did you know that?"

"No."

"It started before Trey was born," she said, squinting at a picture of her mother on the piano across the room. "At least, I think it started then. I'm not really sure about much of it. Only that she killed herself because of Jack."

"Are you sure?"

She looked at him again and smiled sadly. "She left a note. It was meant to reassure me that she loved me, that she knew suicide was cowardly but that she just didn't want to live without Jack. She begged me not to reveal her secret." Annie's expression was bitter. "Her instinct was to protect him to the last moment of her life."

He had been leaning back. Now he sat forward and touched her knee, just one brief, gentle touch. "I'm sorry, Annie."

"He wasn't worth a second of her time, but he stole her whole life," Annie said, her voice shaking. "He was a married man—I reminded her of that many times. Think of Taylor, the children. She was deaf to everything, even to the real possibility that Charles and Lily would likely throw her out of this cottage if they found out. She was enslaved, Stuart. From the moment he seduced her, everything she did, every thought in her head, centered around Jack."

"It must have been agony for you."

"I swore nothing like that would ever happen to me."

"It couldn't, Annie. You're strong and practical and talented. No man could ever enslave you."

"Dear God, I can't believe you said that." She put her hands over her face, then removed them. "Why do you think I'm telling you this, Stuart? Don't you see the similarity? By letting you in tonight, I'm opening myself to the same thing."

"It doesn't have to be that way," he said quietly. "You were strong before. You—"

"It can't be any other way. You're married. It doesn't change anything that Ellie's pissed at you right now." She tossed the cushion aside and sprang off the sofa. "What do you want from me, Stuart! You've been married to the woman for more than twenty years. She decides to go to Washington without a second thought and that's what it takes to make you realize something's missing?" She turned a blazing look on him. "Something's been missing for longer than that, Stuart."

"Yes, and that's what I was trying to tell you."

She gave an impatient shake of her head. "What?"

"I wanted to throw a little cold water on her, so I told her not to get too heated up about the new job in D.C. if it depended on Jack Sullivan staying in office."

Annie shrugged with confusion. "You lost me."

"Yeah, and I can't explain, not enough to make good sense. Put it this way. Jack has been dabbling in some very shady stuff. My sources tell me he's in for a rough time. I've never been a fan of Jack's, you know that. If it wouldn't hurt my sister and the kids, I wouldn't care if he disappeared tomorrow." There was an ironic twist to his mouth. "I guess I said that, more or less, and Ellie went up like a rocket. Bottom line is we're through."

"There's no chance you'll patch it up?"

"No."

"Do you want to?"

"No. I've wanted a divorce for...I don't know how long now. This D.C. job was the last straw. Marriage means one thing to her, another to me. I wanted children, Ellie didn't. She wanted to live in New York or L.A. I didn't. But when I mentioned divorce, she always resisted." He looked up, and his gaze was sad. "That's what I came to tell you tonight."

"Why?"

He stood up and went to her, cupping her face in his hands. "You know why, Annie."

She drew in a breath and it caught in her throat. "You've left her?"

"I've left her."

She closed her eyes. "I don't know if this is a dream."

He bent and touched his lips to hers. He was cold from sitting outside so long, but the kiss was warm. For a moment or two, he simply played with her mouth, touching it with butterfly kisses, nuzzling it in a wordless plea for entry. She sighed, hanging on to him by fistfuls of his shirt.

"Let go, Annie-girl," he murmured with his lips against hers. "We've both waited long enough."

She made a soft sound and he enclosed her in his arms with sudden, urgent strength. She threw her arms around his neck and returned his kiss. Yes, long enough.

THIRTY-FOUR

TAYLOR HADN'T BEEN SLEEPING when Jack and his entourage had finally shown up a couple of hours after she, Gayle and Trey had come home. Dreading what she was in for, she had made herself a pot of black coffee and spent the time pacing. But chastising her wasn't part of Jack's plan this night. He'd wanted her to make an appearance before his friends—not because anyone was interested in what she might have to say, but because he wanted her to play the part of First Lady to his governor-elect.

Taylor stood behind Jack, smiling, as he ushered the last of his supporters out the door. Three in the morning and these people were still rehashing the election, crowing over the brilliance of the campaign and their inspired strategy. Jack, of course, was the center of it all, the sun in their universe. God, if only she could just go to bed and never wake up again.

Or go to Spence and never come back again.

"Okay, we made it, baby!" Jack turned to her, rubbing his palms together. He was almost manic tonight. She had never seen him so hyper.

"You did it, Jack."

He gave her a sharp look. "You sober now?"

"I only had a few sips of champagne, Jack."

"A few glasses, baby. Don't try to shit me. I've got eyes in the back of my head. And when I'm not around to keep an eye on you, just remember I've got people to do it for me."

"Jim Rankin?"

He started upstairs, nudging her in front of him. "Maybe."

"I figured as much when he kept plucking my glass out of my hand tonight."

"For your own good, sugar. I know you felt like celebrating, but you can't handle the stuff." He drove a fist into his palm with glee. "God *damn,* I feel good! It doesn't get any better than this, huh, baby? Governor of the fuckin' state. What would my ol' daddy say if he could see me now?" He chuckled then, shaking his head. "Since he's in hell, I guess we'll never know."

"You shouldn't talk about your daddy that way, Jack." He seldom mentioned his family, and when he did it was never anything good. They were all dead now, and Taylor believed Jack was glad.

"Yeah, well, if he'd been a decent human being, maybe I wouldn't. But since he was a first-class bastard with shit for brains, I say he deserves whatever I call him."

When they reached the bedroom, the phone was ringing. Jack grabbed it and launched into another critique of the campaign. Didn't these people ever sleep? She used his distraction to escape to her dressing room. Distraction must be the reason he hadn't jumped on her with both feet about the champagne. Whatever, she was thankful not to have to cope with one of his tantrums tonight.

While he paced with the portable phone pressed to his ear, she began removing her makeup. She'd lost track of the number of calls he'd made or received since getting home tonight. She listened incredulously while he told someone on the other end to begin planning a fund-raiser to replace his depleted campaign chest. Only nine hours into the job and he was already planning to hit his supporters for more money!

She bent her head and rubbed at a spot on her temple that had been throbbing for the past hour. She shouldn't have ruined a good champagne high with a gallon of black coffee. It could be caffeine, but then again, it could be pure, unadulterated fear. She looked at herself in the mirror.

First Lady of the state of Mississippi.

For Jack, it would be so easy. He was born for this. It was

different for her. She didn't know if she could do it. Change had always been hard for her. What if it was too much? What if she were as disappointing to the people of the state as she was to almost everyone who knew her, especially Jack? They would be living in a fishbowl. What if the whole world suddenly saw their marriage for the charade it was?

Hands trembling, she jerked open a drawer and fumbled around until she located a bottle of pills. She had three of them in her palm, then impulsively shook out two more. She swallowed all five at once with water. Vodka would enhance the effect, but Jack had removed the liquor trolley that was usually in their bedroom suite. She'd have to go downstairs to get some and he would know.

This was panic, that's all. Time. Give it time. It would pass. Everything did. Eventually. Taking a deep breath, she moved shakily to the bed. Now it was just a matter of waiting for the pills to work. She forced her body to be still, though she was screaming inside. Jack was still on the phone, still pacing. She heard the sound of his voice, but through an echo chamber. Laughing. Then brisk with orders. Sharp with interest. More laughing. She would have to remember to take off her kimono before he came to bed. She had to be naked.

Now her drugged heart was thudding sluggishly and the tension in her body was going. Less throbbing in her temple, too. The drug was kicking in. Good. A few more minutes...

Now she was reaching that nice in-between place, the place where she was not quite sober but not quite drunk. A figure formed in the mists of her mind and she smiled in dreamy welcome.

Spence. Oh, yes, Spence...

He touched her face, then slowly bent and kissed her. Now he was loving her, his mouth moving sweetly over her face, her breasts, her belly. Everywhere. She moaned, reached for him, breathed his name....

"What the fuck did you take!"

She blinked in confusion. Jack, not Spence, stood at the bed-

side. No shirt. Pants…he was kicking his pants off. Not now…
not now… She tried to lift her hand to cover her eyes so she
wouldn't have to cope with this. Closing her eyes, she willed
her lover's image to reappear.

"Wake up, damn you!" Jack jerked her up and tore her
kimono from her. "I turn my back a few goddamn minutes and
you're zonked on some fuckin' shit you've got stashed somewhere. This really pisses me off, Taylor."

"I don't want to have sex," she said whining.

He threw her back on the bed and peeled his briefs off.
"That's too damn bad, sugar, because sex is exactly what I *do*
want. A man achieves the fuckin' *universe* and the least his
wife can do is show her love and support." On the bed now, he
held her face hard with one hand. "Unless you *don't* love me,
sweetheart. Is that it? You don't love me anymore, sugar?"

She wouldn't look at him. Couldn't. "Please, Jack, I'm really
tired…."

"I bet you wouldn't be too tired if it was *him,* would you,
baby?"

Fear pierced the fog inside her head. Like a doe sensing a
hunter closing in, she went still as death. "Wh-what?"

"Wh-a-a-at.." He mimicked her. "I'm saying you'd be up for
it in a New York minute if I were somebody else, am I right?"

"I don't know what you're talking about, Jack."

"I'm telling it straight out, baby. I'm talking about your goddamn lover. You've been a very bad girl."

"No, I—"

"Don't lie to me, Taylor." His hand on her face tightened like
a vise. "I could get very upset."

She licked her lips, tried to think. He was just tormenting
her. Taking a shot in the dark.

"You thought I didn't know?"

"Let me up, Jack."

"Why? So you can run to the gazebo and see if he's waiting? Sorry, baby, but it won't happen, not tonight." He moved
his hand from her face to her breast and gave her nipple a hard

twist, laughing softly when she winced. "Tonight it'll be just you and me, lover."

A tear ran from the corner of her eye. "I don't know why you're doing this, Jack."

He lifted a fraction, keeping his hand curled menacingly around her breast, and looked her in the eyes. "You don't know why a man—the fuckin' governor of the state—would be pissed because his wife has been screwing around behind his back for who knows how long? Is that what you're saying?"

She moved her eyes, unable to look at him. "Can we talk about this later?"

"Before or after you screw him again?"

"Wh-who are you talking about, Jack? I don't—"

"The fuckin' *weirdo,* that's who! Spencer Dutton." The hand on her breast tightened until she whimpered. Taylor wrapped her fingers around his wrist.

"You're hurting me, Jack. Let me up…please."

"When I'm ready."

She closed her eyes again. "What do you want from me?" she cried in anguish.

"Ahhh…" He nodded in satisfaction. "Now, that's what I like to hear." He bent and licked the inside of her ear, then bit her lobe, hurting her. "I'm gonna tell you what I like, baby. And we're gonna get it on tonight. It'll be our celebration, just us two, the governor and his First Lady."

"No, please…" Her head was thrashing back and forth desperately now. Sex between them had often been rough, but she'd never been truly afraid before.

"Yes, please." He threw a leg over and mounted her heavily.

"It wasn't what you think," Taylor said, trying to reach him any way she could.

Pinning both her hands, he grinned at her. "Oh? You want to tell me how it was?"

"I…it…it wasn't the sex."

"Oooh, guess ol' Spence has another technique, hmm?"

Yes, tenderness, caring, love. He loves me!

For a second or two, some surviving scrap of pride pierced her fear and humiliation. He might know about Spence, but he wouldn't do anything because of the scandal. She could just get up out of the bed and walk away. Just dress and leave now. To hell with the whole meaningless farce of their marriage. But then what? Face the disgrace? The scandal?

Jack was above her now, poised to enter her without even pretending to prepare her. She reached for the remnants of her dream, blessedly cushioned from the worst by the drug. With her mind in a daze, all he could take was her body. Jack might curse Spence—and her—but he couldn't take her fantasies.

And in her mind, she would be loving Spence.

SUZANNE WAS JOSTLED BY a couple of Jack's eager fans trying to push their way to the front of the crowd as the limousine cruised to a stop in front of the club. She glanced at their faces, struck again by whatever it was about Jack that made people—women especially—so crazy about her brother-in-law. In designer outfits and dripping jewelry, they craned to get the first glimpse of him. Their presence at the fund-raiser tonight probably translated to cash for future campaigns.

Oh, why am I here? she asked herself for the tenth time.

Because Taylor begged me.

Her sister had looked like hell a few hours ago in Suzanne's chambers pleading with Suzanne not to desert her tonight. Something had happened, she told Suzanne. She'd explain later. It must be bad. Anyone could see Taylor was on the edge. She was pale, literally jumping with nerves, and she wouldn't take off her sunglasses. Suzanne had worried that if she didn't get hold of herself soon, she might fortify herself with a drink or two out of desperation.

Why was she so desperate?

Suzanne spotted her now with Gayle and Trey and relaxed a little. She seemed calm enough. Suzanne saw that Annie had spotted Stuart across the steps and was heading toward him. Caleb, as usual, was at her side. Watching them, Suzanne smiled in spite of herself. Some things were right in the world, after all.

The ripple of excitement in the crowd made her turn back to watch what was, after all, the main event of the evening. Jack's limo stopped and he climbed out. As he lifted his arms, people roared their approval. Suzanne noticed that Taylor and Trey lagged a bit, but Gayle ran eagerly toward him. In the clamor, Suzanne nearly missed the sharp *crack!* of the rifle.

She thought later that possibly she had imagined the sound. She recalled only that she stared at Jack in horror as his death played out before her eyes as if in slow motion. For a split second, he'd looked incredulous, and then blood was pouring from his chest. But to her horror, when Suzanne had clawed her way through, Gayle's inert form lay across her father's body.

PART IV

THIRTY-FIVE

December 1997

SUZANNE RODE WITH TAYLOR to the hospital. Beside her, Taylor was lifeless. The person who'd fallen screaming beside her daughter on the sidewalk had vanished, replaced by a shocked, empty-eyed shell. Suzanne had pulled her away the moment the physician had appeared, and Taylor had stood trembling in Suzanne's embrace while the doctor—failing to find a pulse—had pronounced Jack dead. The next vital minutes were devoted to staunching the flow of blood from Gayle's midriff, but by then Taylor had seemed transported to another place. She was still there, cocooned in fear and grief and shock.

So much blood. Holding on to Taylor tightly, Suzanne had watched the physician work valiantly, wondering how a person could survive the loss of so much blood.

But this was not just a person! This was Gayle, beautiful, gifted Gayle. Taylor's firstborn.

The crowd had parted willingly to allow the paramedics through. From their demeanor, Suzanne knew Gayle's condition was grave. They'd worked quickly to get her onto the gurney and then inside the ambulance. They'd refused when Suzanne asked if she and Taylor could ride with Gayle. Taylor had given no response. Then, with the police scrambling wildly in the wake of the shooting, Ben Kincaid had arranged for a cruiser to take them both to the hospital. Stuart and Annie would ride with Trey and Caleb in a second cruiser. Tears had filled Suzanne's eyes as Ben saw them into the car with a reassuring squeeze of her hand. Once under way, Suzanne had pushed her own apprehension aside and taken Taylor's cold hand in both of hers.

Her sister still had not uttered a word.

The situation got worse at the hospital. The bullet that had entered Jack beneath his arm had hit his heart dead-on, then exited and slammed into Gayle, nicking her liver. Most of the blood on the sidewalk had been Jack's, fortunately, although Gayle was bleeding copiously internally. The family was huddled in the waiting room when a nurse came out and informed them that her blood type was a rare one and that the hospital's supply was low. They were told most families preferred to use blood from relatives, people they knew to be free of disease— HIV, hepatitis, other viruses. Taylor, Suzanne, Stuart and Trey were quickly typed, but no one was compatible. Suzanne left the waiting room to call her parents.

The crowd, mostly reporters and curiosity seekers, converged on her. Luckily, a couple of uniformed guards were on hand. One of them kept the crowd back while she made the call. She was heading back to the waiting room when she saw Spencer Dutton step off the elevator. A guard stopped him as he tried to force his way past the area cordoned off for the press. Suzanne was struck by the look on his face. He caught her eye, called her name. She remembered the night of the election, and how he'd spoken with familiarity about Taylor. If there had been any doubt before that he had a deep regard for Taylor, there was none now. She walked to him and touched his arm. "She's in the waiting room, Spence. I'll take you."

"How is the girl?"

"Gayle. Holding her own. She needs blood."

"I'll give."

"She's AB negative."

"I'm O positive."

"Thanks anyway, Spence."

They started back, braving an onslaught of questions and curiosity from all sides. At the waiting-room door, Spence stopped, seeking Taylor's face. The instant she saw him, she sprang up out of her seat. Suzanne had the oddest feeling that her sister wanted to run to him, would have run to him if there hadn't been so many eyes watching. Spence went to her and pushed her gently back into her chair and took the one vacated by Suzanne when she'd gone to make the call. She couldn't hear what he said, but his tone was gruff, the words halting and awkward coming from a man unused to emotion. But Taylor seemed calmed by his presence and her hand found its way naturally into Spence's large, rough one. She began to weep silently, brokenheartedly, as if a dam had broken.

Suzanne exchanged a quick look with Annie, torn between alarm and gratitude. Until now, Taylor had seemed devoid of any emotion. If Spencer could bring her to life again, then that was good. They'd worry about the appearance of things later.

"Dad's on the way," she said, hoping to distract the family. She glanced around. "Where's Caleb?"

Stuart emerged from a cubicle rolling down the cuffs on his shirt. "He's in there giving blood, just in case."

"Oh. Okay." She sat down, staring at the closed curtain as new fear spiraled through her. Caleb was giving blood. What if he was AB negative? Someone had already said that Gayle's blood type was the same as Jack's. If Caleb matched, too, would anybody make the connection?

She spent the next fifteen minutes praying, her hands clasped tightly in her lap. She wanted blood for Gayle, but did it have to be Caleb? Finally the curtain was shoved open and Caleb came out, casually rolling his shirtsleeve down as he chatted with the lab technician. Suzanne rose slowly from her seat, her heart knocking.

"Mom, you're pale as a ghost." He walked over, his face concerned.

"They're trying to find donors," Suzanne said, distracted. "How rare can a blood type be?"

"It's okay, Mom. Turns out mine is a match." Caleb shrugged with a half smile. *So like Jack!* "Go figure."

Suzanne's heart stumbled. She saw the puzzlement in Stuart's eyes, but then Annie nudged him and he turned away. Her heart still racing, Suzanne sank back into her chair and rested her head against the wall.

Dear God, let this day end without another disaster.

HOURS LATER, SUZANNE stood at the window of Gayle's room in the hospital. On the other side of the room, Taylor was stretched out on a settee, an arm thrown over her face. Suzanne had persuaded her to drink some tea and eat a few bites of a sandwich from a vending machine in the hall, but food seemed the last thing Taylor needed.

Suzanne's appetite was gone for an entirely different reason. She'd relaxed a little when everyone finally left the hospital after Gayle had stabilized—thanks to Caleb's blood—and was sleeping naturally. Nobody seemed to note the significance of Caleb's blood type. Maybe after Jack's death, they were simply in a daze. Or ready to believe in miracles. She wasn't so naive as to think they wouldn't see the truth eventually. Caleb, especially. He was always alert to clues about the mystery of his father.

"Hey, how's it going in here?"

"Ben." Her heart gave a little lurch when she heard his deep, quiet voice, and she managed a smile. "Hi, come in."

Taylor lowered her arm. Her eyes were empty. "Hello, Ben."

"Taylor." He looked beyond her to the young girl on the bed. "How's Gayle?"

"Better," Suzanne replied, coming away from the window. She touched Ben's arm and drew him over to the door. "She's stable," she said, whispering. "At least, that's what they tell us. Now she needs rest. After so much blood loss—" She stopped.

Ben put his arm around her shoulders and gave her a warm hug. She leaned against him for a minute, comforted by something in Ben that touched a deep, almost-forgotten memory. How was it that in the worst times of her life, Ben Kincaid was always there?

He urged her through the door. "Come on, let's walk to that

little room at the end of the hall. There's coffee, if you aren't wired to the max already, and no one's there."

She hung back, looking at Taylor, again stretched out in the recliner, eyes closed. "I don't think I should leave Taylor."

"Spence will stay while you take a break," Ben said.

Spencer Dutton rose from a chair just outside the door. Beyond being surprised by his devotion to Taylor, she wondered how long he'd been there. She simply nodded at him and waited until he'd disappeared inside before going with Ben. He told a nurse where they were headed in case Taylor needed her.

The tiny room was blessedly deserted. Ben pointed to one of the chairs and lifted the coffee decanter. "Want some?"

"Not really. You're right, I've had more than enough."

He nodded, poured one for himself. When he sat down beside her, Suzanne leaned her head back against the chair and murmured, "I still can't believe this, Ben. It seems like a nightmare."

"I talked to the doctor, Suzy. Gayle really is out of danger. It'll take a while to recover her strength, but she's young and healthy."

"I know. But Jack…"

"Yeah, one second he's smiling and blessing his fans, the next he's catching a bullet. He always seemed too damn lucky to go like that."

She opened her eyes, stared at the ceiling. "Lucky devil. How many times did I hear those words applied to Jack?"

"Yeah. But a thirty-ought-six is enough to bring down even Jack Sullivan."

"Is that what it was?"

"Yeah, Rankin's men found the weapon abandoned in the park across from the club. Probably right where the guy was standing when he shot it."

"Thirty-ought-six. That's a rifle, isn't it?"

"Big enough to kill a deer. Hell, a bear."

"Big enough to go through Jack and Gayle, too." She bent

her head and rubbed her temple. "Do they have any idea who it was?"

"No."

"Did you talk to his campaign people? Maybe somebody had a grudge against him. People like that usually leave a note or make a phone call if they're ticked off, or it could be—"

"Whoa." He touched her knee. "It could be a hundred things, and I didn't talk to his campaign people. They wouldn't have cooperated if I'd tried. I don't have authority to interfere in the investigation of a murder. The shooting happened in Rankin's jurisdiction, and you can bet your life he won't tolerate anybody sticking his nose in this case."

"I suppose so." She frowned. "But how do you suppose somebody could stake out a place in the woods right across from the country club, wait with a rifle while a couple of hundred people are milling around and then take aim, fire a shot, drop the gun and run away, and nobody sees anything? How can that happen, Ben?"

"Yeah, Kincaid, how can that happen?"

Jim Rankin stood in the doorway watching the two of them, his pale eyes alert. In his knife-sharp creases and the too-short haircut, she was suddenly reminded of an SS officer. Ben leaned forward, set his coffee on the small table in front of the settee and stood up. "Rankin. I didn't expect you to get away from the crime scene before morning."

"What did you expect? That us rednecks would scurry around in the dark trampling evidence like a bunch of Keystone Kops? That what you expected, Kincaid?"

Suzanne was on her feet now. "Do you have any information about the shooter, Jim?"

"It's hard to tell what we have. When it's daylight, we'll have a better idea what went down." He looked back at Ben. "Seems certain the killer fired the shot, abandoned the weapon and merged into the crowd at the fund-raiser. What that boils down to is that anybody there could have done it."

Ben raised a single brow. "It'll be tough trying to single out somebody who might have slipped out and not been missed, then run back after the deed was done."

"Tough, but not impossible."

"I'd look for a motive first if I were you," Ben remarked.

"I'm working on it," Rankin said, looking more like an SS officer than ever. "So, where were you when Jack fell?"

For a second, Ben was silent. Then he flashed an incredulous grin. "Are you suggesting that I had a motive to kill Jack?"

"He was suspicious of you coming back to Percyville. He said you held a grudge over some land your old man lost for taxes. He said you blamed him for it."

"It wasn't my 'old man.' It was my grandfather, and he didn't lose the land for taxes. Jack swindled it from him. That's old news. It happened more than ten years ago. If I wanted to kill him over it, I'd have done it then."

Suzanne put a hand on Ben's arm. "This is ridiculous, Jim. Ben wouldn't shoot anybody."

Rankin looked at Ben. "That right, Kincaid? You wouldn't shoot anybody? A dozen years as a federal agent and you've never killed a man?"

Suzanne made an impatient sound. "You're wasting valuable time here, Jim. You should be talking to Jack's associates, the people in his inner circle. That's where you're likely to find his killer. Unless it turns out to be some deranged person."

He turned to her calmly. "Then you can vouch for Kincaid?"

"I didn't see him the instant the shot was fired, but he was one of the first people to get to Jack once he was down," she said quietly. She knew it wouldn't win her any points to come to Ben's defense, but she was surprised by the pure malice in Rankin's eyes.

"I came to tell you not to leave town, Kincaid. You may not have fired the actual shot, but a man in your line of work has the right connections to get it done."

Suzanne couldn't believe what she was hearing. "Jim, for goodness' sake! Jack had his finger in every political pie in this state. Look at those people before you start accusing family friends."

Rankin turned to Ben, allowing his jacket to fall open and reveal his weapon. "Just remember what I told you, Kincaid. Don't leave town."

Neither Suzanne nor Ben spoke in the silence after Rankin left. Then Suzanne stole a look at Ben and a giggle erupted. She put her fingers over her mouth, but her eyes still danced. "Did you hear that? He got that line from a bad movie."

"Had to." Ben wrapped a hand around the back of his neck, chuckling. "Do you believe this guy? He's got Jack's gambling cronies, pissed-off political rivals, assorted crazies, two-timed husbands—the list is endless—and he's focused on me."

"I wonder why." The humor was fading from Suzanne's face.

Ben, too, was looking thoughtful. "I don't know. Maybe I ought to find out." Seconds passed, then Ben touched her elbow. "Come on. Time to get back to Taylor."

They walked quietly back to Gayle's room, stopping at the closed door. Suzanne drew a deep breath as she faced him. Standing there in the dim light of the corridor, she was aware of the changes in him over the years. He looked like a man no sane person would cross. In spite of that, she was almost as comfortable with Ben as she was with Stuart. Or Caleb. She was glad he'd come tonight. He had a way of taking her back in time, back to when she was a whole person. A complete woman.

Why was that?

"Thank you for coming tonight," she said.

He touched her cheek. "No thanks necessary."

She sighed, liking the feel of his warm hand. She closed her eyes briefly. "Tomorrow will be here all too soon, with everything that Jack's death means. Taylor is very fragile. I don't know what this will do to her."

"She's lucky to have you and Stuart and Annie."

"If it were me, I don't know if that would be enough. The media will be vicious, Ben."

"Uh-huh. Just keep them at bay. Don't say anything and

don't let anybody else in the family say anything. Let Jack's press people handle that part of it."

"I will."

He bent and touched his forehead to hers. "And take some time for yourself. You look like a strong wind would do *you* some damage, too."

She smiled. Any other man this close and her heart would be thudding in panic. Actually, her heart *was* thudding, but it wasn't panic. It was…it was something good. Again she felt a little like the Suzanne before…before the rape. There, she'd said it. Thought it. But she was in a public corridor. Would she feel so safe if she were alone with Ben?

"Hey, you aren't asleep on your feet, are you?"

Her eyes fluttered open and found him so close that she could see the little golden flecks in his eyes. "I need to get back," she said, breathless and confused. She hadn't felt anything like this for sixteen years.

"Okay." He stepped back, and she was aware of a feeling of disappointment. As if something good had been within reach and now it was removed.

"Thanks again," she whispered.

"I'll call," he promised. "Tomorrow."

She nodded. Then he moved with a quickness that she didn't anticipate and kissed her. A swift, warm and deliberate kiss on her mouth, and she was left with the taste and thrill of it to savor for what was left of the night.

CALEB RESTED HIS HEAD on his stacked hands and studied the stickers of the universe that were stuck on the ceiling in his room. They glowed in the dark. He remembered when his grandpa had put them up. He'd been about eight years old. Trey would have been six. Grandpa thought they were neat, and besides, every time they slept over at Riverbend, they'd learn about the constellations. Boy, that seemed like a million years ago.

He looked over at the matching twin bed where Trey lay

balled up like when he was little and Jack had treated him
shitty. On those times, Trey would say how he hated him. How
he wished he was dead. How he wished *he* didn't have a father
like Caleb, because fathers sucked. But Caleb knew Trey didn't
really mean it, because he always had this awful look in his
eyes and he would almost always cry. Until he got old enough
not to.

But he had cried tonight. Your father shot down right in front
of your eyes was enough to make anybody cry. Even Caleb had
teared up a little, especially when he realized Gayle was shot,
too. Then at the hospital, boy, it had really been bad. Gayle
needing blood and not enough of her type. All the grown-ups
with worried faces. Aunt Taylor like a zombie. Even his mom
had been shaken. At least that had turned out okay. It felt good
knowing he had played a part in helping Gayle. These things
happen sometimes, Grandpa said. Just be glad you had the right
stuff, son. Yeah, it felt good.

He suspended thought for a moment. Identified the Big
Dipper. The North Star. Orion.

Uncle Jack was dead. No shutting off that thought. Caleb
still found it almost impossible to believe. Uncle Jack was one
of those people you could never imagine breaking a leg, even.
But being shot dead, that was incredible.

Who could have done it? No matter how many times that
question popped up, he couldn't come up with even a possibility. A dozen times already he'd run through all the questions as
if they were on a videotape. Who killed Jack? And why? Was
it connected to business stuff? Politics? For sure, politics was
heavy-duty dirty. That scene could get messy sometimes. De-
feated opponents held grudges, but that guy Jack beat wasn't
the type to shoot somebody. Or even to have somebody shot.
Then who in Jack's circle was that type? As usual, he got hung
up here. Nobody he knew of would shoot the friggin' governor-
elect.

By now, his head was aching from all the unanswered questions. He lowered his hands, turned on his side and studied his

cousin. Trey moved, sucked in a breath, and it was shaky, like
a little kid who'd been crying a lot. Man, this really did suck.
All the neat stuff that went with being governor would never
be. But at least Gayle was okay.

He crooked an arm around his pillow and burrowed into it,
feeling right about that one thing, if nothing else. What a coincidence, both of them having the same blood type. AB negative.
It was pretty rare. Gayle had inherited it from Jack. The nurse
told him that. He yawned and felt sleep closing in. Wonder who
he got it from? Grandpa always said something...

Oh, yeah. There was no such thing as coincidence.

THIRTY-SIX

WHO KILLED JACK SULLIVAN?

It was the Big Question, and the media were having a field day with it. Suzanne wasn't sure if it would have been a bigger story if the killer had been known, or if the media's not knowing made the assassination even more fascinating. No matter, no scrap of information was too insignificant. TV crews and reporters were everywhere. To escape, the entire family except Stuart had taken up residence at Riverbend. Unless a reporter wanted to be arrested for trespassing, there was no access to the people who'd been closest to Jack. That left the hospital. And even there, it was only when the family was in Gayle's room that they were safe.

"Can you believe this?" Annie said, surveying the grounds and parking lot from a third-floor window. "Those people are everywhere. We can use the staff elevator—the head nurse okayed it—but once we leave the hospital, we still have to get to the car."

Taylor stood before a huge bouquet of pink roses. "I don't care about the press. Thank God I don't have to talk to them ever again."

Suzanne glanced at Annie. "It won't be that easy, Taylor. Jack's assassination is big news. Reporters are clamoring for any tidbit of information and you'll be their prime source. Don't underestimate what they'll resort to to get a sound bite."

"They'll get 'no comment,'" Taylor said stubbornly.

Gayle plucked at the tape securing the IV shunt on the back of her hand. "You've never understood the media, Mom. Dad always said so."

"And now I don't have to understand them." Using a single finger, Taylor touched the card tucked among the roses.

"Mom…" Gayle looked exasperated. "Remember what happened when Aunt Suzy got that stuff thrown on her at the courthouse a few weeks ago?"

"Those were demonstrators. They were protesting for a cause," Taylor said.

Suzanne moved to Gayle's bedside and brushed a strand of hair back from the girl's cheek. "Taylor's right, honey. We're not expecting anything like that. But the questions they ask can be painful and intrusive. We'd like to spare your mother that."

Gayle looked at Suzanne, then at Annie. "But why do you have to leave at all? What's so important that all three of you have to go?"

"The funeral arrangements, Gayle," Taylor said, rubbing one temple wearily. "There are decisions to be made. Suzy and Annie are going to help because it's a hassle."

Gayle sought Suzanne's eyes, her mouth trembling. "Does Mom have to go? Couldn't the two of you do it?"

Suzanne shook her head. "I'm sorry, love. This is something your mother has to do. Don't worry. Grandma and Grandpa are coming to stay with you." She glanced at her watch. "They should be here any minute."

Gayle was shaking her head in distress. "But you heard her. She doesn't want to do it. It's a hassle."

"Don't be ridiculous, Gayle," Taylor said, showing impatience. "Of course I have to do it."

"See?" Gayle clung to Suzanne's hand. "That's why you and Annie should do it. Mom didn't love Daddy anymore." Gayle's eyes—as dark as Jack's—filled with tears. "Nobody in the whole family loved him except m-me."

Suzanne's heart ached for Gayle. She had called for Jack, not Taylor, when she first woke up in the hospital, scared and in pain. When told he was dead, she had retreated into a shell, not unlike her mother's initial reaction. The doctor called it depression. Blood loss did that sometimes, he told them, trying to explain Gayle's apathy. But Suzanne knew better. As did Taylor. It was losing Jack, not blood, that made her seek a black corner in her mind to hide in.

"I loved him once, didn't I, Suzy?" Taylor turned back to the pink roses.

Suzanne met Annie's gaze briefly. "Yes, you loved him."

Tears pooled in Gayle's eyes. "W-why did he have to die?"

"Nobody knows the answer to that, honey." Suzanne took a tissue from a box on the bedside table and gently wiped the girl's face. Gayle took it from her and rubbed her eyes hard. When she finished, her eyes flashed with anger, not tears.

"Well, somebody did it, and if they don't find out who, then *I'll* find out when I get out of here."

"They'll find whoever did it, Gayle," Annie said quietly.

"Yes." Taylor held one of the roses against her lips, trying to hide the way they trembled. "You can't get away with killing someone like Jack."

SUZANNE APPROACHED the gates at Riverbend warily, studying the thick bank of oleanders for suspicious vehicles or—horrible thought—a television van. It was midnight, but no hour was too late for the media. Thankfully, the coast was clear.

She groped for the remote above the visor, relieved that the day was finally over. She was increasingly anxious about Taylor. Annie was with her tonight at the hospital, but there was still the wake and the funeral to be gotten through.

Stuart had met them at the mortuary to help plan Jack's funeral and interment. Sadly, Gayle had been on target about Taylor's interest in putting Jack to rest. It might have been any stranger's casket. Her apathy was so obvious that Suzanne had suggested Taylor go with Annie for a cup of coffee while Stuart and Suzanne finalized the details. Afterward, Suzanne had escaped to her chambers to clear away some paperwork until she could resume her duties after the funeral.

She sighed. Two more interminable days.

Braking almost to a stop, she pressed the remote to open

the gates. Light suddenly flashed from her left. She turned and stared in surprise while her foot went instinctively to the brake. A cameraman materialized out of the oleanders. Beside him, a reporter moved forward, but with the lights blinding her, she couldn't see anything except the microphone thrust at her, a silver bubble on a stick.

"Judge Stafford! May we have a statement?"

It was a woman. Squinting through the glare, she recognized Amanda Mason.

"Judge Stafford! Do you have any suspicions as to who killed Jack Sullivan?"

Ridiculous question. Even if she did, she would hardly tell a reporter. Least of all Amanda Mason. She glanced at the gates and found them barely moving. She squeezed the remote again.

"Judge Stafford, the governor-elect was in your office a few days ago. You appeared to be arguing. Can you personally think of a reason anyone might want to kill him?"

What was the woman suggesting? Suzanne felt a chill. What a coup it would be for Mason's career if she uncovered Suzanne's darkest secret. It might catapult the reporter to the big time while she and Caleb and Taylor and—everyone else— would be in hell. The gates moved sluggishly. Had they sabotaged the mechanism in some way? She punched the remote again.

"Judge Stafford, I'm going to write this story. Now is your chance to explain."

"No comment," she said bitterly.

The gates finally swung wide enough for her to drive through. Suzanne released the brake and accelerated, but stopped just inside and waited for the gates to close to be sure Mason didn't follow. The woman's persistence was frightening. No doubt she'd consider an arrest for trespassing a fair exchange for an intimate look at Jack Sullivan's family.

God. Two more days.

Although security lights blazed on the grounds and illuminated the house, it was a blessedly quiet and sleeping household when she unlocked the door and went inside. With a weary sigh, she dropped her things on a chair, shed her coat and hung it in the closet, then removed her shoes. With one in each hand, she climbed the stairs to check on Caleb and Trey. Both were sleeping. She blessed their youthful resilience, stored her things in her room and went back downstairs.

She hadn't eaten since lunchtime. In the kitchen, she opened the refrigerator and chose a carton of yogurt. Then—still in her bare feet—she drifted through the house, heading for the sunporch. Tired as she was, she preferred the soft night lighting and left the overheads off.

The French doors were ajar, and she was through them before she heard a woman's voice. She stopped, the spoon in her mouth. And then fury erupted. Was it Amanda Mason? How dare she? And how had she managed to get into the sunporch?

She snapped on the light. Taylor and Spence were entwined on the sofa. They stared at her with faces as stunned as her own. Taylor's shirt was lying among the cushions tossed to the floor. Her breasts were bare, dark tips tight and glistening. Spencer lay atop her, and her legs, long and white and shapely, were locked around his thighs. Spencer, at least, was clothed, but his shirt was open and his pants were unzipped.

Suzanne took it all in in one shocked instant.

"Suzanne…" Taylor's voice was high with distress.

"Oh…God…" Suzanne turned away, shaking her head. A moment or two passed and she heard the rustling of clothing, snaps snapping, zippers zipping. She moved shakily to the wall and turned off the light. In the darkness, she leaned her head against the wall and wondered what else could go wrong.

"Suzy…"

"Are you crazy?" she asked, not looking at them, not raising her voice. Still leaning against the wall.

"It's not what you think, Suzy."

"What? It's not what I think?" She straightened and glared at her sister. "You weren't making love? You weren't lying together half naked on a sofa on the sunporch—the *sunporch, for God's sake!*—when there are reporters all over the freaking world just panting to find you? To get a statement—any statement—from Jack's grieving widow?"

"I'm not grieving."

Suzanne huffed with irony. "No shit!"

"I love Spencer."

"You love Spencer. Well, ten minutes ago, I had to practically beat off a reporter with her cameraman hiding in the bushes before I could get through the gates! What if they followed me? What if they're filming the two of you right now? Would the world smile and look the other way just because you love Spencer?"

"I'm sorry, but—"

"And Spencer!" She turned furious eyes on him. "I gave you more credit. Taylor's judgment may be impaired considering everything she's been through, but you know how brutal people can be, especially if the widow of Mississippi's golden boy is discovered to have a lover not twenty-four hours after he's been assassinated." She stopped, out of breath, then slapped her arms against her thighs with exasperation. "I don't believe you two!"

"I take full responsibility for this," Spencer said quietly.

Suzanne rolled her eyes. "Spare me!"

He raked a hand over his untidy hair. "Taylor was so upset. I know how she—"

"I called him, Suzy."

Suzanne whirled on her sister again. "You called him? You *called* him? When, for God's sake? Why? You have moral support here. You've been literally surrounded by family since it happened. Somebody was always with you in Gayle's room. We—" She stopped. Her eyes narrowed. "You're supposed to be with Gayle right now, Taylor. Why aren't you? Who's with her?"

Taylor dropped her eyes. "Annie."

"You left your daughter to meet your lover?"

Taylor was weeping silently now. "I—I h-had to see him. I was so...so c-cold. I just n-needed to *see* him, Suzy." She gave

Suzanne a pleading look. "You wouldn't understand. You've never needed anybody. I just couldn't face it. The people. The commotion. The silly, stupid *pretense* of it all!" She buried her face in her hands, her sobs nearing hysteria.

Spencer took her in his arms, holding her and stroking her hair, rocking her as if she were a little girl. Suzanne watched them, stunned by Spencer's tenderness, by Taylor's despair. Her sister seemed almost childlike as she buried her face in his neck and clung to his shirt.

Shaking her head, Suzanne spoke softly. "What did you tell Annie when you left?"

"That I just h-had to get away for a f-few hours."

Over Taylor's head, Spencer gazed steadily at Suzanne. With his arms around Taylor, he looked ready to slay dragons for her. Suzanne sighed inwardly. After living with Jack's callous disrespect of her, both as a woman and as an individual, it was no wonder she'd fallen into a lover's arms. But Spencer Dutton? He had none of Jack's stunning good looks, none of the charisma that made Jack seem larger than life.

Suzanne sank onto a chair. "I don't know how all this is going to play out, Taylor. If anybody gets wind of you having an affair..." She thought of Amanda Mason and closed her eyes with a shudder.

"They won't." Taylor pulled away from Spencer, wiped the tears from both cheeks, then looked at Suzanne. There was sadness in her beautiful eyes. And acceptance. "I knew it was an incredible risk...what I did tonight. But I just h-had to see him one more time. I'll be okay from here on out. I know what I have to do."

Something in her tone alarmed Suzanne. "What do you mean?"

She sniffed, straightened her shoulders. "Stand on my own two feet for a change. See my kids through this ordeal. Stop leaning on people." She gave Spencer a sad smile and touched his cheek. "Including Spencer."

He caught her hand and kissed it. Even now that they'd been

discovered, he seemed oddly disconnected from the potential scandal.

"Are you going back to the hospital tonight?" Suzanne asked.

"Yes, of course. I intended to all along." Taylor began tucking her shirt into the waistband of her denim skirt.

"I'll drive you," Suzanne said. "We'll relieve Annie. I can sleep at the hospital just as well as here. Don't argue, either one of you," she ordered, and after a moment, they nodded.

"Spencer." Suzanne stopped on her way to the French doors. "Don't leave here until after we're out of sight. And then don't use the front gate. I don't know how you got in here, but don't take any more chances on being seen. Amanda Mason is on a mission. That makes her a dangerous person."

He nodded.

"Come on, Taylor."

With one last lingering look at Spencer, Taylor went.

AN HOUR LATER, SUZANNE lay sleepless on a cot in Gayle's room. On the other side of the room, Taylor slept the still, deep sleep induced by a drug. Suzanne had watched her take it, but she had said nothing. If it would help Taylor get some rest, perhaps it was the best thing. Tomorrow would be a long day, the next even longer.

God, even with Jack dead, his ghost lived on to haunt them. Taylor was a wreck, her children were traumatized, Caleb was at risk and Suzanne was still trying to pretend her own life wasn't screwed up because of him.

You wouldn't understand. You've never needed anybody.

Ah, yes, she did understand. She knew how it felt to be wounded and needy. At least Taylor had found someone to take her beyond Jack's cruelty, while she, Suzanne, had not. Suzanne could almost envy her. As crazy as it seemed, Jack was still orchestrating fear and control from the grave.

THIRTY-SEVEN

IT WAS MIDMORNING WHEN Ben Kincaid got to The Dinner Bell. He stopped just inside the door, made a casual survey of Ed Bell's customers, caught Stuart's eye in the last booth against the back wall and headed that way. He nodded to two cops occupying the first two stools at the counter, recognizing one of them as a former basketball teammate, Howie Gill. The look on Howie's face was not friendly. Rankin was probably feeding his troops bullshit about the big-city federal agent in their midst.

The breakfast crowd had come and gone. The other customers were mostly diehard retirees who had no place more interesting to spend the morning. Ben smiled grimly to himself. Thanks to Jack, they now had a topic of conversation like nothing to come down the pike in Percyville before. And the climactic event—Jack's funeral—wasn't until tomorrow morning at ten.

As Ben slid into the booth, Stuart signaled the waitress to bring more coffee. He glanced at the two cops. "When those two leave, two more take their place. Ed's never been robbed."

Ben grinned. "Some things never change."

The waitress brought Ben's coffee, dropped half a dozen individual plastic creamers on the table, pulled out her pad and, with her pen poised, asked, "Y'all want pie or something, Stuart?"

"Ben?"

"Just coffee."

"Okey-dokey." She ripped the ticket off and slapped it on the table. "Y'all want it heated up, just whistle."

"Thanks, Lila." Stuart waited until she moved away. "When

I contacted you a few months ago, Ben, I never anticipated anything like this. I knew Jack had enemies, big-time, hardball types, but…" He trailed off, shaking his head.

Ben played with his spoon. "In spite of Jack's shenanigans, I think the shooting caught most people off guard."

"Can you tell me anything? Off the record."

"Nothing you couldn't find out on your own."

The two cops suddenly stood up and left without paying. Ben and Stuart watched them amble down the sidewalk to a police cruiser, then followed their progress as they backed out.

"The Bureau has a dozen agents looking into every nook and cranny of Jack's life, Stuart, personal and public. It's a mind-blowing task. He had more than his share of enemies, as you know, but so far none of our feelers have turned up anything remotely pointing to a planned assassination."

"I still can't believe it," Stuart said, rubbing his finger over a crack in the tabletop. "I ask myself why they would want to get rid of him. I mean, he was shaking down a lot of people, even Vegas businessmen, people who play real hardball, but he was ten times more valuable to them alive than dead. He was going to open the door to more gambling, not shut it down."

"It's puzzling." Ben had spent the better part of two days thinking along the same lines, but he sensed something else was bothering Stuart. Ben fiddled with his spoon, then looked up into Stuart's eyes.

"I'm wondering if I made a mistake, Ben. I mean, by contacting the feds about the corruption surrounding Jack, did I start a chain of events that brought this about?"

"How so?"

"Think about it." Stuart hunched a little closer, his hands flat on the table. "When you showed up in Percyville, it could be that Jack panicked. Maybe some of those hardball types he was in bed with worried that he might be forced to save his own ass at their expense. Which you and I know he would do without a second thought." When Ben nodded, Stuart went on, "I guess what I'm saying is that my contacting you might have set in motion events that led to Jack's assassination. And now my sister's a widow and my niece and nephew are fatherless."

"You didn't do this, Stuart. You aren't responsible."

"Yeah, well, maybe I am, maybe I'm not. I still feel like I had a hand in it."

Ben leaned back in his seat. He understood Stuart's battle with his conscience. And with guilt. What he feared could very well be right. Maybe Jack had smelled trouble when Ben showed up, got spooked, sent some signals that worried his shady cronies, and they resolved the problem the old-fashioned way.

What Stuart didn't know was that Ben had been on Jack's tail far longer than the six months that the official file had been opened. He had long suspected Jack of widespread corruption and had been building a case against him, piece by piece, for a couple of years. Stuart's sources had been a gold mine from the standpoint of confirming many of Ben's suspicions about Jack.

But—and it was a big but—the Bureau had gone along with Ben's plan to ease back into Percyville, Jack's home turf. His own divorce and the consequent upheaval of the twins' lives had made the plan doubly advantageous to Ben: he'd be right under Jack's nose and he'd have a chance to let his sons experience life in a safer and more relaxed environment than Houston.

Ha. Percyville had turned out to be a cauldron of political intrigue, and now violence. To complicate things from Ben's perspective, his superiors had been pushing him to settle for what he already had on Jack, which would probably have resulted in discrediting him, but in the court of public opinion, Jack was diabolically clever. And skilled. Ben had been holding out. He wanted to destroy Jack, not just cripple him.

"Don't beat up on yourself about this, Stuart. Most of the stuff you provided, we already had. It was just a matter of time. If Jack got himself killed, it's ten to one he brought it on himself."

"Uh-oh. Percyville's finest." Stuart pushed his coffee away and watched Jim Rankin making his way through the tables. "'Morning, Chief," Stuart said when Rankin stopped at their booth. "You breaking for coffee?"

"Stuart." Spit-shined and military-sharp as usual, Rankin nodded curtly, then cut a glance at Ben but didn't speak. Lila started toward him, but Rankin waved her back. "Nothing for me."

"How's the investigation going?" Stuart asked.

"Everything we're free to divulge was said in this morning's press release."

Stuart lifted both brows. "You mean the eight-line paragraph I got when I went by your office today?"

Rankin was unruffled by the sarcasm. "It was brief. We don't want to tip our hand and send the killer undercover."

Stuart sighed. "I came by your office yesterday and couldn't get anybody in the department to talk to me. Then again this morning. Still no cooperation. Only that canned release."

"You don't get special access just because you're the hometown paper, Stuart. The *Sun* will be treated the same as all other media sources on this thing."

"Not the same, Chief." Stuart's dander was up finally. "Not if the past is any clue. Jack considered the *Sun* a thorn in his side. When he skirted too close to the edge, I called him on it. But coverage of him and his campaign was fair and balanced— I challenge anyone to dispute that."

"We'll have to agree to disagree then," Rankin said, but his rigid demeanor slipped when he added with a smirk, "He won big, so I guess that says more about the voters' insight than your opinions."

"The governor-elect has been assassinated, Chief. The people have a right to know the progress of the case. A very brief press release saying exactly nothing doesn't cut it. Why do I get the feeling you're stonewalling on this?"

From his seat, Ben eyed Rankin over the rim of his cup. "Maybe there's nothing to release."

Rankin turned to look at him as if he'd only just discovered Ben was there. "I don't know how you feds do it, but here we wait until we have all the facts before we go off half cocked."

Ben put his cup down carefully. "Meaning exactly what, Rankin?"

"You came to Jack's hometown to destroy him. You conned your boss into believing you had enough dirt on a high-level politician to bring him down."

"You know that for a fact?"

"Jack suspected your retirement from the Bureau was just a cover, Kincaid. He knew you held a grudge from years ago. He knew you were out to get him." Rankin's expression became a sneer. "But there was nothing to get, was there. You came up dry. Jack Sullivan was a patriot," he said fiercely. "He would have turned this state around."

"He would have sold it to the highest bidder," Ben snapped.

Rankin breathed in sharply. "You wanted to destroy him, but you didn't have the goods, so you had him shot."

Ben leaned back, studying Rankin's face. "You made that allegation two nights ago in front of Judge Stafford. Hear this, Chief. If you repeat it once more without enough hard evidence to arrest me, I'll have your ass."

Stuart's mouth was open. "You think Ben killed Jack?"

A small muscle ticked in Rankin's cheek. "I don't know what to think yet, but something about this whole thing stinks."

Stuart was nodding with exasperation. "Murder stinks, Chief. You ought to know that."

But Rankin was focused on Ben. "Maybe the family would like to think it was for political reasons that Jack was killed, but I don't see it that way."

Ben was very still now. "How do you see it?"

"I see it closer to home."

"What are you suggesting?" Stuart asked, narrow-eyed.

"I think it's personal," Rankin said. "It *smells* personal."

"Oh, *that* kind of stink." Ben looked away.

"Be careful, Chief." There was steel in Stuart's voice. "Your persistence in focusing on Jack's personal life could blind you to real evidence."

Rankin was silent as if considering this, then he nodded. "We'll see. Have a nice day, gentlemen."

"Asshole," Stuart murmured, watching Rankin push through the front doors and climb into a cruiser. "He's got nothing."

"Yeah." Ben watched, too, with a thoughtful expression. "After two and a half days with the same result, I can almost sympathize. Whoever shot the governor-elect got away clean."

Stuart shifted his gaze to the window. "Rankin's got to be drawing a blank in his investigation if he's seriously considering you as a suspect. What a crock."

Ben smiled grimly.

"Although…" Stuart leaned back, regarding Ben with a speculative look. "He could be on your case out of pure jealousy."

"Say what?"

Stuart shrugged. "You stole his girl, Kincaid."

To his chagrin, Ben blushed.

"Uh-huh, Suzanne. He's been hot for her for months, and for a while I thought she might be interested. I noticed because Suzy is oddly uninterested in men in a romantic sense. Yeah, the chief was closing in until you rode into town."

Ben was shaking his head, embarrassed.

"Pfft! He's out. Yesterday's news."

Ben was grinning now. "Coming from you, that's the ultimate insult, Stuart."

"Exactly."

Ben looked down, studied the marble pattern on the tabletop. "Suzanne and I are old friends."

"You're saying that's why she dropped Rankin?"

"We've got history."

"True. You delivered Caleb. That's a helluva history."

"Don't remind me. I was scared out of my skull that day." His gaze drifted to the window and beyond. "She was so brave, so damn *together*. Then Dennis…cut out." He frowned, remembering. "Suddenly she was a single mother, she had law school, life without her partner, the Judge's disapproval. She handled it all." He gave Stuart a wry smile. "I guess I've been a little bit in love with her since I was sixteen."

"No kidding."

"It shows?"

"I used to wonder." Stuart's smile gentled. "Suzy's special, I've always thought so. I'd love to see you sweep her right off her feet, Ben, even if it's a dozen years late." His smile faded. "Something's been missing in Suzy's life for a long time now. I never understood what it was. When she was a teenager, she was more outgoing, trusting. She sparkled."

"I remember."

"I don't know what happened, but something did."

"How did we get on the subject of Suzy?" Ben asked. Stuart had given him a lot to think about. Later.

"Rankin, the spurned suitor, and his suspicions." Stuart spoke reflectively. "You know, it makes sense Jack was spooked when you came back to town. He had strong survival instincts. Better than anyone, Jack knew the power of government when it came to unearthing people's secrets."

Ben thought a moment. "As much as I hate to agree with Rankin, he may have something, Stuart. The problem with Jack's shooting is that there are too many people with secrets, too many people who aren't grieving because the bastard's dead."

"And?"

"If we can't make a connection to something in his political life or his business life, it could be personal, Stuart."

"Such as?"

Ben knew he was getting into territory that might give offense. "It smells personal to me, too. I don't have any suspicions about how or why or who, but it's what I feel."

"Does that include my family?" Stuart asked quietly.

Ben raked a hand over his hair. "Shit, I don't know, Stuart. But just think about it for a minute. I'm not accusing Taylor or Suzanne or Annie or the kids—hell, that's crazy. But something about this nags at me. As if we're overlooking something right under our noses."

"I don't follow you."

"Maybe we should look into Jack's personal life the way we've been scrutinizing his public life."

"Sic the federal government on my family? No way."

"I'm with you there. I meant…let me nose around, Stuart. See what I come up with."

For a full minute, Stuart was silent. He tapped his knuckles on the tabletop. "This is a helluva note, Ben, but I guess I'd prefer you nosing around than Rankin. So go ahead. But you know something? If I found out somebody I loved shot Jack, I wouldn't give a damn. The bastard deserved it."

THE MORNING OF THE FUNERAL dawned bright and beautiful— a golden Indian summer morning of rich autumn color and dazzling sunshine. Even Mother Nature had a crush on Jack, Suzanne thought with chagrin as she came downstairs for breakfast at Riverbend. She was dressed and ready to go and found only Caleb at the table, reading the Jackson paper.

"Where is everybody?" she asked, pouring herself a cup of coffee from the decanter on the sideboard.

"You just missed the first shuttle." He shoved the paper across to her. "Mom, did you see—"

"Shuttle?"

"The governor and the legislature sent a limo—Jack being the governor-elect and all. So they all took off in it. Ben's coming for you and me. He should be here any minute. Mom—"

"Ben?"

"Yes ma'am. Ben. You know, your old friend. The one who edged the chief out of your affections."

Her cup clinked against the saucer as she set it down firmly. "Not you, too. Ben is just a friend."

"That's what I said, old friend."

"He and I are not—"

One of Caleb's dark brows went up. "You're not…?"

She laughed in spite of herself and picked up her coffee as much to hide her face as to drink it. She knew when to fold.

"Okay, that's settled." He tapped the newspaper. "Mom, have you seen this?"

"I haven't even had coffee, Caleb. Reading the newspaper comes next."

"It's an article about me."

She looked at the paper. "What?"

"About me. Here, read it."

She had to blink a time or two to focus. "Governor-elect's nephew saves Gayle's life." Dread settled in the pit of her stomach. For months, the public had been on a first-name basis with Jack's wife and children. Now Caleb. Pulling the paper closer, Suzanne scanned the article with a racing heart. It was a human-interest piece focusing on the drama of Jack's bullet striking Gayle and the good fortune of having Caleb's blood type match. He was a hero and Gayle was the tragic young victim, both thrust into the spotlight by the act of the madman who shot Jack. There was a picture of Caleb taken somewhere in the hospital. He was grinning, rolling down his shirtsleeves, obviously having just donated his blood. His likeness to Jack was so startling that she wondered why the whole world couldn't see it.

Holding her breath, she quickly read on. There was little technical information about blood type and thankfully no mention of AB negative. She lowered the paper. Maybe the public wouldn't figure it out, but someone in the family surely would. And soon. Stuart, she suspected. Annie, certainly.

Please don't let it be Caleb.

JACK'S ASSASSINATION had sent shock waves through the populace, and they reveled in his last rites. The funeral offered the final opportunity to pay homage to a charismatic public figure brutally cut down in his prime—in the words of the outgoing governor. He was Percyville's own, too. As Jack had been part of the Stafford family for sixteen years, his origins had been forgotten, his roots a mere technicality. Eulogies were offered by his political friends, none by his family.

Through it all, Suzanne was intensely aware of Ben at her side. Part of her was ashamed that in such a somber setting she should even think in terms of her own confused attraction to him. She should be worried about Taylor. She *was* worried about Taylor, but her sister was well flanked—Stuart on one side, Annie on the other. Suzanne, Caleb and Ben bolstered Trey, whose grim young face reflected none of the raging conflict he felt about his father. Charles Stafford stood aristocratically impassive, his hand on Lily's shoulder. In her wheelchair, the Judge stared straight ahead, the ravages of her stroke causing the smallest tremor of her hands and head. A stone-faced Spencer Dutton stood directly behind Taylor.

It was finally over, and Suzanne was grateful for Ben's protective hand on her arm as they headed back to the car. It had been a long time since she'd relied on anyone but herself.

The media was out in force, but they'd kept a discreet distance from the family. Until now. Just as Suzanne and Ben reached the roadside, a gaggle of journalists and TV people armed with mikes and Minicams surged forward like horses out of a starting gate. Suzanne recognized only Amanda Mason coming at her, mike extended.

"Judge Stafford, a source claims you were in business with the governor-elect. Would you care to comment?"

Suzanne turned her face into Ben's shoulder. "What source?" Ben asked curtly without slowing his stride.

Mason shot him an annoyed glance, hustling to keep up. "You know I can't reveal that information."

"Then you won't expect Judge Stafford to comment," he snapped. He pulled the car door open and urged Suzanne inside.

Mason peered around Ben's shoulder. "What about your appointment to the bench, Judge Stafford? Was it a payoff?"

Suzanne's head whipped around. "What?"

"No comment!" Ben slammed the car door. Suzanne's

thoughts scattered in crazy directions. In business? Payoff? Dear God.

Mason tapped on the glass. "Judge Stafford, one of your decisions a few weeks ago involved a petition by citizens—"

Ben was in the driver's seat now, starting the car with a roar. "Bitch," he muttered, then accelerated in a splatter of gravel and dust. In the rearview mirror, he watched Amanda Mason lose her balance and grab at a cameraman to keep from toppling into the drainage swale.

Suzanne touched her temple briefly. "Thank you."

"That woman's a menace," Ben said, clenching his teeth. "Jumping you at a funeral, for God's sake. What's happened to decency in journalism nowadays?"

She laughed unsteadily. "It went out with bell bottoms?"

He reached over and squeezed her hand. "Don't let her rile you."

"You sound like the riled one."

"It does rile me to see you singled out by a reporter itching to make a name for herself. You're a judge. Scandal could damage your reputation. It's despicable."

"My reputation?"

He glanced at her, then chuckled softly and faced the road again. "No, Suzy. *She's* despicable. You're pure as the driven snow."

"Gosh, you *have* been gone a long time."

"Compared to most of the public servants I know," he said firmly, "you are. Trust me."

She did trust him. The years they'd lived separate lives should have been more of an obstacle to overcome, but they weren't. If anything, their friendship was enriched by the separation. Almost as if they could genuinely appreciate each other more for the years spent apart.

She looked over at him, liking his profile, the firm thrust of his chin, his strong hands. It had been years since she'd allowed herself to look at a man this way. He was attracted to her, too. And like all the others, he would want to make love. With Ben, it *would* be making love, she told herself fiercely, not having sex. Wonderful things might happen if she could just let herself…enjoy. But would she be able to do it? Or would she freeze or panic? No matter, she was filled with a prickly anticipation, and it didn't feel like fear. God, she would miss him so much when he left.

The pain of that thought brought all her anxiety boiling up again. She leaned her head back and closed her eyes. "What did she mean about being in business with Jack, Ben? Jack is the last person I'd choose to be in business with."

"Tell me about it. Sounds like someone's trying to discredit you."

"But who? Why?"

"I don't know, but I intend to find out." He took the next turn, and then they were on the highway that led back to Riverbend.

THIRTY-EIGHT

IN A MATTER OF HOURS after the funeral, the weather turned nasty. The sky clouded over, then darkened with thunderheads emitting fierce lightning. Rain came down in sheets for a solid hour, then slackened off to a miserable drizzle. Suzanne thought the storm a fitting end. Jack had been the eye of a perpetual storm, swirling events and lives in tumultuous disarray around him.

After helping settle the Judge for a rest, she tracked Annie and Taylor down in the sunporch, nursing mugs of hot tea. "You won't believe this," Suzanne said, pulling the French doors closed behind her. "Mother wants us to have a family thing Sunday afternoon when Gayle gets home. She will be out then, won't she, Taylor?"

"Yes, thank heavens." Taylor reclined in an armchair, her feet on a huge ottoman, watching the rain. "It's only five days, but it seems forever with the funeral and all. The doctor says by Sunday she should be fine, barring complications."

"Have some tea, Suzy," Annie said from her spot on a cushion on the floor. "I think the Judge has the right idea. With the family rallying around Gayle, she won't have as much time to brood over losing her dad."

"Who's with her now?" Suzanne asked, crossing to the tea cart.

"Caleb and Trey," Taylor said.

Annie sipped from a mug. "She's in good hands."

Suzanne found some Earl Grey and poured hot water into a mug. "You'll be staying here at Riverbend for a while, Taylor?"

Taylor stubbed out a cigarette. "I don't want to go back to the house in Jackson right now. Jack's everywhere. Do you think that's weird?"

"No," Suzanne and Annie replied together.

"Suzy, why don't you invite Ben?" Annie suggested casually.

"I thought I would," Suzanne answered just as casually.

All three laughed. "Don't say it, you two," Suzanne admonished sternly. "Between Caleb and Stuart, and even Dad, I've had it with comments regarding Ben and me."

Both women put up their hands and made expressions of wide-eyed innocence. Then, when the silence stretched too long, Taylor sighed dramatically. "In that case, I guess there's nothing to talk about."

All three laughed again, then each became occupied with her own thoughts. Unsmiling now, Taylor said quietly, "Except for Jack. But then, that's all I've heard for five days now—Jack, Jack, Jack."

"It was a big thing, his assassination," Annie said quietly.

Taylor fumbled for a cigarette, then changed her mind. "Tell me. It's been so strange, him being so…absent. I go to bed and finally fall asleep, then…boom. He's suddenly there beside me and he's pushing me to get dressed for another campaign stop. But I'm thinking, no, you're dead so I don't have to do this anymore. Then I wonder if it's true and he's really not dead, so this is a nightmare." She shuddered.

Annie shook her head, not without sympathy. "Now there's a chilling picture."

Taylor turned to look at her. "Campaigning or sleeping beside a corpse?"

Suzanne set her cup down. "Taylor…"

"Did you tell her, Suzy?"

Annie looked at Suzanne. "Tell me what?"

"I guess she didn't." Taylor straightened up and shoved the ottoman aside. "I've been involved with someone for two years."

Annie didn't miss a beat. "Spencer?"

Taylor blinked. "Did you know?"

Annie shrugged. "I suspected, but it's too crazy, even for you, Taylor."

Taylor was instantly defensive. "I don't know why you say that. Spencer's kind and gentle and sensitive, everything Jack isn't. Wasn't. He saw through the charade of my marriage years ago."

"Not crazy because you fell in love with Spence," Annie explained with exasperation. "He's everything you say. But the risk, Taylor! I'm surprised he was willing to take such a chance, even for love."

"He didn't want to," Taylor said, staring at the fingers of her left hand. "I wanted to go to bed with him long before he ever consented. He kept thinking I'd eventually ask for a divorce. He begged me constantly, but I knew Jack would never allow it."

"Be careful, Taylor," Suzanne warned. "If you were overheard, your words could be misconstrued. We don't know yet who shot Jack, but Jim Rankin is doing his dead-level best to connect his death to his family."

Taylor stood up abruptly. "Must you always think and act like a prosecutor, Suzanne?"

"Any prosecutor would be interested to know you're having an affair with Spencer and Jack refused to give you a divorce. Blow off my concern if you want to, but it sounds bad, Taylor."

"Why did you have to wait for his consent, Taylor?" Annie asked. "You could have divorced him whether he agreed or not."

"No, I couldn't." Taylor found cigarettes and lighter in her pocket. "Maybe I shouldn't admit this, but I did something a long time ago. Something terrible. It was an accident, but… Anyway, Jack kept me from filing for divorce by holding that threat over my head. I was scared. He got off on controlling people, and I was no different." She lit her cigarette, inhaled deeply, then added bitterly, "Not that he didn't have a thousand secrets of his own."

"He blackmailed you?" Suzanne asked incredulously. "His own wife?"

"Why not?" Taylor reached for a small ashtray. "He kept a file of dirty secrets on an incredible number of people."

Suzanne frowned. "A real file—actual papers?"

Taylor flicked ashes. "Tapes. He loved to document people's secrets and make plans to use them."

"He was such a *bastard!*" Annie cried, springing up. She went to the streaming windows and stood looking out. After a few moments, she spoke quietly, "One of those people was my mother."

"Eugenia?" Suzanne said.

"Oh, God." Taylor bent her head.

"I know about her and Jack, Taylor," Annie said.

Taylor shook her head mutely. "I'd hoped—prayed—that you didn't."

Suzanne looked on in bewilderment. "Know about Jack and Eugenia? *What?*"

Annie turned. "Jack seduced my mother. She was a lonely woman fearing her forties and vulnerable to his…charms." Annie's mouth twisted. "He was years younger, but she was like a teenager with a crush. She killed herself rather than end it."

"On New Year's Eve," Taylor murmured, looking beyond Annie to the dark, glistening leaves of a magnolia tree.

"Were you there, Taylor?" Annie asked sharply.

"Not at the cottage, no, but—" Taylor shook her head, took an agitated drag on her cigarette. "Oh, God, I hope I can explain this. I knew he was sleeping with someone, that was nothing new. But I never suspected Eugenia. Not until the New Year's Eve party at the club." She got up and began pacing. "I had too much to drink. Spencer was there. He was so sweet to me. We danced and I must have looked happy, something Jack couldn't tolerate. He scolded me and told me to sober up. I was hurt and humiliated, so I drank some more."

Suzanne sank quietly into a chair, her gaze locked on Taylor's face.

"Then I saw Eugenia slip out with Jack close behind. I was furious, so I followed them. He didn't want me to dance with Spencer, a perfectly innocent thing, while he was flirting with every woman there. Even Eugenia." Taylor looked at Annie and spread her hands. "I couldn't believe he would do that with my own aunt. I couldn't believe Eugenia would try to steal my husband."

Annie's face was pale. She turned back to the windows. Now Taylor had gone still, staring out at the rain. "I heard them arguing in one of those little private rooms. He was mad because Eugenia refused to sleep with one of his gambling cronies from the coast. What's the difference, I heard him say to her. She'd been sleeping with him—with Jack—so why not this guy?"

Taylor squinted through the smoke curling from her forgotten cigarette. "I lost it then. I charged in and we had a horrible fight. Eugenia apologized, begged me to forgive her, but I was beyond listening. Jack...well, I can't describe Jack's fury. He hated having to cope with two hysterical women. He had the car brought around and made me drive."

"I thought you said you'd had too much to drink," Suzanne murmured, feeling like a spectator in someone else's nightmare.

Taylor took a quick puff. "Jack decided otherwise. He practically shoved me behind the wheel. I remember crashing into some bushes or something. Running up on the curb. I felt nauseous. I remember thinking I should stop or I would be sick." She bent her head and rubbed her temples, frowning. "The rest is so fuzzy...so...garbled."

"You don't remember letting my mother out at the house?"

"No...God, it's been a long time since I—" Taylor was shaking her head, still frowning. "Somebody screamed. The car was going fast, too fast."

"I can't believe Jack let you drive in that condition," Suzanne said.

Taylor still rubbed one temple, her thoughts focused for the first time in years on a night she longed to forget. "That must have been when I hit the motorcycle."

Annie turned from the window. "What?"

As if just realizing what she'd said, Taylor looked startled. "I...Jack said...I killed that boy on the motorcycle. That I hit him and just kept going. I didn't even slow down, he said. But I don't remember any of it." She gave them a pleading look. Her mouth trembled, and she covered it with one hand as tears streamed down her face. "He...he d-died the next morning in the hospital."

"You weren't driving that car, Taylor," Annie said quietly. "If I'd known you thought you were, I'd have said something long ago. The truth is I'm not sure who was, Jack or my...my mother. But it couldn't have been you." She crossed her arms over her midriff. "Mom left a note. In it, she said you were in the car but very sick. You couldn't have been driving. Mom's guilt was so crushing that I wonder if possibly *she* was. But whoever it was, Jack was in control. He orchestrated the whole thing, and I've always felt he must have been driving. It wouldn't faze him to hit-and-run. I never showed the note to anyone because my mother begged me not to. She feared it would reflect badly on Jack and possibly affect his good name. His 'good name,'" she repeated bitterly.

Using both hands, Taylor wiped tears from her cheeks. "Are you saying I didn't kill that boy? That I've lived with that awful guilt all these years for nothing?"

"You couldn't have. Just think—you were unable to drive, Taylor. Even your fuzzy memory should prove that much."

She frowned, trying to capture a scrap of memory. "I remember throwing up. On the grass. I hit my head somehow. It hurt. There was blood. I—" She stopped, looking stunned. "I couldn't have been driving if I hit my head. I did stop. I did."

"You did." Annie walked over and put an arm around Taylor's shoulder. "I wish I'd said something sooner."

"Then Jack would have concocted another lie. He was so good at that." Taylor's eyes flashed and her voice trembled with rage. "I'm *glad* he's dead! Whoever shot him did us all a favor. I hope he rots in hell!"

"If there's any justice, he will," Annie said, her own lips unsteady. "My mother was weak, but she didn't deserve to die for what she did."

Taylor found a paper napkin and blotted the last of her tears. "I'm glad to know I'm not guilty of killing that boy." She gave Annie a sad smile. "And I'm sorry about your mother."

Annie said a quiet "Me, too." Then she added, "But you're not responsible and neither am I."

"It was Jack," Suzanne murmured, feeling the old bitterness well up inside her. "He was evil."

"Be thankful he didn't make a play for you," Annie said, taking a seat in the chair beside Suzanne. "You'd think he would have, but I guess he decided it was more fun needling you in your professional life." She gave a dry laugh. "You would have cleaned his clock if he'd ever come on to you."

So many secrets.

THIRTY-NINE

IT WAS NOON ON SUNDAY when Ben pulled up at the big house at Riverbend. For a few moments, he made no move to get out. He just sat, hands on the wheel, and thought back to the times spent here when he was a teenager. When Suzy had belonged to Dennis and he hadn't allowed himself to think about how much he'd wanted her to belong to him. He wondered now if he'd come back to Percyville not because he wanted down time for him and his sons after the divorce, not because his roots were here or because it was a decent, law-abiding place, not even because it was a good base to pull together his case against Jack Sullivan; he was wondering if he'd come back because Suzanne was here.

Behind him, the twins were going crazy. They were over-joyed to be invited to Riverbend, mainly because of Caleb. Luke and Jakey still talked about the day they met Caleb downtown and he'd volunteered to take them to the arcade, the local hang-out for kids. Being mentored by Caleb Stafford had given them a boost in prestige. From that moment, anything Caleb said or did was perfect. And, from Ben's point of view, they could do a lot worse than choosing Caleb to hero-worship. Now, spot-ting Caleb coming out of the house, they had the door open and were scrambling toward the steps.

Ben shoved the car door open. "Hold on, guys."

"Hey, it's Luke and Jakey," Caleb said, meeting the two boys on the porch. Luke, bolder than his twin, high-fived the older boy while Jakey hung back, grinning shyly but just as eager. Caleb shadow-boxed a punch or two at him, to Jakey's delight, then looked beyond the twins to Ben. "How's it goin', Ben?"

"Okay, Caleb." He could see Jack's boy, Trey, framed in the doorway behind Caleb. No smile there. "Hello, Trey. Have you met Luke and Jakey?"

Trey nodded. "At the arcade. With Caleb."

Caleb hustled the twins up the steps, where he turned them over to Trey. "Okay, guys, there's a couple of burgers and hot dogs out back with your names on 'em. Trey's gonna fix you up while I say a word to your dad." When they hesitated, Caleb crossed his heart with his forefinger. "I just want to talk with your dad a minute—it's important stuff, okay?"

Luke considered it. "Yeah, it's cool."

Caleb nodded. "All *right!* Trey, would you show these dudes where the food is?"

Still unsmiling, Trey nevertheless did as Caleb asked.

With the departure of the kids, there was a moment of silence. Ben used it to study Caleb. He was a good-looking boy, tall, with the strength and agility of a born athlete. There was a lot of Suzanne in him, the same direct gaze, although Caleb's eyes were so dark they were almost black. Where…?

"I hope that wasn't too pushy," Caleb said, taking the rest of the steps to the bottom with easy grace. "I knew if you got in there and started talking, I wouldn't have a chance to get a word in edgewise. And this is important."

After a moment, Ben motioned toward the front lawn. "Take a walk?"

"Yes, sir."

"This is a beautiful place, Riverbend. I remember the first time I ever saw it. I was sixteen."

"I'm almost sixteen."

Ben smiled. "I know."

"Because you were there the night I was born."

"Well, it's one of those moments you never forget."

"Uh-huh." Caleb wrinkled his nose, thinking. "I wonder if you know anything about when I was…ah…I mean, the time my mother… Jeez, this is tough. Do you know when my mom… ah, got pregnant?" Feeling Ben's quick glance, he added hastily. "I know that's a strange thing to ask, but I don't know any other way."

"How would I know what you're asking, Caleb?"

Caleb scratched the side of his neck. "It's just this—I don't know the name of my biological father. It's not Dennis Scott, which is the name on my birth certificate. And I know you and my mom...well, your friendship's sort of special. You were Dennis's friend and you were in law school with my mom. You were so close that you were with my mom when she had me."

Ben was stunned. Dennis wasn't Caleb's father? Then who? This was definitely deep water. He could imagine Suzanne's reaction if she could hear Caleb now. "Have you talked to your mother about this?"

"I've been talking to my mother about this for as long as I can remember, but she gets agitated when I bring it up. She wants me to forget about it, just accept that I'm a Stafford and that nothing else matters." He stopped and looked earnestly at Ben. "Can you see why I just can't do that?"

Ben released a long breath. "Yeah, I think so."

Caleb nodded, one quick bob of his head. "Okay. Fine. This is good." He started moving again. "So you're willing to fill in a few blanks for me, right?"

"Whoa... Wait." Ben stopped him, putting both hands up. "What kind of blanks, Caleb?"

Caleb chewed the inside of his cheek, then seemed to come to a decision. "Are you my father, Ben?"

Jesus. The water was deeper than he'd imagined. He spotted an ornamental iron bench nearby and gave Caleb a nudge in that direction. "Come on, let's go sit down over there.

"First of all," he said when they were side by side on the bench, "if I were your father, Caleb, I couldn't acknowledge it now, today, in casual conversation. Your mother, for reasons of her own, has chosen to keep that information to herself. There could be several reasons for that."

"Such as?" Caleb looked at him expectantly.

Kids. They were so damn literal. "I don't know, Caleb.

Maybe it's something...I don't know." Personal. Painful. Shameful. Hurtful. Nothing good.

"You didn't answer my question," Caleb said.

He shook his head. "It's not me." He looked directly into those dark, dark eyes. "Not that I wouldn't be proud if you were my son, Caleb."

Caleb nodded, then dropped his gaze to his hands. "I'm not too surprised, although I'd hoped..." His voice was a little husky and his smile a little crooked. "You spend most of your life wondering about every man you meet. Heck, you think it's a good thing some of them *aren't* your father, but once in a while somebody comes along and you think it's okay if he's the one."

Suzy, Suzy, do you see this boy's pain?

"I'm not the one, Caleb," he said gravely.

"Yeah, well..." Caleb brought his knee up to retie his shoe. "How about this? I figure my mom got pregnant about the same time Aunt Taylor got married—in April, you know?" His fingers were busy with laces. "I mean, I was a full-term baby, because that's on the birth certificate."

"Uh-huh." Ben looked longingly at the house.

"Here's my next question. Do you think it could be somebody at the wedding? I figure most of my mom's friends were there, you know, because she was Aunt Taylor's maid of honor." He frowned. "I asked Grandpa about that day. He didn't know what I was getting at, so he was a lot of help...in a general sort of way. But he's only her father, so he wouldn't know about law school friends or college friends and so on, but you would."

Ben sighed and dropped his head back. The sky was a vivid blue. Not a cloud in sight. Meanwhile, the kid sitting next to him had a storm brewing in his soul. Couldn't Suzy see that?

Unaware of Ben's dismay, Caleb continued, "Then, like, six weeks pass and she and Dennis *elope!* I mean, no plans or anything. Just bam and they're married. She's pregnant and it's not his baby and he marries her, anyway. What do you make of that?"

"I make it that your mother has a right to privacy. Even if I had an opinion, Caleb, I wouldn't give it to you. You've got to talk to Suzanne. Tell her exactly what you've told me. Let her see how much this is bothering you."

"She'll just put me off again." He was the picture of dejection as he scraped his thumbnail along a seam in his shoe. "Okay, then, just answer me this one last question."

Ben held his breath.

"Do you remember the wedding? The weeks before had a lot of tea parties and girl stuff—Grandpa told me that—so you wouldn't know, but otherwise… How about the reception? Think if anybody there sort of *looks* like me. I mean, I've looked at the wedding pictures but I can't spot my old man." He gave a wry laugh and flicked a twig to the ground. "Or maybe I don't look like him, but how about one of her professors at law school? You'd know that. She was seduced, she told me that. She said it was a mistake and she just wanted to put it behind her, but it affects me more than my mom, don't you think? I mean, it's one half of my gene pool, for crissake!"

Reception. Out of nowhere a picture flashed in Ben's memory. Suzanne on the stairs, stark fear in her beautiful eyes. Ben reaching for her instinctively. When somebody you loved looked that scared… But she'd recoiled, then fled up the stairs. Running away. Why?

"I guess I'm striking out here, too, huh?"

"What?" Frowning, Ben looked at the boy's face. So like Suzanne and…who else?

"Caleb! Ben!"

He looked up to find Suzanne making her way across the lawn toward them. "It's Mom," Caleb murmured. "She'd kill me if she knew what I was saying to you, Ben."

He reached over and touched the boy's knee. "Come on, let's go. It's time we sampled those burgers, too."

"We've been looking everywhere for you two," Suzanne said, flushed and smiling from her walk.

"Man talk, Mom," Caleb said.

"Oh?" A curious look, focused on Ben.

"Did the twins get burgers and hot dogs?" Caleb asked.

"Of course. Trey took care of them, but they kept asking for you."

Caleb shrugged. "What can I say? I'm irresistible."

At the look on her face, he backed up, putting one hand out. "Hey, it was a joke, Mom."

"Another one like that and you'll write 'I must be modest' a thousand times."

He looked at Ben. "See what a tyrant she is? Hey, Mom, take him out to the gazebo, why doncha? I bet he hasn't seen it in… oh, fifteen years, right, Ben?"

Ben nodded, smiling. "Just about."

Safely past his mother, Caleb turned, walking backward. "Y'all could reminisce about old times."

"Caleb—" Suzanne's eyebrows lifted meaningfully.

"Okay, okay, I'm outta here."

Suzanne smiled as she watched him lope off across the driveway, heading around to the back of the house by the side yard. She fell into step beside Ben, her hands clasped behind her back. "I swear I don't know what's come over Caleb lately."

She was flustered, but it made her softer and more feminine. If that was possible. To Ben, she'd always been one of the most appealing women he'd ever known. Walking with her now, he allowed himself the pleasure of just looking at her. Then he put out his hand. "A walk to the gazebo sounds pretty good to me."

She smiled, and with only a tiny hesitation, took his hand. "We don't have to tell him, do we?"

"No way." Her fingers were delicate and cool in his and a tiny bit unsteady. Was she nervous? He squeezed them reassuringly. "How can we get there without somebody spotting us and knocking me out of a few precious moments alone with you?"

She *was* nervous. He heard the little hitch in her breath and stopped abruptly. He was suddenly damned tired of this woman being so skittish around him. He'd never given her any reason to fear him. Without dropping her hand, he made her look at him. "Suzy, are you afraid of me?"

"No!" Her denial was quick and heartfelt.

"Then is it my imagination that every time I say anything vaguely sexual, you get nervous?"

For a second, there was pure distress on her face. He held firmly to her hand, but she put the other over her mouth. "I'm sorry," she whispered.

He gave her hand a small but impatient shake. "No, don't apologize. Explain. Why does being close to me make you nervous?"

"It isn't you, Ben."

He swore suddenly as he realized her eyes were bright with tears. "Ah, hell, Suzy. I didn't mean—"

Shaking her head, she touched his lips with her fingers. "No, no, hush." She dropped her hand. "I think I would like to explain. Maybe I *should.* Come on. There's a path to the gazebo on the other side of the house."

"IT'S BEEN A LONG TIME since I was out here," Ben said as he stepped into the vine-covered structure. Going to the side, he leaned one hand on a post and looked out. "It's more isolated than I remember."

"It's very private," Suzanne said.

He turned and found that she was backed against the opposite post, her arms tight around her midriff. He faced her fully, his hands at his sides. "You're looking scared again, Suzy."

Her gaze slid from his. "Maybe it's a habit I'll never break," she murmured.

He was stunned to feel how much that mattered. He wanted to get so close to her that it would be impossible to tell them apart, but first she needed to know she had nothing to fear from him. Why the hell did she think that, anyway? "If I come a little closer to you, will you freak out?"

She smiled, shook her head. "No. Maybe."

"Maybe?"

"It's a long story."

He went, resting one hip on the railing. He was close enough to feel the warmth of her, to smell the fragrance of her perfume, something light and flowerlike. She laced her fingers and held them between her breasts, almost prayerfully. "I've never done this before. I'm nervous."

"I could put my arms around you."

She laughed softly. "Not yet."

Not yet. Not an out-and-out refusal. His heart jumped with anticipation.

She drew in a deep breath. "This place holds a lot of memories for me," she said, speaking almost too softly for him to hear. "Some good, some bad. Very bad. I—I— Something bad happened to me out here, and it's been hard for me to put it out of my mind."

"Explain 'something bad.'" He watched her swallow, hard.

"It—it was sexual." She closed her eyes. "Wow, I didn't think I could ever tell anyone about this. For a while right after it happened, I didn't think I would ever get over it. It was always with me. For years. Through law school. My marriage. And beyond. I could be concentrating on a brief or something like that and suddenly I would break out in a sweat. My hands would turn cold. My heart would start beating almost out of my chest." She rested her head against the post. "Anxiety attacks you wouldn't believe. It colored my whole life. Black." For a second, her mouth twisted bitterly.

She straightened up, gave a brisk shake of her head. "But I was a practical person. I'd always been focused. Anything I'd set my sights on, I'd been able to do. Always. I thought I could handle this the same way. I would put it out of my mind, I'd focus on what was important. It would pass. Eventually." She smiled sadly. "Wrong. I had nightmares. I lost the ability to connect to other people. I felt boxed in, isolated. Other women were open and loving, but I was…frozen inside."

"Suzy…" He wanted to touch her but he was afraid.

"Crazy, huh?" She dropped her gaze to the floor, toed a pattern in the dust there. "Would you believe, years have passed and I still have some of those feelings?"

"How many years?"

She shook her head. "You don't want to know."

"When was this, Suzy?"

Again she shook her head.

"Taylor's reception? The day of the wedding?"

A tiny, anguished sound came from her. She put her hands to her face, then turned away. Ben glared over the trees, clamped a hand against the back of his neck, railing inwardly. She was talking all around the details, but he'd bet his life she was raped that day. Or that she'd suffered some kind of sexual abuse that had traumatized her just as badly. Jesus. Was this the reason she didn't answer Caleb's questions? He wanted to touch her. God, he needed to touch her.

He moved closer, bent his knees and tried to see her face. "Could you look at me, Suzy? Please?"

She was shaking her head, sobbing quietly.

"Please, Suzy. Let me hold you."

"It's no use, Ben." She pressed her face to the post.

He moved cautiously behind her, touched her hair. Stroked it gently, gently. He could feel her trembling, but the sobbing was quieting. With his other hand, he touched her arm below her elbow. When she didn't shrink from him, he bent and kissed her cheek. Her skin was salty and yet sweet, fragrant. She inhaled sharply, but she didn't run. He slipped an arm around her waist and eased her back against him. With a soft sigh, she rested her head against his chest.

"You're safe here," he promised softly in her ear.

Her reply was just a whimper.

"You feel good," he murmured, his mouth near her ear.

"So do you," she said with a note of wonder.

"Turn around. Please."

She hesitated only a beat or two, then turned and put both her hands—knotted into fists—against his chest. As much as he wanted to feel the softness of her breasts against him, he knew that would have to wait for the next time. For a few moments, he simply held her there, rocking a little. After a while, he smiled against her temple. "What are you thinking?"

"Is this all we're going to do?" She drew herself up with a surprised laugh. "I can't believe I said that!"

He hugged her, squeezing just a little tighter. "There's a long list of things we could do, but I'll settle for a kiss." She went instantly still. "No, don't do that, Suzy. I'll never take anything you don't want to give." He rubbed her arms, rocked her a little more, cupped her head to hold her where she was. Everything in his body language was meant to reassure her. After a while, he sensed she was calm again. "So, how about it, Suzy? Can I kiss you?"

She nodded, a tiny, almost undetectable motion.

"You're not going to faint?"

She gave a small laugh.

"Not going to run from me?"

"Uh-uh."

"Well, then…" With his lips at her temple, he could feel the hammering of her pulse. His own heart was thudding almost as hard. Damn, he couldn't remember feeling like this since he was a teenager. Then, too, it had been because of Suzanne Stafford, but she hadn't been free to kiss. He'd come full circle.

He brought his lips gently to hers and it was just as sweet as he'd always imagined. She made a small sound and he touched her mouth to his again. "It's okay, sweetheart." He kissed her again, opening up a little, using his tongue to tease the corners of her lips. "You can get into this anytime you want to," he said against her soft mouth, still stubbornly closed. He nipped gently, drawing a little gasp from her, and as her guard fell, he closed his mouth fully over hers.

He sensed her shock and ruthlessly held himself in check, braced for her to end it all. But she didn't. Joy burst inside him. He wanted to thrust his tongue deep, to step between her legs and let her feel how hard he was, but he wanted her to stay. To want more. He felt the moment she mastered panic, then her fists uncurled and she took hold of his shirt, hanging on. She was breathing fast, making little sounds of urgency. Of quickening passion. And if she didn't give him some signal that it wouldn't be welcome, he didn't know how long he could resist showing her just how crazy he was about her.

She said something, and he felt her wriggling to get her hands free. Then they were around his neck and her mouth was opening hungrily to let him in. He gathered her close and was unable to hold back the groan of approval that vibrated through him. The taste of her was sweet, heady, wild enough to make him lose himself for a minute or two, imagining the next step.

Nothing had prepared him for the sweetness of her, for the unrestrained, joyful delight he sensed in her. It fed his own dark passion and need until she caught his face in her hands and stopped him. "Oh, Ben, Ben, oh…oh…" She hugged him in a spontaneous burst of happiness. "Oh, that was so…*good!*"

"It was, wasn't it?" Closing his eyes, he rested his forehead against hers, breathing as hard as if he'd climbed a mountain. In a way, he had.

"Thank you, Ben." She trailed more kisses across his throat, up to his chin, to his cheek, his ear.

He groaned. "You'd better stop that if you don't want me to melt into a puddle at your feet."

She laughed, a carefree sound he realized he hadn't heard from her in years. Then she audaciously pushed her hips against his erection. "This doesn't feel like a puddle."

"God, you've gotta stop." He caught her close and held her still. They stood like that until slowly, he took stock of their surroundings. "Do you realize it's broad daylight?"

"There's a party going on," she said, not moving.

"Where? Out here? Or there?" He gave a hitch of his head toward the big house.

She sighed. "There. And before we have company out here, I suppose we should make an appearance."

He stepped back and surveyed her. She'd never looked so beautiful. "We need to talk," he told her.

She nodded, some of her joy fading. "Okay," she said quietly.

Satisfied, he took her hand and they left the gazebo.

IT WAS NIGHTFALL WHEN BEN finally managed to drag the twins
to the Explorer and head home. The whole Stafford clan had
been warm and welcoming to his boys, and he was grateful. Without any relatives left on his side, Ben's sons would
never know the kind of special relationship he had shared with
Lucian. Caleb's presence, of course, had been the magic touch.
For the first time since coming back to Percyville, Ben had felt
a true sense of belonging.

But he was troubled as he drove, in spite of his elation over
finally breaking through Suzanne's defenses. Dozens of questions raced through his mind. Who had attacked Suzanne
at Taylor's wedding? Was he Caleb's father? Was Suzanne's
trauma the reason her marriage had failed? Where did Dennis
fit in?

Stopped for a red light, he put his fingers over his eyes and
rubbed. He'd spent the past week working on Jack's assassination, but he couldn't rid himself of a hunch that there was a
connection to be made to the family. Why? he wondered, pulling away from the intersection. Since he couldn't make the connection, why didn't he just forget it?

Because something nagged at him. Some clue, some fact
floated out there and he couldn't pull it in. He'd felt it that first
night at the hospital, but with the furor that had erupted over
Jack and then Gayle and the family's terror that—

Gayle.

Ben pulled into the garage at his house and stopped abruptly.
Gayle's transfusions. Nobody's blood type matched except Caleb's. Those dark, dark eyes.

The twins were tumbling out, dashing to the door. Ben sat
where he was and stared at the garage wall. Stunned at the
thought. No. Impossible. That would mean—

Ah, Suzy, Suzy.

FORTY

THE VOICES OUTSIDE SUZANNE'S chambers had finally reached a pitch she couldn't ignore. Jim Rankin was determined to force his way past Betsy. Suzanne gave up the task of reviewing the case she was to hear in less than an hour. Just as well, since thoughts of Ben kept intruding. Memories of the kiss they'd shared edged out the reasoned arguments contained in the documents before her. Even harder to resist were fantasies about what would happen the next time she saw him. With a sigh, she closed the file. Might as well deal with the chief of police now.

She pressed the intercom. "I'll see the chief, Betsy."

"Hello, Jim." She was standing when the door opened, then she came around to the front of her desk, not wanting to give the impression he was welcome. She crossed her feet at the ankles. "What's on your mind?"

"Do I have to have something on my mind to see the most beautiful judge in the state?"

She glanced at her watch. "When I have less than an hour before a trial begins, yes."

For a second, his mask slipped and she thought of those minutes in her bedroom. She was glad Betsy was just outside. His smile was tight. "I know this has been a tough time for you and your family, Suzanne. Jack's death shocked everyone."

"Yes."

"People don't realize that it isn't just his family and the state that's affected when a man like Jack dies, but there are a lot of…ah, loose ends…that can unravel."

"If you mean Jack had his hand in a lot of pies, then I would certainly agree with that."

He nodded. "The trial today being a case in point."

"Excuse me?"

He reached around her and touched the closed file on her desk. "This case is linked to another one that's far more important. Don't say Jack didn't talk to you about it—I know he did. Some major contributors to his campaign have strong personal interest in the outcome." He spread his hands. "Jack would have been here himself this morning, but…"

"But he's dead."

"Unfortunately."

When she didn't reply, he frowned. "These are powerful people, Suzanne. You don't want to cross them."

"Are you saying that no matter what the evidence or the law says that I should go along with what the Kent Group wants because Jack promised them something?"

"Nobody mentioned the Kent Group, but I'm glad you understand."

She straightened and walked to the door, pulled it open and stood back. "If you're finished—"

"I need to tell them something definite, Suzanne."

She said coldly, "Tell them whatever you like."

Rankin came toward her with steel in his eyes. "I hope you aren't planning to do something stupid."

"Not unless you consider following the letter of the law stupid."

"You're going to rule against these people?"

"I'm going to rule as the law dictates."

Rankin's features were as stiff as the creases in his pants. "You're playing with fire here, Suzanne. I'm warning you."

"Warning me?" she repeated. "Or threatening me?"

"You think because Kincaid's around that you can forget everything Jack set up and thumb your nose at these people. Kincaid doesn't have that kind of pull, lady."

"Ben Kincaid has nothing to do with how I rule in my courtroom, Jim."

"How about how you rule in the bedroom?"

She pulled the door wider. "It's time you left, Chief."

"You freaked out when I so much as touched you, but you've been with this guy night and day since Jack died."

"I have a right to choose my friends," she said.

"And he's an old, old one."

"Yes." She looked at him defiantly. "Old and dear."

His voice was low, vibrating with anger. "I know he and his kids spent the day at Riverbend Sunday. He must think he's riding high—you and Caleb falling all over yourselves to be nice, Stuart sucking up, the Staffords rolling out the carpet. And Jack, the only person not dazzled, is dead."

"We disagree about Ben, Jim. Let's just leave it at that."

"You really don't get it, do you." He sneered at her. "Kincaid only came to Percyville to bring Jack down. If you think he's going to protect you when the shit hits the fan, then you're one naive lady. Your secrets will come pouring out along with Jack's. You should keep that in mind."

"My secrets?" She kept her voice calm, but she was shaken. Did he know about Caleb? Had Jack left some kind of record? Her heart racing, she thought of the tapes Taylor mentioned. "What secrets would those be, Jim?"

"I know Jack arranged your appointment to the bench. I know he had you in his pocket."

If she hadn't been so insulted, she would have been relieved. He wasn't talking about Caleb, but about Jack's compulsion to manipulate her.

"Nobody has me in his pocket," she told Rankin. "And threats from your cronies won't change that. Now, for the last time, I want you out of here."

Rankin studied her in silence as if she were a bug of some doomed species. "Don't say I didn't warn you."

"Take me home, Ben."

Ben put the Explorer in gear and pulled away from the courthouse. "Riverbend?"

Suzanne leaned her head against the headrest. "No, my

house in town. Please. Caleb's at Riverbend with Trey and Gayle. He wants to stay another couple of days, but I need my own bed."

"Bad day?" With a glance in the rearview mirror, he turned abruptly down a side street to lose the cruiser tailing him.

"Double bad day." She rubbed a spot above her right eye. "The case on the docket involved political cronies of Jack's. Plus it's linked to a more important one scheduled in a couple of weeks. Unfortunately, I had to give them what they wanted. I had no other option. What galls me is that Jim Rankin dropped by my chambers to apply a little persuasion on behalf of Jack's friends. He'll interpret my ruling as evidence that I caved."

"What kind of persuasion?" Ben gave her a quick glance.

"He said his friends—Jack's old friends—were nasty people and it wouldn't be smart of me to cross them."

Ben swore, softly and richly. "Maybe I need to talk with the chief. What the hell does he think he's doing?"

"I think he's making a futile effort to fill Jack's shoes."

"He's not mean enough or smart enough," Ben said, and gunned the Explorer through a flashing caution light.

Suzanne glanced back at the rear window. "Are we in a hurry?"

"We're being tailed, no doubt on orders from the chief. That guy gives lawmen a bad name."

"Why are we being tailed?" she asked, frowning.

"The truth? I don't think it's anything to do with the investigation, no matter what kind of veiled threats that asshole makes. I think he's jealous as hell because you're with me."

She smiled and relaxed again. "He's jealous, all right. He told me today in so many words that I was going to be one sad lady when you were unmasked and I saw your true colors."

Ben settled back now that he'd lost the tail. He glanced her way and smiled. "So, how bad am I?"

"Right up there with Saddam Hussein, according to Jim. An old and dear friend, I say."

"He's still Jack's flunky. He's doing everything he can to hold the machine together."

"I don't know why."

"Maybe he has political aspirations himself or maybe he's being pressured by the people Jack crawled into bed with."

Suzanne shuddered, thinking how she'd actually hoped Jim Rankin might be the person to help her conquer her fear. "I can't believe I didn't see through him."

"How could you? He wouldn't be the first man to play a role to get on the good side of a woman he wanted."

She turned to look out the side window. "I've been thinking about that. If Jack was calling the shots, he probably instructed the chief to make a play for me. If I went along with it, Jack might have assumed I would be easier to control. He'd been trying unsuccessfully to manipulate me for years."

Ben's eyes were cold with fury. "To get you into bed?"

She laughed without humor. "No, he'd been trying to use my power as a judge. Even before that, when I was in the D.A.'s office, he was always at me to reduce or dismiss a charge."

"Why in hell did he keep on? He knew you would never bend."

Her tone quivered with hatred. "He liked to torment me."

"He was a sick bastard."

She rolled her head on the seat to look at him. "Do we have to talk about Jack Sullivan?"

He turned onto the street where she lived, not replying until they reached her house and he stopped the car in her drive. "Seems to me," he said, crooking an arm over the wheel to look at her, "that we talk about Jack a lot because he looms so large in your life, Suzy."

"Not anymore. He's dead."

"Is he?"

Suzanne found the handle and shoved the door open. "Thanks for the ride, Ben. I'll call Annie to give me a lift to the courthouse tomorrow morning." Without looking at him, she climbed out and slammed the door, but Ben was waiting for her when she walked around the front of the car.

"Case closed, eh?"

She wouldn't meet his eyes. "What's that supposed to mean?"

"Jack. His influence in your life." He waited a moment, then added, "In Caleb's life."

"Caleb's life?" Holding herself together, she made herself look directly at him. "He married my sister. Naturally he's a presence in Caleb's life."

"Presence." He took her arm and gently urged her across the flagstone walk up to her front door. "Got your key?"

Flustered, fumbling, she searched her handbag for her keys, then handed them over, saying nothing as he unlocked the door. Her heartbeat was loud in her ears, and her chest felt as if it were being squeezed by a steel band. Behind her, she heard Ben closing the door, but she was already through the foyer, past the living room, heading down the hall toward the den. Part of her was glad he had stayed, glad he wouldn't just give up and go. But another part waited with dread for more questions and as much as she'd like to get it all out, surely it was better if no one knew. Still, Taylor and Annie had been able to purge themselves of Jack. Why couldn't she do the same?

She jumped when Ben came up behind her and slipped his arms around her waist. "I'm sorry, sweetheart. That was unfair."

Tense, she said, "I just hate talking about Jack."

"Caleb's father."

Suzanne forgot to breathe. In fifteen years, nobody had come close to guessing her secret. Standing stiff with horror in Ben's embrace, she was incapable of making a sound.

"It's okay, sweetheart." He kissed her hair.

She closed her eyes. "It's not what you think."

Again, as he had in the gazebo yesterday, he rocked her gently. "*Now* we can stop talking about Jack," he said, his arms strong and warm around her. "Let's talk about us instead, okay?"

Suzanne lay her arms over his and rested her head against his chest. It was wonderful being close like this and not feeling panic. But would she panic if he wanted more?

"What about us?" she asked.

"I want to make love to you."

Tears started in her eyes and she shook her head mutely. She heard him release a breath, felt his body give as disappointment moved through him.

"No?"

"I can't, Ben. I don't know how."

He smiled against her ear. "You know how. You've just been out of practice for a few years."

"Sixteen."

"Okay, *very* out of practice. But we can overcome that."

"I wish." She turned then and looked into his face. "I haven't been with anybody since Dennis and I divorced." Her gaze fell to the floor. "And the months before he finally walked out were so awful, it makes me wonder why he stayed with me as long as he did."

He used his thumbs to prop her chin up so he could look at her. "Listen, don't let's talk about Dennis, either, okay?"

"I'm trying to explain! To warn you."

"Warn me?" With a lopsided grin he pushed against her, letting her feel his erection. "Too late, darling."

Darling. Nobody had called her darling in a long, long time. Smiling, she put her forehead against his and wondered why she hadn't been smart enough to fall in love with Ben Kincaid when she was sixteen.

She sighed when he kissed her nose, enjoying the feel of his hands moving over her back, cupping her buttocks, but gently, without urgency. Inside she felt the darkness and fear unraveling. Joyously she locked her arms around his neck.

In two steps, he had her pushed up against a low bar stool, then his hands were caressing her face. His thumbs rubbed across her lips, and then her cheekbones, and finally tangled in her hair as he urged her head back and brought her lips to his.

With a sigh, she opened to him and his mouth covered hers, not too urgent, not too hungry, but masterfully just the same, and shivers ran all the way to her toes.

He was breathing heavily now. "Can we go to your bed-room?"

She gazed at him, years of failure clouding her eyes. "I don't think you understand, Ben. I'm not a normal..."

"You're normal." He slipped his hands beneath her sweater and found her breasts. She wore a bra, but it was just a scrap of satin and lace. He didn't even have to unsnap it to expose her.

"I'm no good at this," she insisted as he covered both breasts and trailed lazy kisses down her throat. "I... It's like I just... oh, oh..." She closed her eyes as he flicked his thumbs over her nipples. Now she was hanging on to his waist, delirious with sensations she had almost forgotten, breathing hard. He nipped at her parted lips and kissed her eyes, nose, cheeks.

"You were saying..."

"My...my marriage. It...I was the one at fault. I screwed every...everything up." She sagged against him when his tongue probed into her ear. "God, what are you doing? I've never—"

"Never?" He pushed his hips against her in age-old demand. She clung to him, wishing he would kiss her, really kiss her. Long-denied needs overwhelmed her. With a hungry whimper, she tried to capture his mouth, but he evaded her attempts. In-stead, he took her hands and held them to his mouth, looking at her. "Can we go to bed?"

She almost panicked at the intense look in his eyes. Her heart was racing and she knew her face and skin were flushed. God, he didn't know what he was asking, but if she said no, he would go and she might never have another chance. And in that moment, she realized she was in love with Ben Kincaid. She *had* to trust him. He was the one who could take her beyond fear. Hadn't she always known that?

She felt like a scared virgin entering her bedroom with Ben. Her years of marriage were so long in the past that they might never have been. She might have bolted if Ben hadn't pushed his fingers into her hair and covered her mouth with a deep kiss.

She'd feared undressing, but again Ben took control. While kissing her mouth, her face, her throat, he divested himself of his own clothes and then started on hers. He was good at this, keeping her occupied with kisses everywhere, so that in seconds she stood before him naked. Only then did she realize that he was breathing hard, as if he'd been running. For some reason that delighted her. He wanted her!

Seeing her smile, he brought her body to his in a warm, enveloping hug. The scent of him was deeply arousing. She closed her eyes to savor it and enjoyed the hard, masculine feel of his body pressed to hers. She twined her arms around his neck and rubbed her bare skin against his, feeling wantonly feminine— an almost-forgotten sensation.

Then he was urging her onto the bed, his knee between her legs as the bed took their combined weight. His chest was broad, heavily muscled, furred. For a second, fear flashed in her mind. Ben saw it, dipped his head to kiss her mouth with warm urgency, then raised it to look into her eyes.

"I would never hurt you, Suzy. Tell me what you want."

She lifted her hand and traced his nose, the shape of his mouth, his jawline. "Don't stop."

He shifted to his side and pulled her to him for another deep kiss, and Suzanne lost herself in sensation—the hard, male length of his limbs, his firm, flat belly, the strength of his neck. She was startled by the familiarity of him, as if they were finally where they were meant to be all along. The sheer wonder of it—Ben and Suzanne making love! It was almost too much to believe.

Now his tongue was all over the quivering skin of her body. She felt flushed and wild. She heard her own disjointed, gasping sounds but didn't know what she needed. And then his mouth closed over her, hot and greedy. She cried out in shock. She must be dying, she thought, because the pleasure was too intense to be real. Lights exploded behind her eyes and her

blood pulsed with primitive rhythm as she arched and offered
her body for more. Strained for more. Whimpered in mindless bliss. She'd never felt this way—joyful, liberated, intensely
alive. What kind of passion was this? She called his name and
frantically dragged him up, needing to have him inside her.

But again she tensed with fear when she felt the heat of him
probing against her softness. He sensed it and groped for the
lamp switch. With the light on, he settled back, hoisting her up
until she was on top of him.

"Look at me, Suzy," he said, dragging in deep gulps of air.
He was damp, glistening with sweat. "There's only you and me
in this bed, sweetheart. I want you to know who's loving you."
He brought her face close and kissed her fiercely, his arousal
pushing him beyond gentleness.

She stared at him, knowing she was trapped, helpless, yet
inside she throbbed with unfulfilled passion. He'd stopped her
just short of climax. What was there to fear from Ben?

"We're almost there, sweetheart," he urged, waiting with
his hands holding her hips. She felt him at the gate of her femi-
ninity, hot, hard, ready. Her lips opened to try to say…what?
Trembling, aroused, anxious, she looked into his eyes—richly
brown, warm, enticing. Her own fluttered shut. Ben recognized
that for the surrender it was. He made a deep sound and raised
her just enough to settle her onto him.

He was warm, thick and hard. Trembling, she moved cautiously until she'd taken all of him. "Oh, Ben…" Back arched,
head thrown back, she opened herself fully and began to rock,
driven now by her own passion and need. Deep inside her,
Ben fell instinctively into her ever-quickening rhythm, moving
faster and faster with her, both of them straining headlong to
oblivion. *Hurry, hurry,* she thought, mad to reach the peak.
God, it had been so long.

And then it happened. With her arms high above her head,
she crested in a burst of joy and light. She cried out, and somewhere beyond herself she heard Ben echo her release.

Seconds later, she slid bonelessly down on him, damp and

depleted and happy. Flushed and tingling, she drifted in and out of idle thought, content to feel Ben lazily stroking her hair while they caught their breath, amazed at how her limbs and heart and mind had turned to mush.

He shifted so that she was lying next to him, safe in the crook of his arm. He turned his head and kissed her forehead. "Didn't I tell you? You didn't forget."

She smiled against his flat male nipple. "No."

He was quiet, still stroking her—now the side of her face, her throat. "I love you, Suzy."

She closed her eyes, feeling her heart turn over. "I love you, too, Ben."

His grip tightened. "I think I always have."

She considered that, then said quietly, "I missed you so much when you left. One night I just needed to hear your voice—something awful had happened—so I called and a woman answered." She swallowed the tiny catch in her throat. "I never called again, and a little while after that, you were married."

"I wish I'd been there that night."

"It wasn't meant to be, not then."

"Jack raped you, didn't he?"

She drew in an unsteady breath. "Yes."

He waited until he'd mastered his voice. "Was it at the reception?"

"Yes."

"Jesus. His own wedding." When she said nothing, he went on, "You were running from him when we met on the stairs."

"I was running from everybody."

"And it was that day you got pregnant with Caleb."

"Meaning that if I didn't, I must have had an affair with my sister's husband." She gave a bitter laugh. "Well, I didn't. Caleb was conceived that day."

"You didn't tell anyone."

She lifted a shoulder and let it fall.

"Because of the scandal."

"The wedding was over. Taylor was married to him. I thought I could put it behind me. I didn't know I was pregnant."

Ben cursed. "God, if a man ever deserved to burn in hell, it's Jack!" His whole body shuddered with rage. "I wish the assassin hadn't beaten me to it. I'd have loved to confront him, pound him into shit on your behalf."

For a moment, she traced the silky curls on his chest, then she turned her face up to his. "I'm glad you know. I've been worrying about it. I thought either you or Stuart would be the first to piece it together after the shooting."

"When Caleb's blood type matched Gayle's."

"Yes."

He shifted so that they were face-to-face. "Actually, Caleb set me on the right track. You saw us together yesterday at Riverbend. He's dealing with a lot of unanswered questions, Suzy. You're going to have to tell him."

Her eyes filled. "How can I? What will I tell him? That I had an affair with Jack?" She shuddered. "I couldn't. That I was raped? No child needs to know that. And what would the truth do to Gayle and Trey? Don't say we don't have to tell them— they're going to put it together sooner or later. Everybody is."

"Maybe so, but none of that gets you off the hook with Caleb." He tucked a strand of her hair behind her ear. "Some other kid might not be able to shrug this off, but Caleb will. He's strong. He can take it. And he's been searching long enough, Suzy. He deserves an answer."

"It's so awful," she whispered, closing her eyes.

Ben reached out and pulled her forehead to his. "You're going to have to tell him, Suzy."

FORTY-ONE

SUZANNE AND BEN DROVE back to Riverbend later that night. Before they reached the front door, Caleb had it open. "Mom, Mom, Aunt Taylor's had an accident. She fell in the bathroom and I think we need to call the EMTs, but Grandma Lily says no."

"Oh, God." Tossing her handbag on the nearest chair, Suzanne started for the stairs, but stopped as her mother wheeled into the foyer. "Mother, what's happened to Taylor?"

Lily Stafford was pale and clearly shaken. "You won't believe it, Suzanne. You do your best to rear your children and somewhere along the way they take a wrong turn. It's enough to drive a person mad."

"What are you talking about, Mother? What has Taylor done?"

"Who knows? She's hysterical. I'm glad you're here, Suzanne. Gayle is with me in the sunroom and she is *so* upset. Your father's upstairs with Taylor. Trey's run off into the woods somewhere. You'd better go up and try to do some damage control."

Damage control? "Caleb said she was hurt, Mother."

The Judge waved a hand. "She *said* she fell in the tub."

Gayle appeared behind Lily. Only yesterday, everyone had remarked on her rapid recovery from the shooting. Now she looked fragile and shaky and her color was ghastly. "She's been drinking again, Aunt Suzy."

"Oh, no."

Gayle's mouth twisted bitterly. "Daddy would have her committed again...if he were here."

Lily reached behind her and patted Gayle's hand. "Let's let

Suzanne see to it, darling." Still looking at Suzanne, Lily added, "This time she's really gone too far. You'll see."

"Come on, Mom," Caleb urged, already halfway up the stairs.

Ben squeezed her shoulder. "Shall I stay, Suzy?"

Suzanne grasped his hand. "Would you? Please."

Charles Stafford was in the hall when they reached the top of the stairs, his face gray with strain. He met her with a look of relief. "Suzy, thank God you're here. Your sister needs you."

"Where is she, Dad?"

"She's locked herself in the bathroom," he said, rubbing his hand over the top of his head wearily. "I can't get her to come out or even talk to me. Maybe she'll open for you." He put an unsteady hand on Caleb's shoulder. "Caleb, son, you and I need to find Trey. He's run off somewhere. Can't say as I blame him much."

First Gayle, now Trey. What next? Suzanne turned to Caleb. "Go with Grandpa, Caleb."

"Sure, Mom. You just take care of Aunt Taylor."

When they were headed downstairs, Ben followed Suzanne into the bedroom that had been Taylor's when they were growing up. Between it and an identical bedroom—Suzanne's—was a bathroom. Suzanne went to the door and tried the glass knob. It was locked. "Taylor? It's me, Tay—Suzanne."

No voice came, but there was movement behind the door and some sound. Murmuring? Sobbing? Definitely the clink of glass.

"Taylor? Please unlock the door. Caleb said you were hurt, that you needed a doctor."

"I'm fine."

Suzanne met Ben's eyes, then tried the door again. "Okay, if you say so, but can we talk face-to-face? I feel dumb trying to have a conversation through this door."

"I'm the dumb one." The clink of a bottle against glass. "I'm also stinking drunk."

Suzanne closed her eyes. "That's all right with me, Tay. I want to see you, anyway."

"No-o-o-o..." Taylor gave a thin, anguished wail. "You w-won't when you h-hear."

Suzanne gave the doorknob another urgent turn. "Please unlock the door, Tay."

"Not until I take the p-pills."

Suzanne turned frantically to Ben.

"Do you want me to force the door?" he asked softly.

"Yes, yes. Hurry."

He pulled her aside, and with one sturdy kick, broke the lock. The door swung inward with a crash. Taylor didn't appear surprised. Shoulders drooping, she sat on the toilet seat fiddling with a medicine bottle. Beside her on the side of the bathtub was a glass. A bottle of vodka, half empty, was on the floor. She was all in black—snug leggings, an oversize sweatshirt; even her hair—jet black—seemed part of a macabre ensemble. And she was barefoot. Somehow, the sight of her small feet—her toenails painted a pretty pink—caught at Suzanne's heart.

She rushed forward and took the pills, expecting to find the bottle empty. But it was almost full. "Did you take any of these, Taylor?"

"Not yet." She lifted a hand, listlessly pushed at her hair, then added bitterly, "I don't have Eugenia's guts."

Suzanne gasped at the ugly, purple bruise near her hairline. "Oh, what have you done!" Suzanne cried, reaching out. "Let me see."

"It's nothing." Taylor fought her off, almost losing her balance, then tried to focus on Suzanne's face, her beautiful blue eyes filling with tears. "It was all my f-fault, Suzy."

"Come on, Tay. Let's get out of this bathroom." Obligingly, Taylor tried to stand, but her legs buckled. With Ben's help, Suzanne managed to get her out of the bathroom and across the floor where she sank onto the bed.

For the first time, Taylor seemed to notice Ben. "Hello, Ben."

He smiled faintly. "Hello, Taylor."

"Are you a policeman?"

He nodded. "Yeah. Sort of."

After some consideration, Taylor nodded solemnly. "I'd rather say this to you than to Jim Rankin." She made a face. "He makes me think of Jack."

Crouched in front of her, Suzanne rubbed her sister's hands in alarm. She'd worried that Taylor was nearing a breakdown, and her words were chilling proof of how close it could be.

Taylor turned, looking at the naked limbs of a dogwood tree just outside her window. "You want to know the truth, I think of Jack most of the time, anyway. He's dead, I know that, but his *ghost* is still around to t-torment me. I know that sounds crazy, but it's true. He's everywhere, looking over my shoulder." She dropped her eyes to her hands. "That's why I had to have a drink today." She looked plaintively at Suzanne. "I *needed* it, can you understand that, Suzy? I can't think, I can't sleep, I can't deal with my kids. I…I tried to explain that to Spencer, but he kept saying it was just my nerves, the shock of it all, you know. Gayle and everything." The tears spilled over. "God, my daughter almost died and I'm responsible."

"You're not responsible, Taylor. How can you think that?"

"Spencer just said we should put it behind us, we should just make love and I'd feel better." Pulling her hands free, Taylor wiped her eyes with her fingers. "I could tell he didn't understand how Jack *haunts* me."

Suzanne frowned. "When was this?"

"Just—I don't know. A little while ago."

"You went to see Spencer today?"

"At his place, yes. I went to tell him we couldn't ever be together. It was never meant to be, anyway," she said hopelessly. She put her fingers over her trembling lips. "From the moment Jack discovered we were lovers, we were doomed. That's what I told Spencer, but he just wouldn't accept it."

"Jack knew about you and Spencer?" Suzanne asked.

"Jack knew everything. Not that he cared if I screwed every man between Memphis and New Orleans. It was just his precious public image he worried about. But after he was dead Spencer said we were free. He said I'd trusted him to take care of everything and he had, so why couldn't I accept it and enjoy it."

Suzanne could only stare at her in shock, resisting what her words implied.

"No one would ever put it together, he said. It would be our secret and the two of us would take it to our graves."

"My God, Taylor. Are you—"

"And that's when I knew he'd done it. *Spencer* killed Jack." With her arms wrapped around herself, Taylor let out a thin cry and began rocking, rocking. "I told him I didn't believe him. It had to be somebody else, because it was so horrible. Too horrible for a good person to do. Because Spencer's a good person, a kind and loving person. He is, he is. And Gayle...so innocent, and she loved her daddy so *much!*" Taylor bent low and covered her face with her hands and wept brokenly. "And it's my fault. I ruin everything I touch!"

Her own heart aching, Suzanne stroked Taylor's hair. She'd never felt so helpless. But Taylor was still babbling, her words muffled through her hands. "He s-said he thought I wanted Jack out of my life, that I would be glad he was dead. And I am, I *am!* But I didn't want it to be this way. For *Spencer* to do it. Now I have Spencer's blood on my hands, too, because he'll have to be punished."

Yes, he would, Suzanne thought sadly.

Taylor raised her eyes, sniffing. "That's why I just decided it's no use, don't you see, Suzy? Gayle almost died and Trey's so troubled and our lives are turned upside down. The Judge is disgusted with me, Daddy's worried sick, and even the people of Mississippi have been cheated. And the price I'll pay is losing Spencer. I wanted to take the pills because I don't think I can bear that."

Suzanne touched her hand. "You need help, Taylor. I'm going to call someone to help you."

"I don't want help. I want to die."

446   GOOD GIRLS

"Don't talk like that!" Suzanne said fiercely. She moved forward and wrapped her arms around her sister, feeling her own tears welling up. "You have to think of Gayle and Trey. They're depending on you, Taylor. Jack won't be around to torment you anymore. You can stay sober this time, I know it."

"No, I'm not like you," Taylor sobbed. "I'm a complete failure. I'm a rotten wife and mother and lover and... and...I'm a rotten human *being!*"

Suzanne turned anguished eyes to Ben. "I'm going to take her to a hospital, Ben. I know a place. Would you go downstairs and tell my parents? Then call Annie and ask her to come and stay with the children."

It took only a few minutes to get Taylor bundled into Ben's Explorer. Suzanne sat beside her, chafing her hands and gently reassuring her, but she wasn't convinced Taylor even heard her. She seemed to have passed into a state that distanced her from everything except the depth of her misery.

Ben had the motor running when Charles Stafford came out of the house with a look on his face that made Suzanne brace for more disaster. Ben rolled down his window.

"What is it, Charles?"

"That was Stuart on the phone," Charles said, lowering his voice so that Suzanne could barely hear. "Spencer Dutton's killed himself."

FORTY-TWO

SUZANNE SAT IN HER CHAMBERS waiting to be called by the bailiff for the next case on the docket. It was a week since Spencer's suicide, and she could find only one thing for which to be grateful: Taylor had been hospitalized and consequently shielded from the worst of the scandal. When Jack was assassinated, there had been some reluctant attempt by the media to respect the privacy of his immediate family. Not so after the furor erupted when Spencer died. Although his note exonerated Taylor, it also exposed her infidelity. Now every facet of her life, as well as Gayle's and Trey's, was suddenly fair game. What would they do when it was revealed that Jack was Caleb's father?

Was Jack watching? Suzanne wondered with a shudder. Was he laughing?

She bent her head and rubbed her temples, thinking Taylor might not have been too far out believing his ghost was everywhere. She didn't have to try very hard to imagine him waiting in hell with bated breath for the moment when she told Caleb the circumstances of his birth. As Ben had said, it had to be done, but with so much upheaval in the family, she needed to find the right moment to tell that particular secret. Resting her forehead on her hand for a minute, she sighed, then pushed her chair back to stand up. Tonight. She would do it tonight. She would tell him and then ask Ben to come over for moral support.

Ben. God, the man was on her mind all the time, it seemed. Given all that was going on—Spencer's suicide, Taylor's breakdown, the children, her parents' anguish, scandal, media harassment—

how could she still lose herself in sexual fantasy like this? With a small smile, she moved her hands slowly over her breasts and down to her tummy, remembering the last time they'd been together.

There were still questions and uncertainties about their relationship, though. Since going to bed with him, she had tried to dwell only on the present and not worry about the future. It was unrealistic to expect someone like Ben to want to settle down in a small town like Percyville, even assuming he wanted to have a lasting relationship with her. There had been serious problems in his first marriage. Lord, marriage. Was it only a few weeks ago she had rejected the thought of ever marrying again?

She glanced at her watch and reached to buzz Betsy to find out what was causing the delay, only to find her message light on. With an impatient sound, she punched the button. The reason was probably waiting to be heard. Zoning out over Ben was now interfering with her work.

She listened to a series of beeps before a man said her name and told her he was calling about a case that he identified by docket number. His voice was not familiar. With a frown, Suzanne sank into her chair to hear him out. "This is a friendly reminder of the deal you cut when Jack arranged your appointment to the bench, Judge Stafford." Suzanne's mouth fell open in shock. "It's pay-up time, Judge. And if you were thinking to renege because Jack is dead...don't. A judge's reputation is hard to build, easy to destroy. Yours is on the line now." The voice changed to a menacing tone. "Decide the case the right way or you won't like the consequences." After a pause, he said pleasantly, "Have a nice day, Judge."

For a long moment, Suzanne simply stared at the telephone, then she scrambled up and went to the door and jerked it open. Her secretary gave her a startled look. "There's a message on my voice mail, Betsy. Do you know anything about it?"

"No." The woman stood up. "Why, what's wrong?"

Suzanne glanced in distraction at her desk. "I've been here since eight. When was it recorded?"

"I don't know. I—"

"Think!" She drew a calming breath. "I mean, try to think, Betsy. It's important."

"You were in conference with the attorneys on the McMillan case and I went for a new cartridge for the printer. But I was only gone ten minutes at the most."

"Around nine," Suzanne murmured.

"I think so."

Suzanne turned to go back to her office. She closed the door, battling a sense of deep foreboding. The case was scheduled for tomorrow. It was the same one Jim Rankin had warned her about. The caller had talked pure nonsense, but after all the scandal surrounding her and her family since Jack was killed, the public was still hungry for more. If she didn't do what was demanded, would anyone believe her?

FORTY-THREE

Suzanne prepared to leave her chambers late the next day
with her stomach in a knot. She'd heard the case and had found
for the defendants. The Kent Group's lawyers were clearly unhappy, but no one had spoken directly to her once court was
adjourned. She hoped they had decided to accept the verdict
and leave her alone. There had been only a few people in the
courtroom, the case being one that didn't stir much attention,
but the ramifications were significant.

If she'd ruled for the plaintiffs, it would have been the first
step in a series of court cases sure to be filed to allow various
forms of gaming in small businesses—bars, service stations,
truck stops and the like. Suzanne understood Jack's scheme
now. If he'd succeeded in forcing her to rule favorably—as his
Vegas connections wished—the door would have been opened
statewide. Of course his cronies would try again in another
county with a different judge. And perhaps they would succeed, but today had not been the day, and, for now, her ruling
would stand.

But her stomach was still in a knot. She couldn't quite dismiss Jim Rankin's threats or the message on her voice mail and
wondered if she should have told Ben last night. As she reached
for her coat, she reminded herself he could do nothing to change
the law as it was written. Disturbing as it was, this was one of
those times when the responsibilities of being a judge weighed
heavily. After checking to see that she had her car keys handy,
she pulled the door to her inner office closed and gave a start
when the outer door opened abruptly.

"Ben!" She allowed herself the pleasure of studying him

across the room. He'd been boyishly good-looking when they'd first become friends. Now he was tough and lean, and years of international travel had stamped him with a sophistication that gave her a delicious feeling of anticipation. She could not deny that Ben added the spice of newness and challenge to her life.

"Hi, I was just thinking about you." She was breathless. And something must have shown in her eyes, because without a word he closed the door behind him and went straight to her, pulled her into his arms and kissed her, a ravenous, open-mouthed, mind-blowing kiss.

"Gosh," she said, even more breathless.

With his lips pressed to a spot beneath her ear, he said, "How about a ride home?"

"I have a ride home," she said, hanging on to him weakly. "But you can follow me."

"Owen took the twins to the arcade and I'm without wheels. Temporarily."

"No problem." It felt so right meeting Ben after work, touching him, kissing him. Even the knot in her stomach seemed to ease a bit. She dangled her keys. "You can drive."

She started toward the door, but he stopped her by catching her hand. "Wait a minute, Suzy." She met his eyes and only then noticed the hard set of his jaw.

"What is it, Ben?"

"Before you go out there, we need to talk."

"What's wrong?" Her mind took off like a runaway train. God, what now? "What's happened? Is it Caleb?"

"Caleb's fine." He squeezed her hand. "You're all over the news, Suzanne. I was building some shelves with the television on when I heard your name in a teaser for the five o'clock news. Amanda Mason claims she has documents proving you've protected the interests of some very nasty people whose cases have come before you in court."

"That's ridiculous!"

"She says they deeded you a beach house on the Gulf Coast in payment for that decision on the landfill case a couple of months ago. She also unearthed a recently established trust in Caleb's name, large enough that you couldn't possibly have funded it on your salary as a judge. The trustee is a lawyer who does work for the Kent Group."

"Caleb? A trust?" Dazed, she was shaking her head. "There couldn't be—"

He squeezed her hand again. "It gets worse, sweetheart. Mason claims Jack arranged your appointment to the bench to ensure there would be a judge in his pocket when he needed one."

"I don't believe this," she murmured, needing to sit down.

"You don't own property on the Gulf Coast?"

"No! My house here in Percyville is the only piece of real estate I've ever owned and it's mortgaged to the hilt."

"What about the decisions in favor of the Kent Group?"

"My hands were tied!" she cried. "I had to rule according to the law. Today the law didn't work in their favor. They threatened this if I didn't rule the way they wanted. Doesn't it prove something that it didn't go their way this time?"

Ben's eyes narrowed. "Who threatened you? Was it Rankin again?"

"No, it wasn't Jim. I didn't recognize the voice."

"He phoned you here?"

"It was on my voice mail. He said if I didn't decide the case the right way, they'd destroy my reputation."

"And you didn't tell me?"

"What could you have done? I had no option but to rule as the statutes dictated. I can't knuckle under to threats, no matter how personal they get, Ben. I'd be at the mercy of every criminal who came before me. Would you have advised me otherwise?"

"We could have alerted the right people, and when—if—they followed through on their threats, you would've had some credibility. As it is, Suzy, you're out on a limb."

"Thanks a lot. You can't know how you've relieved my mind."

"Shit." He reached over and hauled her back into his arms. "I'm sorry, sweetheart. I'm frustrated and mad as hell." He drew a deep breath, inhaling her scent. "The woman I love is being victimized by some sleazy lowlifes with money and power and I can't do a damn thing about it."

She pushed against his arms to look him in the eye. "Does this mean you think I should step down?"

He didn't need to see the glint in her eyes to know that was not an option for Suzanne. He laughed softly. "No, baby. You'll step down over my dead body."

She put a hand over his lips. "Don't say that!"

"Bad choice of words." He caught her hand and pulled her to the door, cracked it open and took a quick look around. "Coming on the heels of the assassination and Spencer's suicide, there's potential here to discredit you personally as well as professionally. The press is outside. The guard's keeping them out of your immediate area, but they'll be on you like a bad smell the minute you hit the hallway."

She moved to his shoulder and could see the crowd being held at bay by a privacy bar used to protect defendants from the public. With dismay, Suzanne realized that to the media, she was just as much the accused as if she'd been charged with a major crime.

"Stick close to me, babe." With an arm around her, Ben swept her out into the hall. "Keep your head down. And don't comment."

The minute she stepped outside, the whirr of cameras started. Lights flashed in her face, microphones were shoved obscenely close, questions were hurled from all sides.

"Do you have business ties with Jack Sullivan?"

"Are you or anyone in your family on the board of the Kent Group?"

"Did Jack Sullivan visit you at your new beach house?"

Amanda Mason. Suzanne recognized her voice but doggedly kept her eyes straight ahead.

"Judge Stafford, did you have a personal relationship with Jack Sullivan?"

"No!" she replied with revulsion.

"Don't say another word," Ben hissed in her ear.

"Did your mother really have a stroke, Judge Stafford?"

It was a nightmare.

With the help of two security guards and Ben, she was finally hustled to her car, and with Ben at the wheel, they got out of the parking lot. Once on the street, the tires squealed as Ben accelerated. "Riverbend, I think," he said through his teeth. "Those electronic gates have paid for themselves three times over since Jack died."

"Yes." She was trembling, her stomach now in outright rebellion.

Ben glanced in the rearview mirror and saw only empty road. "At Riverbend you'll be relatively safe from media sharks chumming for your pretty ass."

She groaned. "Charming."

He gave her a wink, then sobered. "This is bad business, Suzy, make no mistake. The longer Mason's allegations are allowed to go unchallenged, the greater the potential for destroying your reputation beyond repair."

"Tell me."

His mouth was a grim line. "Jack set all this up before he died, didn't he?"

She closed her eyes. "Yes. He must have."

"Bastard."

Caleb was waiting for her on the front steps as Ben stopped the car. "Oh, no! Look at his face!" Suzanne wailed. "He knows."

Ben touched her hand. "Don't worry. He's tough, Suzy. This isn't the first time your job has pushed you into the limelight, and it won't be the last. Just give it to him straight. He'll always be your biggest fan."

She got out of the car, but Caleb didn't wait for her to climb the steps. He rushed down to meet her. "Mom, Mom, I've figured it out. Uncle Jack's the one, isn't he? I mean, he's not really my uncle, he's my father. Right?"

"Caleb." She spoke through bloodless lips as her purse fell to the ground with a soft plop. Caleb swept it up without noticing she'd gone pale as milk. He was excited, full of his discovery. "I saw all that stuff on the news, and when that woman asked if you had a personal relationship with Jack, it just clicked in. My blood type's the same as Gayle's, you were always so tense around him, just…lots of stuff." He shook his head and drove his fingers through his hair—so like Jack!—and then met Ben's eyes. "I can't believe I didn't put it together before now, you know? Like, it's been right there in front of me, but Mom's paranoid about Uncle Jack, always has been, so you don't even *consider*— Hey, even that should have been a clue, huh?"

"Caleb, please…"

"But am I right?"

"God…"

"Am I right, Mom?" he repeated stubbornly.

"Yes." She put a hand to her mouth and her eyes filled.

"Jeez, Mom, I'm sorry. Don't cry, okay? I guess you didn't want me to figure it out, huh?"

She was shaking her head mutely.

"But I was bound to sooner or later, Mom. I'm no dummy."

"No." She felt Ben's arm come around her and leaned against him gratefully.

Caleb's expression was anxious now. "Gosh, you're pale. You're not gonna faint or something, are you?"

"No."

"Then are you upset?" His excitement had faded to apprehension.

Upset? She opened her mouth to reply, then closed it again. To Caleb, she must appear shocked or stunned, probably both. And she was. This was the moment she'd dreaded. This was the secret she'd hidden from him all his life. And, God love him, he wasn't flipping out over finding out his uncle was actually his father. No, her son was worried about her reaction.

"I'm not upset, Caleb," she said, gathering herself finally. She blinked away the tears. "You just took me by surprise. I thought you'd be alarmed by seeing me on TV and having all the ugly allegations flying left and right. Instead…"

"Yeah, well, all that stuff comes and goes, the way I see it. I know you aren't for sale to anybody. Not that we aren't going to have to figure out a way to counter their stupid charges, but we'll do it."

She gave a helpless laugh and then hugged him. "You are something else, Caleb Stafford."

"I'm thinking maybe I should change my name."

She pushed away, her mouth falling open. "Caleb! No."

He gave her a gentle punch on the shoulder. "Just kidding, Mom. I'm not exactly panting to have that guy's name."

"Don't say that in front of Gayle and Trey, please."

He rolled his eyes. "Of course not. But I do have a few questions." He lifted his eyebrows. "Okay?"

Ben touched her elbow. "I need to make a few phone calls. Why don't you two find someplace private and have a little talk?"

Caleb looked at his mother. "The sunroom?"

After a moment, she nodded. It was time.

THE KNOT WAS BACK in her stomach. Standing with the door at her back, Suzanne waited for Caleb to choose a place to sit, and when he did—on the floor hugging a cushion—she crossed the room and sat down opposite him.

"This is difficult," she said, holding a matching cushion to her own stomach.

"How 'bout I ask some questions, Mom? I've got about a thousand. You can take your time answering."

She could imagine the questions and knew there wasn't going to be an easy way to do this.

He waved a hand back and forth before her face. "Hello… Mo-o-o-m."

She closed her eyes. "Ask away."

"Did you have an affair with Uncle Jack?"

"No!"

"But you had sex with him?"

"No!"

He frowned. "Are we talking artificial insemination here?"

She touched her forehead, as if dizzy. She *was* dizzy. "No. I know this sounds confusing, but it's true. In a way."

Caleb huffed with impatience. "Well, if you didn't have an affair with him and you didn't have sex and you didn't have artificial insemination, how in heck did you get pregnant?"

She drew a breath and looked at him pleadingly. "Couldn't you just leave it at this, Caleb? I've admitted he's your biological father. What more do you want to know?"

"I want to know how it came to be, Mom. Gayle and Trey are now my half sister and brother. Do you realize that? They're not my cousins anymore, so how come for years you've let me—let us—think that?"

"I thought it was best."

"What did Uncle Jack think?"

"We never discussed it."

He stared. "You never discussed the fact that I was his kid?"

"No."

"Why, for crissake?"

"I didn't even meet your uncle—"

"My father."

She cleared her throat. "Your...your father...until a couple of months before the wedding. I was in law school when Taylor became engaged to him."

"And then *you* had his baby. Some details are missing, Mom."

"Yes. Taylor...she was ecstatic over her engagement. Jack was everything Mother wanted for her. He—"

"Mom, is this about Aunt Taylor or about you?"

She sighed. "All three of us, actually. I was just trying to help you understand how it was that day, how happy she was."

"That day?"

"The day of the wedding." For a second, Suzanne traced the cording around the pillow, lost in the memory of the ceremony and the reception. She could almost smell the flowers, hear the music, see the guests. Taylor had been so happy, drinking champagne with their mother…. "It was such a gorgeous spring day. Dennis was there and he had a little too much champagne. Not that he was the only one. Taylor, too, but— And Ben…Ben was there, too. So many people. After a while it got a little much, so I went out to the gazebo just to be by myself for a few minutes."

"The gazebo."

"Yes. It's pretty deserted out there, you know."

"Yeah."

"I'd been there only a few minutes when Jack appeared." She pressed the cushion against her midriff. "This is so hard, Caleb. I never wanted you to know this."

He leaned forward and touched her knee. "I'm not gonna freak over this, Mom, but I want to know."

"Jack flirted with me." She stared bleakly at the floor. "He'd just taken his vows with Taylor and he was flirting with me! I told him to go back to his bride, but he…you know Jack. He never did anything unless he wanted to."

"What happened then?"

"He…kept on. He wouldn't stop. He just—"

"You said no and he kept going?" When she nodded, he added, "He raped you."

She forced herself to look into his beautiful dark eyes. "I hate telling you this, Caleb. You're nothing like him. You're honest and decent, you have a good heart. You're sincere and…"

He laughed, putting up his hands. "Enough already, Mom." His tone softened with his eyes as he looked into her face. "And I *am* like him in lots of ways. I inherited his stubbornness and his way of focusing on stuff and not letting go. I'm smart in a left-brain way and you're a right-brain person, you say it all the time."

"I don't want you to be like him."

"He was a shitty human being and I won't use him as a role model, I promise." He scratched his cheek thoughtfully. "You think he was just a nutcase? I mean, doing what he did the very day he'd married your sister... Gee, it sounds like a man with a brick or two short of a load, Mom."

"I don't think he was insane." She couldn't have him believing that! "Honestly, Caleb, I think he was one of those people without a moral compass. I don't believe his childhood was pleasant. Maybe things happened then that might explain his personality. He's gone now, so we shouldn't judge him."

Caleb studied the floor, and after a moment raised his eyes to hers. "You didn't say anything because of Aunt Taylor and the scandal, right? The Stafford name and all that."

"It seemed right at the time."

"Maybe so, but he would have been stopped in his tracks if you'd said something. No telling how many people—women— he hurt before he was popped by good ol' Spence."

"Caleb," she said in a chiding tone.

He shrugged. "Sorry. Sort of."

She studied him with a thoughtful look. "I thought you'd be more upset about this, Caleb. I thought it would be horribly traumatic when you learned how much I'd kept from you."

"Well, I wish you'd told me before I wasted so much energy trying to figure it out on my own. I bugged a bunch of people a lot trying to dig up clues, but now I know and it's no big deal."

"Do you really mean that?"

"Sure. Except for the fact that he hurt you and humiliated you, I don't have feelings for Uncle Jack one way or another. Which is probably more than you can say, isn't that right?"

She smiled. "I suppose so, oh wise one."

"Then it's history, okay?" He untangled his long legs and gave her a hand up. "C'mon, old lady, let's find Ben. Incidentally, Mom, that guy's everything Uncle Jack wasn't, you know what I'm saying? Meantime, we need to get busy and figure out how to squelch the current flap surrounding our family."

She put her arm around his hard, young waist and hugged him. "I love you, Caleb."

He grinned. "I love you, too, Mom."

FORTY-FOUR

From her chair in the game room at Pinehaven Retreat, Taylor watched without interest the familiar intro to the six o'clock news. For the past seven days she had felt little interest in what was happening in the outside world. It was all she could do to cope with the turmoil going on inside herself.

She slept a lot, a result of medication. She didn't know and didn't care what they were giving her. Sleep was part of the regimen to help patients over the worst of detox. The problem with sleeping was that she dreamed. And dreams became nightmares. Gayle lying in blood. Jack laughing with devilish delight. Trey drifting like a lost soul. And Spencer cold and lifeless in a coffin. The only thing that could be worse was trying to cope with no medication whatsoever. Then she would be forced to face her demons in sobriety.

She was jerked from her reverie when she heard Suzy's name. She focused hazily on the television screen, recognizing Amanda Mason. For a few moments Taylor resisted the reporter's words, watching instead the movement of Mason's lips in the dissociative way she saw most things these days. But the reporter's words finally penetrated the chemical veil. No drug was strong enough to cushion the impact of Mason's exclusive. Lies—surely everyone would know it was all lies. But even so the scandal would devastate Suzy and ruin her career. Taylor's heart sank with dismal resignation. This nightmare was real.

You think you're having the last laugh...right, Jack?

FORTY-FIVE

"JUDGE STAFFORD'S SON IS named as beneficiary of a two-hun-dred-thousand-dollar trust. The beachfront cottage is valued in excess of a quarter of a million dollars. Repeated attempts to reach Judge Stafford for comment were unsuccessful. This is Amanda Mason reporting live outside the gates of Riverbend."

"What *nerve!*" Annie muttered, punching the mute button on the remote control to silence Suzanne's nemesis. "Why doesn't she just pitch a tent on the side of the road to be sure she doesn't miss a chance to harass you?"

"Two hundred thousand!" Suzanne said in dismay, looking at Stuart. "Is that right?"

Stuart leaned back on the sofa, cocking one ankle on his knee. "If my sources can be believed, yes."

"It's so bizarre." Suzanne rubbed her eyes wearily. "If this keeps up, I'll be disbarred. No judge can survive this kind of publicity."

"She's a barracuda!" Annie muttered.

Ben stood at the window, his hands flat in his back pockets. "We need to find a way to discredit Mason's sources."

"Who do you think furnished her with all this stuff?" Annie asked, beginning to pace.

Ben shrugged. "Could be anybody in Jack's inner circle. Has to be someone familiar with his ties to Vegas. Whoever, he had to be given the nod from the big boys there."

"It's so unfair." Annie dropped down beside Stuart and propped her chin on her hands. "We need to think of a killer strategy."

With a faint smile, Stuart reached over and stroked the baby curls on her nape. "There's been enough killing, Annie-girl."

"I was speaking metaphorically," she told him, settling back in the crook of his shoulder. "How about a press conference?"

"To say what?" Suzanne asked.

"The truth." Annie idly rubbed Stuart's thigh. "Just make a full statement—honesty's the best policy, after all. Tell how you knew nothing about the trust, nothing about the beach house, that your earlier rulings were strictly by the book. Be sure to throw in the part where you were threatened on your voice mail."

"Actually, I saved that message...for what it's worth," Suzanne said. She looked hopefully at Ben. "What do you think?"

"She may have something, Suzy." Ben moved away from the windows. "It just might work."

"It *would* work." Annie was on her feet again. "Just put yourself in front of the voters and give 'em free rein to ask anything they please. And answer them truthfully. We'd all be there with you, right, guys?" She looked questioningly at Stuart and Ben. "They'd see your family and friends solidly behind you. Sometimes when I see a politician in hot water, I think if he'd just admit he made a mistake, say he's only human, stand up and admit it like a man, then I'd forgive him."

Stuart smiled. "The go-and-sin-no-more strategy, huh?"

"But I haven't sinned!" Suzanne cried.

"And folks would see that," Annie insisted.

"Slow down, Annie-girl." Stuart pulled her down beside him and wrapped his arms around her as if to restrain her. "This is Suzanne's life and reputation on the line here, not a new account you're trying to nail down. Standing before a crowd of reporters can be a bloody experience. Give them enough leeway and their questions could become cruelly intrusive."

Suzanne met his eyes and knew that Stuart had made the connection between Caleb and Jack. Ben went to stand behind her. When she felt his arms go around her, she held on tight.

"Bad as it sounds, Suzy," he said, "I think a press conference is the best way to stop the speculation. Otherwise it will only escalate, and sooner or later no area of your life will be private."

"They'll get around to Caleb, won't they?"

"Probably."

"Definitely," Stuart put in.

Annie studied them all with a confused expression. "What about Caleb?"

After a sympathetic glance at Suzanne, Stuart told her quietly, "Jack is his father."

Annie stared at him, then gave a little gasp of dismay. "My God, I should have guessed. I always sensed...something." She looked genuinely baffled when she asked Suzanne, "But how? When? You've always hated him, Suzy."

"It's too long a story, Annie, and too ugly, but I'm trying to finally put it behind me. But," she added bitterly, "it'll be like throwing fresh meat to a pack of hungry wolves if a hint of it surfaces among those reporters."

With a grim look, Annie studied the dark landscape through the windows. "Jack. He was so...vile."

Suzanne nodded. "Yes."

"He hurt so many people—Taylor, you, his children, my mother and me, too, in a roundabout way. God only knows who else."

"Yes."

"Ugly, you said. It was rape, I'll bet. Wasn't it?"

"Yes."

Annie turned her face into Stuart's shirt for a few moments, shaking her head helplessly. "It would've happened after Taylor married him. Because you'd have reported the bastard otherwise."

"Yes."

"She would've been better off, of course."

"Yes."

"But you wouldn't have Caleb."

Suzanne managed a smile then. "Yes."

"Shit."

"In a word, Annie-girl." Stuart drew her closer and kissed her curly head. "I think that about sums up what we all think of Jack."

They were all silent for a few minutes. Suzanne stared thoughtfully through the darkened windows. In spite of the turmoil, the threat to her career, the possibility of Caleb's paternity coming out, in spite of everything, she realized she felt a deep, quiet joy she'd never known before.

For years she had imagined that if Jack had never existed, her life would have been far different. Happier. Simpler, without a doubt. And if Taylor hadn't married him, she would surely have been better off. He had even managed to taint Annie's life. How had they allowed Jack so much power? she wondered now. They *had* allowed it. By taking the path of least resistance, they'd aided and abetted him in wreaking havoc on their lives. By not forcing him to pay for the consequences of his sins, they had allowed him to do as he pleased. It was so easy to see now.

"Twenty-twenty hindsight," she murmured.

"What?" Annie asked.

Suzanne told her, making no effort to excuse herself.

"Don't beat yourself up over this, Suzy," Annie said. "Each one of us kept our secrets for what we believed to be good reasons, and none of them were selfish. I'm sorry it took Jack's death to change things, but, truly, for everything there is a season." She turned to look up into Stuart's face and smiled. "Maybe ours came late, but it's here now."

Stuart lifted her hand and kissed it before looking at Ben and Suzanne. "Annie and I will be getting married as soon as my divorce is final."

"Oh, Stuart, that's wonderful!" Suzanne smiled at them both.

"Yeah, I think so." Stuart kept his eyes on Annie, his expression so loving it brought an ache to Suzanne's heart. "We should be celebrating twenty years together, but I'll simply love her more for having wasted so much time."

Suzanne opened a bottle of wine and they drank to Stuart

and Annie's happiness, but all too soon they were again pondering Suzanne's dilemma. Their minds raced to find alternatives to Annie's plan, to shield Suzanne from the press.

"It's the only option," Suzanne finally said.

All studied the darkness beyond the windows, and no one disagreed.

THE PRESS CONFERENCE started at ten on the dot. With Ben, Stuart, Annie and her father flanking her, Suzanne stepped up to the podium, hoping her knees wouldn't give way. She deliberately didn't lift her eyes to the crowd until the last second. She was afraid that if she did, the courage she had left would desert her. The array of microphones reminded her of snakes waiting to strike.

In truth, the snakes were in the audience.

The noise died down instantly when she finally looked out over the crowd. She searched for a friendly face among the throng. Reporters packed the front of the crowd, others had been pushed to the rear. In the furor of clicking cameras and whirring Minicams, it was difficult to find even a familiar face; certainly there were no friendly ones. She spotted Jim Rankin, unsurprised by the open hostility in his pale gaze. Amanda Mason stood in the forefront, smug with satisfaction.

Suzanne's stomach was once again in a knot. But then she saw Candace Webber far in the back giving her a thumbs-up. And beside her, Betsy. And Grayson Lee, for heaven's sake! Actually, a lot of her friends were lined up along the back wall, she realized with a rush of emotion.

Her hands trembled as she placed the pages containing her brief prepared statement on the podium. For just a moment, the words danced like gibberish before her eyes. She stared in panic, then Ben—standing directly behind her—touched her waist and squeezed it reassuringly. In seconds, her panic passed and she realized she could handle this.

"Ladies and gentlemen," she began. "I have a brief statement regarding the allegations leveled against me yesterday on a local evening television newscast. I—" She stopped, sensing a ripple in the crowd. Her hand went to her breast as she spotted Caleb elbowing his way through a sea of cameras, mikes and people. Her heart swelled with love and pride and anxiety. She rejoiced that he had the courage to face whatever happened here today, but the mother in her cried out at the risk of subjecting him to the callousness of the media.

Please don't hurt my son.

He took the steps up to the press platform two at a time and grinned at her. "Hi, Mom." Hugging her hard, he planted a kiss on her cheek, stepped back and stood beside Ben, his chin firm and his dark eyes focused straight ahead into the crowd.

Suzanne cleared her throat and began again. "In the interest of time—" she gave a brief smile "—yours and mine, I will get right to the facts. It is alleged that in return for favors granted from the bench in my position as an officer of the court I was rewarded with a beach house on the Gulf Coast. I was never informed of that gift, nor did I ever agree to grant favors from the bench to anybody, including the Kent Group. It was further alleged that a trust fund in my son's name was established in the amount of two hundred thousand dollars. I knew nothing about such a fund. I was never informed by the trustees—who are associated with the Kent Group—that such a fund was being established, and neither I nor my son intend to accept any income from that fund. I am certain it will be canceled, but in the event that it isn't, the proceeds will go to charity."

Suzanne paused, allowing a moment for her words to be digested, then turned the page. "To keep the facts straight, copies of this statement will be furnished to you. It lists every case heard by me in the months I have occupied the bench. It includes dates and times, which can be confirmed." She drew a deep breath. "I ask only that you give me the kind of fair scrutiny you would give to any other public figure. When you've done so, I am confident you will find that I have never breached the public trust."

Suzanne folded the statement and looked out over the audience. With the exception of her friends in the back, she encountered mostly hostile or openly skeptical expressions. So much for the impact of truth and honesty. She managed a smile, anyway. "Now I will take your questions."

The words were barely out of her mouth when the reporters exploded in a frenzy of unintelligible shouts. Finally she pointed to a young print journalist she had met a couple of times outside the courtroom.

"Judge Stafford, were you aware that Jack Sullivan was on the board of the Kent Group?"

"No, but I knew the Kent Group was a major contributor to his campaign."

"As his sister-in-law, shouldn't you have recused yourself?"

She spread her hands. "Why? *I* was not a Kent investor."

Amanda Mason didn't wait to be recognized. "What about the fact that Jack Sullivan arranged to have you appointed to the bench, Judge Stafford?"

"It was a surprise to me." Suzanne controlled the impulse to walk off. It was too late for that. "On a day when I was to hear an important case, Jack visited my chambers and told me that he had been responsible for my appointment to the bench when my mother, Judge Lily Stafford, fell ill from a stroke. He reminded me that the polls assured him victory on election day and that if I didn't play ball on this particular case, the appointment that he'd fixed could be just as easily unfixed."

She paused to wait for the resulting furor to die down, then smiled with irony. "I was upset. Who wouldn't be to think the dream of a lifetime hadn't been achieved on merit—as I believed—but because of the machinations of my brother-in-law? But stop and think about it, ladies and gentlemen." Suzanne deliberately did not address Amanda Mason directly. "I had no option but to rule as the law dictated on any case brought before the court. Had I ruled otherwise—no matter what Jack demanded—I would have been overturned by the appellate court. I ask that you review all my decisions before judging me."

She nodded to a reporter from the newspaper in Memphis.

"Jack Sullivan was a powerful politician," he said. "When you refused to play ball, was there any threat of retaliation?"

From behind her, Suzanne felt Ben's fingers flex on her shoulders. She reached up and touched his hand. "I'll let you decide that for yourselves. I'll never be able to prove this, but Jack was surely the person who masterminded the idea of the beach house and the trust for my son. I have no doubt he would have produced the paperwork to try to influence me the next time he needed a decision for his cronies." She laughed without humor. "He was not the type to factor in something like his own death."

Amanda Mason's face twisted cynically. "It's easy for you to say these things about the governor-elect now that he's dead. Why should we believe you?"

"Because she's telling the truth and I can prove it!"

Suzanne's eyes widened with astonishment. Taylor was making her way through the crowd. She looked pale and fragile, but there was a determined set to her chin. As she advanced, she waved something aloft in her hand. A camera?

"Aunt Taylor!" Caleb jumped down, shoving reporters, mikes and Minicams aside as he plowed a path to his aunt. With his protection, she reached the steps without mishap, and Stuart pulled her onto the platform.

Suzanne still stood in shock as Taylor gave her a quick kiss and gently urged her aside. "May I?" she asked, and when Suzanne moved, she turned to face the crowd.

She didn't speak for the first few seconds. When the furor reached critical mass, she lifted her hand, still holding the black object in a signal for silence. In the settling quiet, she gave a dry laugh. "Suzanne and Annie can tell you that I swore I would never speak to any representative of the media after Jack died," she said softly, then shrugged. "Never say never."

A few cynical laughs.

"Can't hear you!"

"Speak up!"

"Closer to the mike!"

Taylor leaned forward slightly. "Do I need to introduce myself?"

Real laughter erupted from all sides.

She nodded, her blue eyes bright with tears. "That's good." She swallowed audibly, her voice unsteady. "Then I guess I don't have to say the famous line, but perhaps I should, anyway. Maybe I should get some practice." She paused. "My name is Taylor and I'm an alcoholic."

Surprise, like an electric current, went through the crowd.

"I presently reside at a rehabilitation clinic in Jackson in a program lasting about three months. I'm here against the wishes of my doctors, but when I saw Ms. Mason's piece on television about my sister, I realized that I was probably the only person who had irrefutable evidence that it was all lies."

An explosion of questions erupted from the listeners. Taylor simply closed her eyes, lifted her hand and waited. When the tumult died down, she pointed to the black object in her hand. "This is a tape recorder. I wonder how many of you who dogged Jack's every footstep through the past campaign noticed his partiality to this thing?" She looked around inquiringly. There were several nods, a few confused shrugs and many blank looks.

"Some politicians never write anything down, some keep diaries, some employ other people for the material that will record their place in history. Jack used a handheld recorder. *This* handheld recorder."

After a moment, she carefully laid the recorder on the podium shelf in front of her. "Everything he planned, he made an audiotape of. Everything he dreamed, he taped. Everything he schemed, he taped." She smiled sadly, then searched the crowd for a face. "Ah, Ms. Mason. I particularly wanted you to hear this."

Mason stirred uneasily. Taylor's dramatic appearance had visibly subdued the reporters. With faultless timing, Taylor flicked the recorder on, and Jack's voice, amplified through the maze of microphones, cursed Suzanne for refusing to decide a case in favor of the Kent Group. Another voice, muffled but understandable, replied. Then Jack's voice again, outlining a litany of schemes designed to force Suzanne to cooperate.

Without waiting for a reaction to Jack's vicious tirade, Taylor handed the tape to Suzanne, then faced the media again. "I was in the room the night that he recorded that, but I don't think the other individual realized it. He's here, however, and I'll bet a few of you recognize his voice. You're wondering why I didn't speak up then, and I'm ashamed to say it was because I was too weak. I had secrets of my own, as you've learned. Jack relied on that. I'm not the only person he manipulated that way. He was a master at getting people to do what he wanted while he mesmerized his constituency with his charm."

She paused again, put a trembling hand to her head, then waved dismissively when there were murmurs of concern behind her. Suzanne tried to slip a hand around her waist, but Taylor resisted, squaring her shoulders and drawing in a deep, calming breath. "I'm not quite finished, Suzy."

She told them of the many nights she watched Jack record the events of the day and make taped notes of his plans for the future. On the night when he came home ranting and raving about Suzanne, she removed the tape from the recorder, dubbed it and replaced it without Jack ever suspecting.

"I hoped this day would never come," she said with a sad look. Then, without giving the crowd a chance to bombard her with more questions, she turned away, leaning on Stuart when he threw his arm around her.

Suzanne found herself once again in front of the microphones, but speechless. This time Ben was on one side and Caleb, grinning broadly, on the other. Amanda Mason turned and made her way toward Jim Rankin, the light of battle in her eye.

"Her source," Suzanne murmured. "It was Jim Rankin."

"Sleazy snake," Ben growled.

Beside them, Caleb waggled his eyebrows Groucho-style. "Hey, looks like we'll be shopping for a new chief of police in Percyville!"

With a rush of joy and relief, Suzanne grabbed both their hands, then spoke into the microphones. "Ladies and gentlemen, thank you for hearing me out." She flashed a smile. "I'll see you in court."

She found Taylor in the ladies' room with Annie. While Stuart waited outside, Suzanne talked to Taylor. She hugged her first, a warm, loving, wordless embrace that expressed her feelings far more than words ever could. "Are you all right?" she asked, concerned by Taylor's pallor.

Taylor smiled shakily. "I've been better, but nothing I've ever done made me happier than facing those clowns and watching them wipe the egg from their faces when I played Jack's stupid tapes."

Suzanne touched Taylor's hair with affection. "I'll owe you forever, Tay. You probably saved my career."

"The debt was mine." Catching a look at herself in the big mirror, she wrapped her arms around herself. "In AA they're big on making amends, did you know that? Coming here today was a first step for me. I owed you, Suzanne. I can't make amends for many things I've done—I can't bring Eugenia back, or comfort the parents of that poor boy who was killed on the bike. I can never atone for behavior that drove a man to shoot my husband and wound my daughter." She stopped and blinked rapidly. "I can't undo Jack's many sins—but this I could do."

Using a tissue, Suzanne wiped her sister's tears. "I'll always be grateful."

Taylor was shaking her head. "I owe you for pushing me into rehab this time, for believing in me, for not washing your hands of me as you must have longed to do."

"No, Tay..."

"Here's a promise, Suzy. I'm going to work to put my life back together. Maybe now that Jack's gone, I can find some peace. Then I'm going to work on being a better mother. My children need me, and I know now that I need them."

Through her own tears, Suzanne smiled. "You're going to be fine."

Taylor straightened. Nodded. "I am. You're right." She pointed to the door. "Now, go out and let Ben take you home and reward you in a way you deserve while I try to do something with this face." She grimaced into the mirror.

Suzanne stood a moment, her heart aching. For the first time in her life, Taylor was alone.

Taylor touched her hand. "Don't worry. I'm going to make it this time."

With a quick, wobbly smile, Suzanne slipped out.

Ben was waiting for her. "Where's Caleb?" she asked, scanning the crush of people still milling around.

"He'll be okay. He'll find a ride to Riverbend," Ben assured her, pulling her by the hand toward his Explorer.

It was slow going. She was stopped frequently as her friends congratulated her and wished her well, but finally she was alone with Ben.

By unspoken assent, they drove to her house in Percyville. It was almost habit now to pass her housekey to Ben, and he unlocked the door. She put a hand out to stop him in the entryway. He gave her a questioning look.

She put a hand to her lips. "Listen…"

"What?" He smiled faintly, puzzled.

"No ghosts."

He pulled her into his arms, holding her against his heart. "Jack's finally dead and buried, huh?"

"Finally." Eyes closed, she simply stood in his embrace and let him rock her gently awhile. "I was so scared."

"With good reason. It was a helluva risk to take."

She smiled against his chest. "Now he tells me." After a moment, she said softly, "Caleb's secret may still come out someday."

He grunted. "And you'll handle it. You're a brave lady."

She turned her face up to look at him. "You think so?"

"I know so."

She laughed with delight, hugging him. "It's true, I will. I feel free, really free for the first time in my life. It's wonderful!"

Their gazes held for a moment. Then Suzanne saw something in his eyes. "Ben? What is it?"

"What are your plans now?"

She gave a confused laugh, trying to read his thoughts. "My plans?"

He shrugged. "You said that for the first time in your life you're really free. What does freedom mean to you, Suzy? Jack's not around to plague you anymore. The sky's the limit in your career. You could be on the Supreme Court before it's over. Caleb's comfortable with his history, so you don't have anything to worry about there. You're still young, you're beautiful and smart. You're feeling liberated now after—"

"Wait, wait." She touched his lips, realizing suddenly where he was going and what that odd expression was in his eyes. She framed his face with her hands. "Are you suggesting that since I'm now quote, unquote, liberated—I assume you mean in the sexual sense of the word—that I might be interested in other men?"

"It makes sense," he said, watching her carefully.

"Not to me, it doesn't."

"No?"

Tilting her head, she regarded him in silence for a long moment. Could it be possible that this fabulous man, this sexy, sophisticated, accomplished man could be feeling just the tiniest bit uncertain?

A little devil suddenly came alive in her. "But now that you mention it, maybe I shouldn't make any hasty commitments. I've only made love to one man in sixteen years. Maybe I should shop around first." Holding his gaze, she ground against the hardening bulge in his jeans. "I sure wouldn't want to ah... shortchange myself."

With a growl, he hauled her up and buried his face in her

neck. "Little tease," he growled, biting her just enough to make her yelp. "I've created a monster."

Laughing, she threw her arms around his neck. His body was warm and strong and welcome against hers. With her head tilted back, her eyes half closed with pleasure, she reveled in the way he was nibbling at her throat. She sifted her fingers through his hair, traced the shape of his ear, laughed softly as he began mindlessly rocking his hips back and forth.

God, she loved this man.

"Wait," he said, pulling back.

"What?" With a fingernail, she traced the cleft in his chin, the outline of his jaw, his sexy mouth.

"Let's get some things straight."

With a husky laugh, she pushed again at his erection. "Things are straight, Ben."

He closed his eyes, breathing with agitation. "Suzy…"

"Hmm?" She kissed his throat.

"I'm not going back to Houston."

She stopped but didn't move from his embrace. "Where will you go?"

This time he caught her face between his hands. "I'm staying right here in Percyville. I'm raising my sons here. I'm a lawyer—I can open a private practice."

She nodded carefully. "That could be a plan."

"I could run for the office of police chief."

A smile played at her mouth. "I hear the job's available."

"And my boys need a mother."

"Caleb needs a father."

He studied her intently for a moment. "What about other children?"

Still smiling, she turned her head and kissed his palm. "I would love to have your baby," she said huskily.

There was an audible catch in his breath as he hugged her tight. "Then it's time we got started."

* * * * *

REQUEST YOUR FREE BOOKS!

2 FREE NOVELS
PLUS 2 FREE GIFTS!

MYSTERY **W⊕RLDWIDE LIBRARY**®
™
Your Partner in Crime

WWLI1B